35674060269694

The
Woman
Inside

Also by M. T. Edvardsson

A Nearly Normal Family

The Woman Inside

. . .

M. T. Edvardsson

TRANSLATED FROM THE ORIGINAL SWEDISH BY

Rachel Willson-Broyles

CELADON
BOOKS
NEW YORK

For Kajsa, Ellen, and Tove.
Always.

THE WOMAN INSIDE. Copyright © 2021 by M. T. Edvardsson. English language translation copyright © 2023 by Rachel Willson-Broyles. All rights reserved. Printed in the United States of America. For information, address Celadon Books, a division of Macmillan Publishers, 120 Broadway, New York, NY 10271.

www.celadonbooks.com

Library of Congress Cataloging-in-Publication Data

Names: Edvardsson, M. T., author. | Willson-Broyles, Rachel, translator.
Title: The woman inside / M. T. Edvardsson ; translated from the original Swedish by Rachel Willson-Broyles.
Other titles: Familjetragedi. English
Description: First edition. | New York : Celadon Books, 2023.
Identifiers: LCCN 2022046424 | ISBN 9781250204622 (hardcover) | ISBN 9781250906182 (international, sold outside the U.S., subject to rights availability) | ISBN 9781250204608 (ebook)
Subjects: LCGFT: Thrillers (Fiction). | Novels.
Classification: LCC PT9877.15.D85 F3613 2023 | DDC 839.73/8—dc23/eng/20221202
LC record available at https://lccn.loc.gov/2022046424

Our books may be purchased in bulk for promotional, educational, or business use. Please contact your local bookseller or the Macmillan Corporate and Premium Sales Department at 1-800-221-7945, extension 5442, or by email at MacmillanSpecialMarkets@macmillan.com.

Originally published in Sweden in 2021 as *En Familjetradgedi* by Forum/Bonnier

First U.S. Edition: 2023
First International Edition: 2023

10 9 8 7 6 5 4 3 2 1

First Patrol on the Scene

I—Officer Larsen—and Officer Hemström respond to the Lund home after the man who lives there fails to report to work.

The large brick house is set back from the road, and a Tesla is parked in the driveway. I enter the yard by way of an iron gate and ring the doorbell while Officer Hemström runs the license plate.

I peer through the windowpane in the door. Some coats and jackets are hanging in the foyer. There are several pairs of shoes on a low rack. I ring the doorbell several times, but there is no response.

Hemström and I walk around the house together. We get the impression that no one is home. All the lights are off and every blind is down, but I notice a gap at the bottom of one of the kitchen windows.

Officer Hemström helps me pull away a few tree branches so I can step into the flower bed, where I stretch up to peer through the window. When I shine my flashlight inside, I see a tidy kitchen. There are two drinking glasses on the counter, and a black cardigan is draped over the back of one chair.

Only when I aim the beam of light at the floor do I discover a person lying next to the table in a semi-prone position. This person's outline is all that is visible; their face is turned away from me. I bang on the windowpane in an attempt to draw their attention, but there is no response.

Officer Hemström calls it in on the radio, reporting that we have discovered an individual but are unable to establish contact, and we receive orders to enter the house to investigate further.

I break the windowpane in the front door, which allows me to reach in and turn the lock. I enter the house with Hemström close behind. We aim the beams of our flashlights around until I find a light switch on the wall.

We continue straight ahead, through the hall and into the kitchen, and as we go we call out, alerting any occupants that we are police officers. On the floor in front of us lies a motionless woman. While Officer Hemström provides light, I examine her and quickly determine that the woman is deceased.

We make a joint decision to search the rest of the house. Officer Hemström checks the living room while I open the doors of bathrooms and closets. Nothing significant is found.

We take the stairway in the hall to the second floor. I sweep the beam of my flashlight through the second floor and find three closed doors.

Officer Hemström investigates the bathroom while I approach the first bedroom. The door is a few centimeters ajar, and I nudge it open with my foot as I aim the flashlight into the room.

The blinds are down, and all lights are off. Against the wall is a bed with a headboard. On the bed is another dead body.

In service,

Ludvig Larsen

Karla

The house is enormous. When I stand on the little path that leads to the door, the roof blocks out the whole sky. The blinds are drawn, and two black birds stare down at me from one of the windowsills. The front door is guarded on either side by a bronze lion.

It's hard to believe that only two people live here. But that's what Lena at the cleaning company said. And I can't imagine there's any reason for her to lie. Even if her eyes did start shifting oddly when she described the clients in the mansion on Linnégatan. Steven and Regina Rytter.

Before I ring the doorbell, I double-check the address on my phone. I take a deep breath as the *ding-dong* echoes through the house. When a man opens the door, I have to clear my throat before I manage to stammer out a few incoherent words.

"That's right," he says with a smile. "I heard they would be sending someone new."

Lena at the office was right. This man really does look like a movie star.

"I'm Karla," I say.

It seems that my attempt to erase the worst of my Norrbotten accent from my voice doesn't succeed.

"You're from Norrland?" says the man. He looks to be somewhere between forty and fifty.

"Yup," I reply, not without irony—I suck in the word on an inhalation, as we do up north.

He smiles anyway, and his handshake is warm and firm.

"Steven Rytter," he says. "I'll show you where we keep the cleaning supplies."

I leave my shoes on the rack and follow him through a wide hall with mirrors on the wall and a chandelier hanging from the ceiling. The furniture is rustic, older; the ceilings are high, and the railing of the massive staircase is covered in beautiful flourishes that must have been carved by hand.

"What a lovely home," I say, regretting my words immediately. I'm here to work, nothing more.

But Steven Rytter doesn't seem to notice my comment. He opens the door to another room. Brooms, vacuums, and mops line the walls, along with rows of detergents and sprays.

"If there's anything you can't find, or if anything runs out, just let me know and I'll take care of it for next time. We're still on for Mondays and Wednesdays, right?"

I nod. Mondays and Wednesdays. Four hours each visit. Which sounded pretty darn excessive when Lena told me—like, who needs a maid twice a week? But now I realize that a house this size will take time to clean.

"Are you a university student?" Steven Rytter scrutinizes me, still with a smile on his face.

Maybe it's silly, but suddenly my body is warm. Me, a student? It's for real now. Guess you can tell just by looking at me.

"I'm going to study law," I say with such pride that I almost sound smug. "This is just a side job."

Even though I'm taking out full loans from the state, the course materials are ridiculously expensive, and apparently in recent years the Lund housing market has gone seriously bonkers. People are paying ten thousand kronor a month for a studio. It's beyond lucky that I found a part-time job.

"What an exciting subject," Steven Rytter says. "I actually considered the law too, but I decided on medicine in the end."

"You're a doctor?"

Steven Rytter nods and smiles. He does actually look like he was plucked straight out of *Grey's Anatomy*.

"Feel free to help yourself," he says, leaving me alone in the cleaning closet.

For a minute or two I'm at a loss as I face all the cleaning supplies. I pick up and examine some of the implements; there are a few I don't even know how to use, or what they're for. But how hard can it be? I've been cleaning our apartment back home since I was four.

When I haul a bucket of brushes and sponges into the hall, Steven Rytter is kneeling by the front door with a shoehorn in hand.

"Do you want me to mop all the floors?" I ask.

Some of the rooms have shiny hardwood floors that I suspect might be sensitive to moisture.

"You can do whatever you like," says Steven Rytter, cramming his feet into his shoes. "Mop if you think it needs it."

The other clients I've cleaned for this week have been awfully picky about exactly what I should do, down to the tiniest detail; some talked about their houses and apartments as though they were their babies, but Steven Rytter seems more or less indifferent. Which is nice for me, of course. Eight hours a week here will mean lots of easy money.

Steven Rytter gets up and smooths out his shirt. We make eye contact for a second, but he immediately looks away and clears his throat.

"Did the cleaning service mention anything about my wife?"

I remember Lena's hesitant face. His wife's name is Regina, but that's all I remember.

"No, why?"

He heads for the staircase and gestures at me to follow him.

"She's in bed, up there."

That sounds odd.

I stop on the first step.

Steven Rytter turns around with his hand on the railing. His movie-star looks aren't quite as obvious now. His head is drooping, and he has shrunken into himself a little.

"My wife is sick," he says.

Bill

've never been late with the rent before. Other bills can sometimes be put off, but rent and electricity have to be paid on time. That's what Dad taught me.

Miranda would be furious if she knew. A few years ago, I got a letter from a collection agency—it turned out to be a mistake, but Miranda acted like the end was nigh.

"There are certain things everyone can manage," she said. "Being on time, saying thanks for dinner, and never buying something you can't pay for."

She and I truly come from different backgrounds.

Most things in life came so easy for Miranda.

She was the one who got us this apartment, a two-bedroom on Karhögstorg in the Järnåkra neighborhood. Four floors up, and not far from Lund city center.

Now the balcony door is open, the sun is shining, and I'm sitting on the sofa with my laptop on my thighs. Once again I log in to my bank account to look at the sad reality.

If it weren't for Miranda, I probably never would have ended up in Lund. She was born and raised here; she was surrounded by family and friends and couldn't imagine living anywhere else.

My childhood was spent moving constantly from place to place. When people ask where I'm from, I usually name a town in Östergötland, but that's mostly just to have an answer—in reality, I've never felt like I belonged anywhere in particular.

I don't have any solid ties to Lund either, but for Sally this is home. I know what it's like for a child to be uprooted and dragged away. I don't want to subject Sally to that. Not under any circumstances. We're staying in Lund.

Miranda and I were supposed to get married. I proposed while we were expecting Sally, but the wedding got postponed. Miranda was dreaming of a big, fairy-tale wedding with an extravagant party, and we just didn't have the money. In the end, we simply ran out of time.

For a long time, Miranda was the one who supported us. I was in the film studies program at the university, worked at a movie theater, and wrote a few reviews and half-decent columns for an online magazine. For almost ten years, I stood in the sales window, tearing tickets and filling colorful cardboard buckets with popcorn. The theater was doing well. We had survived some cutthroat competition, first from the Pirate Bay and then from Netflix and HBO, but when Miranda got sick, I had to turn down more and more evening shifts to take care of Sally. At first my boss was understanding and sympathetic, and rightly so, but when I returned after taking sick leave last winter, there were hardly any shifts left for me. Three months ago, I was let go for good.

The rent reminder arrived in the mail a week ago and caused me to fly into a panic. Ever since, I've been all over town to let folks know I'm looking for work. My caseworker at the employment office may be super friendly and encouraging, but I seriously doubt she'll be able to secure me a job. Not that I'm a hopeless case. I think I'm reasonably good at most things, I'm service-minded and upbeat, and even though

Miranda used to say I was all thumbs when it came to working with my hands, I've never been afraid of getting them dirty. I'm prepared to take whatever's available, as long as I can be home with Sally on nights and weekends, but this city is crawling with hungry young college students armed with top grades and impressive résumés. And the employment office isn't what it once was. My caseworker herself says that most people end up finding jobs on their own. It's all about taking initiative and being well-connected. That's why I'm sitting here checking off my Excel list of local businesses.

When Sally gets home from school, I've got a batch of thin pancakes ready. She spreads them with a thick layer of jam, rolls them up, and eats them with her fingers.

I sit down across from her and try to decide what to do with my hands.

"So I had an idea," I say.

Sally licks her lips, but somehow there's jam all the way up by her ear.

She knows we don't have much money. Even if I'd tried to hide it, she would have seen the situation for what it is. No McDonald's in weeks, no chocolate milk in the fridge. It's been two months since we went to the movies.

"I was thinking we could get a lodger," I say, taking my hands from the table and placing them in my lap. "Just for the summer, maybe."

"A Roger? Like a man?"

"No—a *lodger* means someone who needs a place to live. Maybe a student?"

"And they would live here?" Sally says. "With us?"

"Yes, we would share the kitchen and bathroom. Since you sleep in my room every night anyway, I thought we might as well move your things in there. It would only be for a while. Like just for the summer."

It's actually the worst possible time. Lots of students leave Lund in early June. Most of them don't have to pay rent for their student housing over the summer. But I can't wait.

Sally pokes the end of a pancake roll into her mouth. "If we do, it will definitely have to be a girl lodger."

"A girl?"

She's chewing with her mouth open. "Yeah, kind of like Mom."

My stomach ties itself in a knot and tears burn behind my eyes.

Me, the guy who never cries.

Neither Miranda nor I have ever been good at feelings. When she came home from her first appointment at the hospital, we sat down right here in the kitchen after Sally fell asleep. Very matter-of-factly, without revealing her emotions, Miranda told me what the doctors suspected. She could just as easily have been talking about a cold. We nodded at each other; her calm spilled over onto me, and we declared, together, that everything would be fine.

I'm sure things would have been much worse for Sally if we hadn't managed to maintain that balance through everything that followed. I didn't even lose control during the funeral.

But now that we risk losing the apartment, I can't hold back any longer. I bolt from my chair and hide my face from Sally as I hurry to the bathroom.

Later that evening, I post the ad on Facebook. *Room for rent, short-term.*

As usual, Sally shows up in my room during the night. Just after midnight, I wake up to the sound of her padding feet. Without a word she tucks herself into Miranda's side of the bed, and a moment later her hand finds mine under the covers.

"Dad?"

"I'm right here," I whisper. "Sleep tight, honey."

"Okay," Sally says every time.

It never takes long for her hand to relax in mine and her breathing to grow heavy.

All I care about is making sure Sally feels safe and secure.

Jennica

The patio at Stortorget is swarming with the cheerful Friday happy hour crowd. What was I thinking? The chances of running into a familiar face here are basically 100 percent.

As I walk the last few steps to the restaurant, I try to spot him among the umbrellas surrounding the outdoor bar. Here's something I've learned after five years on Tinder: the question isn't *if* he'll look different from his pictures, but *how* different he'll be.

I'm standing on the sidewalk outside the entrance, digging through my purse for my lip gloss, when a hand lands on my arm.

"Jennica? Hi!"

He was unusually honest with his pictures.

Most forty-seven-year-olds are, like, half-bald with a doughy belly. I'm pleasantly surprised.

"Is it okay if we sit inside? I thought that would be more relaxing."

His smile is so confident and hard to resist.

Together we walk through the stuffy summer air of the restaurant to a table in the back, where he pulls out my chair like a real gentleman. A marked difference from the twenty-eight-year-old IT guy I was out with last weekend.

"Forgive me for saying this, but I'm so relieved." He hangs his jacket over the back of his chair and sits down across from me. "You never know, with Tinder. So much Photoshop and who even knows what."

"It's so nice to hear you say so. I was thinking the same thing."

He laughs.

"Can we make a deal?" he says, placing his large, hairy hand beside the silverware on the table. "If you feel like I'm a total dud, just get up and go to the bathroom after the appetizer. I promise never to get in touch again, or even be the least bit disappointed. Or—well, of course I would be terribly disappointed, but I promise to keep it to myself."

"Ditto," I say. "After the appetizer, in the middle of the meal, whenever you like. Just get up and go. No hard feelings, I promise." A quick wink.

His hand remains on the table.

"I'm sorry," he says. "I never introduced myself. Steven."

"Jennica." I nod and let out a ditzy sort of giggle. "I thought you would have one of those sexy English accents."

"I certainly *can* have one," Steven says in a thick accent. "My mother is from Scotland. Dad wanted to call me Stefan, but she had a terrible time pronouncing it, so Steven it was."

What luck.

"My parents made a similar deal. Dad wanted me to be named Jenny, but Mom voted for Annica."

"Fantastic," Steven says. "We're both the result of compromise. Isn't it great when people get along?"

I force myself to zip my lips.

I have a whole lecture on this very topic on deck in the back of my mind. About how my mother, like so many other women, always seemed to draw the short straw when it came to compromise.

I smile and hope a better opportunity will arise for that lecture.

"Well, we've got one thing in common, at least. It could be worse."

Steven laughs. He browses the menu and quickly decides to order the fish.

"I'm thinking of getting the flank steak," I say.

Steven shakes his head. "That's a tough one. Meat should be thick and tender. Most kitchens can handle a sirloin or a tenderloin. I wouldn't take the chance on a flank steak at this place."

I look at him, astonished.

"It's up to you, of course," he continues. "But don't sit here whining later if you have to saw your way through a tough piece of meat. I warned you," he says with a smile.

I like this audacious character. He says what he thinks. Besides, he seems to know what he's talking about.

"I'll try the fish too," I say.

Steven smiles, satisfied.

"And wine," Steven says. "What's your preference there?"

I shrug. "White? High rating?"

He laughs out loud.

"Maybe a Pouilly-Fumé?" Steven suggests.

That sounds like a breed of horse.

"Excellent," I say.

There are a few seconds of silence as the waiter arrives and jots down our order, and it's painfully long enough for me to blurt out the first question that pops into my head.

"So, you're a doctor?"

What a dumb thing to ask, given that he'll expect me to talk about what I do in return.

"A pediatrician," Steven says. "Before I specialized, I spent two years in South Africa with Doctors Without Borders. It was appalling to see all that suffering, but also fantastic to see the genuine, pure joy in those children's eyes. That was when I decided to keep working with kids."

"So lovely" is my unimaginative reply.

"Tell me about yourself." Steven smiles. "I'm so curious."

What can I say? He saves starving children in Africa while I spend my days pretending to be a student so I don't have to register with the Employment Service, and play fortune-teller over the phone each night.

"I'm still a student," I say, picking at my napkin. "Right now I'm studying international development. I got it into my head that I want to do something abroad, maybe with a nonprofit or something, but I'm not so sure anymore."

"Interesting," Steven says.

His eyes are intense, deep and pale blue, almost transparent.

"I want to know more," he says. "Who are you? The person behind the Tinder profile."

I laugh.

"Come on," Steven says. "I'm too old for games and that kind of crap."

I can't deny that this sounds nice. "I mean, I'm not even thirty yet, so I suppose I'm still trying to figure out who I am."

"That has nothing to do with age," Steven says. "You never stop wondering who you are."

"Maybe not. But it's especially obvious at the moment. I'm the only one in my circle of friends without a family or a career. I guess you could say it's my thirty-year crisis."

At least no one can accuse me of selling myself on false grounds. No wonder my career in telemarketing lasted about as long as a fruit fly does.

"Thirty! Imagine being so young," Steven says. "All jokes aside. I remember what it was like. I'd hardly had a proper relationship by the time I was thirty. I had spent all my time on my studies and the student union life. One day I discovered that everyone else had settled down and become adults. As if I was the only one who didn't come down to earth. It was pretty rough."

"Exactly!"

He really does understand. We raise our glasses in a toast as the waiter brings our fish.

"I read an incredible book last week," Steven says, without putting down his glass. "More than two hundred pages on eels. I thought I had no interest in eels whatsoever, but boy, was I wrong."

"*The Book of Eels*? I've read that one too! Isn't it great?"

"Beyond fascinating. I mean, everyone has heard how all eels are born in the Sargasso Sea, but there was so much more. What an amazing animal!"

"Right?"

I almost have to pinch myself. A date who talks about books! When was the last time this happened?

"What was this, again?" I poke my fork into the white fish on my plate.

"Hake," Steven says.

I look him in the eye. "They're probably not mysterious at all, are they?"

"Not at all," he says, taking a big bite.

It's like slow motion. Something about his strong jaw slowly chewing his food. I'm riveted.

"What?" Steven laughs and wipes his lips with his napkin. "What's the matter?"

"Nothing."

I can't help but laugh too.

But I honestly don't know what the matter is.

By the time we've eaten up our hake, we've discussed everything from climate change and Greta Thunberg to Me Too and Bob Dylan's Nobel Prize. Even though Steven appears to have firm opinions on most things (climate change must be arrested primarily by way of the UN and China; Me Too was much needed on a systemic level, but courts of public opinion are never a good thing; and even though Bob Dylan is the world's foremost rock poet, the Nobel Prize should go to real authors who write real books), he always lets me have my say and seems perfectly genuine when he says he's willing to reconsider his views.

"Would you excuse me for a moment?" he says, pushing his chair back.

"It's fine. We have a deal."

He laughs, and I take out my phone as he disappears around the corner. I send a quick message about the date to the Messenger group that still goes by the name Tinder Central. Then I realize his jacket is gone. Suddenly my heart is pounding. I crane my neck to look for him.

Shit. Of course he made use of our emergency exit. I can't even manage to order a glass of wine properly.

Responses to my message are already pouring in, in the form of emojis that are applauding or sticking out their tongues. As always, only Rebecka dares to actually ask what they all want to know.

Sex?

I reply with a sunglasses emoji.

"Are you texting your other date?" Steven asks.

He's standing behind me with his jacket over his shoulders. Relieved, I put my phone aside.

"I have a Messenger group with a couple of girlfriends, we check in to make sure everything is okay when we're on dates."

"Smart," Steven says. "Can't be too careful these days."

I manage to avoid the sad fact that Tinder Central is a remnant of better days. I'm the only one who still dates. The others are probably at home on their sofas at this time of night.

"Dessert?" the waiter asks, handing us each a menu.

I try to read it, but I can't focus.

"A week ago, I was on the verge of deleting Tinder," Steven says, shaking the last drops of the wine into my glass. "Now I'm glad I stuck it out a little longer."

"Have you been on it for long?" I ask.

"Not really—I've messaged with quite a few people. But there's only a handful I've met in real life."

A handful? What does that mean? Five? No way can I reveal how I've spent years working my way through Tinder, with an ever-expanding age range.

"It was easier in the olden days," I say with a sigh. "When you married the neighbor boy or let your parents pick someone for you."

Steven folds the dessert menu.

"There are too many delicious options."

"Are we still talking about Tinder?"

When he laughs, the tip of his shoe happens to brush my foot under the table. We look at each other.

"What would the lady say to a drink instead?" He leans back with his elbow over the back of his chair. "We could find a cozier spot."

"Well . . . did you have somewhere particular in mind?"

"I'd love to invite you back to my place," Steven says, rising from his chair. "I've got a really nice Hennessy. Do you drink cognac?"

"Definitely."

"But unfortunately, that will have to wait. I've got water damage in the bedroom. Blower fans and dust everywhere."

Typical. Most Tinder guys hardly manage to swallow their dinner before they want to drag me home with them. Now, the one time I actually want to go, it doesn't seem like it'll happen.

"My place is no good either," I say, adjusting my dress. "My roommate and I have a pact. No gentlemen callers allowed."

That's a white lie.

There's no way I can bring a forty-seven-year-old pediatrician to my shabby student studio with its kitchenette in the student housing complex Delphi.

Steven looks a little glum as he hands me my jacket. With one large hand at the small of my back, he guides me out through all the tables.

"How about Grand Hotel?" he asks.

"Sounds good."

I haven't been there since my uncle turned sixty. It's no place for my usual Tinder guys.

I wobble slightly on the stone steps, and Steven reflexively takes my arm. I stare right into his pale blue eyes and feel a tickle low in my belly.

"To Grand."

Excerpt from Interrogation with Bill Olsson

Would you please state your full name?
Bill Stig Olsson.

Can you tell me a bit about yourself, Bill?
I'm thirty-three years old. My education is in film and culture studies, and I live here in Lund with my eight-year-old daughter, Sally.

How do you support yourself?
I write quite a bit for online outlets, reviews and so forth. I used to work at a movie theater, but that ended last spring.

What do you do all day then?
This summer I've mostly been spending time with my daughter. We've gone on little outings to the beach and stuff. One day we went to the 4H farm. At the same time I've been trying to look for work, but it isn't easy.

You're aware of why we're here today, Bill. Two people have been found dead in a house on Linnégatan here in Lund. What do you know about that?

I mean, obviously I've read about it and everything. Lund is a small city, things like that don't happen much here.

When did you become aware of who had died?
I saw it online a few days ago. Naturally, I was curious.

Did you recognize the names of these people?
Not exactly.

So you weren't acquainted with Steven or Regina Rytter?
No, I've never met them. Not that I know of, anyway.

You've never been inside their home on Linnégatan?
No. Like I said, I don't know who they are.

This isn't the first time you've been investigated for a crime.
But, *murder*! You can't be serious!? I would never be capable of hurting another person.

But you're in our database, Bill. We have your fingerprints on file. You were aware of that?
Yes. Sure.

So how do you explain the fact that we've found your fingerprints in several locations in the Rytters' house?
What? No, that can't be right.

Karla

These orange earplugs are totally useless. I haven't slept a wink all weekend. The student housing I've ended up in seems to be some combination of hostel and rec center, with constant partying: music and shouting around the clock.

On Monday morning, the alarm on my phone goes off at seven. With my eyes half-open and the beats of the night still ringing in my ears, I cross the street to the bus stop. The sun has risen large over the city, and the wind yanks at my cardigan. It always seems to be windy here.

The bus ride takes ten minutes, max, but there's time to see a whole lot of the city. Rows of small houses crowding close along narrow, winding alleys; lovely institutional buildings that have been around for centuries. And the magnificent cathedral with its two towers, over-shadowing everything else. There's something Harry Potter–like about Lund.

I'm on my way back to the big house where Steven and Regina Rytter live. Could it really need cleaning again? Even before I got there for the first time, a week ago, it was cleaner than most other houses I've seen.

Lena at the cleaning company squirmed a bit when I asked why they needed a maid twice a week.

"It's up to the client how often they want us to visit," she said.

But she couldn't hide the way her eyes were shifting here and there. Obviously, she was aware that I wouldn't want to question it any further. I was damn lucky to get this job, and I definitely don't want to seem ungrateful or difficult.

It's a bit of a walk from the bus stop. Past a schoolyard full of children playing jump rope under big green trees, in through the black wrought iron gate, and up the path of pebbles that crunch beneath my sandals. Once I've entered the code on the alarm, I step into the hall with a cautious *hello*. No response.

All the doors upstairs are closed. Everything looks just as neat and tidy as when I left last time. I start with the upstairs bathroom, spraying lemon-scented cleaner into the toilet, the sink, and the bidet, and I've just knelt down with the scrub brush when I think I hear something. A sound. A half-muffled whimper.

I get up. Standing stock-still, I listen. The scrub brush drips onto the tile floor.

"Come here." A pathetic voice from the bedroom.

I toss the brush into the sink and hurry over.

"Hello, excuse me," I say.

Regina Rytter is lying on her side in a luxurious bed with a velvet headboard. The blinds are down; the air is dry and stale. Her speech is slurred and slow; I don't understand what she's trying to say, but she seems upset, almost afraid.

"I'm the new cleaner," I explain. "We met last Wednesday, but maybe you forgot. . . ."

"No, no, I haven't forgotten you."

Glassy eyes stare at me in confusion. Her skin is white and fragile as tissue paper, and her every movement seems to be painful. Her sunken cheeks and haggard gaze remind me of Mom.

"My medicine. I need my medicine."

Her hand flutters out from beneath the covers and fumbles on the nightstand. I don't know whether I should help.

"I'm sorry," Regina says, sitting up with effort. "I feel all out of it when I don't take my pills."

I assure her that there's no reason to apologize and ask if there's anything I can do to help.

"Oh, no, go ahead and work. It's important to my husband for everything to be nice and clean."

She fiddles with a plastic pill organizer, the kind with different compartments.

"I'm sorry if I woke you up," I say, backing out of the room as I close the door.

Throughout the rest of the day, I interrupt my cleaning several times to listen for sounds from the bedroom. I work for four hours. Sweeping and vacuuming, mopping floors, beating rugs and scrubbing. Not once do I hear a peep from the bedroom.

What kind of life is this poor creature living? It makes no difference if you have crystal chandeliers and charming grandfather clocks that would be right at home on *Antiques Roadshow* when you don't even have the strength to get out of bed. These beautiful rooms, all these knickknacks and valuables. The clinical neatness. It's just so clear how little it truly means.

When I return to the rowdy student housing complex, I'm exhausted in mind and body. Muscles whose existence I had only been vaguely aware of ache and throb.

The room has a bed and a wobbly chair and nothing more. I sit on the chair, staring out the window as I drink a Coke. Apparently, there's some sort of mental hospital across the road.

It's not long before someone is pounding at my door.

"Hey, Norrland!" someone bellows.

When I unlock the door, a whole gang of guys tumbles into the room. They're smashed even though it's the middle of a Monday afternoon.

"Stop being such a drag," they say. "Come hang with us in the kitchen and have a drink."

"No, I'm beat. I've been working all day. And now I need to study."

In the end I have to shove them back out the door. Whooping, they disappear down our corridor to bother someone else.

When I sink onto the bed with my laptop, my eyes are burning and soon my vision is cloudy.

I can't absorb a word of what I'm reading.

How am I supposed to manage this? Working, studying, and never getting any sleep?

Maybe Mom was right after all. I'm not going to last long here.

I close the laptop with a bang and press my face into my pillow. I feel naked. I grab the blanket and draw it over myself.

It's like a shell is falling away, leaving behind the ten-year-old girl who was forced to grow up way too soon. The girl who cleaned up after her mother on so many levels, who did the shopping and laundry and dishes. Who soon learned to keep secrets. The girl who put herself to bed every night without knowing what would still be there when she woke up.

I squeeze my fists and sob into my pillow. Mom's voice echoes in my head. I will not prove her right. I refuse to give up.

Bill

Sally is on the sofa, her shoulders stiff and her eyes full of expectation.

"This isn't an *Idol* audition," I say. "These people need a place to live."

She rolls her eyes.

"I know, Dad. But it has to be a good person."

Can't argue with that.

Just a few hours after I posted the ad, messages began streaming in. Our first candidate is already on her way.

"Maybe we should take that down," Sally says, pointing at the photograph above the sofa.

Beside the *Goodfellas* and *Once Upon a Time in America* posters, Miranda gazes down at us from the wall. If you didn't know her, you probably wouldn't notice the smile quirking one corner of her mouth, but her sly look gives it away. People were always telling her she looked stern.

"Can we really do that?" I ask. "Take Mom down?"

Sally pouts. She always looks so eerily like Miranda when she's grumpy.

There's no time for further discussion because the doorbell rings.

Sally rushes over, waving her hands in the air. I stop in the entryway and take some deep breaths. I've always been shy, *cautious*, as Dad used to say, especially when it comes to people I've never met.

Sally is basically the opposite of cautious. She gets that from her mom too.

"Hi! Welcome!" she says, flinging the door open wide.

On the other side is a young woman whose eyes are half-hidden behind her bangs.

"Hi," I say, giving her a nod.

She extends a slender hand with stubby nails and no rings. "Karla."

"Hi, Karla."

There's something wary, almost watchful, about her.

"I'm here to look at the room."

"Of course."

Sally is so worked up she can't hold still.

"Are you from Norrland?"

"Yeah, is it that obvious?" Karla laughs.

She's dressed in black head to toe, and her turtleneck is so tight on her throat that it can't be entirely easy to breathe in this summer heat.

I open the door to Sally's room.

"Well, here it is."

I explain that she's welcome to use the kitchen and bathroom as much as she likes. Of course she'll also have access to the living room when we're not there.

"But also when we are here," Sally says firmly.

"Right. Of course. If you want to."

Karla tosses her bangs out of the way, and for the first time I look into her green, catlike eyes. She gives a small smile and something tells me I could get used to having her around.

"How old are you?" Sally asks.

"Twenty-two. How about you?"

"Eight."

Sally is off to the races, and my attempts to interrupt this cross-examination aren't particularly successful.

"Where are you from? Why did you move here? Do you have a boyfriend?"

Karla laughs again and squirms a bit.

"That's enough," I say.

"It's fine," Karla assures me. "I'm from Boden, which is basically at the very top of Sweden, and I moved here to study at the university. And no, I don't have a boyfriend." She blushes as she offers this last piece of information.

I ask where she's currently living. Surely she didn't come down from Boden without a place to live, did she?

"It's some sort of hostel," she says, her face revealing her distaste. "I think it used to be a refugee center."

She tries to explain where it is, but even though I've lived in Lund for a long time, I don't know the city well enough. I've heard it again and again: you come to Lund as a student and end up sticking around, but it's never *quite* home for real.

"Please, Daddy," Sally whispers loudly, tugging at my pants leg. "Can't we pick her?"

Karla and I both laugh. I explain that electricity and water are included in the rent, as are Wi-Fi and twenty-four channels on TV.

"But I'm afraid we can't wait. We need a renter right away."

"I can move in tonight," says Karla.

Sally cheers.

"I need two months' rent in advance," I say.

That's my salvation. Two months' rent will at least cover us for June, and by the time the next bill comes due I'm sure I'll have found a job.

"I can manage that," Karla says.

Sally claps her hands in glee.

"Just one more thing," I say, not eager about this part.

I've already warned Sally, she understands.

"What's that?"

"We're not actually allowed to do this. If anyone asks, you can't tell them you're renting a room from us."

Sally takes Karla's hand.

"We can say you're my new stepmom."

Jennica

t's a strange feeling, descending the stunning staircase of Grand Hotel with sex hair and a quick-fix face. A walk of shame squared when
the young guys at the reception desk nod my way with insinuating
smiles.

It feels nice, letting down my guard. First dates are always a pain,
since you have to be careful what you say and do.

I hurry to the station, my eyes on the ground. I board the number
four bus to Norra Fäladen and send a brief message to the Tinder Central group on Messenger.

A doctor? Not bad! Could be a keeper? Emma responds within a
minute.

I love my friends, I've known them forever, but in recent years all
the talk about how I should meet someone and settle down has led me
to avoid them more and more.

None of us were surprised when Miranda got married and had
a baby relatively young. She'd been dreaming of a nuclear family of
her own since preschool. But the others. Emma and Tina. And even
Rebecka! They were the world's biggest partiers, carefree and horny
and curious. Around the age of twenty-five, though, something struck

them all, a change so sudden and drastic that I suspect it must have been some sort of inherited trait. A small-town girl's inborn drive to find security. Ever since, I haven't quite felt like one of the gang.

We'll see, I write to the group.

I'm not going to give them even a quarter of an inch here.

But on the inside, a flame has kindled.

Steven Rytter is so different from everyone else I've met on Tinder. Most of them weren't even born yet when he finished high school. But that's not all. Steven is more IQ and less testosterone. It's been ages since I met a guy with whom I want to have sex *and* discuss Lena Andersson's latest column in *Svenska Dagbladet*. Not necessarily at the same time.

Here's hoping! Emma sends to the chat.

She adds a fingers-crossed emoji.

I start to compose a response, delete it, try again, delete it again. In the end I just don't bother.

Emma and I became best friends way back in elementary school. In fourth grade we bought identical friendship bracelets and swore we would remain best friends forever. Now we've grown apart; we live such different lives, but I still have that bracelet in my box of important stuff.

As soon as I get home, I mix myself a fizzy painkiller-and-electrolyte cocktail. I scarf down half a burger I left in the fridge and pour out some food for Dog.

He aims a disdainful look my way.

"No, no herring today." I can't afford to spoil him like that.

When I bend down and pat his head, he arches his back and turns away from the food bowl.

Dog is just his name. He's actually a cat. A grumpy and easily offended cat who will probably never forgive me for my bad sense of humor when it came to giving him that name.

"Eat it or don't," I say. "This is all you're getting."

Naturally I talk to my cat. I'm not ashamed of it. He even answers me sometimes. He's unusually smart, for a cat.

Today he just sneers, but sooner or later he'll eat what's on offer.

"That crap is more expensive than fucking baby food."

I plop myself onto the bed with my phone to google Steven Rytter. It's not the first time, of course, but now he's turned out to be interesting enough that I step up my detective work.

Steven is oddly anonymous online. A few photos, boring information gleaned from public records. No social media, nothing exciting at all. I suspect it has to do with his age.

After half an hour I give up and ready myself for today's shift. I typically find that the best conversations happen in the evening, but Saturday morning isn't so bad either. A long, boozy Friday night can put anyone in need of a little spiritual guidance.

It's not exactly a dream job, but I can work from anywhere, at any time. All I need is a cell phone. Plus, the money is pretty decent.

According to the website and ads, which mostly run in so-called lifestyle magazines for middle-aged women, we offer psychic advising. I'm no prophetess, and under no circumstances am I to deliver any sort of predictions. The people who call us are really after something else.

On the website, it says: *Do you believe life is more than just the physical and material world? Sometimes things don't turn out the way we imagined. We encounter roadblocks and ordeals that demand guidance. Our psychic guides provide you with the support and advice you need for further reflection.*

During my job interview, over Skype, I was asked if I possess any psychic abilities. I expected that to say no would be to disqualify myself, yet I couldn't bring myself to lie. Instead, the CEO asked if I considered myself to have *empathic* abilities. I could say that I did without stretching the truth even an iota, and that was enough for them to offer me the job on the spot.

It's not exactly as if I listed Psychicadvice.com as my employer on LinkedIn. In those instances when I tell people what I do, I talk about it like a lark, a gimmick, something I do for fun. Obviously my family doesn't have a clue about it. Dad would be furious. Mom would probably die of shame. People who know me probably assume I live off my parents, but an agreement like that would come with strings attached, strings I want nothing to do with.

After I got my master's degree, I worked as a middle school teacher for a year. It wasn't what I expected at all. By the time half a semester was over, I despaired of ever being good enough. I also had reason to reconsider my belief that all children are worthy of love and do their best to be obliging. The only reason I lasted the entire school year was because of my extreme reluctance to capitulate to my parents and thus prove them right, after their constant harping that a career in education wasn't for me.

Now I'm sitting here with my headset on and glass in hand, waiting for the first call of the day.

Some conversations are delightfully refreshing. Like the guy who called the other night, wondering if he should get circumcised. He wanted to know how women would feel about such a stunt. Did I, perhaps, have any experience in that arena? I ended up recommending he get a Prince Albert piercing.

But most of my callers are women between fifty and death. And they call to talk about men. About what they believe is love, or what they hope might turn into some variation on it. Does he love me? Will he change? Will the two of us ever be together? The answers are always *no*, *no*, and *no*. Naturally I coat my responses in sugar and honey, but these women deserve the truth, no more gauzy delusions about knights in shining armor. If he looks like a pig, walks like a pig, and smells like a pig—surprise! He's a pig.

There are worse jobs. I have fun and get to help people. Maybe not as much as a teacher does, but still.

My phone dings. Tina has sent a new message to Tinder Central.

Give the doctor a chance. I believe in you. Woo-hoo and hugs!

I respond with a heart and a blowing-a-kiss emoji. I hardly have time to put down the phone before there's another *ding*.

This time it's a message from Steven.

Can't stop thinking about you. When can I see you again?

Excerpt from Interrogation with Karla Larsson

How long did you work for the Rytters?

It's not like I was their private cleaner or anything. I worked for a company that has lots of different clients. The Rytters' house was just one of many I cleaned.

But you were always the one who cleaned their house?

Mm-hmm. I moved down to Lund in early June. After that I was their only cleaner. Clients usually prefer to have the same person come each time.

How often did you clean at the Rytters'?

Twice a week. Mondays and Wednesdays.

Isn't that often? Is it typical to clean the same house twice a week?

I guess it's pretty unusual. I don't have that much experience.

Was the Rytters' house especially untidy, or why did they need such frequent cleanings?

I don't know. That's how they wanted it. Based on what Regina told me, her husband was very particular. But it's not as if there was anything strange about the house or anything.

Did you talk to Regina Rytter a lot?
Not that much. She was mostly in bed when I was there. But we chatted now and then.

And Steven Rytter. Did you talk to him too?
Sometimes. He's the one who showed me around and stuff on my first visit.

Did you form any impressions about Steven and Regina's relationship?
I don't know. At first everything seemed fine. Steven seemed like an awfully nice guy. It took a while for me to realize.

For you to realize what?
Well, eventually I realized how things really were.

Karla

'm five minutes late and miss the bus. Instead, I run all the way through Lund, getting lost in the winding, narrow alleys between the small houses where the city's poor once lived—these days, they cost half a fortune. When I reach the square by the big market hall, I turn on the sound on my phone's GPS and let the artificial voice guide me up to the cemetery and past the school.

By the time I finally arrive, my underarms are soaked, my makeup is smeared, and I'm panting loudly. No one responds when I call out "Hello!" so I set to work cleaning.

The bathroom first, that's the routine.

The water in this luxury sink doesn't come from a regular old faucet. Instead, it comes gently gurgling out of what looks like a miniature waterfall. I lean over, rubbing and scrubbing with the sponge. It's not entirely easy to clean when it's already so spotless that you can hardly tell the difference between before and after.

Before I attack the inside of the toilet, I fill my lungs with air and hold my breath. I'm scrubbing hard when the door behind me opens.

"You're really toiling away," says Regina Rytter.

This is the first time I've seen her out of bed, and she's both taller and prettier than I imagined. Her robe looks fluffy and soft.

"I was going to have a cup of tea," she says. "Will you keep me company?"

I'm caught off guard; all I can manage to produce is a no.

Regina stares at me in surprise. A little laugh bubbles out between her dry lips.

"I'm sorry," she says. "You look like you've just seen the walking dead."

"Oh no, I'm sorry."

"That's okay. I do feel like a zombie sometimes."

So awkward of me. I never can hide my feelings. "I just didn't know you were awake, ma'am."

She laughs again, although it appears to cause her pain. "Ma'am? You make it sound like I'm sixty years old. My name is Regina."

She's about to put out her hand, but changes her mind when she sees the yellow rubber gloves that have just paid a visit to her toilet.

"I'm Karla," I say.

"That's right. Do you drink tea, Karla?"

I look at the scrub brush in my gloved hand. "I don't know. I should . . ."

I turn to the waiting toilet, but Regina insists.

"You'll have plenty of time for that too. It's my husband who's the cleaning tyrant around here. He's a doctor; maybe that has something to do with it. It sure escalated after I got sick, anyway. Maybe he thinks I'm contagious."

I stop short.

That's strange. I had gotten the impression that her husband hardly cared.

She's already headed down the stairs and turns around with her hand on the railing.

"Take it easy. I'm just joking. My condition isn't contagious."

I don't know what to say. It feels all wrong to join her for tea. I'm here to work, and this woman doesn't seem entirely stable.

"Come on!" she says, hobbling down the stairs.

Her hand grasps the railing tight, and her matchstick legs tremble as she pauses to rest on each step. She's out of breath; at last she sinks onto a chair in the kitchen.

"I always overestimate my abilities. I wake up and feel more energetic than I have in a long time, but as soon as I exert myself, here comes the setback like a letter in the mail."

That sounds horrible. Regina rests her cheek in her hand.

"Will you help me put on the tea?" She points at the display cabinet in the corner. "You can use those white cups there."

I really shouldn't. I'm here to clean and nothing more. Even so, I put on the kettle and gingerly take out two cups and saucers. They're stamped *Royal Copenhagen* underneath. They must be ridiculously expensive.

"Have a seat," Regina says, pointing at the chair across from hers.

I hesitate, my hands on the chair back. "I don't actually have the right to take a break."

"Says who?" She stares at me, baffled. Then she covers her eyes, sighs, and scoffs.

"Why are you here?" she asks, crossing her arms. Her gaze darts here and there as if she's just woken up.

"I . . . I'm supposed to clean. I'm the new cleaner."

Regina blinks a few times. Then she laughs so hard she starts coughing.

"No, I'm sorry. I meant, why are you here in Lund? I can tell by your accent you're not from around here."

I blush. I look at the fancy teacup and try to work out how to hold it by its little handle. When I take a sip of the tea, I burn my tongue.

"Careful," Regina says, two seconds too late.

The teacup wobbles and drips on the table.

"I'm going to study law," I mumble.

It seems so far away. I can't even manage to drink tea without burning myself and spilling.

"Oh, a future attorney?"

That's what everyone thinks.

"Judge," I say, fanning my mouth.

Regina looks genuinely curious. "That's exciting," she says. "And a little unusual."

She seems to understand what I'm saying. I'm not used to that. Mom, for instance, was under the impression that we have jury trials in Sweden. Then again, she's also mystified about why I want to spend so many years in school.

"I don't think I could handle being an attorney," I say, "having to defend people who've done terrible things."

"You'd rather judge them?" Regina says.

"Yes, if they're guilty. I want to be part of creating justice for all."

Regina leans forward and blows on her tea, which is still steaming. "I wanted to be a cop for a while," she says. "My father thought I was nuts. Cops are underpaid and vulnerable. Plus I was a girl. God."

She picks up her teacup with a chapped yet delicate hand. It trembles so violently the porcelain clatters. I meet her gaze. She can't be much over forty, but her illness makes her seem a lot older.

"Dad was determined that I should study the humanities," she continues. "Maybe that's why I became an economist, just like my brother. These days, though, I'm mostly in management and organizational development. Although—these days? That feels like another life now."

She replaces the cup on the saucer, gazes down, and seems to deflate.

I have to say something.

I slowly take another sip.

It burns me again.

"It's hot," I say. "But good."

Regina stares right through me as though she didn't hear me. "These days I spend most of my time in bed."

I smack my tongue and try to cool it with my breath. Obviously I feel sorry for Regina, but I should get back to work now. If my employer finds out I'm spending working hours drinking tea and chatting, I probably won't last long at this job.

"I hope you get better soon," I say.

I sound like such an imbecile. But what am I supposed to say?

"I just don't know anymore," Regina says. "No one knows anything. The doctors shuttle me back and forth with vague answers. Sometimes I wonder if it's even worth trying. How long can I go on like this?"

I think of Mom and a painful lump rises in my throat.

"I wish I had appreciated my health more back when I was well," Regina says. "You take for granted that you'll wake up healthy every day. But one day everything might change. I was busy living life when this goddamn virus knocked me down. It started out like a regular old flu. Now I don't know whether I'll ever live a normal life again."

She gulps and picks up the teacup, which trembles and clatters. The spoon is halfway out before she manages to catch it.

"My medicine," she says, putting the cup down again without having drunk any. "I forgot to take my pills. Could you maybe run up and get them, Karla?"

"Of course."

Halfway up the stairs, I stop. Even though everything is so new, there's something that feels eerily familiar about this situation, and I don't know if it's a good thing at all. I think of Mom again.

Bill

Friday is the last day of school, and Sally picked out the dress she's wearing for the celebration herself—it has pink and purple flowers. My little baby, suddenly she's eight years old. As the children sing the traditional end-of-school hymn, tears spring to my eyes.

I stood in this exact same place in the schoolyard last year. On my own that time too. Miranda had just been admitted to the hospital. But it wasn't even on my radar that she might not ever come home.

When I look around at the smiling parents in their summery clothes, I get a knot in my chest; rage at the injustice. Who decided that this should happen to our family? Why am I the one who has to stand here by the bike rack all alone, waiting with Sally's zebra-striped schoolbag in hand?

Miranda was my best friend. Without her, I'm half a person. If it weren't for Sally, I don't think I could have gone on.

I was awfully lonely as a child. Maybe that has something to do with it. People always say that childhood experiences leave deep traces that never fade. Since I never knew how long we would stay in any one place, I quickly learned not to form any bonds. Being uprooted simply hurt too much.

Dad was everything I'm not. Intuitive, spontaneous, emotionally driven. He fell in love with everything in life, big and small: people, places, things, interests. It was often too much for an overly sensitive kid like me.

Movies and the internet are what kept me going. Even back in grade school I spent most of my waking hours in front of a screen. Everything was so much easier when you didn't have to look anyone in the eye. I made friends all over the world on Lunarstorm and Myspace. When I was nineteen, I met Miranda on Bilddagboken, kind of like a proto-Instagram. She was a few years younger, but we clicked instantly. I took the train down to Lund a few times, and a year later I moved into her bedroom. I didn't think I could survive a day without her.

Sally receives a rose from her teacher. On the card it says she's valued. I carry the rose the short way home from the schoolyard. Outside the pet store on the square, a gust of wind catches the flower, and I lose my grip.

I chase after it. The petals are damp and rumpled. I try to blow on them to dry them off, but when I run my hand over them the petals fall off one by one. I can't even keep a flower alive.

"I'm sorry, I'll buy you a new one."

Sally is looking at me, wide-eyed. She takes the damaged rose from me with a smile.

"It's okay, Dad. It's still pretty."

That evening we make tacos together. Sally has convinced our new lodger to eat with us.

"Is there anything I can help with?" Karla asks. "Are you sure I'm not a bother? I can just get a falafel in town instead."

Sally is practically insulted. "We bought enough for three people. Dad and I got everything ready."

Karla immediately backs down. "Well, in that case. I'd be happy to eat with you."

Never have I seen someone eat tacos like Karla does. She carefully places each individual vegetable on the tortilla, then folds it up as though it's a napkin made of the most delicate paper.

Tiny, tiny bites, interspersed with sips of her sparkling water.

"Is there a lot of snow where you're from?" Sally asks.

"Not now, in the summertime." Karla glances my way. "But the rest of the year, there's a lot of snow. I've never been much of a skier or anything, but without the snow it would be awfully dark in the winter."

Sally pokes pieces of peppers into her taco.

"What do you like to do instead?" she asks.

Karla takes a fresh sip of water. "Soccer. I like to play soccer."

Sally is clearly impressed. In our family, video games and card games are about as close to sports as we get. Miranda did used to go to the gym, but that was just to work off excess energy and feel a little healthy.

"Do you have any brothers or sisters?" Sally wonders.

Karla says she grew up with her mother. "It's always just been the two of us."

"No dad?" Sally takes a crunchy bite of her taco and half its contents shower onto her plate.

I pretend to be a little upset, both about the state of the table and her nosiness. But really, I'm pretty curious myself.

"My dad got sick when I was little," Karla says, and her voice sounds thin.

Sally puts down her crumbling taco and her face lights up. "My mom got sick too," she says, sounding almost enthusiastic. "Then she died."

Karla brushes her bangs out of her face and looks at me in concern, but Sally is going full speed ahead.

"Some people think you go to heaven when you die, but I know you end up in the ground. They burn up your coffin and plant your ashes deep underground."

"That's enough, Sally," I say.

"But, Dad."

Karla shakes her head. "It's okay. I don't think people go to heaven either."

"See?" Sally says to me before turning demonstratively to Karla. "Is your dad dead too?"

Karla nods. "He died when I was little. I don't remember him at all."

"Really?" Sally looks back at me. "Will I remember Mom when I grow up?"

"Absolutely," I say.

We both look at the photo over the sofa. Miranda watches over us from her spot next to Noodles from *Once Upon a Time in America* and Tommy from *Goodfellas*.

Karla gently tries to explain that she was only a little baby when her father passed away. Of course Sally will still have her memories of Miranda.

"Is your mom still in Boden?" Sally asks. "Don't you miss her?"

"Yes, all the time." Karla's bangs fall over her eyes for the millionth time, and this time Karla lets them stay.

"Then why did you move here?" Sally asks.

"Because she's going to go to college," I say. "I told you that. Karla's going to be a lawyer."

"Or a judge." Karla smiles. "I really want to be a judge."

Luckily, she seems to think Sally's curiosity is more charming than maddening.

Sally rests her chin in her hand and nods in interest. I'm not sure she understands quite what Karla is talking about.

"My dad works at a movie theater," she says, picking a few kernels of corn from her taco. "Naemi and I got to see *Frozen II* four times.

We got free popcorn and as much Coke as we wanted. I can see any movie for free, except the rated R ones, of course."

Karla laughs. "What a great job your dad has."

I don't say anything. I don't even look at Sally. She knows perfectly well that I don't work there anymore. Sure, I've told her that there are other movie theaters, and maybe I can get a job at one of them, but that was before our situation went from difficult but surmountable to totally desperate.

"Have you seen *Frozen II*?" asks Sally, who will soon have rid her taco of vegetables.

"I actually haven't," Karla says. "But I liked the first one."

Sally licks her lips. "The second one is sick. Way better."

After dinner we play a game of Yahtzee on the couch. Sally gets both the large and small straights and yells "I rule!" with her arms in the air once I've added up the points. We stuff ourselves with pick 'n' mix candy and drink Coke Zero and soon Sally is asleep with her feet on the arm of the couch and her head in my lap.

"That looks so cozy," says Karla.

Our eyes meet for a little too long, and all of a sudden she's self-conscious and flips her bangs back over her eyes.

"Please don't feel like you have to hang out with us," I say. "Sally can be a little overeager. I'll have a talk with her."

"It's really no big deal."

Karla smiles as I stroke Sally's forehead. She gingerly rises from the couch but ends up standing there for a second, hesitant. A moment of awkward silence follows.

"Sweet dreams," she whispers.

For the first time in ages, something tugs at me, a quiet urge for physical contact.

"You too," I say.

Karla walks silently down the hall and into Sally's room, which is now hers. The key turns, and she tests the handle from the inside as if to make sure it's properly locked.

It comes over me out of nowhere.

That's the nature of grief and longing. You're never safe from it.

It encroaches like a cold snap, over my shoulders, through my chest, into my legs. Images before my eyes. Everyday life with Miranda. An overwhelming hopelessness.

With the greatest of care, I stand up with Sally in my arms. Her dreams move behind closed eyelids. I carry her to the bed, where I perch on the edge to watch her.

"You and me against the world," I whisper. "You and me."

Jennica

T he agony of feeling like you're the same age as the nineteen-year-olds at a graduation party, until you realize that you get exactly 0 percent of their references and have to google every tenth word to keep up with their chatter.

It's my niece's graduation. Little Lykke, nineteen already. I do some math in my head. My sister is fourteen years older than me—so she's forty-four. So she must have been twenty-five when she had Lykke. Twenty-five? Jesus, she was only a child. I'm almost thirty and I practically pass out when I think about becoming a parent. I can hardly manage the responsibility of having a cat.

"Jennica," says my oldest brother, sticking his head through the tent flaps. "How'd you end up at the kids' table? Are we having a tiny crisis now that we're almost thirty?"

If only he knew.

"You're only as old as you feel," I say, winking at my brother.

"Tick tock, tick tock." He smirks, turning his finger into a pendulum. "I can hear your biological clock from here."

His wife, who is two years younger than me and already a mother of three, inspects me with a disconcerting X-ray eye, as though she can see my ovaries and uterus, how they're dried up and withered away.

"Cheers!" cries one of the freshly minted graduates in the party tent, and as they scream and shout about how fucking awesome they all are, I take the opportunity to sneak out to the garden.

I pass the gazebo and the old gossiping bench, where an entwined couple is in the process of trying to devour each other. Their student caps have fallen off and landed in Mom's beloved rose garden.

A small crowd has formed beneath the plum tree. I accidentally get too close before realizing those are my parents in the hammock, at the center of a group of people.

"Jennica!" my mother says as she catches sight of me.

It's too late to turn around.

My aunt and uncle are there too. My sister's colleague, and a random neighbor. I muster a polite smile.

"Hi there," Dad says, puffing on his cigarillo.

I've managed to stay far away from him all evening. We haven't even said hello until now.

"Come here, and we can visit for a little while," Mom says.

She has taken off her shoes and is using her foot to rock them slowly in the hammock, the contents of her wineglass gently sloshing.

Dad blows out a big white cloud of smoke. "Do you remember your graduation?" he asks.

Mom tries to curb him with a hand on the knee of his neatly pressed suit trousers, but Dad has never understood that sort of subtle communication—that, or he just ignores it.

"Do you remember *anything* about your graduation?" he says, aiming a scornful smile at the crowd of onlookers.

"It wasn't that bad," I say.

Dad laughs. "Her friends had to carry her off the parade float," he says to whoever wants to listen.

Mom doesn't look amused in the least. Dad wasn't exactly happy when it happened either. He couldn't look me in the eye all summer. My sister and my brothers had graduated with scholarships; two of them had been student council president; each of them had sported neatly combed hair and the gleam of a bright future in their sober eyes. For my part, I spent most of my graduation party making out with a toilet bowl.

"What are you up to these days, Jennica?" Aunt Birgitta asks. "Are you still a teacher?"

It might seem like a reasonable question. But not in this family. It's so clear that the word *teacher* is meant to needle my mother. Aunt Birgitta's daughters would never walk their dainty, pedicured feet into a classroom.

"I'm studying international development right now," I say, pasting a smile on my face for Birgitta. "I might go back to teaching later."

I only say that to rile them up. And to preserve the last of the mangled pride I've got left. The truth is, I would rather make a living juggling burning torches on Mårtenstorget than go back to the world of education.

"I think you'd make an excellent diplomat," my mother says.

Clearly she's never seen me attempt to mediate for a gang of tween girls who are fighting over a misogynistic sixth-grade player.

"Are you here alone?" Aunt Birgitta asks.

Her beautiful daughters, my teeth-whitened and Botox-enhanced attorney cousins, haven't strayed more than thirty centimeters from their respective spouses all evening.

"Solo," I say to my surprised aunt. "I'm here *solo*."

That's the honest truth. I very seldom feel alone.

"I read somewhere that the average age of first-time mothers in Sweden is thirty-two," Mom says.

That's her way of defending me. And herself, of course.

"Oh my God," says Aunt Birgitta. "Think of all the increased risks of pregnancy after thirty."

I almost regret that I didn't bring Steven. We actually joked about it via text yesterday. I'm sure he would have charmed the pants off my stuffy relatives. I would introduce him as a pediatrician. Both Mom and Aunt Birgitta tend to cream their panties at the mere sight of a white coat.

"Unfortunately I have to get going," I say to Mom.

Her attempts to convince me to stay are ridiculously transparent. Dad doesn't even try to hide his relief. I kiss my half-smashed niece on the cheek; adjust her student cap, which has fallen askew; and tell her to do everything she'll regret tomorrow.

Then I take a taxi to Bantorget. Outside of John Bull I decline the offer of a wasted guy who asks if I want to fuck. On the stairs to Grand Hotel, I say hello to a guy whose offer I accepted a few years ago.

I leave my coat at coat check and find Steven at a table by the far wall of the restaurant. He stands up and greets me with a hug.

"You're glowing," he says.

I sit down at the window table. "Thanks for rescuing me."

Steven looks surprised. "The graduation party? Was it that awful?"

"Oh, I suppose I'm exaggerating. But I always feel like the black sheep of the family. My siblings have successful careers and lovely families. And then there's me."

I throw up my hands.

"You're young and beautiful," Steven says. "You've got your whole life ahead of you."

He's so easy to talk to. Despite the age difference, it's like we're on the same wavelength.

"How come your Swedish is so good?" I ask.

Steven aims a meaningful nod at the waiter, who quickly fills my glass with sparkling wine.

"I was born in Aberdeen and went to school there, but my father was Swedish," he says. "We summered in the Gothenburg archipelago. You could almost say I grew up in two places. I spoke Swedish each summer, with my relatives and friends and so forth, so it wasn't a big adjustment when I moved here."

"Why did you leave Scotland?" I ask.

The tiny bubbles of the cava bead in my mouth.

"Twenty days of each month are rainy in Aberdeen," says Steven. "Storm winds around the clock. Have you ever been to Scotland?"

I shake my head. "I've been to London."

"Not quite the same thing."

He tells me that he's lived in Lund for the last four or five years.

"We had a house," he says. "But since I ended up alone I've been living in an apartment instead."

"Solo," I say.

"What?"

"You said 'alone.' You mean you're living solo. Alone is more of a state of being. A feeling."

Steven smiles, but he looks far from convinced. "Does it really help to use a different word? Does it make you feel less alone to call it something else?"

His smile vanishes. He puts his glass aside and gazes down at the table.

"Do you feel alone?" I ask.

We haven't really approached this sort of conversation before.

"Sometimes," Steven says.

A notch of darkness appears in his otherwise bright eyes.

"Tell me about your wife," I say. "If you're okay with it, that is."

I'm certainly curious, but I also ask for his sake. It looks like he wants to talk about her.

"I don't know. It's still hard to talk about." A tear appears at the corner of his eye. Each time he says her name he has to avert his eyes and catch his breath.

"It happened so fast. Suddenly she was just gone. I never had time to come to terms with how sick she was. Of course it was a blessing that she didn't suffer, but it was a terrible shock for me."

They hadn't been married for even a year. Their future was laid out before them: kids, car, house, dog, family Fridays. Nothing turned out the way they planned.

"I miss her every minute of every day. But I also know that she wouldn't want me to fall apart. I have to try to stay strong, for her."

He sighs and pinches his nose. As he does, I realize that tears are trickling down my cheeks.

"I'm sorry," Steven says. "I didn't mean to get sentimental."

I place my hand over his and lace our fingers together. "I'm glad you told me."

It's been years since I got so intimate with a man. After just a few dates. It fills me with both fear and hope.

Steven isn't like the other men I've been with.

"What do you say we take this evening elsewhere?" he says.

Apparently the moisture damage in his bedroom has been fixed, and his apartment is only blocks away.

As we leave the restaurant, there are fireworks in my chest. I can't stop smiling. On the steps outside, Steven takes my hand, and he proceeds to hold it all the way down Klostergatan to Stortorget and past city hall. I feel like a teenager with a massive crush again.

Steven lives on the third floor. As he fixes drinks for us in his ultra-modern kitchen, I wander around the apartment.

The bedroom has a king-size bed and a table with a wireless phone charger. I don't see even a hint of any water damage. Was it just an excuse? Why would that be? Maybe he hadn't cleaned either.

"You take minimalism to a whole new level," I say, running my finger across the few book spines on the String shelf in the living room.

A huge TV hangs on the wall, and there's a blanket draped over the arm of the sofa. A few pillows in one corner.

It feels like a model unit.

"How is this possible?" I ask. "Can someone own so few belongings?"

Steven laughs as he comes out with two massive tumblers filled to the brim with mint and lime.

"Ever heard of Shurgard? I have four hundred square feet of storage space outside the city. And a ton of furniture still in our old house, which I never managed to sell."

"But still," I say.

He would faint if he saw my place.

"I guess I'm just not a fan of clutter," Steven says.

He must be such a fusspot.

"My mother thinks I ought to marry someone who likes things neat and tidy," I say, raising my glass.

"Oh my, is that a proposal?"

"Not exactly. But I'm sure you'd win your mother-in-law over right away."

"That's not a bad place to start," Steven says.

I set my drink down on the coffee table and link my phone to his sound system. The music vibrates through my body, and I press my hips to him in a sinuous dance.

"I thought we might take this party elsewhere."

Steven gives me a baffled smile.

"Where's that?"

I take the drink from his hand and suck it down until all that's left is a mint leaf and ice; I place it on the table. With a firm shove I herd him into the bedroom.

Excerpt from Interrogation with Rickard Lindgren

So, Rickard. Regina Rytter was your sister?

Correct. Regina is . . . she *was* three years older than me.

How would you describe your relationship? Were you in close contact?

As children we were pretty tight. I had a knack for getting myself in all sorts of trouble. Regina was always there like a guardian angel. But as adults we didn't have much in common. We've always been pretty different. And it didn't help when Dad went downhill.

Tell me about your father. Is he sick?

He was diagnosed with Alzheimer's a few years ago. At first he was mostly just a little confused, would forget what day it was and people's names. But then he got worse awfully fast. Now he's in a home, and he doesn't recognize me anymore. It's a hell of a disease.

And your mother?

She died twenty years ago. Breast cancer that recurred and spread all through her body.

How did your father's illness affect your relationship with Regina?
I don't know how much you know about my father. He owns a lot of property. He started out as a historian, but in the nineties he wrote a few books that became bestsellers. He invested the royalties in real estate. When he got sick, I took over the real estate company. As long as Dad is alive we can't sell or anything. It was going just fine, though. Until Regina married Steven Rytter.

What do you mean by that?
Oh, Steven is Steven. At first everything was tip-top. It was easy to like Steven. He was pleasant and sociable, intelligent, easy to talk to. It took quite a while for me to realize he has other sides too.

What kind of sides?
Steven likes to be in control. He horned in on just about everything. Obviously he tried to hide it from me, but I could see the changes in my sister. She always took Steven's side. Before that, she never had any opinions on how I ran the firm, but after Steven came into the picture, she wanted to control everything. Steven showed more and more interest in the firm and our real estate. It was a huge pain. Eventually I couldn't handle spending any time with them at all.

Why do you think Steven was so interested in the real estate firm?
It's pretty obvious. Dad's holdings are valued at hundreds of millions of kronor.

Has Steven ever threatened you or acted violent toward you?
No, hell no. Steven was more the devious type.

Do you know if he was ever violent toward Regina?
[long pause]

To be honest, I've never seen Steven blow up even once. He was always composed. What he subjected my sister to was probably more on the psychological level. After all, Regina's mental health became fragile pretty soon after they got married.

What are you referring to?

She stopped working and lost a bunch of weight. She didn't socialize with anyone anymore. At the end she seemed to be living in total isolation at that house. Shit, none of it was even a little bit normal.

Karla

Once again I'm standing in front of the Rytters' mansion, entirely out of breath. Birds are singing in the park next door, and I'm just about to punch in the code to disarm the alarm when the front door flies open and Steven Rytter steps out.

"Good morning," he says.

I reel off a half-assed excuse for my tardiness and hurry past him and into the house.

"You're not late at all," Steven says, looking at his watch, which looks like it cost more than I could earn if I cleaned 24–7 for a whole year.

"Oh, great. I haven't quite learned my way around Lund yet."

"No one ever does." Steven laughs. "Are you enjoying it here, though? You don't start at Juridicum until the fall, do you?"

"No, I've started already."

I explain that I'm taking an introductory course that's almost entirely online. Each week there's an assignment to turn in, and at the end there will be a written test.

"If you get the top grade, you're guaranteed a spot in the master of laws program starting this fall."

"That sounds stressful. Do you really have the time to clean on top of that?"

Easy for him to say. Does he know how much rent is for a room in Lund? Not to mention that I have to pay double rent this month, since I had to get out of that loud student-housing room. I was lucky to find a spot in such a central location at a price I could afford. Bill seems great, and his daughter, Sally, is funny. If worse came to worst, I probably could have struggled along on just my student loans, but I'd really like to be able to treat myself to a meal out once in a while and stop walking around in the same clothes every day.

"I'll manage," I say on my way to the cleaning closet.

"Hold on, Karla! That is your name, right? Karla? There's something I need to discuss with you."

His tone is different. Strained.

Did I do something wrong?

Regina Rytter claimed that her husband is awfully particular about the cleaning, but I've hardly been given any instructions at all.

"It's my wife," he says, taking a few steps into the hall.

I hide behind my bangs.

"She told me you had tea together."

He sounds annoyed. I never should have sat down and had tea on the clock. I really don't want to lose this job.

"I'm sorry, I didn't know . . ."

"It's okay," Steven says, softening.

He comes over and brushes against my arm.

"It's my fault. I should have been clearer about this. You see, my wife is gravely ill and needs constant rest. The tricky thing about her illness is that the least amount of effort will make her symptoms worse. She might wake up and feel energetic, but if she doesn't stay in bed, there's a considerable risk that she'll suffer a major setback."

"Understood," I say, thinking of Mom. "Is there really nothing anyone can do?"

"The doctors are investigating, but it's terribly difficult to diagnose something like this, and even if she does get a diagnosis, there's no guarantee there will be any adequate form of treatment. In the meantime, we can only do our best to manage her symptoms: she has to avoid exertion and take her medications."

I promise to do my best not to disturb Regina. In actuality, I couldn't be more relieved to avoid being social.

"I hope she'll get better soon, anyway," I say.

It feels like such a private matter. I just want to do my job without getting involved.

"It's more common than people think, to get seriously ill after a virus," Steven says. "Some people have to live the rest of their lives with serious complications."

I'd almost forgotten he was a doctor. Obviously he knows what he's talking about.

"So even if Regina seems energetic and wants to chat or have tea, I have to ask you to decline," he continues. "It's for her own good."

"Definitely. Of course."

I bite the inside of my cheek. I knew this would happen when I sat down with her.

I've always had a hard time making mistakes. At any moment I can recall the disappointment in my mother's eyes.

"If Regina wakes up, you can just make sure she takes her medication and goes back to bed again," Steven says.

I nod and promise I will, and he smiles in appreciation.

"I'll let you get to work now." He closes the front door and disappears down the path.

No instructions for cleaning whatsoever.

I seriously doubt this man is a cleaning tyrant. Maybe his wife is more confused than I realized.

As usual, I start with the bathrooms. I brought my earbuds, but I don't dare to plug both ears. If Regina calls out, I don't want to miss it.

I'm thinking of what she said about this illness suddenly shattering her life, that you should never take your health for granted. My mother had it all too but elected to throw it away on drugs. She always says it was my father's death that drove her straight down into hell.

I spent my whole childhood tiptoeing around. In many ways, I had to parent my own mother. But that was all I knew. I learned to lie and cover things up. My fear of losing her was so strong.

When I'm finished with the bathrooms, I start dusting. I dust upstairs and downstairs, then pull out the vacuum.

Whitney Houston is singing "I will always love you" in my earbud. One of Mom's favorite songs. I remember standing on the kitchen counter with my arms around her neck. The sharp odor of wine and cigarettes on her breath as we sang along with the refrain.

I start by vacuuming the kitchen and living room. Next to the stairs in the hall is a substantial bureau made of heavy wood and lovely brass accents. I have to bend all the way over to get beneath it with the vacuum. When there's a clatter from the hose I rush to turn it off. Something is stuck.

I pick up the vacuum and unscrew the hose. Out falls a gold bracelet with pearls. I weigh it in my hand. If it's real, it must be worth thousands.

Should I say something? No. Regina seems to be asleep. I place the bracelet on top of the bureau. At the same time, I realize that the top drawer is ajar, and as I go to close it I discover an entire sea of jewelry: bracelets, necklaces, rings, and earrings. Some are in boxes or cases; others are loose, scattered every which way. Several hundred thousands of kronors' worth of bling.

I don't dare to touch a thing.

So I quickly close the drawer.

I hurriedly vacuum the rest of the house, until all that's left is Regina's bedroom.

I don't know whether I should wake her. Does it matter if I don't vacuum in there today?

Sneaking up to the door, I take a listen. It's been hours without a peep from Regina. It really doesn't matter; I should just head back downstairs and get out the mop, fill the buckets with soap and water, but the silence in there makes my skin crawl. As I reach for the handle of the door, memories come back to me like a bolt of lightning.

Mom's bedroom door, five years ago, and me, cluelessly walking right in. The stench is still burned into some part of my brain: the stuffy, rank air mixed with pungent urine. The empty packs of pills on the floor. Mom's hand dangling over the edge of the bed, slack and pale.

Despite all the times I'd seen her high and passed out, I knew right away this was different. No matter how hard I shook her, tried to rouse her, I couldn't make her wake up. Within thirty seconds I'd found my phone and dialed the emergency number.

Mom recovered pretty quickly. After three days she was discharged and returned home. I had to talk to social services, and they offered me therapy, but I declined.

It took weeks before I realized what had actually happened. The plan was for me to move to Umeå that fall to start attending high school there. I'd done three weeks in Luleå the year before but had to withdraw due to Mom's condition. She thought I might as well go to school in Boden; there was a school there, after all. But I so badly wanted to get away. Just as I was about to move, Mom informed me, red-eyed and full of frustration, that she wouldn't survive if I abandoned her. That overdose was no mistake. Mom's only regret was that she hadn't managed to end it all.

I never made it to Umeå. I ended up studying the social sciences program at Björknäs in Boden, and it would take me another five years to leave.

Now I slowly depress the door handle. The close air hits me, and I squint into the darkness.

Regina Rytter is curled up on her side in bed.

"Are you awake?"

Bill

Days pass before we see Karla again. Whenever she's home, she spends most of her time closed in her room, studying or doing whatever it is she gets up to in there. It's a little weird, having a stranger in your house.

"What is she doing in there?" Sally asks for what must be the tenth time.

At last I lose my patience. "That's none of our business. She's only renting a room."

Sally sulks.

I tell her to go read a book instead while I put on coffee.

After a chat with my caseworker at the employment office, I write a letter, a spontaneous application of sorts, in which I describe myself and my qualifications. I email every last business in and around Lund. Shops, bars, restaurants, offices. More or less shady places. I've already bothered some of them more than once. They must be incredibly sick of me. But what else can I do?

Later that night I'm lying in bed, checking out different apps where people post requests for help with tasks. It might be anything from pruning an apple tree to installing a wall lamp. Sometimes there's a fixed payment; sometimes the task goes to whoever puts in the cheapest bid. I download one app and register myself as a "worker." There are some tasks available in Lund. But what am I going to do with Sally in the meantime?

I toss my phone aside, and Sally startles in her sleep. I feel stuck. Something has to give.

The next day, Sally and I make sausage stroganoff for dinner. She loves to help in the kitchen, and I love to watch as she ties the checked apron around her waist and shoves the stool over to reach the wall cabinets.

"Can't we invite Karla to dinner today?" she says, pulling a red pot from the top shelf.

"I don't know. . . ."

"Come on, Dad."

Sally puts down the pot and hurries over to Karla's door.

"We shouldn't bother her," I say. "It's up to Karla if she wants to spend time with us. I'm sure she has a lot of studying to do."

Sally pouts. "I thought we were going to get someone who wanted to hang out with us."

I know it's my own fault that she's gotten her hopes up. She misses her mother, of course. It pains me to explain once more that a lodger has no obligation to us. We have to treat Karla like any other neighbor.

"Is it too late to get someone else?" Sally asks, her lower lip sticking out.

With a sigh, I cave.

"Okay, fine. Go knock and ask if she wants to eat dinner. But you can't pester her, just ask."

"Yeah, yeah, Dad, I get it!"

There's no harm in asking, anyway. It's just a nice gesture to offer to share food, right?

"We made sausage stroganoff," Sally says before Karla has even opened the door. "Dad says I can't make you eat with us, but you have to eat dinner sometime, because everyone has to. Do you like sausage stroganoff?"

Karla laughs. "I *love* sausage stroganoff."

Her hair is sticking out in every direction, and she's holding a laptop that's plastered with stickers.

"I'm working on an assignment," she says, aiming a dazed look my way. "Are you sure there's enough?"

"There is!" Sally says. "We always make too much."

I set the pot on the table and smile.

"That's true, we do."

Sally and Karla both shovel down their meals as though they haven't eaten in days. It's nice to have company. Before Miranda got sick, we ate all our meals together. It was important, something she grew up doing. The family gathered around the table to talk about topics big and small. Those moments were sacred to Miranda, but without her it's not the same, and it's increasingly common for Sally's and my dinners to consist of fast food and frozen meals.

With Sally at the table, an awkward silence is a rare thing. She continues to interrogate Karla about her life in Norrbotten. We talk about studying the law, and Karla says she's always been passionate about justice. She realized she wanted to become a judge in high school.

"Everyone said it was impossible, that you have to spend years in school and get top grades in every subject. That only made me more determined. One day I'll show them you can do anything if you just set your mind to it and work hard enough."

I elect not to contradict her. I don't want to seem bitter. Presumably I felt the very same way when I was twenty-two and dreaming of a future as a director or producer in the film industry.

"My teacher says that justice doesn't mean that everyone gets the exact same thing," Sally says.

Karla runs her fingers through her bangs. "Maybe not. It's more about everyone having the right circumstances to succeed."

Sally giggles. "That's exactly what my teacher said!"

"You're lucky to have such a smart teacher."

Karla glances at me, and I have to make sure I'm not chewing with my mouth open or letting a smear of sauce stay on my chin for too long. I weigh my words carefully and pretend to be upset when Sally licks her knife.

"Hey, watch your manners."

Sally can't quite hide her surprise. Etiquette was Miranda's thing. I've never gotten worked up about a furtive burp or my kid's feet on the table.

For an hour or so, everything else fades away. I just exist. No thoughts of overdrawn bank accounts or declined transactions, no churning in my belly, no dark clouds in my mind. I can breathe and smile and feel alive.

After dinner, we all do the dishes together. Karla says she has to get up early the next day to work.

"Do you clean someone else's house?" Sally asks. "Why can't they clean their own house?"

"I'm sure they can," I say.

But Sally is persistent. "Then why don't they?"

Karla gazes tentatively at me.

"The woman who lives there is sick. She doesn't have the strength to clean. And her husband is a doctor, and he's almost always at work."

I'm a bit ashamed when I see the mess in our kitchen. Miranda would have been furious.

"Can we play cards now?" Sally asks. "Just for a little while?"

Karla glances at me again. "Okay," she says.

"Just for a little while," I reiterate.

We can't demand too much of Karla's time. At the same time, I haven't seen Sally this happy for a long time.

We sit on the couch, and I cut the deck. Karla teaches us a new game, and Sally never wants to stop playing. Eventually she drops off with the cards still in her hand and her head resting on Karla's arm.

"Man, she reminds me so much of myself." Karla pats Sally's head. "You seem to have such a sweet relationship."

I smile. "We've had a rough time of it. Sally took her mother's death very hard. Me too, of course. It's not easy to be a good parent when you're barely keeping your own head above water."

Karla looks me deep in the eyes. "I think you seem like an absolutely wonderful father."

PARTNER OF MURDER SUSPECT WORKED
FOR PEDIATRICIAN

The Evening Post, Lund

Today Lund district court made the decision to remand the 33-year-old man who is a suspect in the murder of a Lund couple. *The Evening Post* can now reveal that a link exists between the 33-year-old and the murder victims.

According to the prosecutor, police interrogations have fortified suspicions against the 33-year-old. A source with insight into the case tells *The Evening Post* that there is also physical evidence linking the man to the scene of the crime.

"The 33-year-old is under suspicion of homicide with probable cause," says the prosecutor.

She declined to state whether there is any suspected motive for the murder of the pediatrician and his wife. According to the prosecutor, this is a very sensitive phase of the investigation. At the present time, there are no other suspects in the case.

The remanded man resides in central Lund. He has a criminal record and has been previously convicted of petty crime. According to the national registration database, he lives alone with his eight-year-old daughter, but according to a number of sources contacted by *The Evening Post*, a 22-year-old woman lives at the same apartment as well.

At present *The Evening Post* can reveal that there is a link between the man's young partner and the murdered couple. The 22-year-old woman, who was raised in Norrbotten but came to Lund as recently as last spring, worked as a cleaner for the murdered couple.

"It's true that she is an employee here," says the CEO of the local cleaning company hired by the pediatrician and his wife.

The CEO declined to comment further.

The 33-year-old suspect has lived in Lund for almost fifteen years. During his youth he lived in a number of different communities in central Sweden, including a small town in Östergötland.

The Evening Post contacted some former schoolmates of his, but few of them remember him.

"He was in our class for a year or two," says one man, who wished to remain anonymous. "But he didn't really stand out. I don't think he hung out with anyone outside of school. I read on Flashback Forum that he's got a record. Too bad it had to turn out like this."

The 33-year-old studied film and culture studies, but it seems that he largely supported himself on various odd jobs. The man's previous partner, the mother of his daughter, passed away due to illness about a year ago.

"He must have been having a really tough time," says a source who lives in the same neighborhood. "But he seems to be a great dad to his little girl, and I definitely can't believe he's guilty of all this."

A number of other neighbors contacted by *The Evening Post* confirm the image of the 33-year-old as a withdrawn but very pleasant man who was often seen around the area with his daughter. But few were aware of his relationship with the young cleaner.

"I've seen him and his daughter with that gal, but I guess I thought she was a relative or a babysitter," says one neighbor.

The 33-year-old is now in custody while the police investigation continues. The man's attorney declined to comment on the case, citing the ongoing nature of the investigation.

Karla

The wallpaper in Sally's old room is from *The Lion King*. When I need a break from studying, I dream myself away among giraffes, zebras, and flamingos. The legal concepts swirl around me. Everything flies apart.

I wish Mom were here. I even suggested it. One week before I left, I sat down at the kitchen table and took her hands, which had so quickly grown old.

"You can come with me, if you want," I said.

We both knew it wouldn't happen, but I still wanted to say it. I meant it too. At least, I think I did. But most important, Mom could never claim that I didn't offer her the chance.

Now I pull Mom up among the contacts on my phone, which trembles in my hand. It's always been like this. The fear of what I'll encounter when she picks up.

"Hi."

That one little word is all it takes, and I know.

Tonight she's low. Probably took some sedatives.

"I'm so miserable," she slurs. "I'm so fucking alone and useless. I honestly don't know how much longer I can go on."

I try to comfort her and cheer her up, like I always do, like I've done all my life. At the same time, guilt gnaws at me. Mom's misery is awfully contagious, and I'm way too susceptible.

"I went to the doctor yesterday," she says, "but he doesn't give a shit about me. Same as everyone else. No one wants anything to do with me. Not even my own daughter."

"You know that's not true, Mom."

She whimpers and sighs.

I wish I could fend it off, just shake off these pricks of the needle, but they drill their way deep inside. She is my mother, my lifeline.

"Love is actions," she says, "not just words."

I don't want to allow her to control how I feel. She has been controlling my world for way too long as it is. But it's not as simple as just steeling myself. She's sick, and I'm codependent, I know all that. Still, I spend every second doubting whether I did the right thing by leaving her alone with all her misery.

"Can't you go visit Silja and Bengt?"

She does actually have friends. If it weren't for them, I don't think I could have left. Even though Silja and Bengt are addicts too, I know they'll always be there for Mom when they can manage to be.

"I got a new room," I say, telling her about Bill and little Sally. "It's so freaking sad. Her mom died of cancer."

"But I'm alive," says Mom. "Although that doesn't seem to matter to you."

I know what she's trying to do—it's extremely obvious—but it's still hard, almost impossible, to defend myself against it. Mom has always played off my guilty conscience.

"I have to go now," I say, a lump of tears in my throat. "Love you, Mom."

She doesn't respond.

I'm still perched on the edge of the bed, wondering how I'm going to deal, when there's a knock at the door.

"Just a sec!" I say, hurrying to fix my face.

Sally's outside, asking if I want to come play cards.

"I don't know. I need to . . ."

"Please," she says, pressing her hands together as if in prayer. "It's so much more fun with three people."

"Well, okay."

Bill's already on the sofa, shuffling the cards. Coke and popcorn on the table, soft music on the speakers.

I wish my own childhood had looked like this, instead of beer cans and liquor bottles everywhere, cigarettes and pills, snoring ragg-sock feet on the couch, or waiting alone, fear in my belly, behind dark windows.

"Who were you talking to?" Sally asks when I sit down on the easy chair. "I heard you talking to someone."

I stretch my legs out under the table while Bill starts to deal the cards.

"It was my mom."

"Does she miss you?" Sally asks.

"Yes, of course. At least, she misses me a little. But she's doing okay. She's busy with her own life. Mom has always worked a lot. She likes her job. And she's got a bunch of friends. So I'm sure she's doing just fine."

I'm almost surprised. The lies are so deeply rooted that they come right out on their own.

It's not even about shame anymore. Just pure habit.

Sally smiles, and Bill sorts his cards.

"You start," he says to me.

Jennica

have never heard of Joe McNally before, but after half a day at the Louisiana, I'm thoroughly captivated by his photography. Steven has done his homework and is excited to share what he knows. It's like having a personal guide.

Five stars for my life. That evening, I find myself sitting at a champagne bar at the best hotel in Copenhagen. We've just polished off a Michelin-starred dinner and will soon take the elevator up to our suite. In front of me is one of the hottest men I've ever met. He's smart and well-rounded, charming and easy to talk to. And he has this way of looking at me that says he truly cares, that my thoughts and emotions and opinions are important.

I raise my glass and finish the last sip of wine.

"Should we talk about the elephant?" Steven says, taking my hand beneath the table.

"The elephant?"

"It feels like we've got one here in the room," Steven says, opening his pale eyes wide. "Our age difference."

Something dislodges itself and begins to float around inside me. I like his straightforwardness. I haven't exactly been spoiled with frank and honest communication in my life.

"Do you feel old?" I teasingly ask. "Isn't age just a number?"

Of course, while it's easy to say, it's not quite true. I've dated at least one guy over forty before, but Steven is actually closer to fifty.

"You know how it is," he says. "People will talk. What do your parents think, for instance?"

"My parents are on a need-to-know basis when it comes to my dating life."

I can't bring myself to mention that my mother would probably sing a falsetto hallelujah if I introduced her to Steven.

"I guess we'll have to take it as it comes," he says. "Some things just happen. It's not as if I planned to fall for a thirty-year-old."

He touches me under the table. The back of my hand, up the inside of my forearm.

Goose bumps everywhere.

He's fallen for me?

"You're amazing," he whispers into my ear as he pulls out the chair.

As we walk through the restaurant, he walks close behind me, and it feels like people are staring with envy.

One hour later, we're having sex between sheets of Egyptian cotton. Steven doesn't drop my gaze as he enters me. I'm starting to get used to making love like this, slowly and tenderly, like in a movie.

You have to take it as it comes.

The next day, we drive back across the bridge in Steven's Tesla. My hand rests on his thigh, and I can hardly take my eyes off him.

We approach Lund from Norra Ringen. Steven walks me into the parking lot at City Gross.

"See you tonight?" he asks.

I run my hand in under his jacket. "I have to work."

"What? I thought you were a student."

"It's a kind of charity work, you might say. I answer phone calls from people who need someone to talk to. Like a phone-a-friend help line."

It's not all that far from the truth, but this doesn't seem like the right time to bring up mediums or empathic abilities with Steven, no matter how wonderful a time we're having together.

He's still standing outside his car as I go. He waves, and I blow kisses his way until he's out of sight. Who *am* I? I'm acting like a silly teenager.

When I get home, I shed both the ridiculousness and my fancy Busnel blazer. Dog is stretched out on the bed, looking like he owns the place.

"Move."

He gleefully rolls around in the sheets. When I reach out to pet him, he darts away.

"Don't look so damn pleased with yourself," I say.

Then he slithers off the bed and pads over to his food dish. I serve him what smells like dead rat, but it's the only thing he'll eat besides tinned herring.

I lie down on the bed, catch up on the latest news on my phone, and scroll through my social media until it's time to start working.

My first two calls are from women who have been betrayed and dumped by cheating bastards but still want to know if there's any chance these douchebags will want them back. That's one downside of this work—it only bolsters my view of men as insensitive Neanderthals and women as pathetic ninnies. Of course, I've been sure all along that there are good people out there, but it wasn't until Steven that I got firsthand confirmation of that knowledge.

By the time I hang up after delivering an hour-long harangue to a forty-five-year-old biomedical engineer who was on the verge of forgiving her husband's little bout of adultery with an intern at his work, I'm panting and out of breath. It's like I've just run a marathon.

Now that I've convinced her to burn that cheating pig's Armani suit, I'm full of endorphins and my underarms are dripping, but I still feel like a good human. My empathic abilities are top-notch. To think that I get paid to do this.

There's a conversation manual that tells me how to handle various situations that might crop up. Before I was hired, I was told in no uncertain terms that we do not mess around. We are not licensed therapists. At the least hint of suicidal behavior, we must sound the alarm. We don't want any investigative journalists on our case.

Each time the phone rings, I say the same thing.

Welcome, I am your psychic adviser, Jennica. How can I help you?

This is the third call of the night. I already feel emotionally drained.

"Hello?" says a distant-sounding voice.

I take for granted that it's a woman. At least nine out of ten callers are women. But when there's a sudden crackle on the line and the voice comes closer, I realize I was wrong.

It's a man.

"Hi, Jennica."

I must be hearing things.

Mom has mentioned that we've got mental illness in our genes. I guess it's the irony of life that made it burst forth now, of all moments, just as everything is going my way.

"Who is this?" I ask.

"I'm sorry, I couldn't help it."

I can see Steven's amused face in front of me. It can't be true. He's going to lose every ounce of respect he had for me.

"How did you get this number?"

He laughs. "Some online sleuthing. You have a pretty unusual name."

I adjust my headset and shove off Dog the cat, who has stolen my favorite corner pillow. This is beyond humiliating. Steven is a doctor, and here I am, playing therapist on the phone.

"Look, I'm not a real psychic. Or, I mean, I don't believe in this stuff. It's just a job."

Steven laughs even more.

"That's too bad, but maybe you can give me some advice anyway. I could really use some guidance."

I still can't believe he's doing this. I should be furious, but Steven just laughs yet again, and I make up my mind to do the same.

"Sure, I can try to give you a little spiritual guidance."

"Oh, thanks! Here's the thing," Steven says. "I've met this woman, and she's wonderfully smart and funny and charming. But she doesn't seem to understand how fantastic she is."

"A fairly common ailment among the female sex," I say.

"Definitely! But it feels like she and I have something special. Unfortunately, she seems to have a hard time letting me in. I don't know how to get closer to her without scaring her off."

"That's a tough line to walk," I say.

"Mm-hmm." Steven drags out his response. "Do you think I should tell her how much I like her? Or is it too soon?"

Part of me wants to simply drop all the pretense and let Steven know I like him too. I'm well on my way to total infatuation. But another part of me won't allow it. The part that's been through this before, knows the rules of the game, and will never forget how painful it is to get hurt.

"It's probably best to wait," I say. "I'm sure she has her suspicions, anyway."

Steven Rytter is truly one of a kind. When we hang up, my hands and chest are both trembling.

What is happening to me?

How are things with the doctor? Rebecka asks in the group chat.

Emma adds a bunch of question marks and curious emojis.

I sit cross-legged on the bed, with my favorite pillow at the small of my back, and realize that I'm wearing a huge smile.

"Yeah, yeah, I know," I say to Dog, who stares snidely.

Don't want to jinx it, I write to the girls. *But right now it's going pretty fucking great.*

Excerpt from Interrogation with Karla Larsson

I'd like to talk a bit about Bill Olsson now, Karla. What is your relationship to Bill?

I lived with him over the summer. I rented a room there.

How long did you do that?

Almost the whole summer. The first week after I moved to Skåne I lived in some kind of student housing, but I could hardly get any sleep there, people partied all night. Then I saw an ad on Facebook and wrote to Bill. That same day he let me come look at the room.

Do you have any documentation for this?

Documentation? What do you mean?

You must have signed a lease of some sort, right?

It didn't occur to me. Bill wasn't sure if he needed permission from the housing company to rent me the room. But I did pay rent, in any case.

Did you? We've had a look at Bill Olsson's bank transactions and can't find any such deposits.

But I paid everything in cash. Two months' rent in advance.

Is that so? Could it be that you and Bill had a different sort of relationship?

Definitely not! Where'd you get that idea?

Did Bill Olsson ever accompany you to the Rytters' home?

No. He had nothing to do with them. Or . . . no, wait, he picked me up there once.

When was this?

I don't remember exactly. Maybe a week or two before the murders.

And he came inside the house that time?

I wasn't quite finished cleaning, and Regina Rytter was asleep upstairs, so I let him in for a minute. It wasn't long at all.

How would you describe Bill Olsson?

Describe him? I mean, I don't know . . . He's a really good dad to Sally. He's nice and has a big heart. I have nothing negative to say about Bill.

Have you ever known him to be violent?

Definitely not! Bill is the chillest guy in the world.

We know Bill was having financial troubles last summer. Did he ever discuss them with you?

Yeah, maybe a little. That was why he was renting out Sally's room, after all. He needed money for rent and the electric bill and stuff.

He never asked you for help with money?

No, not directly. I was paying him rent, so I suppose I was helping in that sense.

But not in any other way?

No.

So Bill never convinced you to do something you maybe didn't really want to do? Something you came to regret?

No . . . or . . . no!

[crying]

[inaudible]

Bill

've gotten responses to five of the twenty job inquiry emails I sent out. No luck. The owner of a betting shop promises to take note of my interest, and a woman who runs an interior design boutique says she might need someone for the Christmas rush. That's six months from now. I'm about to give up. This is hopeless.

After breakfast, Sally goes down to the playground with some friends, and I sit down in front of the computer. I have to find a job. I'll just game for a little bit first.

Before Miranda was diagnosed, I had only dabbled in *World of Warcraft*, but as she got sick the game started to take up ever more of my time. It was a way to escape when cancer took over our daily life. These days it's my primary source of contact with other human beings.

I don't know if it's been an hour or two hours when the front door opens and Sally comes hurtling into the entryway with tears running down her face. Her friends' wary faces peer through the crack in the door behind her.

"Daddy, Daddy, come quick!"

She's hyperventilating.

"Sweetie, what is it?" I kneel down in the entryway and embrace her. Her little rib cage is heaving.

"What happened?" I ask her friends at the door.

A boy named Mohammad, who's in Sally's class and lives on the next stairwell over, looks like he's about to burst into tears too.

"It wasn't Sally's fault!" he says.

"You have to come downstairs," says a girl in shorts and a hoodie, whose name I'm blanking on at the moment. "The man is waiting for you."

I take Sally's hand and step into my flip-flops.

"But what happened?" I ask her friends.

"We were playing four square," says the girl in the hoodie as we head down the stairs.

"You make a square and divide it into quarters," Mohammad explains. "Then you have to bounce a basketball, and—"

"Yes, I know four square. But what happened to Sally?"

Miranda used to say I am a marvel of patience. When Sally was getting on her nerves and Miranda was about to snap, all it took was a look for me to know it was time to intervene.

By the time we get to the building entrance, Sally has recovered and her breathing is a little easier.

"I accidentally bounced a ball right into a window," she snuffles.

"A basement window," Mohammad clarifies. "It went bang, and then the whole window broke."

"Oh dear."

I unlock the door and let the kids out.

"I didn't mean to," Sally sobs.

"Of course you didn't. Accidents happen."

Around the corner waits a building super from the city property office; he's smoking a cigarette, has his hands-free device in his ear, a broom leaning against the wall. He's blocked off the broken window with a big crisscross of red-and-white tape.

Sally squeezes my fingers.

"I've told them again and again not to play ball here," the super says with a sigh. "A windowpane like this one is a costly affair."

"We need blacktop to play four square," says Mohammad.

The man glares at him.

"It was an accident," I say.

"Right, of course." The super points his cigarette at Sally. "This your little girl? You'll have to pay for the window."

It can't be true.

Sally starts sobbing again. I give the guy a significant look. He bends down and stubs the cigarette out on the ground; sparks fly.

"You've got insurance, don't you?"

Karla

Exactly nineteen seconds before the deadline I send in my first assignment. I've read through it a hundred times, double-checked all my cited sources, and paged through the course books until the pages are full of stains and thumbprints.

This introductory course in legal studies is almost entirely web-based. I can address questions to a study coach and there's a forum where you can discuss things with other students. So far there's hardly a single question there that's received a helpful answer. It's so clear no one is here to help anyone else. People toss out desperate queries about a concept or want to know where in the literature they can find a certain piece of information, but no one seems to want to respond.

When the first assignment is over, a girl named Waheeda posts to the forum. She says how relieved she is that it's finally over and describes how miserable it makes her to constantly be forced to be an overachiever. It's not healthy, how there's no room for even a single mistake. To be allowed to sit for the final exam we must receive a passing grade on every single assignment.

I'm convinced that lots of us are having the exact same feelings as Waheeda. Even so, she doesn't get a single reply.

In the end, I'm the one who writes back.

I feel the same way. It's like there's a knife to our throats every second. I want this SO BAD.

It's only a few minutes before Waheeda responds, and soon we've got a conversation going. To keep from exposing too much on the forum, we switch to Snapchat.

Waheeda is in the same boat. Neither of us got terrible grades in high school, but we were far from good enough to get accepted to the legal studies program the traditional way. Acing the final exam is our only chance.

I KNOW I will be the best prosecutor ever, Waheeda writes. Huge fucking loss for Sweden if I don't get in because of some fucking homework assignment.

She says she thought about becoming a police officer for a long time, but the real power is with the prosecutor.

I'm gonna lock up everyone who truly deserves it. Not just the ones who do the dirty work, but all the people who always get away with stuff because they have money or power or the right last name.

That sounds pretty naive, but I still find her passion impressive. When I tell her about my dream of becoming a judge, she suggests we make a pact and infiltrate a court of law somewhere.

We'll disrupt the whole system!

I realize I'm smiling to myself.

When it comes out that we both like soccer, Waheeda suggests I should come with her to a practice. Apparently she plays for one of the best teams in Lund.

I mean, I haven't played for like five years, I write.

You have to! You KNOW it would be nice to kick someone in the shin after turning in such a huge assignment.

Haha, maybe.

I don't think I really have time to play soccer this summer, but I don't want to miss out on the chance to make a friend. Waheeda seems nice.

When was the last time I had a real friend? I guess I've never exactly been an outsider, I've never been bullied or frozen out or anything, but when the other girls in my class were becoming BFFs I hesitated to let anyone get too close. It seemed so important to keep anyone from finding out about my home life. It's not like Mom ever forbade me from inviting friends home, though. In fact, she encouraged me to, and was always asking why I didn't have friends around. But it was impossible to bring anyone to our house. It was always chaos: beer bottles, pill packs, leftover food, overflowing ashtrays. Besides, I never knew what kind of mood Mom would be in. My greatest dream was to have taco nights, to pile on the couch to watch the Melody Festival together—just one night without screaming and shouting or Mom falling asleep on the sofa.

At least I had soccer. I went to extra practices with kids who were one or two years older and made the countywide team. All my anxious thoughts disappeared for a little while when I was on the field.

As I prepared for high school, I dreamed of starting afresh, somewhere new. By that point everyone in Boden knew everything about me and Mom. At least they thought they did. That was why I wanted to go to Umeå or Luleå for school. But Mom begged and pleaded, saying she wouldn't survive without me, and in the end I stayed. She had already lost Dad. That was when everything fell apart. It would take several years and many difficult battles with my inner demons before I broke free. The angst of it all still comes back to me every day.

When Waheeda asks if I want to come along to one of her practices, my thoughts go straight to Mom. It's in my bones. She has such power over me.

I hover between yes and no for a moment, but then I write back that I'd love to come along.

I have to. This would be a step closer to the normal life I long for. I feel restless in a good way; I open the door and go to the kitchen.

"Oops, sorry."

I'm completely unprepared to see Bill sitting there in the dim light, bent over with his arms resting on the table.

He looks up with red-rimmed eyes.

"I just about fell asleep."

It looks like he's been crying.

He lives with a lot of despair too, of course. At least I still have my mom. I can call her whenever I want. Bill will never share even another second with Miranda.

I shift from foot to foot and try to think of something to say.

"Are . . . you okay?"

Bill pushes his chair back and stands up. He doesn't look at me.

"I'm just tired."

Jennica

HBO has released a new series about missing women in Alaska. I lie in bed with chips and dip and wine, bingeing episode after episode, even as I avoid glancing at the war zone in the kitchenette: the mountains of dishes and pizza boxes, the pyramids of empty energy-drink cans. My friend Tina, whom I've known since preschool, once said that my apartment is like a bachelor pad. In other words: if I'd been born with a penis, no one would have expected any different from me. Ever since then I've thought of it as an important part of my personal battle for equality not to clean too much or too often.

Time and again I find myself zoning out and forgetting about the documentary on the screen. Instead, my thoughts drift to Steven. What is happening? I can hardly concentrate anymore. I picture Steven's pale eyes before me. It's like I can feel his big hands on my body. I feel tingly all over.

My family and all my friends, the whole world, it feels like, wants nothing more than for me to grow up, settle down, have a family, and become one of the same kind of responsible adult humans they all are. At the same time, my circle of friends is normative, to say the least:

lots of eyebrows would be raised if I introduced a forty-seven-year-old widower as my new boyfriend.

I shouldn't worry about it, obviously. I'm almost thirty. What does it matter what people think?

When I get up to refill my glass, Dog the cat swishes over and licks up the last dollop of my garlic dip.

"Hey! Watch yourself or I'll neuter you."

The cat looks content.

Apparently Steven is allergic to cats, which is great news because that means we'll have to stick to hotels and his apartment in the city. Glad to. I'm sure he will have seen more elegant places in the slums of Cape Town. And he'd never get that this bachelorette pad is a statement.

When I take out my phone to change the song, I discover a new message from him.

I've been thinking of you all day. Can I see you tonight?

A flame is kindled deep inside my chest and soon spreads to my skin; I get goose bumps. Each minute without Steven feels like a waste of my life.

Sorry, I have to work, I reply. Can I call you later?

I browse the emojis. A red heart, is that too much? The little hearts spinning through the air? A smoochy face blowing a heart kiss?

All these hearts. They're driving me nuts. At last I decide to forgo some goofy emoji. He's almost fifty after all, what does he care?

When I've got two episodes left in my series, I have to turn off the TV and start my shift. With yet another glass of sparkling wine in hand, my headset on, and Dog on the pillow beside me, I lean back in bed and accept the first call.

It's Olivia, one of my regulars. She's just a few years older than I am. The first few times she called, I mostly ended up beyond annoyed with her; I thought she was totally bonkers. The thing is, Olivia is married to a drunk. Her husband, who's also the father of their two little kids, is a hardworking IT dude who likes cycling and cooking. But most of all he likes to drink.

It wasn't until Olivia described how wonderful her husband is with the kids, and how fantastic their marriage is 90 percent of the time, that I started to understand her, and I actually came to realize that sometimes dismembering the bastard with an ax isn't the only solution.

"You're codependent," I tell her again and again. "You have to stop allowing him to behave this way."

You're not supposed to blame the victim, but sometimes it's hard not to.

This time, Olivia's husband had arranged a weekend getaway for the family at a cozy bed-and-breakfast in Österlen. They rode tandem bikes, explored some art galleries, went on picnics, and sat in hot tubs at night. Then he got drunk.

"He was yelling and throwing things," Olivia tells me. "But really, it was all my fault. I'm so dang careless. When we got to our room, I had lost the key. We couldn't get in. It was late, and the reception desk was closed. We had to stand there for forty minutes, wrapped up in our towels. The kids were freezing and whiny. No wonder he lost his temper."

"But hold on. You didn't lose the key on purpose, did you?"

"Of course not."

Olivia sobs. She often cries her way through our talks.

I bring up Steven's text on my phone and read it over and over. It's not easy to find a good man. I've gotten lucky. And I never gave up. I'm so glad I haven't rushed and settled for just anyone. Olivia is a good example of where that can lead.

"Today he's been wonderful," she says. "He apologized, and then he took the kids so I could do some shopping on my own. What am I supposed to do? I love him. I love our family."

I wish I could give Olivia a straight answer. If it were just her and her husband it would be easier. With children in the picture, everything is more complicated. So many times I've thought about what my own upbringing would have been like if Mom had left Dad. There's no guarantee it would have been better.

"I think you need to talk to a psychologist, Olivia."

I've told her this many times before.

"But I've got you," she says. "I like talking to you so much, Jennica."

There's no reason to give her the rundown of all my arguments yet again. If Olivia wants to throw away her money on calling me, I can't stop her.

After Olivia, I talk to two more women. I try to be as empathetic as possible and give them tips and advice. Toward the end, I even lie in response to a direct question about whether I'm in contact with the other side. What does it matter? If it might make someone feel better to think the tiny nuggets of common sense I offer come from spirits or whatever, I don't see how a little white lie can hurt.

I've just hung up and pulled off my headset when I hear something out on the access balcony. Before I can react, there's a knock at the door.

Dog lays his ears flat and arches his back. We stare at each other. No one ever comes knocking here.

Maybe it's a kid wanting to sell ridiculously expensive cookies for a school trip? Or Jehovah's Witnesses? Maybe I should join up.

There's another knock, louder this time. I realize I'm wearing nothing but panties and a camisole and hurry to wrap myself in my blanket.

"Yes?" I call through the door.

It's not as if this 1960s-era student apartment building has thick, secure doors.

"Jennica Jungstedt?" comes a voice from the other side.

"Yes, what is it?"

"I have flowers for you."

When I open the door, a young guy with snuff on his teeth hands over the biggest bouquet I've ever seen. I'm totally drowning in sweet-scented cut flowers.

There's a tiny card, and I open it.

The name *Steven* with a huge heart. A huge fucking red heart.

Bill

spend all morning immersed in computer games while Sally is off playing at a classmate's house. I don't have it in me to tackle anything else. The real world comes knocking only when the mail slot slams and I realize I forgot to eat lunch.

Under a pile of colorful ad circulars on the floor I find the envelope from municipal housing with a bill for five thousand kronor for the broken window.

What do you do when you're out of money? Ever since Miranda got sick, finances have been tight. The first few months after her funeral I was out sick, and the situation quickly escalated from bad to worse.

I started with our expenses, chasing sale prices every which way and avoiding any purchase that wasn't absolutely necessary. It's fascinating how much money you can save by comparison shopping and making smart choices, buying from flea markets and thrift shops. These days we can forget luxury items like freshly baked bread, pastries for coffee time, new shoes, and cologne. The only promise I made to myself was that things should change as little as possible for Sally.

Over the Christmas holidays I got a massive amount of overtime at the movie theater, and after a few late-night hours playing the slots on a casino site I was sitting on a minor fortune. But money can always make more money, and when you've got a lot of it, it's easy to become blind to its value. As quickly as I had brought in tens of thousands of kronor, I was rid of it again. And then I lost my job. A couple of block-busters flopped, people chose streaming over the theater, and I was soon made redundant. The matinees, which I preferred to work because I didn't have to drag Sally along or find a babysitter, grew fewer and far-ther between, and when I had to decline a couple of late-night shifts in a row, I learned in March that my employment would be terminated.

That was the kiss of death.

All our savings were gone, and soon I wouldn't have a salary either.

I did away with all our recurring expenses aside from the most basic ones. I canceled all subscriptions, got rid of our streaming services, and stopped taking the newspaper. Personal accident insurance and home insurance I would also have to do without. Each cent I could save was valuable.

To bring in money, I emailed newsrooms all over the world to offer my services as a film critic and writer, but I didn't get a single bite. I answered ads that promised extra income for simple tasks. On top of all this, I was a hair's breadth away from investing money I didn't have in a setup that reminded me of a classic pyramid scheme. I took out easy loans and watched the mountain of debt grow. I took out more loans to pay off the old ones. And I sold stuff on Facebook and to secondhand stores. I unloaded everything of value except the TV, my computer, and my DVD collection.

Now I open the app I downloaded. There are a number of new tasks in Lund, and I mark myself interested. It's scut work, and it hardly pays at all, but I can't exactly be picky. I'm prepared to take on anything.

When Karla comes home at three in the afternoon, I still haven't had any lunch.

She opens the freezer and looks through the kitchen drawers.

"Isn't Sally home?"

"She's at a friend's house."

"I was going to heat this up," she says, offering me half of her vegetarian microwave meal.

We sit across from each other at the kitchen table to eat. I try not to let her see how crappy I'm feeling, but the mood quickly grows strained.

"I'm trying to find a job," I say, to break the awkward silence. "It's not easy. My skills as a film expert aren't exactly in high demand."

Karla swallows a bite and drinks some water.

"I would check with the cleaning company, but unfortunately I already know they only hire girls."

I smile.

"Is that allowed? Isn't there some sort of equality law for that?"

I'm trying to make a joke, but Karla is taken aback and fumbles for an explanation.

"I'm just kidding," I say. "No serious cleaning company would hire me."

To show her what I mean, I gesture at the cluttered counter, and Karla laughs, relaxing now.

"The bills are piling up," I explain, placing my cutlery in a cross. "When I was little, we moved around a lot. The minute I made new friends, it was time to leave again. I promised myself Sally would never have to live that way. I really want to be able to stay here. It would be super hard to find another place nearby."

"We didn't have much money either, when I was little," Karla says between bites. "Mom had a rough time after Dad was gone. Still, I never missed the kind of stuff you can buy. What I missed was the other stuff: laughter and hugs, someone to play cards with. Sally has all of that."

I smile. That means a lot to me. Sally is my life.

"Like I said, she can be a little much at times," I say. "You have to say something if—"

"Oh, no," Karla interrupts me. "Obviously she's been raised right."

"Thanks."

Really, I can't take credit. Sally is so much like her mother. Everyone liked Miranda. She was the kind of person who made sure others felt at ease. The one who organized dinners and parties, who paid attention to everyone and noticed the moment someone felt left out. She was often the glue that held everything together, and not just in our family—even among friends and colleagues. In the end, when she was in palliative care, and she was losing so much weight, she still asked how other people were doing. As if she cared more about them than about herself, up until the very end. The last words she said, before she closed her eyes forever, settled it. Miranda whispered through dry lips: *Whatever you do, Bill. Don't do it for me. Do it for Sally.*

Each morning I wake up with those words close to my heart.

I do it for Sally.

Karla gazes down and pokes at her food with her fork. She seems lost in thought.

"What happened with your dad?" I ask, rushing to add: "Obviously you don't have to tell me, if you don't want to."

But it seems like she does want to.

Karla uses her fork to draw tiny circles on her plate. Her black nail polish is starting to chip.

"Both my parents were drug addicts. They quit when I was born, but Dad had a relapse. He died of an overdose before my first birthday."

I can hardly relate to that. I didn't always have it easy with my folks, but neither of them had a drug problem. Even though I seldom saw Mom, she was still there in the background. It must be terrible to grow up like Karla did.

"Did your mother make it through without relapsing?"

She slowly shakes her head.

"After Dad died, Mom fell back into using too. She spent my entire childhood quitting and starting, quitting and starting again."

That must have left deep wounds. Karla seems so chill and considerate, but she's still always cheerful, and she's fantastic with Sally. She's a true survivor, just like me.

"You're a dandelion kid," I say.

She gives me a skeptical smile.

"A what?"

"That's what Miranda's mom always said about me. That I was a dandelion kid. A kid who makes it against all odds. You know, because dandelions are tenacious and can grow anywhere."

It almost seems absurd to compare myself to Karla. Sure, my dad had a few beers now and then, but I don't remember ever having seen him drunk. Dad was like a big kid. He forgot to pay bills, was useless at remembering things and keeping commitments—the idea of a routine was totally foreign to him. But he was never mean. Nothing but love and affection from him.

"I don't usually talk about this," Karla says. "Not a lot of people understand, and I'm not out for sympathy."

I understand precisely.

"Same here. I hardly ever talk about my childhood. It really wasn't until I met Miranda and her family that I realized how strange my upbringing was."

Karla takes a sip of milk and runs her index finger under her nose.

"Maybe it's just as well Dad died. I don't know if I could have taken care of two addict parents. I guess sometimes death sets you free."

I look away. I don't like that.

When we lost Miranda, lots of people said similar things. That she was finally at rest, that it was a blessing she didn't have to feel the pain anymore. I hated everyone who said that. There was nothing positive about Miranda's death.

"I'm sorry," Karla says. "I didn't mean . . ."

"It's fine. I get it."

I look at her again, and she lowers her voice until it's almost a whisper. "It must be so rough. She was so young."

I stand up. I don't want to talk about Miranda. Every little reminder takes me back.

"Thanks for the food," I say. "Are you finished?"

Without waiting for a response, I pick up Karla's plate. The fork slides off and lands on the floor. We both hurry to retrieve it and almost knock heads.

"Oops, sorry," Karla says.

I pick up the fork and carry our plates to the sink. As the water pours from the faucet, the black cloud envelops me. The pain never ends. This emptiness and silence is forever, and forever is a hell of a long time.

After Sally falls asleep, I sit at the computer hour after hour. My wallpaper, Al Pacino as Colonel Slade in *Scent of a Woman*, prompts me to visit YouTube. I'll never get sick of watching that defense speech in front of the school disciplinary committee.

Colonel Slade's ruthless indignation.

I'll show you out of order!

Really, I should watch the whole movie again. It's been a couple of years since I saw it.

On the table in front of me is the bill for the windowpane from the housing office. Soon it's taking up my whole field of vision. I can't seem to ignore it.

How am I going to pull five thousand kronor out of nowhere? I'm sure that's an affordable price for plenty of folks, but for me it's a fortune.

Sally turns over in bed and whimpers.

Shit. I cannot crash into that black cloud again. I have to keep myself from falling as quickly as possible.

Over the past year, I've talked to both a pastor and a psychologist, but nothing worked. It was like strangers were trying to force their way into a world that belongs to me alone. I couldn't even look them in the eye.

If only there was someone to talk to.

For almost fifteen years, Miranda was that person for me. I never thought I would need anyone else.

I browse the internet aimlessly, looking for help lines and therapists. There are psychologists who will accept new patients over the phone. You can even talk to them over chat. Maybe that would work better? I don't know.

In one forum thread about grief, someone recommends a site called Psychicadvice.com. My first inclination is that it's all sheer nonsense, but after I check it out a bit, I soften. At least it doesn't seem to be about fortune-tellers and hocus pocus; instead, it's someone who *will listen and guide you through the labyrinth of life.*

I was always skeptical when Miranda showed her spiritual side. Unlike her, I've never believed in anything you can't see or touch. Miranda used to say my life would be richer if I opened myself up to other dimensions, but I just laughed at her. Now I regret it. There was never any reason to be narrow-minded.

I click on the *Our advisers* link. There are portraits of several different women, who all claim to have psychic and empathic abilities.

One of them looks awfully familiar.

I click on the photo and zoom in.

Hold on. Is that really her?

Her hair is definitely shorter and her face is a little harder, as though life hasn't been totally kind to her. Then again, it's been almost five years since I last saw her. She never came to the funeral. Everyone else was there, but Jennica Jungstedt didn't show up. People said she was sick, but I had my doubts. It would be very Jennica to keep punishing Miranda even after her death.

I lean back, my hand on the mouse.

Jennica Jungstedt has psychic abilities? As if.

In a moment of weakness, I consider dialing the number on my screen. There are still questions I'd like answered. Then I notice the price: 19.90 kronor per minute. Forget that!

Sally whimpers from the bed again. She tosses and turns, dreaming.

I turn off the computer and crawl in beside her.

Excerpt from Interrogation with Jennica Jungstedt

Would you please state your full name?

Jennica Joanna Jungstedt.

Can you tell me a little bit about yourself?

I'll be thirty in December. I was born and raised here in Lund. My studies have been kind of here and there, English and international relations. I worked as a teacher for a while, but now I'm a student again. I live on Magistratsvägen. At the Delphi student housing complex.

What is your relationship with Bill Olsson?

I don't know if I'd call it a relationship. I grew up with Miranda, Bill's late fiancée. Miranda and I were in the same group of friends for years, but for the last five years we had no direct contact. Then she got cancer and died. It's a tragic story.

From what we've heard, your relationship with Miranda ended rather abruptly.

It sounds drastic, but yeah. Yes, that's about the size of it. Miranda screwed up. I had to end our friendship after that. Life is too short to waste time on people who hurt you.

But you've been in touch with Bill Olsson?
Not until this past summer. I was surprised when I heard from him, to say the least.

Karla

Heaven or hell? You never know with Mom.

When people talk about "living in the now" and "just being," it's like I break out in internal hives. The worst periods of my life have been when things seemed calm on the surface, when Mom was doing well and life sort of just flowed on. Those are the times when I was always counting down to the next disaster.

I call Mom on the morning bus to the Rytters'. As usual, my hand is trembling.

"Karla? Sweetie!" she answers.

I immediately relax.

Mom tells me she got up super early and is on her way into town to run some errands. It's not entirely easy to tell if she's on anything. Maybe it doesn't matter.

I proudly declare that my first assignment got a passing grade.

"You're amazing," Mom says. "To think that my little girl is going to be a lawyer."

"Judge," I correct her.

"Right, right, I'll be happy either way. I've always said you've got a head for studying. Big things will happen for you."

We keep chatting until I step into the Rytters' foyer. It's quiet and empty. The lights are out and no one responds to my *hello*.

With one earbud in, I get to work on the toilets, as is my habit. As I haul the pail up the stairs, Regina comes out of the bedroom.

"Are you back again?"

I quickly pluck the earbud from my ear.

"Hi!"

"I must have been fast asleep," Regina Rytter says, rubbing her eyes.

She's wearing satin pajamas, and her hair is unbrushed. Her voice is off, and I recognize that foggy gaze. She's clearly in some other reality. Presumably she is under the influence of some strong medications.

I think about what Steven said. The least exertion can lead to serious setbacks.

"Your husband said you should lie down to rest again," I say.

She fixes her gaze on me. The fog disperses and is replaced by an icy, severe look.

"I will not let you declare me incompetent. I may be sick, but I'm still fully capable of making decisions on my own. My husband has a tendency to exaggerate. He likes to be in charge."

I put down the bucket so hastily that the water sloshes over the edges.

"I was going to keep working on the bathroom."

I point at the closed door. I just want to be done as quickly as possible so I can leave.

"That can wait," says Regina. "It's so *Steven* to try to sway you before you've even started here. When we got married I told myself he was different, but men are all the same. Stay away from them for as long as you can."

With one hand gripping the railing, she teeters her way down the stairs. "Come on!"

I take one last look at the soapy water in the bucket. I should stay up here and clean.

"A cup of tea never killed anyone," Regina says.

I can't bring myself to protest, so I follow her to the kitchen. Regina opens a cupboard, and the china inside clinks gently.

"Love is dangerous," she says. "It's so easy to delude yourself when you first fall in love. You'd think I would have noticed all the red flags, given that I grew up with a narcissist for a father and a brother who turned out the same."

She fills the kettle and sets out delicate cups and saucers.

"I assume you don't know of my father?"

I shrug. "Should I?"

This is all giving me bad vibes. The swanky house and these people. I promised Steven I would send his wife back to bed. If she would just let me do my job in peace . . .

"Helmer Lindgren. Does that name ring a bell?" Regina fixes her eyes on me. "He was a history professor at first, but that wasn't enough. When I was little, he started writing popular history books that became bestsellers. He was on TV every other week, and Mom quit her job to be his agent full-time. With the money he earned he bought real estate, and today his firm is one of the biggest in southern Sweden."

"I guess I should have heard of him."

She laughs. "Maybe you're not all that interested in the Swedish Empire and the Caroleans? Dad's favorite subjects."

"Not exactly," I confess. "Although I did get A's in history."

I had taken for granted that it was Steven's money that bought this magnificent mansion, and all the beautiful furniture and the jewelry in that drawer. I guess it's not a sure thing that he ordered the cleaning services either. Maybe I really should listen to Regina more.

"My dad was a very special man," she says as the kettle whistles. "He commanded a room from the moment he entered it. To me he was more like a fictional character than a father. I could watch him on TV and feel proud, but I never really knew him."

She pours steaming water into our cups and tells me to have a seat.

"I'm talking about Dad in the past tense," she continues, "as though he's no longer with us. Because for me, he hardly is."

I think of my own father. Most of the time I manage to convince myself that nothing would have been any better had he lived. But, of course, there's no way to know. My mother's grief for him broke her.

As the tea steeps, Regina pokes a few pills from her pill organizer. I hand her a glass of water, and she smiles in gratitude, then swallows the pills.

"You sure are sweet. We had another cleaner before who wasn't pleasant at all."

So there was a falling out with my predecessor. She must not have done as Steven asked. Or maybe she did? It actually sounds as if it's Regina who wasn't satisfied with her.

I stir my tea carefully so it won't slosh over the edge.

No matter what I do, someone will be upset. I really don't want to lose this job.

"I'm actually not much of a tea drinker," Regina says, sipping the scalding beverage. "But I stopped drinking coffee when I got sick, and I just never went back."

I blow on my tea.

"I'm not really that big a fan either," I say, taking a sip.

At home we mostly had Coke and beer. Mom drank Nescafé once in a while, but it was just to get a burst of energy or stay awake.

Regina takes a sip, makes a face, and laughs. I can't help laughing too.

I look around the kitchen with its white tile walls and granite countertops, the massive coffee machine, and the display cabinets full of beautiful china. Back home in Mom's kitchen, the cups, plates, and glasses all crowd into the sink alongside scraps of food. The countertop is marred by a couple dozen stab marks from the time one of Mom's exes had a mental breakdown.

"I started having such bizarre dreams when I got sick," Regina says, shifting in her seat. "They're still with me. I gave up coffee and cut back on sugar, and Steven got me a whole bunch of medicine, but the dreams just keep coming. Sometimes they're so vivid I think it's actually real life."

"Gosh, that's awful," I say, pushing back my chair. I don't want to seem rude, but I'd rather not hear more.

"It's like living in a bubble," she says. "I'm totally wrapped up in my own little world."

"I should really get back to cleaning now," I say, standing up. The cup wobbles, but I manage not to spill.

"Listen," Regina says. "What did Steven tell you, anyway?"

I set the teacup on the counter and look at her. "What do you mean?"

She rubs her eyes, blinks a few times, and squints. "He must have said something, right?"

I shake my head as I put both our cups in the dishwasher. "Just that you're sick."

She gives me a look that says she doesn't believe me. It makes me uncomfortable, and I say again that I need to keep working before I vanish up the stairs.

Soon I'm sitting on the floor with the bucket and spray bottle at my feet. Paragraphs from my law textbooks and homework spin inside my head; Bill and Sally, sausage stroganoff, playing Skitgubbe on the couch. It's all one big mess. Steven Rytter admonishing me, his wife, who seems generally crazy.

I think about the conversation with Mom. She sounded so cheerful.

There was a note of hope I didn't recognize in her voice, one I'd never heard before. Maybe things are turning around for her. And here I am, in this unfamiliar house fifteen hundred kilometers away. I should be with Mom instead.

Bill

At last, I get my first job on the app. I pull my old bike out of the basement storage area and let Sally hop onto the luggage rack. Wheels squeaking and chain grinding, I pedal past the ice-cream-eating stroller moms in Stadsparken, pass the Högevall baths, and head down Nygatan and up toward Bantorget.

My first task as a "worker" involves assembling a bookcase for a young woman in a newly built house north of town hall. Sally bounces around and sings; she helps me out, and we laugh when we accidentally attach one of the cabinet doors upside down. The woman hides in the next room and says she definitely would have done this herself if it weren't for an infected finger. Three hundred kronor lands in my account immediately for my trouble.

All day we go around the city, completing tasks. Often you only have a minute or two to jump at the offer, and you have to bid low to keep someone else from nabbing the job. Sally and I drag a set of patio furniture out of a garage, sanitize a vomit-covered couch, and help an elderly professor of literature install Skype.

By evening we're ravenous, my legs are stiff with lactic acid, and my bank account is 850 kronor richer. We pick up a large pizza and invite Karla to join us, but she declines and says she has to study.

Once I've put Sally to bed, I sit on the couch and rewatch season one of *Game of Thrones*. It's past midnight when I toddle to the kitchen and open the fridge.

"You sneak food too, huh?"

Karla stands in the doorway, barefoot and wearing a hoodie that's three sizes too big.

"You can have my chips, if you can't find anything else. In the cupboard," she says.

I have to stand on tiptoe to reach them.

"I can't eat up your chips."

"We'll share," she says.

I pour the chips into two bowls. Karla stops in the hall, then follows me to the couch and sits down.

"I can't study anymore. It goes in one and out the other," she says, pointing to her ears. "Nothing sticks."

"I'm sorry if we were bothering you," I say.

Even though we've hardly been home today.

"It definitely isn't because of you two." Karla smiles.

"Do you have to clean as much as you do?" I ask. "After all, it uses up both time and your focus."

She nods and takes a bite of a large dill chip. "I'll talk to the company. It's not really working out. How did things go for you today?"

"Oh, fine." I tell her about our tasks. "It might not make anyone rich, but right now every little bit counts."

"Maybe you shouldn't take Sally along," Karla says. "I'd be happy to help out by watching her."

"Stop. You already have too much on your plate."

"Isn't there like a rec center she could spend the day at?"

She looks at me as though I should know better. Does she think something will happen to Sally if she comes along on a few tasks?

"Rec centers cost money," I say. "And Sally likes to come along. We had a lot of fun today."

Karla digs in her bowl for more chips. "Although sometimes you tell your parents you like doing something when really you'd rather not do it. I don't know how many times I swore to my mom I loved going along with her to parties and bingo and I don't know what. I was only telling her what she wanted to hear."

I'm speechless. Is she seriously comparing Sally's situation to having a parent on drugs?

"Thanks for the offer," I say in a neutral tone. "It's ridiculous that Sally has to deal with this, but if I don't bring in money, we can't stay here."

Crunching from Karla's mouth. She fiddles with her watch.

"There must be some other place," she says. "Something cheaper?"

"Not in the city. We'd have to move out to Eslöv or Hörby. Here in Lund, everything costs a fortune and there are long waitlists for housing everywhere. And moving is the last thing Sally needs, now that she's just started to recover."

Karla nods. "There must be help, though, right? Can't you talk to social services?"

My hand jerks. Chips land on the floor.

I try to think of something to say, but Karla seems to understand. Social services is not an option.

"What about your family?" she asks. "Can't you borrow money from them?"

Family? I don't know if that's the right word.

"My dad died years ago, and I'm not really in contact with Mom. She left me and Dad when I was five, remarried, and had new children. Besides, I've already borrowed money from her."

Karla stirs her chips around. "Miranda's family? Sally's grandma and grandpa? Don't they want to help?"

I twist away so she won't see my shame.

Miranda would never forgive me if she knew. Her parents were always nice to me. Vanna and Heinrich opened their home and welcomed me so warmly when I lost Dad and had nowhere to turn.

"I already owe a ton of money to everyone and everything," I say, without going into detail.

Last spring, Sally asked about her grandmother and I had to lie. As soon as I get a job and things are a little more stable, I'll ask Vanna and Heinrich for forgiveness.

"What actually happened?" Karla asked. "To Miranda?"

I stare at my feet. My socks are more beige than white, and one has such a large hole that my big toe is poking out.

"One morning she just said her vision was a little blurry. She went in to get it checked out and got referred to a neurologist. Two weeks later she came home and told me that they'd found a tumor in her brain."

I scrape my fingers against my knee, tell her that it came as a complete shock. There you are, just living your life, the daily grind, as they say. Each day ticks by, gray and ordinary. Tedious in that way anyone who has been plunged into hell learns to appreciate and long for. Sometimes the fact that nothing ever happens is for the best.

"When was this?" Karla asks. "How old was Sally?"

"She had just started first grade. Miranda and I never talked about it as though it wouldn't all work out. Radiation and chemo. Surgery, of course. Then everything would go back to normal."

Karla squirms. Her eyes look misty.

"It never went back to normal," I say.

She leans forward and pats my knee. "It's going to be okay," she says. "You won't have to move."

I try to smile. "Hope not."

Slowly, Karla stands up with the bowl of chips in her arms. "I guess I should try to get a little more studying in."

As soon as she's back in her room, I end up in front of the computer, logging into the bank. I've got seven hundred kronor left after the pizza. Not bad for a single day's work.

What about taxes and stuff? I'll have to worry about that later.

I stare at the numbers. Seven hundred. That won't cover the broken window by any stretch of the imagination, but it's a decent start. I could make it grow. It's worked before.

Without overthinking it, I surf over to my old favorite casino.

My body is one big rush. This is better than *World of Warcraft*. It's almost better than sex. My pulse throbbing as the wheels spin; the total triumph when I hit the jackpot.

Half an hour later, I've more than quadrupled my starting capital. Seven hundred has become three thousand. When I log out I feel dizzy and I stagger over to the bed. Sally is relaxed, asleep, half her face buried in the pillow.

All my tension, every ounce of discomfort, is blown to pieces and flutters like confetti through my agitated brain.

"Daddy loves you," I whisper.

For the first time in ages, I've accomplished something. I'm on the right track. Something like pride swells in my chest.

It's impossible to fall asleep like this.

Jennica

'm on the evening shift. I fluff the pillows in my bed, open a bottle of bubbly, and dig half a bag of nuts out of the cupboard. Dog the cat watches over me like a grumpy Sphinx from under the TV in the corner. He stares huffily at the enormous bouquet, colorful in red, pink, green, and yellow.

"You never thought you'd see the day, right?" I say. "Me getting flowers?"

I'm not a flowers kind of girl. The only houseplants I have are cactuses and succulents, which don't take much more in terms of nurturing than breathing on them now and then. I don't like taking on responsibility for living things. I probably would have preferred not to have a cat either, if only he hadn't persisted in hanging out on the breezeway outside my door for weeks, meowing like someone was about to strangle him. At first I tried to chase him off. I even sprayed water at him, but he wouldn't give up. He's been here ever since.

"You're not jealous, are you?" I say when he keeps staring at the bouquet. "You know you're always number one in my book."

I chuckle, but Dog has no sense of humor. He just yawns and turns his butt to me.

Today I received an email from the Department of Human Geography and Human Ecology. The tone was almost threatening. Apparently I'm not taking enough credits and have to arrange a makeup exam and a few assignments before the fall semester starts to keep from being kicked out of the degree program. I haven't decided how to respond yet. I don't like threats, but I need some way to keep busy this fall, and I'm definitely not about to start teaching again.

The evening's first call comes from Maggan, a regular who calls at least once a week to discuss her children. She thinks it's great that I'm the same age as her twin daughters. This time, one of them has chewed Maggan out because she "happened to say the N-word" within earshot of her grandkid.

Ever since I was old enough to think for myself, it's been perfectly clear to me that my family is fucked up. So it's good to get some perspective sometimes. Through my job as a psychic adviser, I am constantly reminded that there are always people who have it way worse.

After half an hour with Maggan, I get a little bit of downtime before the phone rings again. I quickly toss back the rest of my wine and put on the headset.

"Welcome to your psychic adviser, Jennica. How can I help you?"

There's crackling on the line. A faint voice in the distance. It sounds like a young girl.

"I don't know," she says. "I've never made a call like this before."

I think of the conversation manual. It comes to me automatically.

"What prompted you to call today?" I ask.

A shuddering breath, then silence. I give her space.

"I'd like to contact my sister," she says at last. "She went over to the other side three weeks ago."

I'll never get used to this. The earth is just crawling with people who seem to believe you can talk to the dead. I suppose grief and sorrow can make anyone desperate. But if I could truly contact the spirit world, I'm positive I could find a better way to cash in on it than sitting on a bed in this 180-square-foot room with a headset on.

"I'm sorry," I say. "But I think there's been a misunderstanding."

I stretch out my legs, and Dog leaps onto the bookcase, where he crams himself in between Buddha and my unread show copies of Dostoyevsky and Solzhenitsyn and other Russians with names I can't pronounce after a bottle of cava.

"Look, I'm really sorry to say this," I say, "but I can't convey anything to your sister. I'm not that sort of medium."

Honestly, I feel sorry for her. Who knows how you'll react to the loss of a close relative? I'm sure I would try anything too.

"But . . . I thought . . ."

Her voice is like broken glass.

According to the company's instructions, I should refer her to one of my colleagues who does claim to have contact with the other side, but I've had to talk to some of them at various work functions, and it would not be kind to subject this grieving girl to them.

"Do you know what? I think you should talk to someone close to you about this. Or maybe seek professional help? A counselor or a psychologist?"

"But . . . I want to . . ."

"Unfortunately, I can't help you," I say, perhaps more harshly than is necessary.

Something has been set in motion inside me. I zoom out and see myself from above, as I sit there with my nuts and wine. If Mom and Dad could see me now. I think of my sister and my older brothers. Even before I started school, comparisons started pelting down at me from all directions: Mom and Dad were the worst, but even my aunt, my teachers, and our friends measured me against the ruler of my siblings. The result was always the same: I was lacking.

I hang up and wiggle off my headset. I don't want to take any more calls. It feels so dishonest, as if, instead of helping people, I'm just a cog in a vast machine that wants to make money off people's grief and need for support.

I get up when there's a knock on the door.

Did Steven send more flowers? I realize I miss him.

Dog looks like he wants to kill someone. Unclear whether that someone is me or Steven or someone else entirely.

I wrap myself in the blanket and waddle to the hall.

"Yes?"

"It's me."

It takes a few seconds to hit me. He's here. He's standing outside my door. I quickly scan the room. The floor is covered in pizza boxes and stacks of books; the kitchenette is piled with the dirty dishes I'd planned to tackle tomorrow. It doesn't exactly smell like roses in here.

Steven is Grand Hotel and everything bright and fresh. If I let him into this pigsty, he will never want to see me again.

"Is that you, Steven?" I say, cracking the door so slightly that there's no way he can see anything but my lovely face.

"Hi . . . ? Is this okay?" he asks.

I paste on a big smile. No, it's not okay to drop in on people out of nowhere. But of course I don't say so.

"It's fine."

Sure, he's told me that he's allergic to cats, but I need a better excuse.

"It's my roommate," I tell him, jerking my head back. "I told you, we have a deal. It's a very delicate situation. We never let any men inside."

"I get it."

Steven looks skeptical. Disappointed.

I have to think of something, and fast. I refuse to throw away everything we've built up.

"I just can't invite you in," I say, tilting my head and winking. "But if you give me two minutes I'll change and be right out. Let's go grab a bite, my treat."

I can't actually afford that, but who the hell cares right now. I have to do something.

"That sounds nice," says Steven.

I turn back in to face my room and call out.

"Yes, I know! We're leaving in a sec."

Dog stares at me from the bookcase.

I make a dubious face at Steven, nod at him to stay where he is, and close the door. It takes me less than a minute to hop into a summer dress, run a brush through my hair, and pack the necessities in my makeup bag.

"Yes, he's old," I say to Dog. "But age is only a number and yada yada."

When I come out, Steven is casually leaning back with his phone in hand. I glide along the access balcony and down the stairs alongside him.

"Did you drive? Or should we call a cab?"

Steven looks at me, puzzled.

"We'll take a cab," he says after a moment. "The car can stay put for the night."

We go to the long pier in Bjärred. When I was little, Mom and I would come here for soft serve. At the very end of the pier is a restaurant. The gulls shriek, and I suck the sea air into my nose. Across the bay is the Malmö skyline, the bridge and Turning Torso.

We are shown to a small table for two near the bar.

Steven orders the daily catch for each of us, without asking.

"Why don't you have a boyfriend?" he asks then.

I burst into laughter. "What?"

"You've hardly told me anything about your exes," Steven says. "There must have been tons of interested parties over the years. How come you're single?"

I moisten my lips with outrageously expensive wine.

"If you ask my dad, it's because I'm a lazy tomboy who would rather lie in bed all day watching Netflix. Or maybe it's because I'm an incompetent socialist who never progressed past the stubborn stage and makes unreasonable demands of those around me."

"Are you?" Steven asks, pretending to be horrified.

"Lazy and incompetent?"

"No, a socialist."

We both laugh.

"In Dad's eyes, anyone left of Margaret Thatcher is basically a communist. It's totally impossible to talk politics with him, to be perfectly honest."

It's a never-ending balancing act, trying to figure out how honest to be.

"I'm sure you're exaggerating," Steven says.

"I'm sure."

Steven doesn't need to know that the few exes whom I actually allowed to meet my father had to be prepped with a two-hour briefing first.

"I'm sorry we can't hang out at my place," I say, suddenly serious. "It feels so fucking stupid, but I can't break my promise to my roommate."

I tell him that the apartment at Delphi is very temporary, that I'm looking for a different place.

"Hopefully by the fall. Can you hold out for that long?"

Steven laughs.

Everything is so simple with him.

"I get it. I lived in a similar room at Ulrikedal once upon a time. Those places are usually charming, but not exactly bright and airy."

"Seriously? You fucking studied here too?"

"Only for one year, I studied in Glasgow the rest of the time. And there wasn't much fucking," Steven chuckles. "Neither here nor there. I spent most of my time at the library, studying."

"I don't believe that for a second."

"It's true. I wasn't very gifted, or 'book smart,' as my mother put it. I had to make up for it by reading everything five hundred times. Besides, it takes two to fuck, and basically no one ever volunteered. I guess I'm just one of those late bloomers."

We laugh again. Long and loud. I like laughing with him.

The waitress brings our cod and, across the dark sound, the lights on the bridge turn on.

"I'm going to have dinner with some good friends in Malmö on Friday," Steven says. "I'd love for you to join us."

It almost feels like a solemn moment. Like a statement. You don't introduce just anyone to your friends.

"That sounds fun," I say.

We linger until the lights dim and the staff starts picking up chairs. In the back seat of the taxi, Steven places his hand on my thigh. With the other hand, he gently brushes a lock of hair from my cheek.

"Do you know what you do to me, Ms. Jungstedt?"

My index finger glides slowly across the deep grooves of his face. I like that firm husk, those rough cheeks.

"It's crazy," he whispers. "This hasn't happened to me since . . . since Regina."

He blinks a few times. Maybe it's kind of a downer, but apparently I make him think of his wife.

Obviously I've googled her. Regina Rytter didn't leave a lot of traces online: an old Facebook profile that never got taken down, and a photo of uncertain origin where she's posing with Steven. Regina was beautiful, with the looks of a classic model: curly blond hair, blue eyes, full lips.

"You can let us off here," Steven says to the driver.

We've just pulled up at Mårtenstorget. There's a starry sky, and the wine has put a pleasant rush in my head. A drunk is snoozing on a bench in front of the dancing water feature outside the art museum.

As soon as we're out of the car, I drape myself around Steven's neck and kiss him.

Excerpt from Interrogation with Vanna Schumacher

Would you please state your full name for the record?

Vanna Schumacher.

We'd like to talk to you about Bill Olsson. What is your relationship with Bill?

At present we don't have a good relationship at all, unfortunately. I mourn the fact every day.

When did you first get to know him?

It was years ago. Miranda was only seventeen when Bill moved in with us. They'd met each other online, and Bill was having a tough time. His father had just died, so my husband and I allowed him to live with us.

How would you describe Bill?

He's very kind. A bit withdrawn, maybe somewhat naive. My husband has never been the biggest fan of his, but Bill truly loved Miranda. There's no doubt about that.

So you are the maternal grandmother of Bill's daughter, Sally?
That's correct.

But you have no contact with Sally?
Almost none.
[crying]
Everything fell apart when Miranda died. My husband discovered that some money was missing. He accused Bill. That was a stupid and rash thing to do. How I wish we had handled the situation differently.

What money was missing?
Miranda had set aside some money in mutual funds. The plan was that they would go to Sally when she came of age. But when my husband looked into it, it turned out Bill had sold the funds and withdrawn the money. There was nothing left.

What did Bill have to say about this?
He swore he would pay it all back to Sally when she turned eighteen. I guess Bill had a very tough time of it, financially, when Miranda got sick. She was the breadwinner, and while she was in the hospital, Bill couldn't work much. He borrowed some money from my husband and me. It was when we tried to get that money back we discovered that most of Sally's account was gone.

Most of it? How much are we talking about?
At least a hundred thousand. I'm sure my husband could give you a more exact number.

Has Bill paid back the money he borrowed from you and your husband?
No, we haven't seen a whiff of it.

When did you last talk to Bill?

Sometime last summer. It must have been around the beginning of July. I was really happy to hear from him when he called. We talked about going to the big playground in Stadsparken with Sally. But then he got around to the real reason he was calling.

What was that? What did he want?

To borrow money, of course.

Karla

My heart pounds as I cross the street outside the sporting fields. I really don't know a thing about Waheeda; we've only been exchanging messages for a few days. Still, I know right away that that's her standing in the parking lot with a retro duffel bag over her shoulder and one foot braced on the wall behind her.

"Judge Karla!" she cries the moment she spots me.

Her giant hair bobs side to side. Her laugh sounds like birdsong.

"Are you sure I can just show up like this?" I ask as she shows me the way to the field.

"Of course," Waheeda says. "It's not like we're playing in the Champions League or something."

A couple of girls are jogging around the grass, passing the ball to each other. Others are kicking a ball or doing tricks in small giggly groups. Some are taking practice shots at the goal.

Waheeda tosses her bag down and sits on the sidelines to pull on her bright yellow cleats, and just then the only man on the field, a chubby forty-year-old with a sun-bleached cap, comes over and slides up to us with a skeptical smile.

"Hey, Coach!" Waheeda says. "I brought a friend."

He looks me up and down.

"Hope that's okay?" I say.

"Have you played before?" he asks. "This is division two, after all."

Waheeda laughs. "What do you think? She played in fucking Piteå. Ever heard of them, maybe? Karla just moved down here from Norrland, can't you tell? She's studying law just like me."

The coach runs the back of his hand over his nose and makes a snuffling sound.

"Piteå? Aren't they in Allsvenskan league?"

"I mean . . ." I'm about to protest when Waheeda bounces up off the grass and drowns me out.

"You better snag her fast. Otherwise LBK might get her. Have you got one of those contracts for her to sign?"

The coach nods and introduces himself with a lazy handshake.

It's nice to be back on the field.

Everything else fades away.

I don't have to think about work or school, of Mom back home, of Bill or Sally.

It's not like I have great ball sense, but my old coach used to praise my winner's brain, my ability to fight hard. Even though I'm small, I've never been scared to get right in there and battle even the beefiest opponents.

"I never expected it," Waheeda says as we share a bottle of water in the grass after practice. "You look like a princess but play like a goddamn king."

Waheeda herself is the team's shining star, with her athletic legs and brilliant ball-handling techniques.

I pull a little grass as the bowlegged coach waddles our way.

"Want to come to the next practice too?"

His glasses are fogged up.

I look at Waheeda, who looks up at the sky and lets out a peal of laughter.

"Sure," I say.

Of course I do. At the same time, I have another assignment to work on, and my cleaning job wears me out more than I'd expected.

"Is there a signing bonus?" Waheeda asks the coach, who takes off his glasses and aims a serious look at me.

"Chill," says Waheeda. She gets up and pats him on the shoulder. "I'm just kidding."

The coach laughs.

"Thanks for letting me tag along," I say to Waheeda as we stroll toward the parking lot.

"Don't be silly," she says, elbowing me. "See you!"

As I hop on the bus outside the hospital, my chest seems to open. The driver is playing dance-band music on the speakers, and the bus pitches down the hill and straight into the sun.

Once I've showered, I sneak into my room. Bill and Sally are at the table. I don't want to bother them. Still, I've hardly closed the door behind me when there's a knock.

"It's me," Sally calls through the door. "Want to play cards?"

I actually need to be spending every second of the evening on my next assignment, but I'm not feeling inspired at all, and I don't have the heart to disappoint Sally.

"Just let me get dressed," I say.

In gray sweatpants, a camisole, and wet hair, I settle onto the couch as Sally deals the cards.

"Was it a good practice?" Bill asks.

"Yeah." I'm beaming. "It was fantastic."

Sally's eyes grow wide.

"I want to start playing soccer too, Dad," she says.

"What? You've never . . ."

He looks at me like this is my fault, while Sally crosses her arms and makes a face.

"Sure, sure, of course you can play soccer if you want to," Bill says, patting her arm. "I just didn't think you were interested."

"I wasn't," Sally says. "But *now* I am. You're always saying it's good to be able to change your mind. You have to, if you find out you were wrong. I think I was wrong about soccer."

Bill smiles and winks at me.

"Looks like someone's got a fan."

Then we play cards, and Bill and I are both the kind of people who let Sally win. Not to avoid sore-loser drama, but to see the glee in her eyes when she performs her winner dance, hips swaying and hands in the air.

"I'm the king!"

When Bill turns on the TV, it doesn't take long before Sally is resting her head in his lap. She stretches out her little feet and asks me to move closer to Bill so she can cuddle with both of us.

"How much does it cost to play soccer?" Bill asks.

"I'm not quite sure. A couple hundred kronor, maybe?"

We both look at Sally.

Bill breathes heavily through his nose.

"It pains me so much to have to say no to things like that, but we just can't afford it."

I am all too familiar with that refrain. So many cleats I had to borrow or get as hand-me-downs from my teammates' parents. It wasn't until I was a teenager that I realized the club still let me play even though Mom hadn't paid the membership fees for years.

"Maybe we can look around on Facebook? Sometimes people give away tons of kid stuff."

Mom hated taking things for free. That's how she was raised. You had to pull your weight and always pay your fair share. In her world, it seemed like it was almost less shameful to steal than to accept gifts and charity.

"You're right," Bill says. "There must be some way to make it happen."

I've already gotten out my phone to look for buy-sell-trade groups around Lund.

"We can definitely make it happen."

Bill nods.

"The worst part is that we might not be able to stay," he says. "Sally's doing so well here. I hate to have to uproot her from this sense of security."

I'm sure it has to do with Bill's own upbringing. He doesn't want Sally to end up as rootless as he is. On the other hand, it would only have to be one single move, out to the countryside somewhere.

"I'm sure you can find somewhere cheap and nice that both of you like."

Even as I say them, I regret my words. Obviously I would be out a place to live. I'm never going back to that student housing with its twenty-four-hour nightclub.

"Sally changed after Miranda died," Bill says. "She snapped shut like a clam and refused to be apart from me for longer than a few minutes. It wasn't until this past spring that things turned around and she started laughing again. Her teachers have been amazing. And her friends, and their parents. That's why it's so sad that we might have to move."

Bill covers his eyes and swallows hard.

I don't know what to say.

I wish there was something I could do for them.

Bill

Sally borrowed *Harry Potter* from the library. Before we crawl into bed and start reading, I tell her that her mother plowed through these books when she was in high school.

"How old was she then?" Sally asks.

"Seventeen, eighteen."

"Wow! But the librarian said I could read it."

"I'm sure you can."

We read about poor Harry being treated so cruelly by his cousin, aunt, and uncle. Sally becomes so upset that she grabs the book.

"Did you ever get bullied, Dad?"

"Hmm, not really."

I wouldn't call it bullying. Other kids were seldom straight-up mean to me. I never managed to form any relationships, neither good nor bad ones, before Dad thought it was time to move on.

"Was Mom bullied?" Sally asks.

"Mom? No, I definitely don't think she was."

Miranda was good at sticking up for herself. People used to say she had a thick skin, although she hated that expression.

"Your mom was a superhero," I say.

In some ways, I really did think of her that way.

For better and for worse, maybe.

Sally hands the book back and smiles.

"You're my hero too, Dad."

I keep reading, with a lump in my throat. Sally soon falls asleep, and I insert the bookmark.

Karla's out with some classmate of hers, and the apartment is empty and quiet. I sit at the desk in the bedroom and listen to Sally breathing in her sleep.

The computer is being slow. I shut down some programs that are eating up memory in the background and start closing some old tabs in my browser.

Miranda didn't like to show weakness. Sometimes it went a little overboard; she kept everything bottled up. In some ways, we were alike on that front.

I think about what happened at that one party, and the chain of events it unleashed. It affected her more than she wanted to admit. It must have felt horrible when all her friends turned their backs on her. Jennica Jungstedt succeeded in manipulating every one of them.

I stop at the tab with the psychic adviser site, where she's staring at me from the screen. She's wearing a friendly smile, but I can see right through her.

They were a pretty tight gang. Miranda, Jennica, and a couple of other girls. When I moved to Skåne they were all in high school, and I suppose I didn't exactly win them over when Miranda started to choose cozy nights in with me over parties, dance, and booze.

Jennica and I had hardly even spoken to each other, at least not on any deeper level, before that twenty-fifth birthday party that turned everything upside down. I really don't want to think about it—I've managed to keep it at arm's length for so long, but when I see Jennica again, I'm dragged right back to that night, and agony washes over me.

Our psychic guides provide you with the support and advice you need to move on when life is hard.

What a joke. The Jennica I remember, the one I'd heard about all those years, is completely incapable of empathy and compassion. I will never forget how she fixed her eyes on me on that beyond-horrid night. She had no consideration for the fact that I had been betrayed too.

That boyfriend of hers, Ricky, was basically a small-time criminal. I can still see him clear as day. The hair that curled at the back of his neck, that nasty, self-satisfied smile.

Sure, Miranda found other friends through work and Sally's preschool, but it was never quite the same. She had grown up with Emma and Rebecka, and she frequently mentioned that she missed them and their company.

Out of sheer rage, I pick up the phone and dial the advice line. It rings on the other end, and I clench my jaw.

"Welcome to your psychic adviser, Jennica. How can I help you?"

She sounds unbelievably phony. Miranda said more than once that she had never trusted Jennica.

"My partner . . ." I begin, but I don't know what to say after that.

"Yes?"

I should hang up, but something has taken over me, a power I can't curb, an uncontrollable fury. I stare at the picture of Jennica. She may be smiling and playing the part, but she can't hide the callous and arrogant parts of herself. Without a second thought, she turned her back on a friend with whom she'd grown up and shared everything. Miranda was never really part of the gang again, after that. It was a stain on her life she had to carry to the grave.

"I'm listening," says Jennica. "Take your time."

"She's dead."

The words are harsh, without the least bit of window dressing. But I want to make it clear. She should damn well know what things have been like for the past few years. I'm going to let it all out. If she has even the tiniest fragment of a heart, she should apologize.

"I'm very sorry to hear that," she says. "Do you want to talk about it?"

I want to scream. If Sally weren't sleeping right next to me, I would roar at the top of my lungs.

"You're not sorry at all!" I hiss between my teeth.

If she were sorry, she would have come to the funeral. She wouldn't have treated Miranda like garbage and turned all her childhood friends against her.

"What are you talking about?"

She sounds just as arrogant as before.

"You claim you can communicate with the dead." I spit the words at her. "If that's the case, then you can apologize to Miranda."

There is silence for a moment. Jennica breathes in my ear.

So this is her job. To revel in other people's misfortune and pretend to give advice. Wonder what her fancy family thinks of that? I've never met her parents, but Miranda told me quite a bit about them. Apparently her father was some sort of hotshot in the business world, and her mother was a pampered wife who went to gallery openings and played golf. It seems Jennica's older brothers have followed in their father's footsteps and made their own fortunes. All the siblings are highly educated, with fancy titles and splashy cars. Miranda led me to believe that Jennica was something of a black sheep in the family.

"Bill?" she says. "Bill Olsson, is that you?"

Miranda described her as a lost soul who yearned for affirmation.

"You're a fucking fraud." My voice betrays me.

"Why would I apologize to Miranda?" Jennica doesn't seem to have changed at all. "She's the one who let me down. Have you forgotten that?"

"Bullshit. Miranda essentially got raped that night. You all pressured her to drink until she was out of it, and Ricky took advantage of the situation."

I've tried to keep his name out of my mouth over the years. I'm suddenly dizzy and nauseated.

"That's not what happened," Jennica says.

"You defended him. You chose a guy over your childhood friend." I'm fighting tears. I don't want her to hear me bawl. "Then you turned everyone against Miranda. Didn't you see how alone she felt?"

I spin in my chair and look at Sally. She's kicked off the blanket and is hugging her teddy bear, which has faded and grown stiff after all her tears.

"She lied to you," Jennica says.

I refuse to listen to this.

"You can't even apologize!" I shout.

Sally opens her eyes and whimpers. "Daddy?"

I hang up and crouch beside the bed. Sally hugs her bear to her chest, and my fingers run through her soft hair. Her little forehead is damp with sweat. I have to try to calm down, but my rage at Jennica Jungstedt is hard to hold back. I take a deep breath. At least now she knows.

"You're not leaving, are you?" Sally whispers, blinking in concern.

"I'm not going anywhere."

Jennica

When I tumble into Espresso House, out of breath, with my hair ruined by a summer downpour that came out of nowhere, I find that Emma and Tina and their kids have already claimed a corner booth. Emma's little Silvio is crawling around with a sustainable toy dump truck and Tina's Lotus is strapped into a high chair before a buffet of rattles, stuffies, wooden cars, and puzzles. As if thirty seconds of inactivity might destroy this child's brain.

"How's it going?" I ask.

"Fine," says Tina, as if in passing.

"I'm slammed," says Emma.

It's almost a miracle that they've managed to come. Ever since they had kids, the tiniest coffee date has turned into a whole project.

"We just made it before the rain," says Emma.

As usual, I'm five minutes late. This time, it cost me a soaking-wet mane and running mascara.

We sit in silence and observe the kids for a while. I pour way too much raw sugar in my cappuccino and eat the foam with a spoon.

Emma, Tina, and I can typically talk about anything. We grew up together. I'm the one who fashioned a pad out of toilet paper when Tina got her first period in sewing class in fifth grade. Emma was the one who held my hand every night for a whole week after I got my heart broken for the first time. We never kept any secrets from one another. Now we don't seem to have much to talk about besides their children.

"Lotus hasn't been eating well for two nights in a row now," says Tina. "I'm starting to wonder if I should give her formula."

"Oh, no," says Emma, as though little Lotus were hovering between life and death.

I don't say anything. I imagine very few babies die of anorexia and malnutrition in Sweden, but what do I know? I'm not a mother.

"How are things otherwise?" Tina says.

She hardly has time to look at me before Lotus demands all her attention again.

I have to bang my hand on the table to alert them that I have something important to say.

"Whoa," says Emma, stroking Silvio's forehead.

The little boy stares at me in wonder.

"You'll never guess who called me yesterday," I say.

That's why we're here, after all. This is why I messaged them.

Emma and Tina are two of my oldest friends. Along with Rebecka and Miranda, we built a pretty unique coalition in our school days. Most other girls could only hang out in pairs. But we stuck together, all five of us. Up until my twenty-fifth birthday.

"Okay, dish," Emma says once Silvio has crawled off with his dump truck.

I put down my spoon while I pause for effect.

"Bill Olsson. Miranda's partner."

They gape at me, bewildered.

"Bill?" Tina says. "Why would he call you?"

"How is he?" Emma asks. "I've been thinking of Sally a lot lately."

"He called my work number."

"What?"

Naturally, Emma and Tina are among the few people who are aware of my work situation.

"He called the advice line?" Emma says. "Didn't he know it was you?"

"He did. He was furious, he hurled accusations at me."

"For what?"

"Because you missed the funeral?" Tina says.

"My twenty-fifth birthday."

They each whirl to look at their respective babies, as if to assure themselves that nothing dangerous will get caught in their kids' subconscious minds.

"He was raving on like a madman, talking about rape. As if Miranda were innocent in all this," I say. "He's put her on some sort of pedestal."

"He did that early on," says Tina.

Emma nods. "Bill worshipped Miranda."

"He probably still does," I say. "It seems like she fed him a pack of lies."

"Just let it go," says Emma. "I'm sure he's in a terrible state after everything that happened."

"Of course he is. But what right does he have to call me up and accuse me of things? Someone ought to tell him the truth about his saint of a partner."

"I hope he can move on," Tina says. "For little Sally's sake."

She takes a bite of her beet-salad sandwich and yanks a soft toy from Lotus's mouth. "No biting."

"Listen," Emma says. Her eyes glitter with curiosity. "I want to hear all about your hunky doctor."

She leans forward with her arms on the table as I tell them about Steven. Tina chews with her mouth open. I've posted photos in the group chat before, but now I let them scroll through some new pictures on my phone.

"He definitely doesn't look forty-seven," says Tina.

Emma inspects one of the photos at close range.

"You said he was married before, right? But no kids?"

"No, no kids. His wife died about a year ago."

"It's so lucky they didn't have kids," Tina says, wiping drool from Lotus's chin.

It's unclear who's the lucky one here. Steven, or the nonexistent children? Or maybe mostly me?

"Hope it sticks," Emma says.

I don't know if she means it this way or if I'm just reading too much into it, but it feels like a warning. Like, *make sure you don't fuck this up too*. Like I always do.

Then, suddenly, Emma's in a huge rush. Apparently Silvio should have gone down for a nap five minutes ago. It's as if every new parent gets a dash of insanity at the maternity ward. Tina, who used to scarf down macaroni and cheese when we got home from the bar in the middle of the night now gets anxious when she realizes that her beet-salad sandwich has messed up her meal cycle and made her full when she has to eat lunch soon because it's noon.

When we leave the café, the sky is clear and blue. Little puddles linger, a reminder that the beautiful weather is fickle. You have to enjoy it while you can.

A patrol officer has parked halfway up on the sidewalk and is about to lug a sleeping homeless person from the ground.

Emma covers Silvio's eyes as they take the crosswalk toward the station.

I hide a burp behind my hand and get on my bike.

On Friday I'm going to meet Steven's friends for the first time. I hope they're child-free.

Excerpt from Interrogation with Waheeda Bashir

Could you please state your full name?
Waheeda Mounira Bashir.

How do you spend your days?
I'm a student.

And you live here in Lund?
I've lived here my whole life.

Can you explain how you got to know Karla Larsson?
We were in the same introductory law course. It was an online class, but both of us lived in Lund. So we wrote back and forth on the course forum for a bit, and then I added her on Snapchat. She had just moved here and hardly knew anyone. I asked if she wanted to come along to my soccer practice with me. I swear, that girl looks like she's about to break, she's so skinny, but she's strong as an ox on the field.

Did you know she had a side job as a cleaner?
Yeah, of course I did.

Did she tell you anything about it?

She said she had to scrub toilets and stuff. It sounded pretty gross. People should be ashamed. Can't they clean up their own shit?

Did Karla talk about her clients with you?

Umm . . . yeah, there was that one. The doctor. There was something sketchy about him.

Did she mention his name?

Yeah, it was that guy. Steven.

What did she tell you about Steven Rytter?

She told me what he was doing to his wife.

Karla

close myself in my room to study. About every ten minutes, Waheeda sends me a snap. Half the time she's freaking out over some concept she doesn't understand, and half the time she's found some new filter she just has to try out. I love how she makes me laugh.

I've got Bananarama on my headphones, so I don't hear the first few knocks. But in the silence between "Cruel Summer" and "Love in the First Degree," I hear pounding on the door.

"Bill? Sorry, I was listening to music."

He's out of breath. His hair is flopping over his forehead, and he's dripping with sweat.

"An amazing task popped up on the app," he says. "I could earn fifteen hundred kronor in two hours. But . . ."

He turns around. Sally's curled up on the couch with a book.

"It's fine. I can watch her," I say.

Bill sighs deeply.

"Are you sure? I already talked to her, and . . ."

"It's no problem," I assure him.

Sure, I should be using the time to study, but my brain needs a break now and then. And it's actually fun, hanging out with Sally. She always puts me in a good mood.

"Go on," I say to Bill. "We'll be fine."

I teach Sally how to play a new card game called Bluffstopp, and soon she has mastered dropping cards under the table without my noticing.

"How long are you going to live with us?"

It's my turn to shuffle. I cut the deck a few times.

"I'm not quite sure."

"I think you should stay forever."

I laugh, but Sally stares at me in all seriousness.

"Someday I'll probably want to move into my own apartment," I say. "Maybe I'll meet a boyfriend. Who knows? You won't want to live with your dad for the rest of your life, right?"

"Will too." Sally crosses her arms and looks away. When I lean toward her, she pulls away even more.

I've never seen her like this.

"Hey . . ."

She snuffles, and I move closer. A tentative hand on her arm.

"I never want to move away from here. Dad says we might have to move to the country if he can't get a job. Then I'll have to start at a new school and all my friends will still be here."

The tears are flowing, and I hug her tight.

Bill was right. Moving now is the last thing she needs.

"It might not happen. Your dad might find a new job."

She gulps.

"I think he should go back to working at the theater again. I used to help tear tickets."

"That sounds fun."

Sally tugs her sleeve over her hand and wipes her face.

"Can they really make you move if you definitely don't want to?"

"Don't worry about it," I say.

Every day, as far back as I can remember, I've carried around this feeling of instability. Like a ticking time bomb in my chest. No child should have to live like that.

"Why can't everything just be okay?" Sally says.

I take her hands.

"It will be okay," I say.

I hope I'm not promising too much.

The next morning, I'm back at the Rytters'. I've decided to give it one last chance. If anything else weird happens, I'll call Lena at the cleaning company and ask her not to send me here again.

The huge house is dead silent. The door to Regina's bedroom is closed. I've just started vacuuming when my phone vibrates in my pocket.

It's Silja, Mom's friend.

I freeze, my foot on the vacuum.

"Is something wrong?"

"No, no, everything's under control," Silja says.

Her voice is raspy from forty years of smoking.

"I promised your mother I'd call and have a chat with you."

"Okay."

I lift the vacuum over the threshold to the living room and then drag it behind me like a disobedient dog.

"She's decided to quit, Karla. We made an appointment with social services. I'm going to help her get into the methadone program."

It almost sounds like school. The legal studies program, the methadone program. Mom and I have discussed this before.

"That's only switching one addiction out for another. Mom knows what I think about it."

Last time I picked her up from the police station, she swore that everything would be fine if only she could get into the methadone program. She had been stoned on Valium and had stuck a mascara in her bra at Coop.

Silja sighs in my ear.

"You should come home, honey. Your mama needs you. She's really motivated this time, but it's a big step to take."

I honestly want to believe it will work. I want to be there for her, but last time Mom went away for treatment it ended up with them calling and waking me up in the middle of the night. She was missing for two days. The longest days of my life.

"She's serious this time," Silja says. "I know your mama. You really should come home and lend a hand."

"We'll see," I say.

There's no point in discussing this. I'm not about to give up on my dream. Not now. Not like this.

Once we've hung up, I drag the vacuum back to the hall. I'm just about to bend down to get under the bureau when I discover a pair of feet on the stairs.

I drop the vacuum hose to the floor.

Regina Rytter is standing on the middle of the staircase like a statue. She blinks a few times and her eyes grow a few shades brighter.

"Kajsa?"

"Karla," I correct her.

"Right," she says, running her hand through her hair. "I don't know what I was thinking. What a strange dream I was having."

"It's fine," I say. "But it's probably best for you to go back to bed."

Without much protest, she turns around, and I follow her up the stairs.

"Promise you'll let me know if you run into any problems with Steven," she says. "It's impossible to please that man."

I don't know if I want to hear more. I don't want to get involved in their lives. I've got my hands full with Mom. At the same time, I can't just ignore Regina when she's feeling like this.

She walks into the bedroom and sits on the edge of the bed with a blanket over her knees while I make a move to close the door.

"Hey," she says. "Hold on."

I find that I can't look away.

It's not hard to believe that Regina was beautiful once, but now she's pale and bony, and her hands shake as she looks for her pills on the nightstand.

The plastic pill organizer is on the floor.

I bend down and pick it up for her.

"Oh, thanks. You're so sweet."

Regina smiles and fiddles with the lid. "Have you found a place to live?"

"Sorry?"

She looks at me and blinks. "It's never easy. There are never enough student rooms."

I explain that I'm renting a room in an apartment.

"Of course," she says. "Lots of retired people rent out rooms."

She pops a few pills in her mouth and takes a drink.

"The guy I live with isn't retired, though. He's only thirty-three."

She puts down the glass and gingerly settles in with her head on the pillow.

"Then what does he want with a lodger?" she asks, curious. "You're being careful, right? Plenty of people out there take advantage of students."

"No worries there. Bill lost his job. His partner died a year ago, and he has a little girl to take care of."

"Oh my God!"

Regina's hands fly to her head.

"There's always someone who has it worse, isn't there?" she says, making a face. "Although that's really a strange way to think. I don't really think it's much comfort."

She rubs her temples and grimaces.

"Are you okay?" I ask.

She groans. "My head is about to burst."

"Try to get some rest," I say.

She closes her eyes but can't seem to get comfortable. It's clear that she's in pain. I wish there were something I could do.

I tentatively place one hand atop the blanket.

She keeps making faces and writhing.

It takes a few minutes for the tension to ease. Her breathing gets heavier, and her head droops to the side. I slowly tiptoe out of the dim bedroom.

When I get downstairs, I stop before the crystal chandelier on the ceiling.

It's nuts. Looking at this amazing mansion from the outside, you'd imagine happiness and success lived within its walls. And here it looks like this. Darkness and disease.

I turn to the bureau, all full of bling. Expensive pieces of jewelry just lying there collecting dust, things no one would be likely to miss if they disappeared.

Just think what a single piece would mean for Bill and Sally.

They say that opportunity makes a thief, but that's an oversimplification. There are always other circumstances. When I helped Mom swipe beef tenderloins from the market, she always defended herself by saying it didn't affect anyone else. Once we broke into a house and stole computers and cell phones. That time, she said at least they could afford the loss.

It wasn't fair, she said, that some people have things in excess while others don't have enough to make it through the day.

As a kid, I never managed to poke holes in Mom's definition of justice. Now I know better. Still, I slowly open the top drawer of the bureau.

I'm no thief. I'm a law student, I'm going to be a judge. All the rest of it belongs in the past.

I picture Sally, sleeping safe and sound in Bill's lap.

I'm no thief.

Jennica

After an extra-long Friday lunch with Mom, I bike home to my Delphi apartment at top speed. Dog is on the bed, licking himself in the most improper places.

"Hello! Take care of that during your alone time."

I stare him down. Then I think of the vibrator under my bed and am ashamed at my double standards.

Four hours and two face masks later, I'm sitting in yet another taxi. The restaurant is smack-dab in the middle of Malmö's canals, squares, and cobblestone streets. It's fine dining with a tasting menu and accompanying drinks.

The couple we'll be dining with is already seated.

Steven's good friend Andreas is down from Gothenburg on business. While they embrace, pat each other on the belly, and talk about how much weight they've lost since last time, I say hello to Pauline, a woman of around thirty-five or forty, with a model's body and a boob job.

I'm ashamed at my own appearance. Next to Pauline's sparkling pumps and salmon-colored lace dress, I look like I'm on my way to a dance-band festival out in the sticks.

"It's so very wonderful to meet you," Andreas says, grabbing me in an awkward hug. "I'm so happy for you and Steven."

I glance at Steven, who's busy kissing Pauline on the cheek. What has he told them about me?

"Your last name is Quiding, right?" I say. "Any relation to Mariana Quiding?"

That was the first thing that popped to my mind when I heard the name. Mariana was Dad's colleague for years before it came to light that they were having an affair. That was the first time I was aware of Dad's infidelity. I'll never forget that nasty old bitch Mariana, who was invited into our home a number of times, where she smiled right in Mom's face.

"No, I don't know any Mariana," Andreas says. "Quiding is an old family name, which we reclaimed when we got married."

As the first appetizer is served, Steven and Andreas recount their friendship, practically in unison. They've been buddies since high school, and their friendship has survived although they haven't lived in the same city for almost twenty years now.

"I thought you went to high school in Scotland," I say.

Steven and Andreas exchange a quick glance.

"No, no." Steven smiles. "I went to Hvitfeldtska in Gothenburg."

"A ladies' man even then." Andreas laughs. "They've never been able to resist you."

It's so cheesy, but I grin politely along with the others.

"You poor thing. Here I thought you were a late bloomer."

Andreas just cracks up. He offers a toast, and I throw back the whole glass. Getting royally smashed is the only thing that could save this gathering.

"Steven means an awful lot to me," Andreas says.

"Right back atcha," says Steven.

"That's how it goes, with some people. Even though we don't see each other very often, I know you're always there for me."

They gaze at each other across the table, looking almost like a pair of lovebirds. I don't know whether to laugh at them or be jealous.

"It makes me deeply happy to see Steven back on track again," Andreas says, turning to me. "After everything he's been through. He certainly deserves this."

He launches into a speech about how sad it was to watch Regina become ill. It happened so fast. From a delightfully adventurous person who was so full of life at every moment, to an emaciated shadow of a human at the brink of death.

I lean closer to Steven, whose eyes have grown shiny. How can I ever replace his wife? She should have been the one sitting here with her hand on his knee.

I feel inadequate.

It's only a matter of time before he sees right through me and this is all over.

Obviously I'm curious about Steven's background, but this is all so uncomfortable that I don't ask any questions.

"My wife is exactly the age now as Regina was when she got sick," Andreas says.

Pauline looks at him without batting an eye.

Andreas has a terrible case of a verbal diarrhea. Without pausing to take a breath, he babbles on about their daily lives, jobs and yoga and trips to New Zealand. Apparently they have two teenage sons who are good at American football.

Pauline doesn't make a peep.

She's nothing but an accessory.

With every passing minute, the urge to kick Andreas in the crotch grows stronger.

"Steven has always been fantastic with our kids," he says. "Do you like children, Jennica?"

The question catches me off guard.

"Oh, sure," I say, glancing here and there, not quite sure if Andreas and Pauline have a sense of humor to speak of. "I guess most kids are fine. I'm pretty sure I would like my own."

There's a false ring to Andreas's laugh, and Pauline gives me a hollow stare. More or less as expected.

While the waiter presents the next course on the menu, something with seaweed and grapefruit, I shoot an apologetic glance at Steven and try to think of something sufficiently entertaining to say to smooth things over.

"Did you leave the teenagers alone in Gothenburg all weekend?" I attempt, poking my fork at the piece of kelp on my plate. "I hope the house is still standing when you get home."

Andreas has a sudden coughing fit and hides his mouth with a napkin. Meanwhile, Pauline takes a quick sip of wine.

"No, I mean, I'm not the mother of his children."

Andreas alternately coughs and laughs.

"Pauline and I aren't married. We're just friends."

I gape at them.

Naturally, by now I've figured out what's up. Even so, it's as if I want to keep that insight at arm's length, possibly to keep from spewing out exactly what I think and how it makes me feel.

Friends, my ass. This asswipe is sitting at a fancy restaurant in Malmö with a fucking Barbie doll while his wife takes care of the kids back home. I've suddenly found myself in the middle of the very same shit my clients call to sob about every day.

The six remaining courses mostly taste like bile. I don't say anything and avoid Pauline's gaze while Andreas holds court and keeps talking about Steven like he's some sort of demigod.

Was this how Dad spent his evenings while the rest of the family sat at home in front of the TV, missing him? All those business dinners and trips. Important meetings, always impossible to reschedule. Brussels, London, New York, Borås. There was always somewhere else to be besides home.

A full-body shudder, and I drain the glass the waiter so recently topped off with an acidic wine from the southern Rhône.

When it's finally over, I can't get out of the restaurant fast enough.

I don't want to make eye contact with Andreas. He wants to hug and kiss cheeks, but I wriggle out of his arms.

As soon as Steven and I are alone in the taxi, I let loose.

"Never invite me along to something like this again."

He loosens his tie.

"Was it the mussels? I thought they were terrible too, but it's so hard to—"

"I don't give a shit about the mussels!"

Steven is startled. He's grabbing his tie with both hands like it's a noose.

"Was it Andreas? He can be pretty intense, but he—"

"He's a goddamn cheating pig."

Steven falls silent.

I take a couple deep breaths to calm down. The taxi merges onto the highway and Steven pulls off his tie.

I have to tell him about Dad.

"I was only in first grade when I figured out what was going on. My siblings are a lot older. They were able to handle it differently, but it was fucking traumatic for me. I spent my whole childhood wondering why Dad didn't love us, didn't want to be part of our family. And why Mom never said or did anything about it. Sometimes I'm just as furious with her."

The taxi driver is playing loud music, and I snap at him to turn it off.

"That's terrible," Steven says.

"That's exactly what your buddy is up to."

"No, it's not."

He stuffs his crumpled tie into the pocket of his suit jacket.

"Of course it is. Andreas's wife is home in Gothenburg with their children, while he's running off to restaurants with a goddamn bimbo."

"It's not quite that simple," Steven says. "Pauline and Andreas have known each other for ages. She's not a bimbo."

"Okay, maybe it's not her fault."

Although she certainly bears some of the guilt too. She knows Andreas has a family.

"I don't like what he's doing," Steven says. "For me, infidelity is out of the question. But everyone's different. Monogamy doesn't work for Andreas, and his wife is aware of it. They have something of an unspoken agreement."

"That's some fucking bullshit." I think of Mom.

"I'm not defending it."

"That's exactly what you're doing. An agreement has to be reciprocal, doesn't it? Can it even be an agreement if it's unspoken?"

I pointedly turn to look out the window, where I watch the golden fields fly by. The big windmill and the farms before the exit for Lund.

Would Dad have said the same thing? An unspoken agreement.

Steven's hand gropes between our seats.

"I'm sorry, Jennica. You'll never have to see Andreas again. It's not as though we spend a lot of time together. He lives several hours away."

He places his hand on my back, slowly strokes between my shoulder blades. It tickles and makes me warm.

I hate people who pout and act petty to get sympathy. That's not me.

"Obviously you aren't responsible for your friend's actions," I say. "But it's important that we have the same views on cheating."

Steven continues to rub my back.

"I hate cheating," he says. "In my eyes, it's the most incomprehensible thing. If you don't love each other anymore, you might as well separate."

His hand stops at my nape, and his fingers find their way under my neckband. I can see the driver staring at us in the rearview mirror.

"Sorry, go ahead and start the music again."

Without batting an eye, he turns up the volume until the whole car is bouncing.

Steven laughs and kisses the back of my neck.

When we get to his apartment, he pours a nightcap and turns on some Bruce Springsteen. I turn off the old-man rock and put on Lana Del Rey. Steven's large hands on my hips. We sway together, my head against his shoulder. His warm, safe scent in my nostrils.

Slowly he guides me to the bedroom. My dress pools around my ankles, and he strokes my breasts. Our lips brush. His tongue is gentle but firm.

There's no confusion about who will lead. Steven's gaze is steady, and each movement is purposeful. Very soon I'm on my back with Steven on top, holding me tight as if in an embrace. Not for a fraction of a second does he look away as he coaxes and rocks until he's so deep inside me that my body is a millimeter away from dissolving into atoms. Each time I'm on the very edge he pulls out and kisses me greedily. When the grand finale arrives, my head falls back and I scream until the walls shake.

And wow, missionary. I'm elated. Calling a guy a "missionary" used to be the worst sort of diss on Tinder Central. But this version is absolute heaven.

"Damn, do I ever like you, Jennica Jungstedt," Steven whispers.

He's on his back, panting, with tiny beads of sweat in his chest hair. Our hands are entwined in a firm knot.

Bill

Ever since my conversation with Jennica Jungstedt, I've been walking around with an annoying feeling in my body. An itchy, prickly feeling I can't shake.

Why did she say Miranda lied? I don't get what she would have lied about. It makes me crazy that Jennica seems perfectly unbothered. My call was nothing but a momentary inconvenience, a reminder she would have preferred to go without. I shouldn't waste my time on her. She'll never accept responsibility for what she did, she'll never apologize.

I sit on the balcony, keeping an eagle eye on the job app. At last I get a task with an old lady on Vävaregatan who needs help installing an alarm on her street-abutting house. Sally stays home in the courtyard, playing, while I cycle off through Stadsparken, under the Trollebergsvägen viaduct, and north past the train station.

Outside the courthouse it's a circus of police cars, uniformed guards, and a big crowd in front of the entrance. I rubberneck out of curiosity, but it's not until I get to the woman's house that I find out what's up.

"Don't you read the paper?" she says. "It's the trial for that case in Kärrlösa."

It rings a bell somewhere in the recesses of my mind, but that's about it. I don't ask any more questions, not wanting to seem ignorant, but the old lady keeps talking anyway.

"Those two hooligans who broke into a man's house out in the countryside. He shot them both."

I've heard about the case before, of course. There was a lot of noise about it online when it first happened. People thought the man should be set free immediately. The burglars had only themselves to blame, he'd only been protecting his personal property.

"That's why I'm installing an alarm," the woman says. "I don't have a shotgun."

It's a cheap system from Jula, with a vibration detector and motion sensor. Probably nothing that would scare off hardened criminals. But I keep my thoughts to myself.

The lady shows me where she wants the alarm installed, and then I teach her how to use the remote. I get two hundred and fifty kronor cash for my trouble, and everyone is happy.

The sun blazes like a fireball in the sky. I can smell someone grilling in their yard. The bells of Allhelgona Church ring out.

I've just gotten on my bike when my phone rings. I put my feet down and search my pocket for my phone.

"Hello?"

"Is this Bill Olsson?"

The man says he's calling from Spegeln Cinema in Malmö. He received my email and thought I seemed interesting.

"Wonderful!"

"You seem to have some solid experience," he says. "I need someone who can start more or less immediately—next week."

"I'm sure I can make that work," I say.

The hours will be primarily during the daytime, Monday through Friday.

It's almost too good to be true.

"You wrote that you worked in Lund for many years," says the man at Spegeln. "So you must have had Anette Stehn as your boss?"

All the air goes out of me.

I collapse against my handlebars.

"Yeah. Yes."

It's no coincidence that I didn't list Anette among my references.

"I know her pretty well," says the man at Spegeln. "I'll give her a buzz later today."

"You do that," I say.

Suddenly it doesn't look very promising at all.

That evening, Sally and I make spaghetti Bolognese while Karla is at soccer practice. I read from *Harry Potter*, and Sally and I both fall asleep.

I wake up when I hear the front door; I fly out of bed, ashamed for some reason.

Karla looks at me, perplexed.

She's standing in the entryway in a strapless summer dress, dark red lipstick, and smoky eyes.

"I went out with some of my soccer friends," she says.

I check the time on my phone. It's past midnight.

"I think I fell asleep," I say.

Karla holds up her hand. "Wait a sec. There's something I want to show you."

She steals into Sally's old room and comes back with something in her hands.

"Look," she says. "It was my grandmother's."

I rub some sleep from my eyes.

She's holding a gold ring with a sparkling stone that looks suspiciously like a diamond.

"Is it real?"

Karla nods.

"You can have it. I'm sure you could sell it for ten or twenty thousand kronor on Tradera. It should at least cover next month's rent."

Karla

enter the alarm code and open the door to the Rytters' mansion.

It's quiet and dark. No one responds when I call out.

As I get started on the bathrooms, I listen to Rick Astley and Bonnie Tyler. As usual, I have only one earbud in.

The music takes me back to nights in the kitchen back home. It was always thick with smoke despite the exhaust fan. I would sit in a worn easy chair under the window, doing my homework. Mom always said she was proud of me, that I was the light in all her darkness.

This time she really wants to quit using. According to Silja, at least. I so badly want to believe her. What if she were to fail because I'm not there to support her? It's so egotistical of me not to jump on the first train back home.

I spray a few last spritzes of lemon cleaner and rub at the porcelain around the faucet of the bidet, then close the door on the bathroom and start in on the dusting.

Soon I've arrived at the bureau in the foyer. All the drawers are properly closed.

I can't believe I took the ring. Thinking of poor Sally put my entire ability to consider the consequences out of order. My regret hasn't given me a moment of peace since. I had left all of that behind me. Besides, I'm well aware the court authority always does a background check before a candidate is appointed as a judge.

Soon the duster is dancing across the last of the gleaming surfaces.

I have to put the ring back. I'll just tell Bill I changed my mind. There are other ways to save Sally.

Upstairs, the door to Regina's bedroom is open. I avoid the creaky doorsill in the hall and tiptoe by.

In the bedroom adjacent to Regina's I make the bed and fluff the pillows. There's a half-empty glass on the nightstand; I think it's water at first, but it smells like wine. I assume Steven usually sleeps in here. Does he sleep alone, or does Regina move over here at night? I bend over and sniff the pillowcase to determine if it needs washing.

"What are you doing? Where is Steven?"

I whirl around and yank the earbud from my ear.

Regina is in the door behind me, her hair messy and her eyes sharp.

"I was going to wash the sheets."

"Why? Where is Steven?"

Her eyes dart here and there.

"Isn't he at work?" I say. "It's only late morning."

She sways and grabs the doorframe.

"Are you okay?" I ask. "You should lie back down."

She breathes deeply and slowly, her hand on her chest. "It'll pass in a minute."

"Come on, let's go sit down," I say, offering my arm.

She squeezes my biceps hard as we stagger out to the couch.

"I'm sure you think I'm lying," Regina says, "but eighteen months ago I was in better shape than most forty-one-year-olds. I worked out five days a week. Tabata and boxing. Steven and I spent a lot of time outdoors. I love hiking and kayaking. We did a lot of mountain biking together."

I can just picture them: an attractive couple with tons of money and unlimited opportunities. The kind most people only dream of. Her illness seems to have ruined everything.

"No one understands how much damage a virus can do," she continues. "High fever, vomiting, pain all over. I lost my sense of smell and taste both. It was the worst thing that's ever happened to me, but of course I expected it would go away within a week or two."

Her breathing comes in starts; she presses her hand to her chest.

"It just kept on. After four weeks in bed, I felt well enough to get up and go out. But then the setback came crashing down and everything got so much worse. It's been like this ever since. Every time I feel like I have more energy and try to do something other than lie there in the dark, it comes back ten times worse."

I can hardly imagine. Not even Mom has it so bad. We've always had brighter days, times when she felt better and things actually began to approach normal.

"It's been like this for a year and a half?" I say, failing, as usual, to hide my feelings even a little bit.

"My life changed completely in just a week," Regina says. "Steven and I used to have a glass of wine on the weekends. We would go to restaurants, the theater, concerts. Now, at the very most, all I can manage is half an hour of watching TV."

I've read in the paper about people who end up sick in the long-term after viral infections, but I honestly didn't know it could be this bad.

And now I've gone and stolen from her besides.

"I was a social butterfly, I had lots of friends," Regina continues.

I turn toward the String shelves on the wall. Thick American coffee-table books about interior design and cooking crowd there with Klong vases and Kay Bojesen figurines of the sort I've only ever seen on Instagram.

"At first, lots of people got in touch," Regina says. Her voice fades and she takes a sharp breath. "They felt bad for me, of course. Flowers and chocolates showed up here. But eventually people lose patience, when you can't see them or even talk on the phone. I can't blame them."

She catches my eye and stares right through me. Mom always says I can't hide even something as tiny as a mosquito bite.

I thought I had put this all behind me. Stealing, lies, and secrets. I thought I was a different person now. But once a thief, always a thief. As soon as I get the chance, I'll put the ring back in the drawer.

"I have to keep cleaning," I say, and I start to get up, but Regina grabs my knee.

"Stay right there," she says.

Her voice is unexpectedly sharp.

"You'll still make it through what you need to do," she says.

I avoid her eyes.

"I've almost given up hope," Regina continues. "No one wants to take responsibility for my health. They just pass me around. Most of them seem to think it's all in my head. If Steven didn't have good contacts, I'd hardly be able to get my medicine."

"That's totally bizarre."

It's the Swedish health care system in a nutshell. I've accompanied Mom to any number of clinics, to sterile waiting rooms with felt sofas at the addiction clinic and the emergency psych clinic, to private centers with colorful fish in aquariums and plucky slogans in the entryway. We've been referred here and there and back again, triaged to wait and wait some more.

"You have to put your foot down," I say. "You can't keep going like this."

She leans back and nods, her eyes at half-mast.

"I know. But it's not like I have the energy to take it all on. Sometimes . . . sometimes I just want it to end."

I shiver. I see Mom before me and have to bite back the pain.

"You can't give up. Think of all the people who love you."

Mom's suicide attempt is a wound that will never heal. For a long time it held me in its firm grip. I was scared each time I came home to a closed bedroom door. It took years of therapy before I could finally accept that I wasn't responsible for what happened.

Regina bends forward.

"No one loves me anymore."

She sounds like Mom. But she really seems to mean every word.

"What about Steven?" I say.

"It's been a long time since Steven loved me. No one would be happier than him if I disappeared."

Bill

Sally and I spend a whole morning on the beach in Lomma. Although I don't like the heat and I hate getting sand in between my toes, and even though my skin can't tolerate the sun, we have a couple of wonderful hours together.

"How many days of summer vacation are left?" Sally asks.

We count together.

Then we dig a big pit in the sand and fill it with water from the sea.

"Oh, Dad. I hope summer never ends."

Late in the afternoon, she's still got sunscreen on her face and her long hair smells like salt as we ride the bus to Malmö.

Waiting on the lower level of Malmö's Central Station is a guy who is interested in purchasing Karla's grandma's diamond ring. There's something shady about the way he never makes eye contact with me, but he inspects the ring with extreme care, and after a few moments of quiet deliberation he offers me fourteen thousand kronor for it.

Fourteen thousand!

On the bus on the way home, I log in to the bank's mobile app and pay for the broken window. Even after that, I have ten thousand kronor left in my account. Suddenly it's much easier to breathe. Not even thoughts of Jennica Jungstedt can spoil my good mood. I'm smiling so hard my muscles hurt, and I ruffle Sally's hair again and again until she shoves my hand away and wonders what's up with me.

"I'm just happy."

Maybe *relieved* is a better word.

That evening I'm sitting on the couch with a wet towel across my sunburned shoulders while Sally looks at TikTok on my phone.

"Why won't she come home?"

It's almost ten o'clock, and Karla has been out all day.

"She's young. I'm sure she's got a lot of things to do."

"What kind of things?"

I should have known this would happen. It's only been a few weeks since Karla moved in, and Sally is already way too attached to her.

"I want to show her my tattoos," she says, stretching out her arms, which are full of temporary tattoos.

"I'm sure they'll last until tomorrow."

I help her brush her teeth, and then I read her two chapters of *Harry Potter*. Sally falls asleep in the middle of a scene that's so exciting I have to keep reading to see what happens.

Just as I'm tiptoeing out of the bedroom, I hear Karla at the apartment door. I sit down on the couch with my phone and prepare my little surprise.

It's only a loan, of course. The money from the ring belongs to Karla, and I'm not the least bit interested in charity. Still, these thousands of kronor are going to bail me out for the rest of the summer.

Karla stops at the arch that leads to the living room, crosses her ankles, and leans her shoulder against the wall. Her tank is knotted just above her navel, and as usual, her bangs fall over her eyes.

I have a hard time sitting still. I have to show her the numbers in my bank account.

But when I stand up, I realize something is wrong.

Karla peers at me. "Don't hate me."

"What?"

She's wringing her hands. "I changed my mind."

"What do you mean?"

"The ring," she says. "I changed my mind about the ring. I don't want to sell it."

It takes a moment for me to catch on.

She's changed her mind.

"But, you can't. I already sold it."

"What?" Karla stares at me.

Her face has gone pale.

"Look at this!" I say, dashing over with my phone. "I got fourteen thousand kronor for it!"

Karla looks pained.

"I'm sorry, but I just can't sell it. Can't you buy it back?"

My mouth feels like cotton; I don't know what to say. She should have thought this through earlier.

"Of course, I can make that happen." I close my eyes and swallow. "But . . . why did you change your mind? Did something happen?"

"What do you mean? No."

I had thought, of course, that she was 100 precent okay with selling the ring. It didn't seem like she had any attachment to it whatsoever. Something must have changed.

"I . . . I mean . . . it . . ."

She brings her hand to her forehead and her eyes flutter. Slowly but surely, her face crumples.

Obviously I underestimated the sentimental value of that ring.

"Take it easy. It'll all work out."

I don't know what to do with my hands. In any case, I don't dare touch her.

"I just don't know how it ended up like this," Karla sobs.

"We'll figure it out," I say. "I'll get the ring back."

She looks at me, her eyes red slits.

"It's not my grandma's ring."

"It's not?"

"I'm sorry, Bill. I'm sorry! I took it from one of my clients. They're super rich and they probably won't even notice it's gone. But I'm no thief. I don't want to be a thief."

I try to comfort her as the news sinks in. It hadn't even occurred to me. I never would have imagined.

"It'll be okay. I'll email the buyer and he'll just have to give it back."

She sits down on the couch and gingerly rubs the area under her eyes.

My image of Karla is transforming.

She stole from a client. A diamond ring that could very well be a family heirloom. And now she's got me all wrapped up in it as some sort of goddamn fence.

Maybe it's because she's so tiny and innocent-looking that I let myself be fooled. I don't really know her.

She tells me she stole the ring from a doctor who lives in Professorsstaden. It was purely by coincidence that she discovered a whole drawer full of jewelry and diamonds.

"So you just took it?"

It seems so stupid. Sooner or later, they'll notice the ring is missing and obviously Karla will be the first person they suspect.

She buries her face in her hands.

"I was thinking of you and Sally. I don't want Sally to have to go through any more crap."

"But this is no help."

I hope the guy who bought the ring doesn't try to learn more about it. If we get busted, some of this shit is going to rain down on me too.

"The jewelry is just *there*," she sobs. "It's not like it makes those people any happier. He works all the time, and his wife is super sick. She stays in bed all day long and her husband told me not to talk to her."

I scratch my cheek, tearing at the stubble with my fingernails. It must be possible to buy the ring back without making the guy in Malmö suspicious enough to start snooping. I'll have to come up with some excuse.

"At first I thought they wouldn't miss it anyway," Karla says, gazing at me with her red eyes. "These people don't live like you and me. They live in an actual palace. They've got to be filthy rich. But the woman is sicker than I thought at first. She's on some really powerful medications, and sometimes she's totally out of it. I can't stand the thought that I stole from her."

This just gets worse and worse. It's almost unreal.

Karla opens the Maps app on her phone and shows me satellite pictures of the ritzy country-mansion-style villa; it's right next to the botanical gardens.

"What was their name, did you say?"

I google Steven and Regina Rytter, but there are few traces of them online. There doesn't seem to be anyone with those names officially listed as living in Lund. Either they're registered somewhere else, or they're unlisted for privacy. If they're as rich as Karla claims, that might explain it.

I do, in any case, manage to find some old pictures. Dr. Steven Rytter is smiling in all of them. His muscles bulge beneath his polo shirt, and he absolutely radiates success. His wife, Regina, is apparently the daughter of author Helmer Lindgren. I've read a few of his books.

I sink onto the couch, still scratching at my stubble. These people aren't just anyone. If the theft comes to light, both Karla and I will be in trouble.

One of the images shows Steven and Regina together. Both of them look healthy and happy, but something seems off. There's something false about it. I don't think there's a single similar picture of Miranda and me.

"I'll get the ring back," I say.

Karla tucks her skinny legs beneath her on the couch. She grew up among addicts. I'm sure this isn't the first time she's stolen something. But I'm not about to get dragged into her shit.

I write a lengthy message to the guy in Malmö who bought the ring. With a healthy dose of weepiness in my tone, I explain that my friend changed her mind and wants it back. This is all about its sentimental value, not its monetary value. I claim that it's a memento from her grandmother.

Karla reads the message before I send it.

"Do you think he'll agree to it?" she asks.

"He seemed decent."

It's a white lie.

"I really hope so," she says. "Thanks for being so understanding. I hope you don't hate me."

I force myself to smile.

"Of course I don't hate you."

I'm sitting on the couch and surfing the internet when Karla heads off to brush her teeth. My eyes land on the photo of Miranda. I have to get my life in order before anything escalates further. I can't let Miranda down. Not again.

Of course I will be able to find a job. Something permanent. I may be down and out for the moment, but I'm not a loser, and I have no plans of becoming one.

Miranda once told me Jennica Jungstedt called me that. She had mocked me for my film studies and said I should get a real education and stop sponging off Miranda and her family. It's like Jennica has no sense of self-awareness. Talk about throwing stones in glass houses. Miranda seemed to take it in stride; she never had outbursts and seldom even showed she was upset. She was always so understanding, saying that Jennica had had a tough childhood. I was the one who was furious. I was the one who secretly clenched my fists.

I close my eyes and listen to the water running in the bathroom.

The toilet flushes. For a moment, I picture Miranda moving around in there. These simple, everyday sounds coming and going, the result of unconsidered routines, sheer ordinariness, stuff you never think you'll one day miss. In the blink of an eye, they make you sick with sorrow and longing.

Why me? Why am I the one who has to sit here, broke as hell and missing my wife?

There must be some logic to it. Some sort of justice. If only I didn't have to worry about money on top of everything else that happened.

Before I fall asleep, I log in to my email and discover a new message from the man at Spegeln Cinema.

After a conversation with Anette Stehn at Filmplaneten in Lund, I regret to inform you that you are no longer under consideration for the position.

Excerpt from Interrogation with Anette Stehn

Would you please state your full name for the record?

Anette Stehn.

Can you tell us about your job?

I run the Filmplaneten cinema here in Lund.

Is it true that Bill Olsson is a former employee there?

Bill worked for us off and on for over a decade. At first I suppose it was meant to be a side job while he was in college. Most of our employees are students. Lots of them come and go. But Bill was one of the few who stuck around for a long time. He loved movies. A true cinephile.

How would you describe Bill otherwise?

He was a good colleague, well liked by everyone. It was terrible, what happened with his partner. She was so young. Bill took family leave because of it, but the rest of the time his work was exemplary. Never any red flags. Which was why I was so shocked when things turned out the way they did.

You filed a police report against Bill Olsson last spring.

Yes, that's right. I had no choice.

Can you tell us what happened?

During the winter, things began to go missing from the cinema. Movie passes, gift cards. Things that turned up for sale on Blocket. The first time I reported it, nothing happened. The investigation was closed. So then I put up a hidden security camera.

And we've been given to understand that those tapes were handed over to the police. What did you discover?

That Bill was the one stealing. He confessed to all of it. He'd been saddled with a lot of debt after Miranda's death. But I fired him on the spot. Later he was found guilty and ordered to pay fines.

Jennica

'm half watching a series about a woman whose husband threw her off a balcony when Steven calls.

"Did you see *Stoner* is playing at the city theater tonight?"

I did see that, actually. I keep walking by posters in town. But I haven't been to a single theater performance since, like, grade school, when Mom dragged me along to pedagogical, moralistic plays at the children's theater.

"You've read the book," Steven says. "You liked it, didn't you?"

"I loved it." One of those epic tales of a perfectly ordinary life. "But I hear it's been sold out for ages."

"Doesn't matter," Steven says. "I've got two tickets right here."

I sit straight up in bed.

On the screen, the balcony woman, who survived against all odds, describes how she found God and forgave her husband, who is the father of her children and *also dumped her over the balcony railing like a sack of garbage from five stories up.*

"*Forgave* him? You ought to have hired someone to shove a spear up his ass."

I turn off that trash.

"Huh?" Steven laughs. "What are you talking about?"

"Sorry, just my roommate."

The cat looks offended. I stare at him aggressively.

"Shall we meet at six thirty and have dinner after?" Steven asks. "Then we can discuss the play."

"Sounds like a plan. I can always tide myself over with a pan pizza." Steven laughs again. Obviously he thinks I'm joking.

We talk about *Stoner* some more—the book was forgotten for decades and enjoyed a fairy-tale rediscovery long after the author's death.

When I glance at the time, I realize that my shift began ten minutes ago.

"Sorry, Steven, I have to go now."

I've probably already missed some calls.

Olivia sounds panicked when I answer.

"I've been calling and calling. What's going on?"

"I'm sorry, I was stuck in an important meeting," I lie. "But now I'm all ears."

Olivia is the regular who's married to a drunk. She typically wears her heart on her sleeve, but it's worse than usual today. She's shouting so loudly that I have to lift my headset away.

"I've done something awful. It's unforgivable!"

"What happened?"

"I hit him. Do you hear me, Jennica? I punched him, with my fist, right in the face. He got a bloody nose."

This sounds out of character, to say the least. On the other hand, about damn time she manifested some sort of reaction.

"I was snooping on his phone. I know that's wrong, but I had this strong sense that something was up. And my gut feeling was right! He's been fucking some girl at the office. There were a bunch of nasty pictures on his phone. And texts about what he wanted to do to her."

I turn my face to the ceiling and close my eyes. How much shit can one person take before it boils over? I was in my teens when I found a postcard from one of Dad's mistresses who wrote that she missed him and signed with a heart. It made me want to puke, and I laid all the blame at the feet of the woman who was trying to steal my father. By the time Ricky and Miranda made me a victim of infidelity, I was old enough to realize that they were equally guilty, the both of them.

"You shouldn't have stopped at just one punch," I tell Olivia.

She sounds totally wrecked.

"I hit him in the face. The kids saw the whole thing. I'm so incredibly ashamed of myself!"

"You shouldn't be. You didn't do anything wrong."

"But I hit him. That's assault."

I cut her off.

"It's called self-defense."

Olivia doesn't seem convinced.

I launch into a firebrand speech about how men have oppressed us women for millennia, and that sometimes we must resort to drastic measures, up to and including violence. She shouldn't blame herself.

"A guilty conscience is the patriarchy's best friend. Don't you forget it. Stop feeling sorry for him, that bastard actually got off easy."

It's unclear whether I'm getting through to her. Olivia sobs and snuffles until I can hardly tell what she's saying.

When we hang up, I sigh loudly and demonstratively at Dog.

He meows dejectedly.

How can you stand it? he seems to be saying.

After my shift, I spruce myself up a little before taking the bus downtown.

Steven is waiting outside the theater. Shirt, tie, jacket. He smells like he just showered.

He holds my hand throughout the entire performance. In response to certain lines, he squeezes my fingers and we look at each other in understanding. *We have to talk about this later.*

At intermission we drink bubbly, and when the play is over we walk arm in arm past the hubbub of Stortorget.

I find myself waiting to be asked *What did you think?* Or *On a scale of one to ten, how good was it?* But Steven isn't that type. I love it.

At Mat & Destillat we eat plaice with artichoke and lime puree.

"Did you know that artichokes have nothing to do with choking?" I ask. "It's actually from Arabic. I always thought it was because you'd choke if you tried to eat the whole leaf."

Steven shakes his head and smiles.

"Come on!" I say. "You totally would."

He asks if I took any interesting calls at work today, and I'm about to tell him about Olivia when I realize that Steven wouldn't understand. He knows all about theater, art, and literature. But he has no clue about all the shit that goes on behind the scenes. I bet he'd come up with some platitude about how there's never an excuse for violence, or that two wrongs don't make a right.

Then I happen to think of Bill Olsson.

"I did actually get an interesting call the other day."

I tell him about Miranda, my childhood friend who got a brain tumor and died, and how she left behind a little girl and this guy Bill, who she got together with when we were in high school.

"Why was he calling you now?" Steven asks. "That was a long time ago."

"He was a real wuss, and he lived off Miranda," I say. "She cheated on him, but I guess he never figured that out. He swallowed her story hook, line, and sinker, and I ended up being the scapegoat when everyone stopped hanging out with them."

I tell Steven about my twenty-fifth birthday party.

"I had rented a place out in the country. There were like eighty people invited. Back then I was dating a guy named Ricky; we'd been seeing each other for a few months, and I was super into him."

Steven doesn't need to know that I stalked this guy on social media for six months and then "happened" to walk past his workplace just as he was leaving one night. I've had a crush or two over the years, but Ricky was my first real boyfriend project.

"Miranda and Bill had had a baby and were living this, like, family life," I say. "Miranda probably hadn't partied for ages. She had a little too much to drink. After dinner, she told some of my friends she was thirsty for Ricky."

Steven frowns; his well-groomed eyebrows furrow.

"She hit on your boyfriend?"

"She was obviously drunk, but that's no excuse."

Miranda and I had played Barbies together. We built forts in the woods and collected kisses from the boys at preschool. Any form of cheating makes me want to hurl, but I will never get over the fact that one of my best friends betrayed me, someone I had known for my whole life, someone I trusted 100 percent.

"They danced a little together that night, but that didn't really bother me. She was my friend, and her boyfriend was there too. Then, sometime way past midnight, Ricky and Miranda vanished. I found them in a bathroom."

"You're kidding."

"I wish I was. I ended my friendship with both of them. Miranda tried to get in touch a few times in the following years, wanting to make up, but I couldn't forgive her. I just couldn't do it."

"But her boyfriend . . ."

Steven sets his silverware on his plate. He's already figured it out.

"I guess Bill never really caught on to what was going on. Miranda lied and blamed the whole thing on Ricky."

"And he bought it?"

I take a sip and wipe my lips with my napkin.

"So it seems. He worshipped Miranda. She could do no wrong. But the other girls in our gang, Emma, Tina, and Rebecka, more or less took my side, and within six months Miranda had completely drifted away from us. I know Emma and Tina were in touch with Miranda after she got sick. They visited her at the hospital and went to the funeral. But for me, it was a clean break."

"I understand," Steven says. "You have to be able to trust your closest friends."

"Right? And here this nutcase calls me up years later. It seems he found me online."

Steven touches his chin thoughtfully.

The darkness has closed in around the trees in Lundagård outside, and down the street is the glow of the cathedral.

"It bothers me," I say, drinking up the last of my wine. "That he's got the gall to track me down and hurl accusations at me."

Steven shrugs.

"Maybe you should tell him the truth." He sits up straight and adjusts his chair a bit. "When Regina died, I had an excessively positive view of her. When we met, I fell head over heels in love with her, I was totally enchanted. It's only now, afterward, that I can see how blind I was. Regina had tons of downsides too. Jealousy, a need for control. She secretly read all the messages on my phone and accused me of flirting with other people, even though I only had eyes for her. The realization that she wasn't a saint after all helped me work through my grief."

I lift my hands behind my neck. The button of my pants is about to burst.

"You haven't discovered anything wrong with me, I hope? My position here on your pedestal is solid?"

Steven laughs.

But I'm sure he does have a point.

To be honest, I feel more and more furious when I think about Bill's accusations. Maybe it would even be doing him a favor, to tell him the truth.

Karla

Waheeda holds open the door to the sushi place. It doesn't smell very good. We'd planned to meet up in order to study together, but Waheeda hasn't eaten all day and has somehow managed to convince me to give sushi a try.

"Walla, are you messing with me? You've never had sushi? What do you mean?"

She waves her hands around by her head as though she's trying to swat away a swarm of flies. I still can't ever quite tell when she's being sarcastic and sort of doing a parody of herself.

"Raw fish isn't really my thing," I say.

"Oh, come on. Give it a shot!"

She helps me pick some good pieces to try, and it really is surprisingly tasty.

"Don't you like it?" Waheeda asks, kissing her fingertips clean. "We can go to the falafel stand instead."

"No, no, it's fine."

"Seriously? You look like you just took a bite of poo."

I laugh. She really does have a way with words.

"No, I was thinking about something else entirely," I confess.

I still haven't heard from Bill about the ring. Maybe the man who bought it doesn't want to give it back. I just hope he doesn't start trying to figure out where it came from.

"Tell me!" Waheeda says. "Some serious drama or what?"

I finish chewing and swallow it down with some water. I don't know how much I should tell her.

"There's this client I clean for a few times a week. A doctor and his wife. Something weird is up with them."

I explain that Regina is sick and mostly bedridden. I say she imagines things, hallucinates, and has trouble telling the difference between dreams and reality. All the while, as I talk about it, Mom is there in the back of my mind, but I don't mention that part.

"She claims she's afraid of her husband," I say. "But I don't know what . . ."

"Hundo p, he hits her." Quick as a wink, Waheeda goes from clowning to dead serious. Both her expression and voice take on a harsh edge. "One hundred percent!"

She tosses her voluminous hair.

"You think so?"

"Does Santa have a hipster beard? Obviously he hits her."

"But what kind of monster would do that to a sick, fragile person?"

"Oh, you have no idea," Waheeda says. "The world is just crawling with monsters. There are even evil doctors. Someone should do something about it."

She's right. I can't allow this to continue. If Regina brings it up again, I have to convince her to seek help. I was only thirteen when Mom's boyfriend at the time, he was a drummer in a metal band, hit her in the face with a bottle. She refused to report him to the police, but at least I managed to get her to kick him out for good. I wouldn't be able to live with myself if something happened to Regina Rytter and I didn't do a damn thing about it.

When I'm down to just two pieces of sushi, Waheeda asks if she should give me a hand and snatches one.

"Time to get cracking, then?" I ask.

We really need to study. This assignment has to be turned in by 11:59 P.M.

I haul my copy of the code of statutes and my course reader onto the wobbly table while Waheeda logs in to her laptop.

"Check this out," she says, turning the screen toward me.

Shooting in Kärrlösa Brings Three-Year Prison Sentence

"Our justice system is fucked," Waheeda says. "The real gangsters walk free and we chuck ordinary people who were only defending themselves in prison."

No one in Lund has been able to avoid hearing about the case in Kärrlösa, a small village up on the plains that was struck by a horrific tragedy when two local teens tried to break into the home of a seventy-year-old man. Without warning, the old man took out his shotgun and shot both burglars to death on his doorstep.

"'The court states that the young men were armed and that the man had reason to fear for his life,'" Waheeda reads aloud from the article. "'The situation was such that the man scarcely had time to consider his actions. Even so, the use of deadly force was inexcusable, and as a result, the seventy-year-old is sentenced to three years' imprisonment for manslaughter.'"

I lean over her shoulder.

"'In order to justify the use of deadly force in self-defense, there must be no available alternatives to avert the attack,' legal expert Leonard Emsäter tells *The Evening Post*."

"What the hell was he supposed to do?" Waheeda says. "Ask them to please put down their guns? Invite them in for coffee and say that he knows it's not their fault things turned out this way? That it was surely the system? That they probably had a terrible childhood?"

Annoyed, she raps her knuckles on the table.

"What does the law say?" I ask.

In fact, I have more to say on the subject, but Waheeda is so agitated that I'd rather avoid that discussion.

I think the court's reasoning sounds pretty sensible. Do we really want a society where people are allowed to defend their property by any means they like?

"Must be in the criminal code," Waheeda says, flipping through the code of statutes.

I remember a case in the United States where a man shot his four-year-old daughter to death because he thought she was a burglar. I should tell Waheeda about it. Argue for my beliefs. But I've never liked debating. It so quickly leads to raised voices and bad blood. And I definitely don't want to risk my newfound friendship.

"Listen," Waheeda says, reading aloud from the code of statutes. "'A right to self-defense exists with respect to: an initiated or impending criminal attack on a person or property.'"

She pokes the book with her index finger so hard that the delicate paper crinkles.

Meanwhile, I keep reading. It's very clear that you're never allowed to use a greater degree of violence than the situation calls for. In addition to determining how concrete the threat was, the court must also weigh whether one had the ability to remove oneself from the scene of the crime, the possibility that one could call for help, and the possibility that one could aim to hit less-vital parts of the body.

"There's nothing wrong with the law," Waheeda says. "It's all about how you interpret it. The old men on the courts need updating. They need more people like you and me."

Excerpt from Interrogation with Eldar Kahrimanović

Would you please state your full name for the record?
Ensar Eldar Kahrimanović.

Could you tell us a little about yourself?
I'm thirty-one, I work in sales, IT, and cell phones. Married with two small children. What else is there? I live in Limhamn in Malmö.

How did you come in contact with Bill Olsson?
I answered an ad he posted. It was for a ring, which I made an offer on.

Did you buy the ring from him?
We met at Central Station. I checked to make sure the ring was real and then I Swished him fourteen grand.

Did you ask for a receipt?
No, do people usually do that?

Did you ask to see a receipt for the original purchase of this ring?

Come on! It was an old ring that belonged to some relative. Obviously he didn't have a receipt.

Then what happened to the ring?

The next day I got a message. He had changed his mind. He was blubbering about how his friend was so sad because it was her grandma's ring or something. I decided to be nice and told him I'd give the ring back if he transferred the money back to my account.

Is that what happened?

No, the money never showed up, so I kept the ring.

What did you think about that?

That there was something pretty fucking shady about that dude.

Bill

Ever since Miranda died, each morning is the same. I wake up with a start and turn over to make sure Sally is there and breathing. Early on, she would open her eyes right away, as though she could sense my worry in the air, but now that she's moved into my bedroom permanently and we spend the whole night lying close together, she seems to sleep more deeply and feel more secure. These days I have to touch her, or even shake her gently, before she opens her sky-blue eyes to say:

"Hi, Dad! What did you dream about?"

Miranda is the one who started the dream routine. If you didn't remember your dreams, you could simply pull something from your imagination. I was never much good at it, but Miranda could always concoct fantastic stories.

"I dreamed about Karla," Sally says, rubbing the sleep from her eyes. "I dreamed that you got married. I was a bridesmaid in your wedding, and Celine Dion came and sang 'My Heart Will Go On.'"

Miranda's favorite song, hands down. I asked the cantor to play it at her funeral.

"Karla is our lodger," I say. "We have to give her space."

I say it to protect Sally, but I realize I've raised my voice, and she pouts, wounded.

"You can't help who you dream about, you know."

"No, of course not. That was silly of me to say." I smile and stroke her cheek.

"Karla is my friend," she says.

"No, she isn't. Karla is . . ."

"A lodger, I know."

I place a gentle kiss on her arm and tickle her until she's writhing with laughter. We don't know nearly enough about Karla, but I do know she's a thief and a liar.

"Come on, let's make scones," I say, throwing off the covers.

After breakfast, Sally runs down to the courtyard, slathered in SPF 30 and armed with a cap and a water bottle.

I go out to the balcony and lean against the railing. It's quiet and deserted down there. Lund is in its summer lull. Most students have gone home, and everything is on pause until September.

I sit in the shadows and surf around the employment office listings for a while, but that only makes me depressed. I decide to play *World of Warcraft* instead. By the time the phone rings, I've whiled away a couple of hours.

Blocked number. I answer the phone with a curious *hello?*

"Is this Bill?"

It's a woman. I don't recognize her voice.

"Yes . . . who's this?"

I get up and gaze out at the courtyard. No sign of Sally.

"It's not okay to just call people up and accuse them of things out of nowhere," says the voice in my ear. "I get that you're having a hell of a time and obviously I wish Miranda had never gotten sick, but she was the one who betrayed *my* trust. We were childhood friends! What she did was totally fucking unforgivable."

It's Jennica Jungstedt. I can't believe she's called me back to yell at me some more. Isn't she ever going to apologize?

"You turned everyone against her. You didn't even come to the funeral." I spit the words. From a nearby balcony, an older couple turns to stare.

"I didn't think you would want me there," Jennica says while I aim a fake smile at the neighbors.

"Miranda was a victim." I go into the apartment and close the balcony door. "She was unconscious when that bastard Ricky raped her."

"That's what she told you? Then why didn't she report him?"

Miranda threw up a number of times that night. We took a taxi to her parents' house; they had been watching Sally. Miranda said she could hardly remember what had gone on in that bathroom. She cried hysterically and begged me to forgive her for drinking too much. She just wanted to forget about it and move on. She said she couldn't handle prolonging it all in any way. I respected that.

"Miranda was super drunk, absolutely," says Jennica. "But she wasn't exactly out cold when I caught them in the bathroom. Quite the opposite. Ricky said she's the one who started it."

"Bullshit!" I stub my toe on the couch, and it burns with pain. "Obviously he was lying. If you still don't get that, we have nothing more to discuss here."

I hang up on her and land on the edge of the couch, grabbing my throbbing big toe. I'll never get an apology from Jennica, and it was a stupid idea to call her in the first place. And what does it even matter? Miranda is dead.

My eyes burn as tears spring to them.

Miranda didn't cry that night after Jennica's party. She was terribly upset, but she didn't want to talk about it. Even though Sally was so little, she was afraid she would understand, that it would get lodged in her subconscious. Miranda always avoided conflict and emotional outbursts. In that way, we were the same. We didn't even cry when she got sick. For more than a year she stayed strong through operations, radiation, and chemotherapy. And I played along. We had our usual conversations, our usual laughter; we let life go on as though that tumor didn't exist. Only when Miranda was gone did it become real on a totally different level; only then did it really hit me, what had happened.

I wasn't prepared for the loneliness. Miranda had always been there. She was my safety net, my confidante, my best friend. Sure, I had some old colleagues from the movie theater I chatted online with, film people I'd gotten to know on the internet, and a classmate or two from the past, but no one I could truly talk to, no one to share my deepest self with.

It's been so long now. When Miranda had just died, it was okay for me to feel like shit. You have the right to fall apart when someone has just died. But people won't shut up about how time heals all wounds, and by the time a year has gone by people have started to get sick of you. The kid gloves come off.

How long is grief supposed to last? People seldom wonder out loud, but sometimes all it takes is a glance or a certain tone of voice.

I was dependent on Miranda. We had almost grown into one person. When she disappeared, so did my security.

I look at the photo of her on the wall. The three tiny dots on her cheek. Birthmarks. I have almost identical ones. We used to joke that it was a couples' tattoo.

She never would have cheated on me.

I open my laptop again. There's a new message from the guy who bought the stolen ring. He writes that he understands the situation and is prepared to return the ring as soon as I transfer the money to his account.

I suggest we meet the very next day. Then I log in to my bank account. The available amount stares me in the face. Almost ten thousand. That's a lot of money, a hell of a lot. But it could be more.

I bring up the casino page.

Fuck.

I don't want to. I really shouldn't. But my fingers are itchy. After all, I know I can easily double or triple that money. The extra cash would save our summer. And then Karla can have the ring back and move out.

Obviously it's a gamble. A risk. But I've succeeded before.

My fingers tremble.

I really shouldn't.

Excerpt from Interrogation with Bill Olsson

We've taken a closer look at your finances, Bill. How would you describe your financial situation?

It's not great. It's been really tough since last spring, when I had to quit the movie theater.

You're saddled with quite a lot of debt.

Yes, a couple hundred thousand kronor. But I've always made payments on time. I'm not subject to any garnishment from the Enforcement Agency.

How have you supported yourself since you left the movie theater?

I had to cut out all unnecessary expenses. Then I took on a number of odd jobs via an app. But most important, I rented out a room in our apartment.

How would you characterize yourself, Bill?

What do you mean?

Well, what sort of person are you?

I don't know. Pretty ordinary, I suppose. Like most people.

Do you ever have violent outbursts?

Definitely not. Ask anyone. I don't get fired up for no reason.

Does the name Jesper Lövgren mean anything to you?

Yeah, yes, of course. But whatever he told you, I'm sure it's not true.

What do you mean?

Jesper Lövgren lies. He's done it before.

When has he lied?

After Miranda died, I tried to get help from social services. You know, for a while I could hardly get out of bed each morning. Jesper Lövgren was the counselor for our case.

Lövgren filed a police report on you. What happened?

I wasn't myself. My wife had died and . . . I was called in for a meeting with social services. They accused me of being a bad parent and threatened to take Sally into care. I lost it. I said some inappropriate things and threw some documents on the floor. It was in no way a threat or the "violence against a civil servant" that Jesper Lövgren wanted to make it into. The prosecutor closed the case and cleared me of all suspicion.

But you lost your composure? Is that an accurate characterization of what happened?

I lost everything. My wife had just died, and they were threatening to take my daughter away from me.

So you do sometimes lose control?

no comment

Jennica

When I wake up, Steven has folded his pillow in half. He's lying on his side and gazing at me as though I were an entirely unexplored branch of the family of man.

"I wish I could stay here with you all day," he whispers, slipping his hand under my blanket. "But I have a little patient who's been waiting for this day for months. A six-year-old boy with a serious kidney condition who needs surgery."

It's truly admirable. I wish I could make a difference in people's lives for real instead of sitting on the phone at night convincing older women to leave their cheating husbands.

"There are buns you can warm up in the oven," Steven says. "And fresh-squeezed orange juice in the fridge."

I could get used to sitting in Steven Rytter's citrus-scented kitchen, my knees tucked up beneath me, eating breakfast with the breeze wafting in from the open window.

Steven has changed everything. In recent years I have tried to keep my hopeless dating and roving love life private, but now I long to tell everyone the news. I want to change my relationship status on

Facebook and post kissy pictures with Steven on Instagram. I want to shout for the whole world to hear, serve up the details, and dig deep into all my feelings.

I hardly recognize myself.

Soon the coffee has gone cold in my mug, but I stay in the kitchen with my phone, thinking of Bill Olsson. At least now he knows the truth about Saint Miranda. I just don't have the energy to care about it any more.

After chatting with Tina and Emma for a while, I type Steven's name into the search field on Google, the way you do sometimes even though new stuff hardly ever pops up. I browse distractedly through the results. There's a picture of Steven and Regina where he has his arm around her. They look so happy. Just a year or so later, she was dead.

I enlarge the picture so much it gets all pixelly. Under it is the name *Regina Lindgren.* That must be her maiden name.

I quickly copy and paste it into the search field.

Hundreds of results.

I scroll down a little and the site Hitta.se catches my eye. The white pages. *Regina Lindgren, 43 years old, Lund,* it reads. When I click on the link, an address I don't recognize pops up. Linnégatan, in Professorsstaden—a stone's throw from the botanical gardens.

Regina Lindgren resides here along with Steven Rytter.

A shiver runs down my spine.

I set my feet on the floor and bend forward.

I get the creepy-crawlies as I click on the map and zoom in. A mansion with a huge yard.

It must be a mistake. A glitch in the system. Steven did mention that he and Regina lived in Professorsstaden, right? It just hasn't been taken down from the site. I've definitely heard tales of how difficult it is to get someone's information off the internet after they die.

Once I've spiffed myself up in Steven's bathroom, I hop on my bike and pedal west, past Stortorget. It's teeming with people. The weather's pretty nice, not warm enough for the beach, but perfect for a jaunt downtown. I make it only as far as the crosswalk by Gleerups before I change my mind. I might as well bike the other direction. It's not even out of my way.

I'm awfully curious about that house on Linnégatan.

Karla

und University Library might be the most beautiful building I've ever seen. For a few moments I stand in the small
park outside, taking pictures of the grand brick palace with its
magnificent windows. Green ivy climbs the facade, and the
three towers remind me of a cathedral.

When Waheeda said we should meet up at UL, I had no idea what
she meant at first.

"UL! The libe!"

"What? What are you talking about?"

"The u-ni-ver-si-ty-li-brar-y," she stammered out, in what was apparently supposed to be some version of standard Swedish.

We take over a table, spreading out our books and laptops. Although the sign says only drinks with lids are allowed, Waheeda cracks
open an energy drink and stuffs her hand into a bag of cheesy puffs.

"Check it out," she says, scooching up close to me with her laptop.
"Going back to what we talked about last time. Have you heard of the
castle doctrine?"

"As in, like, a king's castle?"

"Exactly," Waheeda says, scrolling so quickly through the text on her screen that I don't have time to read a single word. "Your home is your castle."

"That sounds like something Americans would say."

"Bingo, Watson. As usual, the Americans are way ahead of us when it comes to common sense."

I scoff. Sure, I dig jeans and Coke and fluffy pancakes with maple syrup, but to be honest I find Waheeda's USA-mania to be pretty alarming.

"What?" she says, her hands in the air.

"Oh, nothing. Tell me about it."

She squints at me in suspicion before she goes on.

"The castle doctrine gives you the right to protect yourself if someone breaks into your home. Like, that old dude in Kärrlösa, he would never have gone to prison if the castle doctrine existed in Sweden. If someone breaks into your home in the US, you have the right to respond with violence. Shouldn't that be a matter of course here too?"

"Should it?"

She reads aloud from a site that doesn't exactly look scientific.

"'Stand-your-ground laws or no-duty-to-retreat laws give people the right to use deadly force to defend themselves against serious bodily harm, kidnapping, rape, or other serious crimes.'"

She stops and looks at me.

"I'm listening," I promise. "Go on."

"The castle doctrine applies in all fifty states if you are attacked in your own home, but in thirty-six states there are stand-your-ground laws that allow you to protect yourself with deadly force no matter where you are attacked."

She stuffs her mouth full of cheesy puffs. The crumbs shower onto her laptop. I'm afraid they'll get caught in the tiny cracks around the keys.

"Well, say something," Waheeda says, nudging me with her elbow. "What do you think?"

"I mean, that's basically the 'shoot first, ask questions later' principle."

I tell her about the man who thought he'd found a burglar and then shot and killed his own four-year-old.

Waheeda chews with her mouth open.

"But that never would have happened in Sweden. Our gun laws are totally different."

"Apparently some people keep firearms at home, though," I say, thinking of the old man in Kärrlösa.

"But, yalla, read this," Waheeda says, plunking her computer in my lap. "They've done studies in the US and found that the stand-your-ground laws didn't lead to any kind of increase in the murder rate. It's about the principle of the thing, their views on criminals and victims. In Sweden, we consider the criminal first and foremost. People here seem to think that due process is only about the rights of the accused. The victims are forgotten."

"But it must be possible to keep two thoughts in your head at once, right?" I say. "One thing doesn't have to rule out the other."

"In my homeland, the victim is central in the administration of justice. When someone is murdered, the victim's family can demand remuneration from the killer. If an agreement, a reconciliation, can't be reached, then you have the right to revenge."

"Revenge, though? I don't know. That's not what justice is all about, is it?"

"About, of course it is!" Waheeda forms her lips into a pout, as though I've offended her. "Think about the woman you clean for, the doctor's wife. If she gets fed up with all that mental and physical abuse, and decides to get back at him—isn't that justice? That dictator would get what he deserves."

"I guess I want to believe society has come a little further than that," I say.

"Listen." Waheeda moves so close that I can smell the cheesy puffs on her breath. "That's not a good argument. As if any sort of progress can only be a good thing. Anything that isn't Western gets dismissed as 'uncivilized.' Justice isn't a scientific concept. You can't read your way to it in books. When I was, like, ten, there was this boy in my same courtyard who shoved me into the bushes and stuck his hand inside my underwear."

Something is happening to Waheeda. Her voice loses strength and her confident gaze starts to waver.

"I went straight to my big brothers and told them what had happened. At school I had been taught that you should talk to a grown-up, maybe report it to the police, but for me it was obvious I had to tell my brothers first." She yanks at her fingers, popping the joints. "What do you think happened? Did they go to the police? No, they had a serious talk with that kid. Next day, he shows up to school with a black eye. After that, he treated me like a fucking queen and no one has groped me ever since."

She takes a sharp breath. I look down and fiddle with my bracelet.

"I'm so sorry something like that happened to you," I say. "But I don't believe in a society where justice is built on revenge and people take the law into their own hands."

Waheeda swipes her hand over her forehead and lowers her voice.

"That's easy enough to say. Until it happens to you."

By the time I get home at eight thirty that evening, my brain is totally empty. Bill is sitting at the kitchen table, messing with something on his computer. He hardly responds when I say hello.

I grab a Red Bull from the fridge.

"I'm sorry," Bill says, "but I don't think we're getting that ring back."

"What?"

"The guy didn't want to give it back."

"What's wrong with him?"

Bill stares blankly at his screen.

"It's too bad," he says. "But it's not like I can force him to."

"Can I have his number?" I ask. "Or email, or whatever you've got?"

"Sure, but it probably won't help. His mind was totally made up."

"Let me try, at least. Can I have his number?"

"Shhh! You'll wake Sally." Bill angrily brings a finger to his lips.

I stop and listen for sounds from the bedroom.

So many nights I woke up to screaming and fighting. Mom's druggie friends or boyfriends, exploding over some minor thing. I used to pull my pillow over my head and pray to God that it would stop. No child should have to experience that kind of fear.

"Maybe I can talk to that woman. Regina Rytter," Bill says. "I'll explain that it's all my fault. If we're lucky, she won't go to the police. I can pay for the ring."

"No way. You don't have any money. And obviously Regina would realize I'm the one who stole it."

"Fine, fine." Bill rests his chin in his hands, apparently brainstorming. "I'll call and talk to the guy in Malmö. I'll try to convince him."

"But I can call him. Maybe—"

He abruptly cuts me off. "I'll do it."

The determination in his voice surprises me.

In my room, I throw myself on the bed. My whole body hurts. Maybe I've overestimated my chances of turning over a new leaf? Once a thief, always a thief. There's no breaking free. I think about the chat Waheeda and I had about justice. Mom is always talking about karma. If you're a good person, with your heart in the right place, the universe will reward you. Justice as a logical result, a law of nature. I haven't seen much evidence of that. Maybe it's like Waheeda says. If you want justice, you have to make sure to help yourself.

Excerpt from Interrogation with Karla Larsson

I have a photograph here that I'd like you to look at, Karla. Do you recognize this object?

It's a ring with a small stone. It looks like a diamond.

It is a diamond.

Okay.

Have you seen this ring before?

Hard to say. I've seen lots of rings that look similar. This could be one of them.

This is Regina Rytter's ring. She inherited it from her mother. Do you know if you ever saw it at Regina's house when you were cleaning?

I can't say for sure. I don't notice my clients' belongings that way. But I could very well have seen it at some point.

This ring was listed for sale on the internet in late June. We were able to trace the seller. It was Bill Olsson. How do you explain that?

I don't know. I don't even know if I've seen that ring before.

Were you aware that Bill was going to sell Regina's ring?

What do you mean? Like I said, I know nothing about that ring.

Was that why Bill killed Steven and Regina? Because they discovered he was stealing from them?

No, no! Bill didn't kill anyone. He wasn't the one who stole the ring.

Who stole it, then?

It was me.

Jennica

'm not actually a fan of bicycling; it seems beneath me, as an adult. I mean, why else did God invent the taxi? But when you're raised in Lund, cycling is a birthright, along with mother's milk and holy water. Everyone pedals their way around here. The city is built for cyclists. There are one-way streets everywhere, and there are no parking spots anywhere. It can't be a coincidence that lots of students live on the north side, so it's downhill to the student unions with their banquets and pubs but uphill all the way home.

In September, the alleys around Lund's student unions—the nations—are suddenly full of twenty-year-olds on granny bikes or army bicycles, savvy global citizens who have come straight from high school to study project leadership and take over the world. As curious, hungry, and immortal as students before them, down through the ages. But now the summer has poked a hole in the student bubble and the kids have exchanged academic departments and nation pubs for strawberry fields and apprenticeships at their fathers' firms. Instead, two nuns stroll peacefully over the cobblestones by the Catholic church.

I take the bike path between the cemetery and the botanical gardens.

The houses in this neighborhood go for at least ten million. Dad has always wanted to live in Professorsstaden, but Mom thinks it's too snobby.

As I cross Östervångsvägen, I send a lingering gaze over to the mansions on Linnégatan. Somewhere around here is the house where Steven used to live with his wife.

This isn't the real Professorsstaden. Not according to Dad, anyway. He likes to say that the border of the neighborhood is actually farther north, but that idiot Realtors seem to think that half of Lund is part of it.

I walk my bike onto Linnégatan, along the sidewalk opposite the house. I can imagine Regina standing at the gate and kissing Steven goodbye in the mornings. Something like jealousy twists inside me. How is it possible? I never get jealous, especially not of someone who's already dead.

I try to figure out which of the big villas belonged to Steven and Regina. There's a black Tesla in one of the driveways. Must be a coincidence.

The house is largely hidden by a lush garden, but you can glimpse some of the upstairs windows. The blinds are down. There's a whiff of creepy abandonment about it.

I stop and lean to the side to see the car's license plate.

My stomach sinks.

That combination of numbers is all too familiar.

I bump my bike down off the sidewalk and am just about to cross the street when the gate before me opens.

"Jennica?"

I squeeze the handlebars. I'm dizzy, almost ready to pass out.

Steven dashes over to me.

"What are you doing here?"

"I was on my way home, but then I spotted your car."

He puts his arm around me and tries to kiss me, but I shove him away.

"The question is, what are you doing here? Weren't you supposed to be operating on a sick six-year-old's kidneys?"

He raises his hands and backs away, a wounded expression on his face.

His voice is thick with disappointment.

"I will be. But I had to talk to my renters. They're having issues with the vents. I have to call in a handyperson."

Renters, vents, a handyperson. I can't make it all make sense.

"This is your house?"

I push my bike to the driveway and peer between bushes and trees at the big mansion.

"I've told you that, haven't I? I never managed to sell it," Steven says.

That does ring a bell.

"Oh, right."

He gazes at me curiously, and I feel myself blush.

"Is everything okay?"

I shake my head at myself. The lovely brick villa is tucked in among juniper and lilac bushes. I see a hammock and a small arbor.

Suddenly I see a young woman in one of the windows. As soon as she's popped up, she's gone again.

"It's a very nice house," I tell Steven.

"It is, yeah." He plucks his car key from his pocket. "But for me it's all tied up in such horrible memories. I prefer to stay away as much as possible."

"Makes sense."

"I should actually put it on the market again," Steven says. "But I feel kind of sorry for the family that's settled in here. They don't have that kind of money. And the daughter's about to start her last year of high school. But once she's graduated I guess I'll have to deal with it."

"That's so kind of you," I say.

Overly kind, if you ask me.

Steven rubs the key between his fingers.

"It'll be quite a job to get rid of all that old furniture and stuff. Regina was something of a collector."

He always casts his eyes down when he's talking about his ex-wife.

I place a comforting hand on his arm and glance up at the house one last time. Two pathetic lion statues flank the entrance. Must have been Regina who wanted them there. I shudder.

"I have to get going now," Steven says, and his car beeps as he unlocks it. "That operation."

I get only a few meters on my bike before the gears start giving me trouble. Outside the botanical gardens, I climb off and kick at the chain a few times. That usually does the trick.

A couple of curses at it and I'm soon on my way again.

Almost thirty years old and relegated to a half-broken bike. When Teslas exist.

Karla

'm standing in the Rytters' living room with the duster in my hand when my phone rings.

"Mom? Is everything okay?"

With the phone to my ear, I sink into an egg-shaped easy chair that gives me a view of the yard, where the morning sun is sparkling on the grass.

"Not okay at all." She's slurring her words. Clearly she's taken something. "Those fucking idiots at the treatment center are refusing to give me any methadone."

I have to turn down the volume on my phone.

"Mom, can we please talk about this later? I'm at work."

"You don't care," she says. "If you cared, you wouldn't have taken off and left me on my own."

She sobs and sniffs. I really have let her down. I've lost hope. Obviously she noticed.

"Mom, I—"

"Stop *Mom*-ing me! Just stop. I can't take it anymore."

She weeps. The sound fades in and out. It's like she's dropped the phone and picked it up again.

"Hello? Mom? Can you hear me?"

Silence.

I call again, but all I get is the busy signal.

As I rise from the chair to keep dusting, the front door opens. I take a few steps into the hall.

"Hi, Karla."

Steven Rytter is walking my way in a floral shirt and a handsome suit.

"Hi . . . ?"

He looks at me, his face grim.

Did he hear me talking to Mom? I look around in confusion.

"I just want to make one thing clear to you," Steven says. "To make sure there are no further misunderstandings."

He's smiling, but his eyes are flinty.

I hide behind my bangs.

"I've asked you several times now not to bother my wife," he says emphatically. "Can I trust that you will comply with this request in the future?"

"Of course, I apologize. I tried to tell Regina, but she was determined we have tea together. Even though I don't even like tea."

It's clear even to me that I'm talking too fast. I can't afford to lose this job.

"We've had other cleaners who had trouble leaving Regina alone," Steven says. He's not smiling anymore. "They were immediately replaced."

So that's why. Regina said it was for some other reason entirely. What was it, again? She'd said my predecessor was unpleasant.

"I'm sorry," I reiterate. "It won't happen again."

Steven takes a step toward me. He's so tall. I have to crane my neck to look him in the eye.

"Just tell her to take her medicine and go to bed. Do we have an agreement?"

I shudder. Waheeda's words echo in my mind. She might very well be right about Steven Rytter. I hardly dare to think about what he could do to Regina, someone so sick and so frequently out of it thanks to her meds.

"Now you may get back to cleaning," Steven says.

It's a struggle to return his fake smile.

As soon as he's closed the door behind him, I twitch aside the curtain in the hall window. Steven has just opened the car door down in the driveway. Beside him stands a woman with a bicycle. They seem agitated as they converse, and they're gesticulating wildly. She's young and beautiful. She seems upset with Steven. Who is she? A mistress? Suddenly she turns around and discovers me.

I let go of the curtain and hurry back to the living room. The dust rag is balled in my hand. I squeeze it hard. After a few minutes I dare to go back to the window. The car is gone now. So's the bike. And the young woman.

When I turn around, Regina is standing in the hall. She's got one hand on the bureau with the jewelry drawer and is tipping sideways a little. She looks at me, dazed.

"You have to lie down again. Your husband is really angry at me."

She coughs, her hand to her chest.

"I can't find my medicine."

"Come on," I say, taking her by the arm.

We walk up the stairs together.

"What did Steven say?" she asks. "Was it about the ring?"

I freeze. It can't be true. They've already realized it's missing.

"What ring?" I try to sound nonchalant.

Regina looks at me, her eyes hazy.

"A delicate little ring with a diamond solitaire. You haven't seen it?"

"No, I'm sorry."

I guide her on up the stairs, hiding my face as best I can. Mom has always said I'm like an open book, can't keep my feelings off my face.

Maybe it would be easiest just to confess everything? That I'm a waste of a human, with no morals whatsoever.

"It's my mother's engagement ring," Regina sighs. "It's always been in the top drawer of the bureau down there, but now I can't find it. I'll have to talk to Steven. Maybe he's seen it."

I don't dare to look at her. What have I done? We have to get ahold of the guy who bought the ring. Regina needs it back.

She sits on the edge of the bed and brings her hand to her forehead.

"I've got a splitting headache. I need my pills."

I don't see the pill organizer. It's usually on the nightstand. I pull out the drawer and dig around, bend down to look in the crack between the bed and the wall. It's like there's a horror movie playing in my mind. All the times I've turned our apartment back home upside down, hunting for pills when Mom is screaming from withdrawal.

"Do you remember when you last had it?"

"It's always right there," she says, pointing at the nightstand. "Please hurry up."

I throw myself to the floor and wiggle under the bed to look, I overturn blankets and sheets, but I still can't find it.

Regina sighs and moans.

"You'll have to run down and get some from the medicine cabinet."

In the bathroom downstairs is a large commode, and in the cabinet farthest to the left I find a bottle of pills, a couple of little boxes, and a few loose blister packs. Hopefully Regina knows which ones she should take.

As I rush back upstairs, I read the packages.

Diazepam, Xanax, lorazepam, oxazepam.

Are these really the right pills?

After twenty years with an addict mother, I know a certain amount about medications. Diazepam is the same thing as Valium. For a while, Mom had half the pantry full of it.

"I found these," I say, and I hardly have time to show her the pills before Regina grabs them away.

She tears open a box of diazepam.

"Water," she mutters, shoving two pills into her mouth. "There's a glass in the bathroom."

Before I hurry off, I check the packages again. Lorazepam. Isn't that the same as Ativan? Pretty damn addictive, according to Mom.

"Are you sure these are the ones you usually take?" I ask.

"Yes, of course. Get me that water!"

Bill

Once Sally is asleep, I lie there with *Harry Potter* on my belly and stare at the ceiling.

Sally moves gently in her sleep.

Sometimes I can hardly look at her, for how much she looks like Miranda.

One evening, when Sally was still a baby, we were lying here, in this very same bed, under this very same roof, and Sally was sleeping beside me as she is now.

"What would you do if Sally and I died?" Miranda asked.

It feels creepy to think about now.

"I wouldn't want to be alive anymore either," I recall answering.

I was being 100 percent honest.

My eyes burn.

John Milton is so fucking right in *The Devil's Advocate*. If God exists, He must be a sadist.

Jennica Jungstedt has always been a terrible person. She caused all sorts of drama in their friend group when they were younger. I'm not at all surprised she continues to hurl accusations at Miranda, even in death. Claiming Miranda was the one who started things with Ricky at that horrid party.

Miranda was no flirt. I always trusted her, never saw any reason to be jealous.

I gently pick up *Harry Potter* and insert the bookmark, which looks like a rat with a long tail. Sally got it from Miranda for Christmas.

I forgave Miranda immediately after that party. It never crossed my mind not to.

Just a few days later I heard about Jennica's reaction. She'd dumped Ricky, of course, but she placed an equal amount of blame on Miranda as well. She never wanted to see us again. At first I thought it wasn't really a big deal, but eventually I realized that she'd managed to turn the other girls against Miranda too.

Never again did we speak of that party, or of Ricky. I was disgusted by the whole thing.

Still lying beside Sally, I log in to my banking app to check the balance again. As if it could suddenly multiply on its own. As if this were all just a nightmare.

As quickly as the money for the ring landed in my account, I managed to make it vanish.

What do you do when you start losing money at the casino? You raise the stakes, take greater risks. Just one last round, one last spin. Hope doesn't abandon you until all your money is gone.

But you're not out of money just because you're out of money. There are loans to be had, quick ones with sky-high interest rates. You can re-up your account in five minutes.

And then, one last bet that's meant to put everything to rights.

I should know better.

Sally is sleeping on her side, breathing heavily. She makes tiny snores as she sucks air into her little nose; she sounds just like Miranda. I could gaze at her forever. I know every last line in her face, the dimples in her cheeks, her freckles, the way her lips bow under her nose. If it weren't for Sally, it probably would have been game over by now.

The next morning, I snag a task on the app worth two thousand kronor. A guy in Gunnesbo wants some boards and other junk removed from his property. I cheer out loud, and Sally sings as we pedal off on the bike.

The man who hired me is waiting on his front steps, his arms crossed. He's in his fifties and is wearing a straw hat on his head.

"You brought a kid?" he says.

Sally slips back and huddles behind me.

"All this needs to go?" I ask.

The driveway is full of plywood and planks; it must be the debris from a torn-down shed.

"I'm assuming there are more of you coming," says the man in the straw hat. "You'll need a car for this."

"We can handle it," I say, aware that I'm not doing a very good job concealing my doubt. "It's not that far to the dump. We can make several trips."

In reality, I know it's a lost cause. Even if we work our asses off all day, Sally and I could probably only haul away a third of the rubbish, max. There's just no point, without a car. You'd almost need a trailer too.

"Forget it. I'll hire someone else," says the man in the straw hat. "You can't let the little one carry all that."

Two thousand kronor, up in smoke, but I'm not about to dwell on it. Sally and I settle on a bench in the shade while I look for new tasks on the app. At last I snag one: an older couple in Annehem needs help installing a router.

The sun is scorching as Sally hops onto the luggage rack. I struggle up the hill past Gunnesbo Station, and when we get to the top I'm so sweaty that my T-shirt has gone from turquoise to dark blue. The router is easy as pie, at least, and that's three hundred kronor plus twenty for a tip for Sally.

"I'm sorry I have to drag you along like this," I say as we walk back into the blazing heat.

Sally just laughs.

"But it's super fun, Dad. And I just earned twenty kronor."

She cheerfully waves the bill in the air.

When we get home to Karhögstorg, my sunburned neck is smarting. Outside the Hemköp grocery store, the woman who always sits there panhandling has been given a bag of empty returnable cans by some passerby. She's been sitting there for years now, day in and day out, from opening to closing time. Time has left its mark on her: her skin is grooved and rough; her eyes are dull.

"Hello, hi," she says, as always.

"Hi!" says Sally, and she tugs at my arm and whispers, "Do we have some coins to give her?"

"I'm sorry," I say aloud.

Sally rustles her twenty kronor, but I press the bill back into her pocket.

We cross the square slowly. Some kids have chalked a hopscotch court onto the asphalt, and they're in the middle of a game. Sally asks if she can stop and play for a bit.

"Sure, but don't go anywhere else. I'll call down when dinner's ready."

My legs are like spaghetti after all that pedaling. The stairwell smells like food: cooking meat, herbs, and garlic. I'm starving, but I'm not sure we have anything at home.

As I step into the elevator, my phone vibrates.

"Is this Bill Olsson?"

My immediate instinct is to hang up, but the woman on the other end launches into a spiel so eagerly that I don't get a chance. She tells me she's calling from the electric company.

"We're contacting you in regards to three unpaid bills. We have sent a number of reminders by mail, but according to my records we have yet to receive any payments."

"They're coming," I say, just as the elevator stops on our floor. "Things have been awfully hectic for a while now. I lost my job, but if you could just have a little patience . . ."

I dig in my pocket for my keys.

"I must inform you that this constitutes a serious breach of contract," the woman says into my ear. "According to the law, we have the right to cut off your electricity if you don't pay."

"Listen," I say. "I have a young child at home. She's eight years old. You're going to cut off the electricity to the home of a little kid? How could you be so unethical?"

She immediately becomes defensive. She's only doing her job, and ethics have nothing to do with it.

"I'll pay," I say. "Just give me a couple weeks."

I quickly unlock the apartment and kick off my shoes in the entryway. I'm hungry and sweaty, tired and irritable. When I walk into the kitchen, Karla is leaning against the counter with a glass of water in hand.

"Isn't Sally with you?" she asks.

Her eyes are wide. Something is going on.

"She's down in the courtyard. Why?"

She takes a sip of water and pours the rest into the sink.

"Regina Rytter discovered that the ring was missing."

I stop mid-step. All my emotions vanish; only emptiness is left. I can't handle this anymore.

"How?" I ask. "How is it possible?"

"Apparently it was her mother's engagement ring."

I can only shake my head.

"You promised to get it back," Karla says. "Did you talk to the guy in Malmö?"

I take a deep breath and look away.

"I haven't had time. I'll call him tonight, I promise."

"Shit, how could I be this stupid?"

Karla sounds panicked. I have to get that ring back somehow.

I cautiously turn back around and look at her.

"And that's not all," she says breathlessly. "Regina couldn't find her pills, so I helped her get some from the medicine cabinet."

She stumbles over her words and falls silent.

"And?"

My stomach growls again. I haven't had a proper meal all day. In the fridge is a carton of yogurt that expired two days ago.

"My mom's been taking benzos my whole life," Karla says as I stick my nose into the yogurt container. "The same kind of pills Regina's on. They're really strong; they make you tired."

"Okay?"

I don't know much about prescription drugs, even though Miranda was pumped full of chemicals. When she was admitted to palliative care, there was a doctor who prescribed antidepressants for me, but I never even got the prescription filled.

"Do you think this is still edible?" I ask, letting Karla smell the yogurt.

"It seems okay."

I squeeze it all into a bowl and start shoveling it into my mouth as Karla messes with her phone.

"Isn't it weird for Steven to give Regina medications that make her so tired?" she says.

"Steven? Her husband? He's the one who gives her pills?"

A doctor prescribing medicine to his wife? Sounds sketchy.

"Regina said the doctors who examined her didn't want to write her any prescriptions."

I think about what to say to the guy who bought the ring. If I say it's stolen, maybe he'll get spooked and agree to hand it back over, against a written note of debt.

Karla hands over her phone.

"Look at this," she says. "This is one of the things Regina is on."

She's brought up a page of information about a drug called diazepam.

I skim it quickly.

Diazepam is used to treat anxiety, panic disorder, and insomnia. Common side effects include drowsiness, confusion, tremors, and withdrawal symptoms. Less common side effects include muscle weakness, memory loss, difficulty concentrating, problems with balance, dizziness, headaches, and slurred speech.

"Regina Rytter has all of those," Karla says.

Also listed as side effects are psychosis and hallucinations, emotional blunting, delusions, and nightmares.

"Diazepam is a type of benzo," Karla continues as I scrape the bowl with my spoon. "It's the kind of stuff that can make you really out of it. The Rytters' medicine cabinet is full of these."

Maybe it's a good thing she's popping so many pills.

"If we're lucky, she'll forget about the ring again," I say. "Seems like she's pretty muddled, to say the least."

Karla aims a reproachful look at me as I put the empty bowl in the sink and run the water.

"Well, at least one thing's for sure," she says. "Benzos aren't any help for chronic exhaustion."

Jennica

Repressing things is one of my top talents, closely followed by self-flagellation and procrastination. So it's no coincidence that it's getting close to the start of the semester by the time I finally get on my bike and coast down the hills to the university library to check out course books for that blasted Analysis of Developmental Acid exam I have to retake.

I seriously consider sitting down in the reading room with its green table lamps to page through these books, but I decide enough is enough. Just obtaining the books in the first place is plenty of productivity for one day.

Instead, I bike home to Delphi.

My apartment stinks; it's a mysterious odor whose origins are hard to determine. Food, sweat, garbage. There are clothes and other objects strewn absolutely everywhere. I really should tackle the mess, but I just open the window wide and spray away the rest of the smell with my cheapest perfume.

Dog hops onto the bookcase and stares at me as only a truly affronted cat can.

I throw myself onto the bed and browse the documentaries on Netflix. I search for cults, murders, and disappearances, but there's not much I haven't seen already.

At last I land on one about a family from Norrbotten. An ordinary family: middle-class parents whose two kids became mysteriously ill with flu-like symptoms that never went away. Life became pure hell. The girls couldn't go to school, they had to quit dance and piano lessons, they couldn't even play anymore. The parents were beyond desperate and did everything they could to figure out what was going on, but the doctors couldn't come up with any diagnosis for the children. No treatment helped. And before anyone in their lives realized how bad the situation was, or how far gone they were, the parents decided to kill their children and then themselves. A self-described expert talks about a form of psychosis, a folie à deux, where two people share the same delusion. It's so easy to resort to that sort of explanation. I know a journalist from one of the evening papers called the case a "family tragedy" and caused a shitstorm in the comments section. I close the laptop, feeling empty.

"What's for lunch?" I ask Dog.

I'm really not all that hungry. I seldom am, but I've learned to eat at somewhat regular intervals anyway.

"No, not herring."

The cat grunts in disappointment.

"Pizza? Okay. Why change things up when you know what you like?"

I cook it in the microwave and sprinkle oregano on it when it's done.

Then I shovel it down, sitting halfway up in bed. Meanwhile, I find a new documentary. This one's about a father who threw his three-year-old daughter off a cliff to her death. No one had any idea; no one had noticed anything wrong. The man himself could hardly explain what had happened, aside from saying that his anxiety and intrusive thoughts had gotten to be too much.

Isn't that always the way? No one notices a thing until it's too late.

I think of Bill Olsson, of his and Miranda's little girl, Sally. I haven't ever met her more than a few times, but as I recall she was a carbon copy of Miranda when she was little.

Miranda and Bill got together when we were in high school. Even back then, I was skeptical. Bill was a little older, had already graduated, and had left his hometown to move in with Miranda and her parents. After that, we hardly saw Miranda except at school. Bill was a special sort. Not social in the least. He just wanted to sit at home, watching movies and playing video games. I thought he was a little creepy. Of course, I put on a pleasant face and kept my mouth shut. Miranda was my friend. She was in love, and I'm sure no one expected it to last until death did them part.

Miranda was halfway out of our friend group even before my twenty-fifth birthday. As the years passed, she slipped further and further to the edge of our circle, and of course, it all culminated in her having a baby while the rest of us went on with Tinder Central.

It wasn't my fault that she lost all her childhood friends. She took care of that on her own. Miranda and our other girlfriends were the only ones who knew my father had been unfaithful. She knew how I felt, how that cheating had affected my whole life, when she went into that bathroom with Ricky.

A few years later, Miranda was on her deathbed and Emma asked if I wanted to come along to visit her. But I couldn't. Some things cannot be forgiven.

I shift my focus back to the screen. When the mother of that little baby who was thrown off the cliff starts sobbing with her altered voice behind a black screen, it's all just too much.

I turn off Netflix. A burned piece of crust is all that's left of my pizza.

. . .

That evening, I dig out a bag of lentil chips I hid from myself behind the pans under the stove. I pour a glass of wine and collapse on my bed with my headphones on. A shift of work is exactly what I need.

First, I have a good chat with a woman whose relatives are all angry with her after she decided to dump the spouse who's been treating her like shit for more than thirty years.

Then Maggan calls. This time there's a hullaballoo because she went out for coffee with her younger daughter and, with all good intentions, told her she should consider a healthier alternative than a brownie with whipped cream.

"She still looks like she's pregnant, even though it's been two years since her youngest was born," Maggan says. "Is it so terribly wrong for me to point it out? She hardly seems aware of it herself. And here she used to be so slim and pretty."

Sometimes it's hard work to be sympathetic. I put my hand over the microphone of my headset and take a deep breath before I respond.

There is not a mean bone in Maggan's body, yet everything she does turns out so wrong.

"You should never comment on another person's appearance," I say.

"But she's my daughter."

"That doesn't matter. She's an adult. She's allowed to eat brownies for breakfast every morning if she likes. She's allowed to look like a blue whale, without attracting any comments from you."

"A blue whale?"

I can't help but sigh.

"Just think about things before you say them in the future," I say.

We end our call, and Dog glares at me in alarm as I reach past him to take my glass of wine from the shelf.

"What is it, buddy? Do you want to come cuddle?"

He yawns, stretches out his front paws, and turns his butt on me.

That wretched creature is about as interested in cuddling as I am. It's almost like we're made for each other.

Steven sent a couple messages while I was working. When I finally find the time to write back, he responds promptly.

Pack an overnight bag. I'll pick you up in an hour.

CAUSE OF LUND COUPLE'S DEATH RULED DRUG OVERDOSE AND BLUNT FORCE TRAUMA

The Evening Post, Lund

The Evening Post can now share details of how the pediatrician and his wife died. According to a police source close to the investigation, the woman perished as a result of repeated blows to the head, while her husband died from suspiciously high levels of narcotics in his system.

The Lund double murder has alarmed many in the university town. Outside of the couple's mansion in Professorsstaden is a vast sea of flowers, candles, and cards. Some are from former patients of the man, who worked as a pediatrician at Skåne University Hospital in Lund.

"It's unbelievable, what happened," says a woman whose child was recently treated by the doctor. "You can't even feel safe in your own home these days."

The doctor, 47, and his wife were found deceased in their home after the hospital reported that the man had not shown up for a scheduled surgery. The police suspect that both the pediatrician and his wife were victims of homicide. A 33-year-old Lund man is in custody under reasonable suspicion for the murders.

The woman, 43, was the daughter of a well-known author and Lund businessman and, according to sources, had been suffering from a mysterious illness in recent years.

"It was tragic," says a neighbor who wishes to remain anonymous. "She was extremely active until she was struck down by a virus that caused some sort of autoimmune disease. I've hardly seen her at all over the past year."

The Evening Post's source reveals that the pediatrician, who also worked with Doctors Without Borders, died as a result of a prescription drug overdose.

"The autopsy revealed a fatal dose of narcotic substances in the man's body," the source says.

According to the prosecutor, the remanded 33-year-old remains a suspect in the case. As *The Evening Post* previously reported, the suspect's live-in partner worked as a cleaner for the deceased couple, but at present she is not under suspicion of any crime.

Bill

t's as though a huge bird of prey is caught in my chest, flapping its wings to force its way out. I try every possible position in the apartment: I sit on the couch, lie on the bed, try to shut out my fears by playing *World of Warcraft*. Nothing works. At last I have to get out.

I just leave. I take long, determined strides on my way to nothing. As though I'm trying to escape myself.

If I don't pay the electric bill, they'll cut off power to the apartment. And rent is due again soon.

In the gravel alley along Södra Esplanaden, I encounter a sweaty jogger clad in neon yellow Lycra. He's panting and tapping at his heart-rate monitor. An energetic Labrador puppy sniffs curiously at my worn shoes, a gift from Miranda years ago.

I wish I had someone to talk to. I wish Miranda were here. It's no secret that I was financially dependent on her, but it wasn't until recently I realized how far beyond money my dependency went. I let myself be absorbed into her to such an extent that I lost parts of myself.

Two men are standing outside Spyken School, arguing loudly and gesturing wildly. I cross the street to keep from getting too close to them; I wait for a green light and head north, skirting the cemetery.

The sun is high in the sky. This is the hottest summer in recorded history. They say something's wrong, that the ice caps are melting and the grass is yellowing, as if nature is in revolt.

I turn in to the botanical gardens. It's been ages since I visited here. I remember one picnic with Miranda's parents. Sally had just started walking, and I had my hands full chasing her down paths and through flower beds.

A young couple is sitting on a bench under a gnarled tree. One of them has thrown her leg over her girlfriend's lap; she plucks the cap from her head. They laugh. The capless one tosses her hair. She reminds me a little bit of Karla.

I should tell her the truth about the ring. I have to swallow my pride and confess that both the ring and the money are gone forever. Karla already knows I'm a good-for-nothing failure.

Sweat trickles into my eyes as I leave the gardens and find myself on a narrow street lined with fancy mansions. There's a huge giraffe sculpture on one semicircular balcony. The hedges are trimmed to perfection and the stone paths are straight and tidy. This is what they call Professorsstaden. A hundred years ago, it was nothing but a field when the university folks started building their villas here. Today, professors can't afford the neighborhood; CEOs and business bigwigs have moved into these grand homes.

Steven and Regina Rytter live around here somewhere. I take out my phone and start to google as I walk south.

"Watch where you're going!"

A woman with a cane snaps at me when I almost walk straight into her.

"I'm sorry."

I've just found the Rytters' house on Google Maps.

I catch a glimpse of the street sign between green trees and bushes:

Linnégatan. I stop for a moment, looking at my phone and trying to figure out which house it is. Then I follow the sidewalk as the soulless GPS voice guides me on.

The Rytters live in a beautiful brick house with a copper roof and lion statues flanking the entrance. In the driveway is a sparkling clean Tesla that's hooked up to a charging station.

I slowly walk by. All the blinds are drawn, and the house is dark. When I reach the next intersection, I turn around and walk back the same way. Behind the iron gate, a narrow path leads to a front door with transom windows. When we were looking at pictures of the house, Karla told me they've got one of those keypads that's connected to the alarm system. I assume Karla has a code to get in.

Steven's a doctor and works almost all the time. His wife just lies around sleeping, totally zonked on drugs. Karla told me the bureau is in the foyer, just inside the door. The top drawer is stuffed with expensive jewelry made of gold and silver, pearls and diamonds. It would probably be so simple to sneak in and help yourself. You could leave marks on the doorframe to hide the fact that you actually had the code. A break-in could explain why the diamond ring is missing, and shift suspicion away from Karla.

The Rytters must be swimming in money, anyway. I'm sure they have great insurance as well.

I trudge back across the street, toward the botanical gardens again and on into the cemetery, where I sink onto a park bench. The bird of prey is flapping its broad wings inside my chest. Its claws tear at the insides of my ribs. I take deep, long breaths.

What am I doing? This is insane. Things have gone so far that I'm seriously sitting here contemplating burglary.

I should find a job instead. I bend over my phone and scroll through the ads on the employment office page: no educational requirements, no experience requirements.

Lots of places are looking for telemarketers or meeting bookers, where the pay is 100 percent based on commissions. I have too many morals and not enough moxie to fool people into purchasing various kinds of subscriptions and other shit they don't need. But I also can't afford to be picky.

There are a number of openings for personal assistants. I haven't looked too closely at these in the past; I'm not sure if I can handle taking care of another person again after everything that happened with Miranda. Besides, I was under the impression that you needed some sort of training for a job like that, but it seems you don't. Most agencies state that personal chemistry is the most important factor of all.

My attention is drawn to one ad in particular. The client is a multiply disabled middle-aged man who needs around-the-clock care. I send an email to the contact.

When I stand up, I realize I need to hurry. I have to pick up Sally in ten minutes.

Karla

As I wait for the bus, I call Lena at the cleaning company.

"I wonder if I'm allowed to switch clients."

I hope she takes this the right way. I don't want to seem difficult.

"Switch? What do you mean?"

"Well, in case I don't quite like working with a particular client. Is it possible to clean for someone else?"

Lena doesn't say anything for a few seconds. From the start she's been great to work with, but what if I've crossed a line?

"Is it the Rytters?" she asks.

"Yes, it is."

My breath is shallow. What if Steven has already complained?

"What happened?" Lena asks.

"Nothing in particular." I don't know how to explain. "It's more like, it just feels off. Regina is seriously ill, and her husband doesn't want me to bother her, but it's not easy when she wants to talk to me all the time."

"I understand. I'll see what I can do."

"Oh, thank you!"

I'm so glad Lena gets it. Now I'll be rid of all my problems. If I'm lucky, the ring thing will work out too.

My bus pulls in at the stop, and I take a few steps out onto the sidewalk.

"But you'll continue to clean for them until I've checked whether it's possible to switch," Lena says.

"Of course."

I'm sure I can handle going there another time or two.

I touch my card to the reader and take the bus to the sporting fields, where Waheeda is waiting with her cleats in one hand and a Red Bull in the other.

The grass on the field is scorched yellow and stiff. I have a hard time focusing.

After practice, I pull off my shoes and socks on the sidelines. Waheeda thumps down next to me, panting and heaving, her hand to her heart.

"It's just pounding," she says, releasing her hair, which has been up in a big bun atop her head.

The coach lumbers over and clears his throat.

"I'm awfully impressed by you, Karla. You're really too good for this level. You should be playing at a higher tier of the league."

I pick a few pieces of grass from my shoes.

"Aw, you're exaggerating."

"Not at all," the coach says, adjusting his sun-bleached cap. "Same for you, Waheeda. As I've told you time and again."

"I know. Obviously I'm too good for this team, but who has time to practice ten times a week? I'm in school too. I'm going to be a prosecutor."

"You know I'm happy to have you on our team," says the coach. "But it's a pity to let such talent go to waste."

He's really trying to meet my gaze, and I force myself to give him a dorky smile.

As soon as he's gone, Waheeda whacks me in the arm.

"Don't be so shy, habibti! You have to learn to take a compliment."

"Oh, he's exaggerating. Didn't you see that bad pass I made? It almost turned into an own goal."

"Stop it!" Waheeda says, nudging me ahead of her down the slope toward the locker rooms. "Forget studying tonight. I don't want to know a word more about intellectual property law. Want to get pizza instead?"

I don't take much convincing. We go to an Italian restaurant at a leafy courtyard downtown and down some nice, crispy pizza, chatting and laughing with blankets over our legs and shoulders. For the first time in I don't know how long, I feel warm and alive. No worries.

"If we both get into the program we can get a student room together," Waheeda says. "You and me in a complex or something. That would be sick."

It sounds like a dream. First we just have to nail that damn final.

We stay put until the waitress starts wiping down our table and Waheeda has to run to make it to the last bus.

By the time I get home to Karhögstorg, it's almost midnight.

I try not to jangle the keys coming in, and I place my shoes gingerly in a corner. The door to Bill and Sally's bedroom is closed; the whole apartment is quiet and dark.

I just have to brush my teeth.

"Hi." Bill's voice in the darkness. His eyes glow.

"You're still up?" I whisper.

"I couldn't sleep."

He's on the far end of the sofa, looking petrified. The screen saver spins on his laptop.

"Did something happen?" I ask.

He doesn't move a muscle.

"I got hold of the guy who bought the ring," he says. "We're screwed."

"What do you mean?"

"He sold it to someone else."

Jennica

We ride in the limousine as the sun sinks above the sea and makes the rapeseed fields shine like gold. Steven puts his arm around me on the leather bench seat, opens a bottle of Dom Pérignon, and toasts the future.

"Have you been here before?" Steven asks as we exit the highway north of Helsingborg.

Kullen is a peninsula that reaches like a crooked finger between the sound and the Kattegat strait.

"My grandpa had a summer house in Arild," I say, sipping my champagne. "I spent quite a bit of time there when I was little."

"I love Arild," Steven says. "It's so much more authentic than Torekov and Båstad."

But we're not on our way to Arild. Our destination is a surprise. Steven has revealed nothing, but we're traveling along the southern coast of the peninsula, heading for the point of the finger where an old lighthouse towers over rocks and caverns. The sign reads "Mölle." I've never been here before, but I've heard it's beautiful. The limo chugs its way up the steep hill along narrow, winding roads, to reach the seaside hotel.

"I like this old style of hotel," Steven says. "Where the rooms aren't all identical. Where the beds still creak and there's a Bible in the night-stand drawer."

I swallow the last of my bubbly.

"I thought you were an atheist."

"Absolutely, I am. But that has nothing to do with the Bible, does it?"

"What do you mean?" I ask with a skeptical smile.

"The Bible is cultural history. The bedrock of all Western civiliza-tion. All literature is a response to it in one way or another."

"Maybe it's worth a read, then," I say.

Steven smiles.

"Definitely, I think it is. I read the Koran last summer. It's fasci-nating literature, really beautiful passages. But that doesn't mean I'm planning to kneel down and face Mecca five times a day."

By the time the limousine pulls up outside the hotel, I'm feeling a little tipsy from the champagne. Steven has booked the top-floor suite, with a view of the bay and the picturesque harbor. I open the doors of the south-facing French balcony and inhale the salty evening air as Steven lands in an easy chair and lights a cigar.

"We have a table in the restaurant waiting for us in forty-five min-utes," he says.

His cigar smokes from its spot in a large ceramic ashtray. Steven doesn't actually like to smoke, but the luxurious aroma speaks to him.

"I can't stand regular cigarette smoke," he says, crossing his legs.

He plays old-man music on his phone as I take a shower and fix myself up. Bob Dylan and Tom Petty. Half the space in the bathroom is taken up by a Jacuzzi tub that Steven has hinted he'd love to try out after dinner.

An appetizer of lobster and mussels is followed by duck confit and a full-bodied pinot noir from Alsace. The restaurant is packed down to the last chair, and we've got by far the best table, with a view of both the dining room and the surroundings.

"I really should be studying for that exam retake."

"Oops," Steven says. "I thought you were the type to ace every test on the first try."

"Almost every test, except when I forget to buy the textbook and only have time to skim through it in the hallway right beforehand."

Steven pokes a toothpick into the corner of his mouth.

"I can get you a taxi back if you'd rather spend the night studying. I myself was considering an evening walk down the hill and then a nightcap in the Jacuzzi."

"Hmm, you never make it simple to decide."

We laugh and toast each other. Neither of us has room for dessert. Instead, we stroll hand in hand down the steep steps to the fishing village. The moon is halfway above the sea's horizon, and I have trouble keeping my hands off Steven.

When we get back to the room, I shove him onto his back on the bed and pull my dress over my head. His cock is about to burst when I land on top of him and grind against him in slow waves. The tiniest movements make the lines of his face smooth out as he heads for the ultimate dissolution.

After he comes, he goes down on me with a hunger I've hardly experienced before. I grab the back of his neck with both hands and press him against me until I explode and see stars.

The next morning, I wake to find that Steven has opened the balcony doors to the dawn and lit a cigar.

"What day is it?" I ask.

His robe gapes, revealing his nakedness beneath.

"Tuesday." He smirks. "Have you got anything on the agenda?"

My thoughts are every which way; I try to get them in order.

"I have to work tonight. And I have to study too," I sigh. "Don't you work today?"

"I have an operation this afternoon. But we'll have time for lunch after we check out, won't we?"

Definitely, I think.

In the meantime, we take a bath in the small Jacuzzi and I get goose bumps when Steven runs soap and kisses over every inch of my body.

What this man does to me hasn't happened since I was a teenager. It's wonderful and jittery and frightening. I want to show us off to the world, the way you do when you've been desperately trying to find something and you finally get your hands on it and, to be safe, affix a sticker with your name on it. I want to shout it out, declare that he's here now and he's mine. It's childish, of course, but it would be awfully nice to take Steven home to Mom and Aunt Birgitta, my cousins and siblings. And Dad.

I wrap myself in the hotel's terry-cloth robe and straddle Steven in the easy chair, my hand on his hairy chest.

"Can you see yourself meeting my family?" I ask. "It wouldn't have to be formal or anything. Maybe coffee in the garden?"

His pale eyes seem to go flat. He reaches for the cigar.

"Of course I'd like to. Eventually. There's no need to rush, is there?"

He holds the cigar between his fingers and follows the wreath of smoke as it rises toward the plasterwork on the ceiling.

His hesitation worries me. What if his feelings aren't nearly as fervent as my own? I've been in his situation more times than I want to recall: dudes who caught feelings early on and came on way too strong. It's such a terrible feeling.

"It was a silly idea," I say. "We don't need to stress about it."

"We'll be chill," Steven says.

He takes a quick drag from the cigar and coughs.

"It's almost a punishment, having to meet my family," I say.

Steven cups the back of my neck and kisses me. He tastes like an ashtray, but I don't care.

"They did a hell of a good job with you, anyway."

I don't know if he can tell that my smile is a little distant. The thought that his feelings aren't as strong as my own has taken hold of me.

That afternoon we head back to Lund. I keep my eyes closed for more than half the drive, to avoid talking. The taxi drops me off outside City Gross and Steven holds me for a long time there on the street.

"When can I meet your roommate?" he asks.

I think of Dog.

"She's not very social."

As I walk up to Delphi, I feel tipsy, even though I haven't had anything to drink since last night. A neighbor outside the pizzeria has to say hello twice before I notice and say hello back.

In the apartment, my roommate is splayed on the floor. The kitchenette is crammed with wine bottles and pizza boxes; I really have to tackle that mess.

"I might have to put you up for adoption," I say, patting the cat's belly.

Steven's allergies are truly the worst kind.

"Or else maybe this dream will be over soon."

Dog aims a strange look at me. He seldom lets me pet him for this long. It's as if he can sense that I need the comfort.

I can feel it clearly. Steven and I are getting ever closer to a fork in the road. And I know just how that typically goes.

Bill

give Sally a ride to visit Naemi from her class. They live in a renovated row house on one of the side streets near the E22 highway. Her mother is on the PTA and typically organizes all the fundraisers for the teachers. I know she works in health care.

"We were going to drive to Max for lunch," she says. "Will that be okay with Sally?"

"I don't think she'll have any problem with that."

I take out my wallet and take a symbolic peek inside.

"I'll have to Swish you the money," I say.

Naemi's mother protests. It's their treat. But I say I'll send the money anyway.

When I get home, I collapse onto the couch.

What's left to do now?

Find a new apartment. Get down on my knees and beg social services? The very thought of it turns my stomach.

On the wall above the shelf of DVDs is Al Pacino, the closest thing to an idol I have. He's in the role of Michael Corleone in *The Godfather Part II*. I think about what Corleone would have done in my situation. What would Tony Montana from *Scarface* do? Or Charlie Brigante in *Carlito's Way*?

All these films where the main character commits the most serious and morally objectionable crimes. For some reason, they're the ones I've been drawn to, the characters I love.

As long as Miranda was alive, it never occurred to me to take something that didn't belong to me. Miranda wouldn't even cross the street against the light. Her father was known to be something of a self-appointed cop in their neighborhood. He would take video of kids riding mopeds in the bike lane and look up their license plates online.

The first time I took something from the movie theater was just before Christmas. Someone had forgotten a stack of gift cards on the table behind the cash register. It was sheer impulse. Sally wanted an iPad of her own for Christmas; it was the only thing she'd asked for. And I so badly wanted to give her one. Once I'd stolen one time, and realized how simple it was and how quickly my anxiety vanished afterward, it became almost automatic. I took cash, comp tickets, and gift cards. Not until Anette confronted me did I fully understand what I'd done. My shame was an abyss. Even so, I degraded myself even more by begging and pleading for her to let me keep my job.

I gaze at Don Corleone again. There's a form of rational and straightforward justice in the Mafia that's always spoken to me. As long as you know your place and follow the rules of the game, there's no reason to worry, but revenge is sure to await anyone who turns to deception or lets their head get too big.

In reality, the entire concept of justice is strange, given that the world is demonstrably anything but just.

Miranda looks down at me from her photograph.

The first and perhaps only time we had a relationship crisis was when she discovered I'd lost money on online gambling. She screamed and cried. If it ever happened again, she would leave me. I suspect she would never forgive me for all the mistakes I've made in recent times.

That evening, I make pancakes for Sally under the humming kitchen fan. My brain is still idling. It's like my head has been packed in a thick layer of Jell-O.

"Isn't Karla home?" Sally asks.

"I don't really know where she is."

Sally sighs. She devours her rolled-up pancakes with jam and cream in the middle. Sticky mouth and grateful eyes.

I'd do anything for her.

"Naemi wants to start playing soccer too," she says, wiping her jammy lips with the back of her hand.

"That's fun."

I stare at the kitchen wall. Of course she deserves the opportunity to play soccer. There must be a way.

"I'm going to ask Karla if she can practice with me in the park," Sally says between bites.

I turn around with a big smile. "What about me? Don't you want to play with me?"

Sally's eyebrows shoot up. "You can play soccer, Dad?"

I laugh and kick at the air.

Fifteen minutes later, when Karla gets home, we play a few rounds of Thirty-One. Sally wins three times in a row and busts out her victory dance.

"Time for bed," I say.

It's almost eleven thirty.

"But it's summer vacation," Sally protests.

She howls with laughter as I carry her into the bedroom.

After half a chapter of *Harry Potter*, she's sleeping like a log and I tuck her in thoroughly before sneaking back into the hall.

Karla is standing outside the bathroom, barefoot and without makeup, in a hoodie.

"My boss says I can stop cleaning at the Rytters', but I was going to talk to Regina about it tomorrow too," she says, biting her nails.

"Okay. What are you planning to say?"

"She needs to know Steven is giving her benzos. My mom has been on that crap for more than twenty years. I know what it can do to a person."

"I get it."

Just as long as Regina doesn't start sniffing around for the ring now. Easiest of all would be not to say anything at all, but Karla wants to do the right thing, and I can hardly get in the way of that.

She mutters "Good night" and goes to her room. I sit on the couch. My heart is pounding, and my knees are jumpy. I'm having trouble sitting still.

I google Steven Rytter again and look at the satellite images of that sweet mansion. I've never cared about material things before, but it bothers me that someone like Steven Rytter can splash millions of kronor around while my daughter and I can't even make rent.

In one picture, he's standing with his arm around his wife. He's smiling at the camera, his eyes sparkling. Regina is so lively and pretty by his side. Could they really be missing a ring worth fourteen thousand kronor? That must be chump change to them. To Sally and me, right now, it would mean everything.

Steven looks like a man who has it all. It's hard to believe the person in that photo would be purposefully drugging his wife. I click his disgusting smile off the screen. There's no way he could understand what it means for the person you love to become seriously ill and waste away. I'd give anything to get Miranda back, and here he's treating his wife like that.

I have to get up. I pace back and forth for a while, then stop in front of my DVD collection. I'm looking for something to take my mind off everything, and I choose one of my favorite Al Pacino flicks: *Insomnia*. It's a remake of a Norwegian film that starred Stellan Skarsgård. Officer Will Dormer, played by Pacino, arrives in Alaska to investigate the murder of a teenager. While chasing the killer, Dormer accidentally shoots and kills his colleague, but in a weak moment he blames the teen's murderer, played by Robin Williams. After that, Dormer receives a phone call from the killer, who blackmails him. It's Pacino at his best. I love the scenes where he paces back and forth in the night, tortured by insomnia and the midnight sun.

I suppose it's pretty ironic that I can't sleep after the movie, even though it's soon two and then three o'clock.

I think about Steven Rytter again. Is he keeping his wife sick on purpose? I picture Miranda, her dry lips in her hospital bed in those last days.

Slowly my brain downshifts. I'm getting tired, but some of my thoughts remain clear and sharp. One of them lingers long enough to appear in my dreams.

How far would Steven Rytter go to keep his secret?

Excerpt from Interrogation with Bill Olsson

I'd like to show you something, Bill. Do you recognize this letter?
No, I don't know what it is.

You haven't seen it before?
No.

So you're not the one who wrote it?
Definitely not.

We found this on your computer, which we seized when we searched your apartment. Do you still claim you didn't write it?
I told you, I didn't.

The document had been deleted, but our technicians managed to recover it. How did it end up on your computer if you're not the one who wrote it?
I . . . don't know. On my computer? Which one?

Your laptop. The one that was on the coffee table in your apartment when we searched your apartment. Did anyone else have access to it?

Not that I know of. Although these days I suppose it's not that hard to gain access to a computer via spyware. Anyone could have planted it there.

Why would someone want to do that?
I . . . have no idea.

Are you saying you're the victim of a conspiracy, Bill? Do you think someone is trying to set you up for something, although you're actually innocent?
No, maybe not. I really don't know anymore.

My experience, after fifteen years as an investigator of aggravated crimes, is that the simplest explanation is often the correct one. But there are exceptions, to be sure. Was your computer password-protected?
No.

So anyone with access to it could have used it? Where is the computer typically located?
I mean, I mostly keep it in the bedroom. Sometimes I forget it by the couch.

So you continue to maintain that you were not the one who wrote this letter?
I've never seen it before.

Karla

still haven't heard from Lena.

I take the bus, as usual, and it's quiet in the Rytters' house when I get started on the bathrooms.

I pick up a ceramic bird so I can dust beneath it; I move bottles of oils, conditioner, and soap from the bathtub, which has little gold claw feet. It's hard not to compare this with our bathroom back home in Boden. The scratched linoleum, the lime-stained bathtub, and the brown streaks in the toilet.

While I'm bent in half to reach behind the toilet, there's a gentle knock on the door. I startle and accidentally whack the back of my head on the edge of the tub.

"I'm sorry, I didn't mean to scare you. Are you okay?"

"I'm fine."

My whole skull is throbbing. I'll probably end up with a goose egg.

"So stupid of me," Regina says.

She must have combed her hair. And for the first time she's wearing a pair of pants and a shirt instead of pajamas or a robe.

She stares at me. Accusingly.

"They called from the cleaning service. A woman named Lena."

Suddenly all my pain vanishes. Now I'm facing a very different sort of headache.

"Why?" I say, dropping my bangs. I'm still crouched down between the toilet and the tub.

"She said you asked to stop cleaning here."

I turn to face the tile. I can't believe Lena told Regina.

"Look, I . . ." Tears burn behind my eyes.

"Is it because of the ring?" Regina asks.

I cautiously turn my head and meet her gaze. Now Bill is going to be in trouble. And Sally.

"What?"

She sees right through me. "I know you took it. A ring doesn't just disappear."

I gasp for air. My eyes spill over, and it doesn't help to bring my hands to my face. I'm done for.

"I knew it from the start," Regina says.

This is a disaster. I never should have moved here. I should have stayed home in Boden, should have been there for Mom. Now I've ruined everything for so many people. Tears stream down my cheeks, and I'm hyperventilating.

"Hey." Regina puts a hand on my shoulder. "It's going to be okay. We'll work this out."

I'm sobbing like a baby. My whole body is shaking.

"I just wanted to help Bill. You'll get the ring back, I promise."

Regina removes her hand.

"Bill? Did he force you to steal?"

"No, definitely not. I'm the one who . . . I'm sorry."

Regina strokes my back gently. Her face has softened, her eyes are warm, as though she understands.

"Tell me about Bill."

My mouth starts moving a mile a minute, and I pour it all out: Bill and Sally, how he lost his partner to cancer and then lost his job at the movie theater. When I found the drawer full of jewelry, I saw a way to fix it. I'm no thief, but throughout my childhood I was told that you've got to do what you've got to do, and that some people have so much that it doesn't make any difference if a little bit of it goes away.

"So silly, right? But I thought people who lived in a house like this must be ridiculously happy all the time. Like on Instagram."

Regina smiles slightly. She keeps stroking my back.

"Give the ring back and we'll forget all of this."

How am I supposed to do that? I'll have to call the guy in Malmö myself, try to figure out who he sold it to.

"And I'd really like you to keep cleaning for us," Regina says.

I don't know whether to be grateful or scared.

"What about Lena?"

"She doesn't know a thing about this. You can say it was all a big mistake."

Regina sounds unusually lucid. She wants me to stay, even though I stole. She likes me. It must be my caring nature. I've been honing it for two decades by taking care of Mom.

"We won't tell Steven about the ring either," Regina says firmly. "He would be furious."

I look her in the eyes. They're sharper than before. All the haziness is gone, and she doesn't seem at all under the influence. I want to ask her about the drugs, but there's always the risk that I'm just imagining things and it'll make everything worse. Obviously she knows what kind of pills she's on.

"What are you thinking about?" she asks.

My tailbone aches. I grab the bathtub and stand up. I've been sitting on one of the little gold claw feet.

"Those pills I got for you last time," I begin. "They're . . . I mean . . ."

"What about them?" Regina asks.

I shouldn't say anything, I definitely shouldn't accuse Steven of anything. I've already interfered way too much.

"Oh, never mind."

I take a step forward, but Regina blocks the doorway, holding the handle.

"Tell me. What about the pills?"

I stare down at the gleaming tile floor. I have no choice.

"Those pills I got you from the medicine cabinet. Are you sure they're what you typically take?"

"Yes, they are. Steven's really the one who keeps track of my medications. He fills the pill organizer for me."

She really doesn't know what she's putting in her body. Or, more accurately, what Steven is feeding her. I look around in desperation. White tile everywhere, the air is hard to breathe.

"Those are benzodiazepines you're taking," I say. "Strong stuff, controlled substances that make you tired and dizzy and can cause hallucinations."

Regina plasters a superior smile on her face. "What an imagination! What do you know about my meds?"

"I grew up with an addict mother," I say, my eyes darting here and there. "Ever since I was a baby I've been surrounded by drugs. My mother uses benzos to escape reality and more or less go into a trance."

I force myself to look at Regina. The anger and irritation seem to slowly drain out of her.

"How awful. It makes me sad to think you had to experience something like that."

In one way, it's like I relax when she says so. For my whole life I've tried not to see myself as a victim. I've put so much energy into appearing strong. Outwardly, in the view of others, but also to myself. I never allowed myself to grieve. I don't want anyone to feel sorry for me. But Regina isn't looking down on me. She knows I managed to break away.

Mom chose to abuse drugs. Time and again she's made that choice.

For Regina, it's different. I have to make her understand what these pills are doing to her. She could have a different life. Without Steven.

She lets go of the handle and takes a few wobbly steps into the hall. Her hand fumbles for the back of the sofa.

"You must be mistaken."

I hurry after her.

"Maybe it's a misunderstanding," I say. "But the stuff I got for you were benzos."

Regina walks into the bedroom. She's looking confused again, the way she usually does.

"Why would Steven give me pills like that?"

I stop in the doorway. The blinds are down, the bedspread is tossed to the side of the bed; the air is sickly and warm in my nose. I hesitate, stammer. There can only be one explanation. Steven doesn't want her to be healthy. But she'll have to draw that conclusion on her own.

"Benzodiazepines are really only meant to be used for short periods, for acute problems," I say. "All the symptoms you have—exhaustion, confusion, headaches, dizziness, memory problems—all of those are common side effects of benzos."

Regina is standing by the bed. She looks at me with wide eyes.

"You mean it could all be because of the pills?"

She bends over the nightstand, pulls out the drawer, and rummages through it.

"I don't know," I say, leaning against the doorjamb. I'm feeling dizzy myself. "But they can't possibly be making your situation any better. How long have you been taking them?"

She turns around, the pill organizer in hand.

"At least a year. Maybe a year and a half. When I couldn't shake that flu and my headaches were about to do me in, I begged Steven to do something. I have no idea what he gave me, but it took away the pain and I was able to sleep. Then there were more and more pills. When I started feeling worse again, he added more."

"Benzos are addictive," I say. "After a while, you develop a tolerance. Your body demands higher and higher doses."

She nods, but she can't seem to focus her eyes. All the color has drained out of her.

"I don't get it," I say. "Why doesn't he just leave you?"

Regina shoves a pillow out of the way and sits on the edge of the bed.

"He can't. He won't get a single cent if we get a divorce."

"But he's a doctor. It's not like he'll end up on the street."

She rests her chin in her hands and mutters.

"Steven loves luxuries and extravagances. A doctor's salary won't go far when you're accustomed to that lifestyle."

"But still . . ."

"I'm sure he's just biding his time," she says, looking up.

She seems unreasonably composed. Maybe because she hasn't taken any pills for a while.

"Biding his time for what?" I ask.

"He's waiting for my father to die. As long as Dad is alive, he and my brother control the company, but when Dad dies my brother will have to buy me out or hand over half the firm. We're talking billions."

It seems sick. Monstrous. Steven Rytter must be such a psychopath.

He looks so pleasant, attractive and charming, always with a smile. But isn't that exactly how psychopaths are? They're super used to manipulating those around them.

"You should call the police," I say.

Regina stares at me like I'm nuts.

"And what will happen when Steven finds out?"

"Isn't there anyone else you can talk to, then?" I ask. "Maybe your brother?"

She shakes her head firmly.

"No one will believe me. Steven can talk his way out of anything. He'll say I've gone crazy."

"But you'll be protected," I say. "If Steven has been drugging you, he'll go to prison for several years."

"You think so? Is that really how it works?"

"I mean . . . well . . ."

I don't want to lie. It should work that way, but I can't give her any sort of guarantee. Is it even possible to prove any crime here? After all, she's taken all those pills of her own accord.

Regina doesn't look away. I can see her fear behind the shock.

"He's going to kill me, Karla."

Bill

The letter carrier stands, for a moment, with her hand in our mail slot, as though she's looking for the right mail. I can only see the gap and hear her humming through the door. At last a pile of ad circulars, free papers, and envelopes tumbles onto the doormat and the slot closes with a bang.

I quickly sort out all the junk and find a brown envelope with a handwritten address. It's so thoroughly sealed that I rip the envelope when I open it.

As I read, my emotions mutate and board a roller coaster. The paper trembles in my hand.

Hello,

My name is Selma Argonova and I work at the administrative desk of social services. We have received a report expressing concern for Sally. When this happens, our procedure is to invite the child and their guardian in to discuss the information in the report.

I have booked an appointment for you and Sally on August 22 at 11:00 A.M. We estimate that this meeting will take approximately one hour.

It must be Miranda's parents again. Vanna and Heinrich. Last time, in any case, they were the ones who filed a report. They claimed that my gambling was affecting Sally. I still haven't forgiven them.

Because it can't have anything to do with the power company, can it? And the landlord would hardly file a report of concern.

Karla's box of muesli is still on the table. It couldn't be her, could it?

I consider calling up Selma from social services right away. If I'm honest about the state of things, she should understand. Maybe social services can help and pay some of our bills. It hardly makes me a bad father just because I'm having a tough time financially. Sally is in good hands.

After a while, I calm down.

It's better to wait.

I make noodles and use the last of the homemade grill seasoning on them, not the terrible blend that comes in a bag. Sally and I eat before Karla gets home from soccer. The fact is, there's only enough for two.

Sally settles on the couch with her iPad and when Karla arrives, I accost her in the entryway.

"What's going on?"

"We have to talk," I say.

We close the door behind us in Sally's room, and I let her read the letter from social services.

"It's only a meeting," she says. "I'm sure it's no big deal."

When she hands the letter back, she brushes my hand. Her eyes are wet.

"It'll be okay," she says, embracing me. "You're a wonderful dad to Sally. Nothing's going to come of this."

I try to slow my breathing.

Maybe she's right. Then again, Karla knows nothing about the last time social services got involved. That conceited pig Jesper Lövgren, who said that grown men shouldn't play *World of Warcraft*.

"Regina knows I stole the ring," Karla says.

I deflate.

"How?"

"I have no poker face. She saw right through me."

"Did you bring up the pills?"

"She really doesn't want to report it to the police," Karla says. "She's not going to tell anyone. She's afraid of Steven."

Of course. It must be a terrible shock. I picture Miranda; she was ripped away from me, we couldn't be together any longer. But Steven Rytter is stuffing his wife full of sedatives.

I think of the flashy mansion in Professorsstaden, the pictures I'd googled: Steven Rytter in his white coat with a stethoscope around his neck, his arm around Regina, and that smug smile. Suddenly it's like the walls are closing in on me. I feel trapped; the air goes stale. That bird of prey is back in my chest, its wings beating and claws scratching.

"Do you want to do me a favor?" I say to Karla. "Could you put Sally to bed?"

I put on my athletic jacket and cap. Sweat is pouring from my underarms.

"Sure." There's a hint of surprise on Karla's face. "If that's okay with her."

"She'll be overjoyed. There's just a thing I have to take care of."

I shower Sally with kisses, then dash down the stairs, the words from the social services letter echoing through my head. My brain is crying out for fresh air.

Up to this point, the summer has been a pressure cooker, but after a whole day's worth of rain, the humidity is still hanging in the air and it's easier to breathe.

I bike north along Stora Södergatan, turn off at the Stäket building, and pass Mårtenstorget, where the patio dining is starting up again on the square after being on hold for the damp weather. I stop for a red light at the intersection by Spyken, one of the city's big high schools. A city bus is splashing up so much water from its tires that I have to move aside.

Only when I'm leaning over my handlebars near the southern entrance to the botanical gardens, and staring across at Linnégatan, do I admit to myself that I've been on my way here this whole time.

I dismount my bike and lead it along the narrow sidewalk, trying to look like a regular person on their way somewhere. When I pass the beautiful house with its copper roof, I sneak a peek at the windows on the second floor. There, behind the blinds, Regina Rytter lives out her days hidden in drowsing darkness. I think of Miranda's final weeks of palliative care, how life was slowly wrung out of her.

I clutch the rubber grips of my handlebars harder.

When I get to the school's parking lot, I stop and head back the same way. This time I don't take my eyes off the Rytters' house.

Suddenly there's movement in the bushes in their yard. The shape of a man in the dim light.

When the black iron gate swings open, the breath catches in my throat and I cough. My first instinct is to hop on my bike and pedal away. But the man stepping onto the sidewalk pays no attention to me. He closes the gate and marches off toward the botanical gardens.

He holds his back straight; his stride is long and resolute. His mane of hair billows as he crosses the street. I have no doubts—this is Steven Rytter I have in front of me.

Out on the bigger road, he stops to let a car pass. I'm only a few meters behind him, and I have to slow down as he walks by the cemetery.

I think about Sally.

I should bike back home.

Before Steven crosses the street toward Spyken, he swivels his head and looks around. We're so close that our eyes meet. A fraction of a second, no more.

I'm not a spiteful person. Ever since I was a child, I've dealt with other people's cruelty by ignoring them. No one liked to tease me, because I would neither cry nor fight back. My even temperament comes from the heart. But now, as I look at Steven Rytter and think about what he's subjecting his wife to, I feel, for the first time, an anger that borders on hatred.

He's right at the intersection.

By the time I climb onto my bike, my fingers have turned red from gripping the handlebars.

Out of the corner of my eye, I see Steven Rytter approach a young woman and put his arms around her.

Karla

Waheeda and I have just finished eating breakfast at a café near Juridicum when Lena calls.

"I spoke to Regina Rytter," she says. "Is it true that you worked everything out?"

"Yep, sure is."

Lena seems astounded, and I'm not surprised.

"Regina says you talked it over and you're in agreement that you will continue to clean their home."

I can't protest. It was awfully cool of Regina not to tell her about the ring.

"That's right. We worked out our issues."

A heavy sigh in my ear. "Great," says Lena. "Then we'll just keep things as they were."

"Right, sounds good."

I glance at Waheeda, who's looking at her reflection in a shop-window and picking at her teeth with one fingernail.

"We should head up there and study," she says once I've hung up.

She turns around and points at the grand university building at the top of the street.

It's an online course, the only part we have to do in person at Juridicum is the final exam, and it feels like we're breaking an unwritten rule when we trot up the broad stone steps and in through the door.

It feels like people are looking at us askance.

"In a few years, everyone here will know who we are," Waheeda says.

She marches through the room as though she owns the place. Over to a table and out with a chair. Books in a stack and her computer in her lap.

Our latest criminal law assignment is the most interesting one so far.

"Honestly," says Waheeda, who always talks a little too loud, "I don't get why the death penalty is so controversial. It's not like you'd punish adultery or shoplifting with death. But a man who kills and dismembers a woman, or takes the life of an innocent child? Why should we let someone like that live? Does he deserve a second chance?"

She's making her opinions sound more uncomplicated than they actually are. It's obvious the moment you scratch the surface. I've come to realize that Waheeda likes to argue in black-and-white terms. It's an effective way to get a reaction.

"We coddle criminals so much in this country," she says, opening a bag of Bilar candy and handing it across the table to me. "I hope you don't become one of those judges who thinks more about the perpetrator than their victim."

It's hard not to think of Steven and Regina. I fall into silent reflection, and it takes about half a second for Waheeda to notice.

"What's wrong? Was it something I said?"

I close the book of statutes and take a few gummy cars.

"It's that client I told you about. Regina, whose house I clean. I think her husband is keeping her drugged up."

"The doctor, you mean? I knew it!"

It all pours out of me. I tell her about my discovery in the medicine cabinet and how Regina doesn't want to go to the police because she's afraid of him.

Waheeda smacks her hand on the table and some candy flies out of the bag. The group of girls at the next table turns to stare.

"That fucking son of a bitch! You remember what I said, right?"

Of course I do. However much that matters.

"Do you think I should report it to the police?" I ask. "Even though Regina doesn't want to?"

Waheeda waves her arm. "No, no, the cops won't do a damn thing. What if he goes crazy and beats her to death?"

A piece of candy gets caught in my throat. I cough, and Waheeda thumps me on the back.

"You're probably right," I say. "It's too risky to report it."

"You should record them," Waheeda says.

"How?"

She taps a nail on her phone. "Voice memo. I record everything all the time, just to be on the safe side."

"What? What do you record?"

"Stuff people say. You never know when you'll need evidence."

I laugh, not sure how seriously to take her. "You haven't recorded me, have you?"

"Of course not." Waheeda's laugh is loud and hoarse.

The girls at the next table glare, annoyed.

I page through the course reader but have trouble focusing. I can't settle down, can't structure my thoughts. It's like my brain is full. After two hours, I still don't know how to get started on this assignment.

"Goddammit," I say.

No legal studies program for me. What was I thinking? No one in my family has ever set foot in a university classroom. I'm nothing but a thief and the daughter of a junkie.

"Hey, pull yourself together!" Waheeda says, staring at the blank document on my computer. "Just start."

"But I don't understand anything I'm reading. I have no idea what it means."

"Stop it! Hasn't anyone told you how fucking smart you are? It's like you don't quite understand how you're on a totally different level from basically everyone else."

"Oh, stop."

"It's true!" Waheeda says. "You're a goddamn genius! It's just so sad that no one's ever told you so."

I can't help but laugh.

"Stop clowning and buckle down," Waheeda says.

She watches me like a hawk and refuses to leave me alone until I finally hit some keys and write a first sentence. Once I've begun, the words pour out of me and I know exactly where my essay is going.

"Thanks," I say to Waheeda.

"What for?" she says, rustling the empty bag of Bilar.

"For believing in me."

She crumples up the bag and tries to make a basket in the trash can in the corner. Wide miss.

"Sorry," she says. "I only believe in God. La ilaha illallah."

On the way back to the apartment I call Mom. I haven't heard from her in a few days. I call several times, but she doesn't pick up. At last I send a text.

Hope everything's ok. Call me when you can.

I'm ashamed of not being there for her. Now that the methadone program turned out not to be happening, she really could have used my help. She seems serious this time. She wants to quit all that crap. What kind of daughter am I, not going back home to help out?

In the apartment on Karhögstorg, Bill is slouched in a folding canvas chair on the balcony. Sally doesn't seem to be home.

"How's it going?" I ask.

Bill is wearing a faded undershirt and a Yankees cap. He looks like he's been crying.

"Maybe it's just as well if social services takes Sally away. I'm a horrible dad anyway."

He blinks into the sun and takes a sip of Coke. I touch his shoulder tentatively.

"Ow, I've got a sunburn."

I quickly withdraw my hand.

"You're a great dad. No one's going to take Sally away."

I too grew up with a fear of social services. Mom taught me early on never to talk to the police, but soc was worst of all. In retrospect, I wonder if it wouldn't have been better for both of us if we'd asked them for help instead. But it wouldn't even enter my mind to report Bill. Even if his financial situation is crap, Sally is a thousand times better off than I ever was.

"I biked past the Rytters' house last night," Bill says, tugging his cap lower on his forehead.

"You did?"

After our talk, he was in a big hurry. I thought he was heading off to some job or something.

"It just happened. I was in the neighborhood, and I happened to see Steven."

A chilly wind hits me in the face. It smells like someone's grilling in the courtyard.

"Where?" I ask.

"He came out the gate and was walking toward downtown. I followed him for a bit."

Bill leans forward, propping his elbow on his knee. His dejected mood has been replaced by something sharp, almost angry.

"Why did you do that?" I ask.

Of course it would bother him. Bill had to watch as Miranda got sicker and sicker and eventually died, while Steven is hurting his wife on purpose.

"He met up with someone," Bill says.

"Who?"

"He's having an affair."

Bill doesn't drop my gaze. His eyes are narrowed, his jaw clenched.

"How do you know that?" I ask.

He straightens up, and the canvas chair wobbles.

"I saw him with a young woman. They were hugging and clinging to each other. It was pretty clear."

I'm not exactly surprised. It would explain a lot.

"What did she look like?"

"I'm not quite sure. I only saw her from the back."

Of course Steven is cheating.

"That's why he's drugging Regina," I say.

Bill stands up and rests his hands on the balcony railing.

It makes sense. Steven is stuffing Regina full of sedatives so he can cheat on her in peace.

"Unless a miracle happens in the next few days, we're going to lose our power and then the whole apartment," Bill says.

I stand next to him at the railing. We gaze down at the courtyard. A couple of kids are standing under the trees with a long jump rope. It takes me a minute to spot Sally, who's in line to jump. Just before her turn arrives she catches sight of us and waves both hands cheerfully.

"I don't believe in miracles," I say.

A couple of years ago, Mom was in the same plight. It seems like just yesterday she was lying in her bed, wrecked from sobbing, and telling me the situation was dire. She was flat broke and the Enforcement Agency would be showing up any minute. We would be evicted and, if worse came to worst, I would end up in a foster home.

There was a solution, of course. When it comes to drugs and money, Mom has never lacked imagination or initiative.

"Me neither," Bill says. "But maybe there's something we can do?"

I open my mouth but quickly close it again.

I shouldn't say anything.

"Look, Karla!" Sally calls merrily from the courtyard. "I'm the king!"

She hops over the rope as it smacks the asphalt.

"I don't know," I say to Bill.

Excerpt from Interrogation with Karla Larsson

Please take a look at this. This is a document we found on Bill Olsson's computer. Do you recognize it, Karla?

No.

I'll read it to you so it's included on this recording.

> To Steven Rytter,
>
> We know you're cheating on Regina and that you're drugging her with benzodiazepines.
>
> If you don't want the police and your wife to find out what you're doing, follow these instructions:
>
> Don't tell anyone about this letter.
>
> Transfer 50,000 kr in Bitcoin to our btc wallet at the address 3PnPi7xFVEv5hV7K by Friday, August 14, at 11:59 P.M.

I want you to think carefully now, Karla. Are you sure you've never seen this before?

No. I don't know. Or, well . . .

What do you mean? Do you recognize this letter?

Yes.

Do you know who wrote it?

Bill.

Why did he write it?

He needed money fast, or else he was going to lose his apartment. They'd threatened to cut his power and social services wanted to have a meeting about Sally. Bill had to move around a lot when he was a kid. He didn't want the same to happen to Sally. He was desperate.

This is new information you're telling us, Karla. Why haven't you mentioned this before?

I was terrified when you arrested Bill. When we first found out Steven and Regina were dead it was like a total short circuit. I was stunned. Like, murdered? Who would have killed them? It took a while for me to figure out what had happened.

Could it be that Bill influenced what you've said in these interrogations?

How? Bill is in jail. He's not allowed to talk to anyone but his attorney. I wish I'd told the truth from the start, but it's a little late for regrets now.

Has Bill ever threatened you, or acted violent toward you?

Definitely not. Bill's not like that.

This isn't the first time you've been involved in extortion, Karla. Is that right?

I'm not involved in any extortion. Bill wrote that letter.

But you've been accused of extortion before?

I was only a child. I was fourteen.

Were you innocent that time too?

No.

Jennica

After twenty minutes of paging through the textbook on development aid, I give up. It's Greek to me. If I had attended any lectures beyond the obligatory introductory meeting, maybe I could have grasped at least some of this muddle. Now it's hopeless. I'll have to look around on some online forums to make any sense of it.

As luck would have it, I have to stop soon. Work calls.

The evening's first conversation is with a woman I've never talked to before. Like most first-time callers, she declares at length, and without much conviction, that she never should have called and that she really doesn't believe in psychic abilities.

"But the fact is, I met an amazing man. He's turned my whole world upside down. But yesterday I found out he has a wife and kids. He's been lying to me. He says he doesn't love his wife anymore and wants to leave her, but I don't know. What should I do?"

"He's not going to leave his wife," I say.

In my years as a psychic adviser, I've ended up in at least a dozen conversations like this one. For decades my own mother has turned a blind eye to my father's nasty behavior. She's neither naive nor stupid.

She simply knows far too well how much pain it would cause and what far-ranging consequences there would be if she let herself admit something was wrong and decided to do something about it.

"How can you be so sure?" says the woman on the phone.

"Does it matter?" I ask. "Even if he did leave her, against all odds, what's to say he wouldn't do the exact same thing to you? How could you ever trust him?"

She hesitates.

"Yeah, I thought the same thing. But . . ."

There's always a *but*.

Before I got this job, I had no idea how far people are willing to stretch the limits of their values. As long as they've fallen for someone hard enough. Normal, sensible people will play second fiddle for years, or stay on some sort of love-related standby, and allow themselves to be treated like dirt just so they can jump right in the moment they're desirable. Women who have seen men act like prehistoric animals can find the wildest excuses to forgive and forget.

"Get out while you can," I tell the woman on the phone.

She doesn't seem entirely satisfied with my psychic advice, but I don't give a shit. I'm not about to become some sort of help-line advocate for unfaithful jerks and cheaters.

Then Maggan calls and showers me with love and gratitude, and everything feels fine again.

She and her daughter had a talk and reconciled.

"I told her she can look any way she wants," Maggan declares in her inimitable way. "She can be an elephant or a blue whale if she likes. I love her just the way she is."

Although Maggan didn't exactly follow my advice, I suppose the end result is what matters, and apparently it all concluded with a heartfelt discussion about upbringings and love, expectations and demands.

"It never would have been possible without you," Maggan says.

I think about the placebo effect in medications. What I do isn't all that different. People just need to believe that someone's got their back and loves them unconditionally. That's probably also one of the reasons it's so difficult to realize that you've been deceived, or that you're deceiving yourself.

"People are pretty simple," I say to Dog the cat. "They say it's a myth that we only use ten percent of our brain capacity, but I do wonder."

Dog scratches his nose and turns his tail to me.

"No need to be fresh," I say. "Your brain capacity is limited for sure."

I open a bottle of wine and put on a documentary. Then Mom calls to ask if I want to come to dinner on Saturday. My brain screams *no*, but the balance of my bank account makes me squeeze out a *yes*. Mom isn't typically a tough sell when I need a little loan.

Bill

can't sleep; I'm sitting in the kitchen and watching the day awake outside the window.

My doubts and my thoughts are like thorns in my brain. No matter how desperate I am, I've crossed a line I never thought I'd be looking at from the other side. Each time regret sets in, I picture Steven Rytter, his fake smile, those expensive suits, the diamond ring, and the twenty-million-kronor house.

As if in a trance, I stagger into the living room and glance at Michael Corleone on the wall. He must have been plagued with regret as well.

I knock gently on Karla's door. She's got an energy drink in hand and lines etched in her face. Probably not from sleep, but from hunching over textbooks and her computer for hours.

"Want to read it?" I ask.

Karla is sitting on the chair at the desk. She closes the thick book of statutes, back cover up, and I hand her a printout of the letter.

Her eyes skim the few lines.

"You can't send this, Bill."

She's right, of course. But what am I supposed to do?

"It's punishment for what he's subjecting Regina to."

I try to think like Michael Corleone. In a few days I'll likely have enough money to get Sally and me through for quite some time. And the only one who will be harmed is that bastard Steven Rytter.

"No one will ever know," I say. "The money can't be traced."

Karla takes a sip of her energy drink. She looks at me with a determined expression. "You can't send it, Bill. In this country, it's the courts that hand out punishment. It's not up to us."

She opens her law book again, and I close the door with a sigh.

Soon I'm in bed beside Sally, but it's impossible to sleep. I toss and turn as I ruminate. Then I go to the kitchen and pour a glass of Coke. Outside the window, the darkness is starting to give way.

My whole body is one big knot. My skin is about to burst.

Eventually I wake up on the couch, all out of sorts. The morning light paints stripes across the posters on the facing wall.

"Dad," says Sally, in her pajamas, her hair unbrushed. "I thought we could have a yard sale."

She's filled a cardboard box with toys, stuffed animals, and old puzzles.

"We have more stuff in storage that we could sell, don't we?" she says.

It's true. Miranda and I stashed away all the baby items that looked halfway decent. Everything that was meant for the little sibling who never appeared.

"I thought maybe you'd want to sell Mom's stuff too?"

Sally is aware it's a sensitive subject. She presents her suggestion with an impressive amount of tact.

"Where would we have a yard sale?" I ask, stretching.

"On Södra Esplanaden, you can sell there on Saturdays."

I don't want to make any promises. We'll see. A yard sale isn't a bad idea. The problem is, I haven't opened Miranda's wardrobe even once since palliative care. All her stuff is right there where she left it. Almost as if the apartment were waiting for her.

Before she got sick, I would meet her in the entryway at the end of the day. She always texted when she left work, and I had twenty minutes to tidy up and do the dishes. Most days I was waiting by the door when the elevator stopped outside. It was one of the high points of my day. Hugging her, nuzzling my nose into her bright curls, and feeling the warmth of her body.

I suppose I'll never know exactly what happened with Ricky at Jennica's twenty-fifth birthday party. The thought chafes deep in my chest, but I intend to make friends with that uncertainty. Whatever happened, I love Miranda unconditionally.

It feels horrid to have to go through her dresses and shoes, jewelry and belongings. Will someone else wear that black-and-red dress that made her breasts absolutely irresistible? The earrings I gave her for a graduation gift? I'd rather burn it all.

"Do you want to spend the day with me today?" Sally asks.

I almost burst into tears. What is wrong with me? Something is about to crack. And I'm the guy who didn't even cry when my father died.

"I always want to spend time with you, honey. What do you want to get up to?"

Sally considers. "I want to go to the zoo."

That sounds expensive and takes a certain amount of planning. We strike a compromise and bike up to the St. Hans 4H farm, where there are pigs and goats. A few girls are practicing rabbit show jumping and Sally gets to try it out too.

It's amazing to see her laughing and smiling.

I'm lost in thought when Sally comes rushing over.

"Daddy, do you remember what you promised me when Mom was having surgery?"

That whole period is a blur for me. I try to recall, but it doesn't matter. No promises I made during that time have been fulfilled.

"You said I could get a cat."

"Oh, right."

That rings a bell. But all I can think about now is how much a pet would cost.

"It's not that simple, to just get a cat," I say. "It's a big responsibility."

I definitely don't want to be the kind of parent who sees everything in kronor and ore, but at the moment I don't have much choice. But it doesn't matter; I don't have time to say anything. Sally can see it on me.

"I actually think I've changed my mind. I don't need a cat," she says. "A rabbit would be just as good."

I smile and hug her, promising that we'll see.

For lunch we have Danish hot dogs on Stortorget. A woman I recognize walks by. It's not until several minutes after we said hello that I realize she must have been on staff at the hospital. One of all those doctors and specialists, nurses and aides who passed through our lives in recent years.

I stop in front of the yellow mailbox outside Åhléns. My heart pounds as I take the plastic-wrapped envelope from my backpack.

"What are you doing, Dad?"

I smile at Sally. My whole body is screaming.

"I just need to mail a letter."

That evening, when it's time for Sally to go to bed, she wants Karla to read to her.

"Karla needs to study," I explain. "She has to take a super important test soon."

"What about tomorrow? Maybe you could take turns and read to me every other night?"

I brush a lock of hair from her face, then take *Harry Potter* from the nightstand.

"Did she do a good job reading?"

"Super good. But she didn't do those cool voices like you do."

I only make it through half a chapter before she falls asleep. Her little chest bobs in slow waves beneath the covers. I wish I could give her everything she deserves.

I kiss her on the forehead and cautiously stand up. On the balcony, I prop my feet on a stool and lean back as the sharp line of the horizon slowly pares the sun down to nothing. For two minutes I close my eyes and let the silence fill every nook and cranny of my brain.

Soon Steven will receive the blackmail letter. He won't have any choice. Fifty grand is nothing for him anyway, maybe a month's salary. In *Insomnia*, blackmail makes Al Pacino's character, Will Dormer, sick with anxiety. I imagine that Steven Rytter's not that type at all. He'll pay up and forget about it. A man who cold-bloodedly drugs his wife in order to cheat on her and live on her family's money can't have much of a conscience.

When I log in to my email on my phone, I find a new message from the home-care agency. A recruiter wants to know if I can come in for an interview this very week.

Karla

awake with a pounding headache. I spent most of the night sitting up studying. If it weren't for all Waheeda's encouragement I probably would have thrown the Swedish Code of Statutes out the window to become a full-time cleaner. This dang final exam is inhumane.

At last I force myself to get up, crawling out of bed even though it's not even seven o'clock yet. I'm sure Bill and Sally are still asleep.

There's a new text from Mom.

Good news! They're letting me start methadone after all. Love you.

I read it several times. I shouldn't judge the efforts she makes. Everyone is an addict in some form or another. Maybe this time it will actually work.

After a while, I write back that I love her and wish her good luck.

Talk tonight.

When I get on the bus, I'm suddenly boiling hot and pull off my sweater. My heart is pounding and sweat is just pouring off me. I turn the fan on the ceiling to max speed, but the air is too thick to breathe. At last I get off one stop early. My hands on my knees, I force myself to take slow, deep breaths.

A woman stops to ask if I'm okay.

"Thanks, I'm fine."

The worst of the sweating is over and my heart slows down. Still, as I trudge toward the Rytters' house, I remember Waheeda's tactic and, just to be safe, I start the voice recording before I stuff my phone in my back pocket and disarm the alarm.

"Hello?"

The foyer greets me with silence, and I go upstairs.

There's a soft mumbling coming from Regina's bedroom.

"May I come in?" I ask.

"Yes."

She's lying on the bed, fully dressed, staring at the ceiling.

"How are you doing?" I ask.

"Horrible. I haven't taken any pills for two days now. It's like my body is on fire. My whole skull is vibrating and my throat stings when I breathe."

It's all so familiar. I don't know how many times I watched Mom writhing her way through withdrawal.

"I can't take it anymore," Regina says, clenching the sheets hard.

I take the pill organizer from the nightstand.

"You can't just stop cold turkey," I say. "This kind of medication has to be tapered slowly."

I help her with the lid and she swallows a few pills down with big gulps of water.

"You have to tell someone," I say.

The glass sloshes as she sets it back down next to the bed.

"I can't. What would I say? To whom?"

Her eyes dart this way and that. Her fingers are like claws against the thin sheets; her shoulders go stiff. A hissing sound, deep in her throat.

"Is there anything I can do?" I ask.

What if she truly is crazy?

What if the medicines made her paranoid?

She lets go of the sheet with one hand and grabs my arm instead. Her bone-dry lips are a fish gasping for breath.

"I think Steven has someone else."

Something clears behind the fog in her eyes.

"What makes you think that?"

"He's been sending a bunch of texts. I saw them on his phone."

Her voice is dry and dusty. I hand her the glass of water again and try to find a smooth way to free myself from her grip.

"He hardly even tries to hide it. I saw exactly what he'd written. They see each other all the time."

I think of the girl with the bicycle I saw in the driveway. It must be her. Probably the same young woman Bill saw Steven with the other night.

"You don't know for sure he's cheating," I say. "There could be some other explanation."

I can hear how naive I sound, but I don't want to cause Regina any more pain than I have to. When I was around twelve, Mom got her heart broken by the only man who ever helped her get clean. I sat by her bedside to comfort her, even though I was too young to understand. I begged Mom and God not to let her relapse. Neither of them listened.

Regina's hand slips away from my arm and lands on the edge of the bed.

"Have you talked to him?" I ask.

She rolls her eyes and blinks.

"I can't, obviously. What do you think Steven would do if I did?"

Excerpt from Interrogation with Karla Larsson

Would you like to describe the extortion?
　　Of Steven Rytter?

No, the other instance. The one you were found guilty of. Who did you black-mail that time?
　　I truly regret the whole thing. It was a terrible thing to do. He was so nice and he cared about me, and I took advantage of it.

Who was he?
　　My soccer coach.

You claimed he was too forward and he touched you?
　　Really, I was the one who started it all. I secretly recorded a couple of video clips and demanded that he pay me. Otherwise I would report him to the police. I was only fourteen. If people in Boden got the idea he was a pedophile, it would be all over for him.

So he paid up?
　　Mm-hmm. The first few times. But eventually he got fed up and went to the police.

And you confessed everything in that first interrogation?

I've never had a good poker face. I had to tell the truth.

But you were only fourteen. Why did you do it?

For the money. My mom had problems. She's been an addict my whole life, and she could never manage to hold down a job. This time, it was really bad. She was behind on rent and we were going to lose our apartment.

So you did it for your mother?

Yeah. Yes.

Jennica

t's not until I'm all ready to go that I realize it's not just going to be me and Mom and Dad tonight. All of my siblings are invited too. And Aunt Birgitta and her doormat of a husband. I'm a millimeter from begging off sick from this spectacle, but my account is in desperate need of topping up and I don't get paid until next week.

When I get down to my bike, some idiot has parked his moped in the way so I have to squeeze past. I swear out loud. Once I've wriggled by, I realize I'm not alone.

"Try counting to ten," Steven says. "It's not good for your health to get all worked up like that."

He's standing in the shadows outside the garbage room.

"Jesus, you scared me."

I lose my grip on the handlebars and my bike tips over. Steven hurries over and rights it for me.

"Where are you going?"

"To Mom and Dad's," I say. "What are you doing here?"

"I thought I would surprise you and take you out to dinner."

His Tesla is haphazardly parked on the other side of the bike path, in the turnaround.

Part of me just wants to make out with him. I have seriously missed him. But this thing where he just shows up—it's such boomer behavior.

"You could have sent a text," I say.

"Then it wouldn't have been much of a surprise."

He smiles cautiously, takes a step forward, and kisses me on the lips.

I give the pedal a little kick to make it spin. Either I say screw it to the family and enjoy a cozy dinner with Steven, or I give him another chance. If he declines another offer to meet my parents, I'll know exactly what's up.

"I mean, I totally understand if you say no, but you're welcome to come along. I'm sure Mom would be overjoyed."

Steven looks at my bike and then at his car. He fiddles with the key.

"I'll come," he says. "But let's skip the bike, huh?"

Fifteen minutes later, we're pulling into Dad's driveway in the Tesla. My brothers lean over the fence to get a good look.

"This is Steven," I say with my best sunshiny smile.

Mom and Aunt Birgitta act like giggly teens at their first boyband concert. Dad and my brothers clear their throats and keep their distance.

"You'll have to excuse us," Mom says. "Jennica is so secretive. She hasn't mentioned a word about you."

"We've . . . I've . . ."

Steven gently interrupts me and explains, in a few words, who he is and how long we've been seeing each other. Mom and Birgitta exchange glances.

"A pediatrician? How wonderful!"

The party tent from my niece's graduation is still standing, and my sister quickly makes sure another place is set.

My family's behavior is unexpectedly civil and decent. Soon we're enjoying a relaxed atmosphere. Steven is a social genius who can converse just as naturally with my siblings as with my reserved uncle. There's laughter and joking. Glasses are refilled and the volume gets louder.

Mom has catered in rack of venison and rosemary potatoes, and my sister has baked a lemon cake for dessert.

With a glass of whiskey in hand, I zone out and enjoy myself. For a while I pretend we're a perfectly ordinary family. No one is too drunk, no one is shouting, and no one belittles or ridicules me even once.

Then my oldest brother asks if Steven has children.

"We never had any," he says. "My wife fell gravely ill very suddenly."

A respectful silence takes over the tent. Sad expressions and downcast gazes.

"I'd rather not talk about it," Steven says.

My brother is chagrined, and my mother makes a valiant effort to change the subject but ends up putting her foot in her mouth and tying herself into knots.

At last Steven comes to the rescue by saying something totally irrelevant that makes the whole table crack up.

Birgitta and her husband take a taxi home, and as the clock approaches midnight, the rest of us make a move too.

Dad gives Steven a firm and lengthy handshake.

"What a nice guy," he whispers when we hug.

Steven drives slowly down the street. I shoot him a sidelong glance and wait for him to say something. Instead, he turns on the radio.

We cruise through Lund without a word. People are bicycling home. Some are walking arm in arm. A few are singing merrily as they go.

On the radio, an artist from Värmland is talking about the joy in the small things. He says something clever about how beauty is in the details we seldom take the time to notice.

When Steven parks in one of the alleys north of Mårtenstorget, he stays put with the engine off and his hands on the wheel.

"I like your family," he says. "They're delightful."

A smile takes shape, and I sink back in my seat with a sigh of relief.

"Let's not exaggerate," I say. "You just wait until they show their true faces."

Steven smiles.

Then he turns to me, suddenly serious in a way that alarms me. Immediately I fear the worst.

"Listen," he says. "There's something I have to tell you."

I close my eyes. My stomach cramps.

"Just say it, then."

Steven places a hand on my elbow. "I don't know where to start."

A dozen different catastrophes have already taken place inside my mind. This has been too good to be true. Tonight was the final straw. Obviously it could never last.

"Someone is trying to blackmail me."

I open my eyes and see how shaken he is.

"What? Why?"

"When Regina got sick, the doctors didn't understand and refused to help her. At first they wouldn't take her seriously. They thought it was psychosomatic and referred her to a psychiatrist. They gave her antidepressants but wouldn't prescribe antianxiety meds or painkillers. I couldn't stand to see her feeling so terrible."

"Okay . . . ?"

I desperately press myself to the backrest. How could this have led to blackmail? It seems improbable, to say the least.

"So I prescribed a few drugs for her myself. I got some colleagues to help. I'm not proud of it, I was breaking every last rule, but I did it for Regina's sake. I couldn't stand to watch her suffer."

"I understand."

Anyone would have done the same.

"But now someone is threatening to expose me. Someone who learned that I prescribed those pills. An anonymous letter showed up in the mail. They're demanding fifty thousand kronor, or they'll go to the police."

I lean toward him and take his hand. I've never seen him like this before. Raw in a way that both frightens me and speaks to me. He's about to open up to me. A new level of *us*.

"But it happened a long time ago," I say, lifting his hand and stroking it. "Why are they only bringing it up now?"

"I don't know."

Even his voice is different, almost boyish.

"You're not going to pay, are you?" I ask.

Steven lowers his head. "I don't know what to do."

He stares into the dark night.

"But who sent the letter?" I wonder. "Who would do something like that?"

Steven's hand grows tense and heavy.

"I have my suspicions."

Karla

There's a full moon, and I sleep for only three hours, max. The final exam begins at 9:15 A.M. at Juridicum. I rattle off terms and statutes to myself as Bill fries eggs for breakfast.

"Sunny-side up," Sally says, digging in with knife and fork. "You know what, Karla? On Sunday, Naemi and I are starting soccer. I get to borrow Mohammad's Messi cleats. Want to come watch?"

"You're *trying it out*," Bill says loudly, to be heard over the kitchen fan. "Then we'll see if you think it's fun."

"I know, Dad, I know."

Sally shoots me a look of exasperation. *Dads.* As if I have any clue about those.

"Don't bother Karla now," Bill says. "She has to take that important test today."

Before I leave, Sally wants me to turn around so she can kick me in the butt for good luck. Her little foot hits me right in the tailbone, and it aches all the way to Juridicum.

The exam hall is dead silent. All I can hear is Waheeda biting her nails. I read through all the questions first, thinking and reflecting, before I begin to write down my answers.

I feel positive the whole time. The words pour out of me. It seems so ridiculously easy that I wonder if I misunderstood something.

Then I glance over my shoulder and see Waheeda rolling her pen through her curls above a blank sheet of paper.

Come on, I want to screech.

When time is up and the exams collected, we slowly shuffle toward the stone steps, which are bathed in sunlight. No one says a word; the air is full of tension.

"Guess I better plan on a career at Mickey D's instead," Waheeda says.

She sits down on a step with her pen in her mouth.

"You can't give up yet," I say. "I'm sure it went better than you think."

Waheeda chews on the pen.

We stay put as people keep streaming down the steps. We don't say anything; we just sit in silence. I've never heard Waheeda be so quiet for so long.

How am I going to survive four and a half years of the legal studies program without her? If I even get in, that is.

"How does it feel?" Bill asks when I return to the apartment.

He's on the couch with his computer. His feet are on the coffee table; there's a hole in one sock.

"Okay. I think it went fine, actually."

"I'm sure it went great," he says with a smile.

Of course, he has no idea.

I make a quick lap around the apartment and ask where Sally is.

"She's out playing in the courtyard."

That's perfect. I need to tell Bill everything.

"Do you have a minute? We need to talk."

I sit down next to him on the couch, and he takes his feet from the coffee table.

"Is something wrong?"

He's tense, his shoulders pulled up toward his ears.

"I spoke with Regina yesterday," I say. "She already knew Steven was cheating on her."

"How could she have known that?"

Bill massages the base of his skull.

"It seems she was snooping on his phone," I explain.

Bill presses his thumb into a tendon on his neck. His pale T-shirt has a circle of sweat at the armpit.

"Did she confront him?"

"She's afraid to."

He lets go of his neck and looks down.

"I sent the letter."

"What? You're joking."

I asked him not to do that. Obviously Steven will suspect me. I'm basically the only person who talks to Regina, the only one who could know about the pills she's taking.

I felt so good today, during the exam. There is actually a decent chance I'll be accepted to the program. That letter could ruin absolutely everything.

"I know, I know." Bill rocks back and forth, his hands on the back of his head. "I was desperate. But don't worry, I'll confess to everything. You won't be involved at all."

Excerpt from Interrogation with Bill Olsson

We know you're the one who wrote the letter, Bill. Karla told us. She stole a ring, which you later sold, and then you wrote this extortion letter.

I know, I know. I was desperate. I did write it. I sold the ring and wrote that letter, but I absolutely did not kill anyone.

Why were you so desperate?

I was taking every odd job I could get, but that money wasn't enough. When Karla told me how Steven Rytter was treating his wife, it almost felt like he deserved it. After all, he had all the money in the world.

What happened with the extortion?

What do you mean?

Did Steven pay you any money?

No. No, he sure didn't.

Why not?

I never sent the letter.

Bill

reat that you could come in on such short notice."

The woman from the home-care agency is called Hanna-Linnea. She's wearing a knitted sweater in all the colors of the rainbow, and offers me lukewarm coffee that tastes like water.

The office is above a kebab place in a run-down building right downtown. There are two desks, each with a computer, and a small, rickety table with chairs for visitors, which is where we sit.

"This week has been a little chaotic around here," Hanna-Linnea says. "Two of our PCAs quit without warning, and we've had trouble covering all the shifts."

She explains that the position she's offering demands a lot of patience and kindness, because this client isn't always cooperative.

"He has a lot of difficulty with communication. Of course, it's terribly frustrating when you can't express what you want to say."

For some reason, I've simply taken for granted that the man's issues are congenital, but Hanna-Linnea clarifies that he's had a stroke.

"He was living a perfectly normal life up until three years ago. But now his wife and his friends have all deserted him. Truly distressing. His kids hardly even visit anymore."

I think of Karla and her mother. Of Sally. Lots of us parents have strayed down the wrong path, one paved with unfortunate circumstances and good intentions. Some of us have sacrificed our children. For some, it's probably too late; for others, the bells are still tolling.

"I understand you are available for night shifts too?" Hanna-Linnea says, failing to stifle a yawn. "So you'll start at ten P.M. and take care of bedtime, then your shift will be over at six thirty in the morning. It's usually pretty quiet. You can bring a book or entertain yourself on your phone. Really, it's mostly about being available in case something happens."

It's hardly the job duties that have me worried. Nor is the pay an issue. Instead, I'm thinking back to all the days Miranda spent tucked in bed. I was on leave from the movie theater and wanted nothing more than to help her. It was awful, not being able to do anything. At last Miranda begged me to return to work.

"That sounds good," I say.

There must be a solution. I seem to recall that the city has a rec center that's open at night; Sally will have to sleep there. Worst-case, if that doesn't work, I'll have to smuggle her into the client's home.

"This is our standard employment contract," Hanna-Linnea says, reading what's printed on the paper before us, line by line.

I don't listen.

My thoughts are occupied by Steven Rytter. Has he received the letter by now? Can he trace it back to me?

"Is there any chance you can start next week?" Hanna-Linnea asks. "Things don't usually move this fast, but as you can see, we're in a bit of a pickle here. Several of our usual alternates are students who have gone home for the summer. I'd really love for you to meet the client as soon as possible, if that's okay."

"I'm sure that'll be fine," I say, shaking her hand. "We'll work it out."
We have to.

"Just one more thing. I need you to provide your criminal record for a background check."

My hand freezes. She notices at once. Her eyes become wary, and she pulls back her right hand.

"No problem," I say, squeezing out a wide, fake smile.

My thoughts roil and rattle inside my head. All evening I walk around with my head full of Steven Rytter and that crazy letter. When it's time to read to Sally, I skip sentences and forget to do the voices.

"What's with you, Dad?" she says.

"I'm sorry, honey. I'm just tired."

It's hard to sleep that night. I pace back and forth like a lost soul. Chow down a sandwich in the kitchen, brush my teeth, eat an ice cream and brush my teeth again.

When I come back to the bedroom, Sally is lying at the very edge of the bed. Her little fingers are clasped around a corner of the pillow. She twitches in her sleep, muttering and clucking her tongue.

We've made it through so much. We'll manage this too.

I gingerly try to move Sally to keep her from slipping right off the bed and onto the floor. She whimpers and opens her sleepy eyes.

"What's wrong, Dad?"

"Nothing," I say. "You were having a dream."

"I woke up, but you weren't here," she says. "It wasn't a dream. It was for real."

I sit on the edge of the bed and stroke her forehead.

"I was just out there, sweetie."

She lets go of the pillow and takes my hand.

"You can't go away, Dad," she says, gazing at me.

Everything that matters is in those eyes.

"I'm not going anywhere," I say.

Then I rest my head on the pillow until Sally's eyelids grow heavy and she blinks more and more often.

I make a silent vow to myself that I will never put us in a situation like this once more. I will never ever end up here again.

I just hope it isn't too late.

I kiss Sally and tiptoe out of the room.

In the pitch-black hallway outside stands Karla. The Adidas logo on her hoodie glows.

Slowly, carefully, I close the bedroom door behind me.

"It . . . It's . . ."

"Shhh," I whisper, letting go of the handle in slow motion. Sally is an extremely light sleeper when she's only just dozed off.

When I turn around, I realize Karla's shoulders are shaking. Her eyes are wide with fear.

"What's wrong?"

My pulse hits the roof.

Steven must have received the letter. He's exposed her.

"I . . . I . . ."

She is breathing heavily; her words catch in her throat.

This is all my fault.

I can't help but throw my arms around her.

"It's going to be okay," I whisper. "I'll take the blame."

"Let me go."

She yanks my arms away and shoves me off.

"I have to go home."

Mascara runs down her cheeks.

"Hey, please, what's going on?"

"It's Mom. She had an overdose."

Jennica

When I wake up, the apartment smells like a sauna. It's impossible to keep the windows open at night on account of the fucking birds' so-called singing, and the fan I got cheap from Biltema is as noisy as a nuclear power plant. After I've hit snooze six times, my dear neighbor bangs on the wall until I roll out of my damp sheets and put my foot directly into the slimy food in the cat's dish.

"I will donate you to the fur factory," I say, glaring at Dog, who smirks contentedly back from his favorite spot on the bookshelf.

Once I've let some air into the room and put some caffeine in my blood, I glance through the development-aid textbook a few more times. But my brain doesn't have any room for academic blather. It's full of Steven. He's taken all of me by storm.

I've never met a man who makes me feel so satisfied with my life. Over the last month I've cut my dose of SSRIs in half and I've almost completely stopped comfort-eating chips and chocolate. He's turned absolutely everything around. He even got my ultra-picky family to fall for him.

I hadn't even made it home last night before Mom sent a text with three exclamation points. She's elated. And my sister already called to congratulate me. She thinks I should propose as soon as possible.

"Before he discovers what a freak I really am?" I say, half joking.

My sister doesn't even laugh.

After we hang up, it strikes me that maybe she's jealous. Her own husband may be filthy rich, a Mensa member since he was a kid, and presumably neither violent nor a cheater. But next to Steven, he looks like the boy in your junior high grade who no one ever wanted to dance with.

Steven sends a selfie. He's wearing a white doctor's coat and looking hotter than ever. For several minutes I just sit there drowning in the picture. I should be 100 percent happy. Still, there's something there in the background. A feeling that Steven might, any second now, call my bluff and realize the mistake he's made.

I send a big heart in response.

Tonight I intend to convince him to report the extortion attempt to the police. Even if Steven does suspect it's their old cleaner who sent the letter, and that there's no reason to be worried—apparently she's a lost little junkie chick from Norrland. Still, that's concerning enough to report it. Sick people like that shouldn't be allowed to run free.

After half an hour I give up on studying and call Emma. I suggest grabbing coffee downtown, but she's afraid it will take hours for her and Silvio to get out of the house and into the city by bus. Can't I come out to her place instead?

"Okay. Sure."

One bus trip and short walk later, I'm ringing the doorbell to their row house in Gunnesbo.

We sit on the floor with Silvio. I would have been his godmother, if the baptism hadn't conflicted with a trip to Ibiza.

"I'm so ridiculously fucking happy right now," I say, picking up little blocks and handing them to Silvio so he can bang on them with a plastic hammer.

"Please," Emma says. "Language."

Ever since Silvio was born, she's gotten, like, religious. She used to have a dirtier mouth than the construction-major guys.

"But I'm very happy for you." She smiles.

"He's wonderful," I say. "I can't believe he wants to be with me."

Suddenly Emma's gaze goes sharp.

"Stop undervaluing yourself. You're a catch."

"Thanks."

I wish it were true.

Emma keeps picking up blocks from the floor.

"So when do we get to meet this dream guy?" Emma asks.

She gives me a clever smile, and I feel a pang in my chest. Steven and I have hardly even talked about my friends. What would he say if I brought him to Emma and Antonio's?

"All you have to do is invite us," I say, pretending nonchalance. "I've actually met one of his friends already. On a double date."

She doesn't need more details. I don't want her to get the wrong impression of Steven. And that night in Malmö was both the first and last time I socialized with Andreas Quiding.

"I'll talk to Antonio," she says. "I want to go on a double date too."

We laugh. Silvio stares at us in surprise.

"What if he's my Antonio?" I say.

Then I think about the extortion. Antonio's a lawyer. Sure, he doesn't deal with criminal matters at all, but he still must have some clue about this stuff. Maybe he would have some advice.

"Steven told me something really crazy." For some reason, I lower my voice. "Someone's trying to blackmail him."

Emma drops a block to the floor.

I relate the whole story of the cleaner who found the medications Steven obtained for his deathly ill wife.

"That's so scary," Emma says. "But it must have been a long time ago, since his wife is gone now."

"Yeah, it's weird. Do you think Antonio could help him somehow? Or should we go to the police?"

Emma can't hide her suspicion. I never should have said anything. Now she'll come up with a whole lot of ideas about Steven.

"How long ago did his wife die?" she asks.

I don't exactly know.

"Well, it was at least a year ago."

Emma looks even more suspicious. "What did she actually die of?"

Silvio whines and points at me to put down my block so he can keep hammering. I try to recall what Steven told me.

"I don't actually know."

Silvio bangs furiously on the blocks.

"You don't know?" Emma says. "You don't know how she died?"

"It was some kind of virus. That's how it started, anyway."

All the blocks fall down, and Silvio, frustrated, bangs his plastic hammer on the floor.

At last Emma takes the hammer away and he lets out an enraged howl.

"I've heard of people who end up with a long-term illness after the flu," says Emma. She works in the medical field, although she's been on parental leave for a pretty long time. "But it seems unlikely that she would die of that after a whole year had passed."

Excerpt from Interrogation with Emma Hansdotter

Would you please state your full name for the record?
Emma Lovisa Ingrid Hansdotter.

Can you tell me a little about yourself?
I just turned thirty and my husband is called Antonio. We have a fourteen-month-old son named Silvio and a baby on the way. We live in Gunnesbo, here in Lund, and I'm a radiographer, but I've been home with Silvio since he was born.

And what is your relationship to those involved in this investigation?
I mean, I've known Jennica Jungstedt my whole life. We became best friends in elementary school, and we hung out together every day for more than fifteen years. We were almost like conjoined twins, basically totally dependent on each other, the way young girls can be.

Do you still spend time with Jennica?
Not like before. It sounds like such a cliché, but I guess we've grown apart. Jennica still lives like we did when we were twenty—going out

every weekend, lots of Tinder dates, and so on. After you have kids, you develop different interests and values.

But you are still in touch?

Oh, for sure. We message several times a week. It's just that we don't see each other as often. Time runs away from you, and there's so much else that has to get done. But we've seen each other a few times this summer, anyway.

Has Jennica mentioned Steven Rytter to you?

Yeah. She fell for him hard. That's how I understood it, anyway. Jennica doesn't usually talk about men or relationships, so when she started babbling on about this Steven guy, well . . . I could see it in her eyes.

Did Jennica know Steven was married?

Definitely not. He told her his wife was dead.

But she found out that wasn't true? She found out Regina Rytter was alive?

Yeah, after a while.

How did Jennica react to that?

She lost her mind.

Karla

don't get a hold of Silja again until later that evening.

"How is she?" I ask.

All I know is that Mom was taken to the emergency room at Sunderbyn. Silja and Bengt found her unconscious on the couch and couldn't wake her. Over and over, I'm hurled back in time. Memories of her lifeless body in the bed, and that floppy hand dangling near the floor. I've never been so scared in my life.

"She's stable," Silja says. "The doctors seem calm. If it were up to your mother, she'd already be on the train home."

I lean back on the bed, my legs crossed.

"Tell her to listen to the doctors. She can't leave the hospital until they give the all clear."

"Of course," Silja says. "But you know your mother. Once she makes up her mind . . ."

Mom hates being admonished and told what to do. She's like a stubborn two-year-old sometimes. If you forbid her to do something, it won't be long before she tests the limits.

She has to grasp how serious this is. I don't want to lose her.

"I'm taking the train up tomorrow," I tell Silja.

She expects Mom will be overjoyed.

"It'll be so nice to have you home again. You'll be staying for good this time, right?"

I don't answer. I can't say for sure. On the one hand, I want to be there for Mom. On the other, I definitely don't want to go back to my old life.

The tears come as I pack my suitcase. In such a short time, Bill and Sally have found a place in my heart. I will miss them. I'll miss Lund and Waheeda and the soccer team. Hopefully I won't get into the legal studies program. That would make my decision much easier.

I cautiously tiptoe down the hall to keep from waking Sally, who just fell asleep.

"When are you leaving?" Bill asks.

He's standing by the kitchen sink with his back to me, clattering the dishes.

"Tomorrow afternoon."

He takes a saucepan from the sink and scrubs it furiously until suds are everywhere. He seems angry.

"I . . . I . . ." I don't know what to say. I hate disappointing people.

"I never should have sent that letter," Bill says. "I need to talk to Steven Rytter."

He scrubs so violently that the water sprays all over.

"Give me the number of that guy who bought the ring," I beg. "Maybe I can convince him . . ."

Without warning, in one quick movement, Bill lifts the pan and slams it back into the water. Water splashes onto his T-shirt.

"I can't." He takes a dish towel from the plastic hook by the stove and dries his hands and shirt. "I lied to you."

"About what?"

"After I sold the ring, I got it into my head that I could earn a little extra at an online casino. I gambled away all the money."

His voice is measured, but he won't meet my gaze.

• • •

I have to sit down. What is he saying? My money? I thought it had gone to electric bills and rent.

"I'll pay you back, every single ore," he rushes to say. "I promise."

But that's not the important thing. This is about trust. I thought Bill truly wanted to be responsible. I made myself into a thief for him, and here he fritters away both the ring and the money.

All I wanted was to be helpful and do the right thing. For Mom. For Bill and Sally. Even for Regina. How could it have turned out like this?

"It wasn't the first time." He turns his back to me and starts drying the dishes. "I've gambled quite a bit over the years. Even when Miranda was alive. Sometimes it goes really well, and I've won big, but it ends in disaster every time."

I heave a sigh and stand up again. I feel betrayed. When I turn around, Sally's at the kitchen door.

"Dad?"

Bill immediately drops the towel and hurries over to her.

"Aren't you asleep?"

"I woke up." She looks at me, bewildered. "Someone was shouting."

"You must have been dreaming," Bill says, leading her back down the hall.

Before he closes the bedroom door, our eyes meet one last time. The blue of his eyes has paled, and grief trickles out.

Like tiny drops of glass.

Bill

must have fallen asleep on the couch eventually. I wake up to find the sun streaming through the window. The open balcony door lets in a chilly breeze. I'm fully dressed, and my jeans are sticky with sweat.

My left leg is asleep. I stagger into the bedroom and place a hand on Sally's arm. She immediately opens her eyes and blinks.

"I had a dream about Mom."

Somewhere inside my head there's a spark. A quick, vague flash of my own dream. Steven and Regina Rytter's contorted faces.

"Mom was alive and I was going to have a little sister," Sally says.

She smiles, beaming, as though the dream might almost replace the reality we never got to experience.

"Tell me what you dreamed," she says, hopping off the bed and into my arms.

Another memory from the night before sweeps by.

"You and Karla were playing soccer. I was cheering in the crowd."

Sally giggles as I put her down on the chair and find some under-wear and a dress. When I look up, her face has taken on a completely different expression. Her lips pout.

"I don't want Karla to go. She's coming back, right?"

"I don't know. She probably doesn't know herself. Her mother is sick."

The question is, how will Regina and Steven react if Karla suddenly disappears?

"I hate it when moms get sick," Sally says.

I stop and listen outside Karla's room. She's probably still asleep. It's still early, and recently she's been toiling day and night ahead of her final exam, all while working her cleaning job.

I serve Sally breakfast in front of the TV and ask her to lower the volume. An extremely perky host with an annoying voice is teaching kids how to make slime. I tolerate this for five minutes.

Then, instead, I end up in front of Miranda's wardrobe in the bedroom. I haven't opened it in more than a year, but the time has come.

My hand closes around the handle. I stare at the closed door. My chest constricts.

In the end, I simply do it. Miranda's scent wafts out and brings tears to my eyes. Through that fog I can see the blouses, tops, and dresses she used to wear. The memories gush out at me with such force that I have to grab the doorjamb for support.

Those first few months at the computer. Chatting. Evenings giving way to nights. Video clips and songs sent back and forth. I recall the longing I felt each time those little dots blinked, showing she was composing a new message. Then, my father's death and my move to Lund. It's like I never had time to grieve. I was too in love. We used to cook together in Miranda's parents' kitchen. She introduced me to ingredients I'd never heard of: truffles, tapenade, Gruyère, foie gras, and caviar. We drank wine in the park at sunset and listened to live jazz. When Miranda was cold, she would stick her hands under my shirt. If I try, I can almost feel her cold fingers against my belly.

As I pack her clothes into cardboard boxes on the floor, a vent inside me seems to release. Something new awaits me. Purging belongings is not the same as forgetting.

Jennica

I sit on the edge of my bed with my laptop, waiting until the last possible moment. Presumably I am just making things up. On the other hand, my intuition is usually spot-on, and right now it's sending a really strong message. Something is wrong.

I woke up like a hundred times during the night. My mind keeps spinning and messing with me. At last I gave up and took a pill.

Emma was the catalyst of all this. There's something off with Steven's story about Regina. I search online and find that viral infections are more deadly than you'd think, but mostly among older people, and always around the time of initial infection. There are plenty of people who have symptoms for months or years after the fact, but those symptoms are typically pain and exhaustion. Nowhere does it say you can die after a whole year has passed. Something else must have happened to Regina.

It's just before nine in the morning when Steven sends a text.

Good morning, sexy. Hope you have a wonderful day!

My thumb rests on the call button. But I have to be smarter than that. Maybe I'm just imagining things. He'd think I was being paranoid and weird.

Ditto. XOXO, I respond instead.

Then I google Regina Lindgren, and the address on Linnégatan pops up again. It says she'll be forty-four in November. I search all the social media sites for Regina Lindgren or Regina Rytter. I try various spellings, but there's no hit. When I try "Regina" and "Lund," my screen fills with images of an old actress.

Dog jumps down from the bookcase and rubs past my feet.

"What do you say?" I ask him. "Should I ask Steven flat out what happened to his wife?"

Then I happen to think of Steven's buddy Andreas. He had the same last name as that nasty bitch Dad cheated with. Quiding. There can't be that many people with that name.

Bingo, straightaway. He's on Facebook.

Tie, jacket, and back-slicked hair in his profile picture. I taste bile just looking at him.

He's posted about a hundred pictures over the years. I scroll through them quickly. In most of them, he's got a glass in hand, always wearing high-end clothes, on large boats, in fancy restaurants, an arm around a beautiful woman, leaning over the hood of a Porsche. Expensive watches and sunglasses.

Andreas Quiding has 140 Facebook friends. I go through them in alphabetical order until I get to a Gina Lindgren. My heart pounds. The profile picture is sepia-toned and a little pixelated, it shows a pretty blonde in her midthirties. I click on the name, but the profile is private. I can't see anything. Gina Lindgren. I enlarge the picture and look into her pale eyes, comparing her to the images of Regina Rytter. The girl on Facebook is considerably younger, but it could be her.

Dog sits at my feet and I bend over to scratch him behind the ear.

"I'm sure I'm overreacting. Don't you think?"

Even if it were Regina's Facebook profile, it doesn't tell me shit. Surely it's not unusual for dead people to still be on Facebook.

Dog looks at me with sad eyes.

I put the laptop aside and page through my textbook a little, trying to stop thinking about Regina. I bolt down a dry sandwich and drink a fizzy vitamin drink, not for the health effects but for the taste.

The window needs cleaning. There's a large blob of bird shit in the corner, spiderwebs along the sill, and streaks left by rain and grime. The sun is shining directly on the pane, illuminating every last speck. It's high summer out there, and I long for fresh air and sunshine.

I put on leggings and my Rolling Stones T-shirt, pack my bag with a blanket and shades and my textbook, and get my bike from the rack. Then I whiz down through the tunnel under Norra Ringen.

Maybe I can sit and study in the botanical gardens. If I don't make it through this retake exam, I'll be kicked out of the degree program.

A peewee soccer team is dashing around the field at Smörlyckan, in red and yellow vests, chasing after the ball. I follow Tornavägen south, past the math buildings and Hallands Nation, down to Öster-vångsvägen and in through Professorsstaden.

I think of the mansion on Linnégatan. The young woman I saw in the window. Seeing me in the driveway seemed to light a fire beneath her—what if it's not at all like Steven said, that he's renting the house to a family?

A big truck has stopped in front of me on the street. Its reverse lights are on, and it's beeping. At the last second I decide to take a left and avoid it. When I reach Linnégatan, I automatically slow down and peer over at Steven's mansion.

In the driveway is a black car.

I stand up on my pedals and try to catch a glimpse of the make or the license plate. My heart beats harder.

It's a Tesla. It's Steven's car.

I ride up onto the sidewalk and climb off my bike outside the gate.

There could be some logical explanation.

Maybe he's come to work on the vents again. He was going to hire a handyman. Obviously the homeowner has to be present when that sort of thing is being fixed. This doesn't necessarily mean something fishy is going on.

The iron gate is stubborn and creaky. I've taken no more than three steps toward the house when the door flies open.

Steven's face is red. His shirt is flapping. He runs toward me.

"Jennica?"

I stop and stare. Steven slows down and tries to read my expression.

"Is there a problem with the vents again?" I say.

He shakes his head. "We need to talk."

Behind him, the house is quiet and deserted. Beneath the copper roof, all the windows are darkened by blinds. Not a single decoration or ornament is visible. Not a sign of life.

"Did your renters move out?"

Steven nudges me gently in the side. "Come on, let's talk."

He holds the gate open. My legs give way, and I feel like I'm floating. Everything around me goes fuzzy.

"I'll tell you everything," he says. "I promise."

I wobble as we cross the street toward the botanical gardens. Steven takes my arm. It's plain to see that this was too good to be true. Men like Steven Rytter don't exist in real life.

We stop by the information board at the entrance. He stuffs his hands in his pockets and looks at me, his eyes gentle.

"I was a pig. There are so many things I regret. If only I could turn back the clock."

"What do you mean?"

In fact, I don't want to know. It's better to stop time here. I want to keep living in this world where Steven is a fairy-tale prince and everything is sunshine, happy-happy.

"When I met you that first time, I never would have dreamed something could happen between us," Steven says, gazing at the ground. "If I had known, I never would have lied. But once I did lie, it was impossible to take back what I'd said."

I can see where this is going. There's no stopping it.

"What did you lie about?"

He kicks at the gravel.

I recall the first time we met up, outside the restaurant at Stortorget. He had me at that first glance. Never would I have guessed it would turn out like this.

"My wife. Regina."

I turn around so the sun is shining straight in my eyes. Red, yellow clouds, and tears. I blink frantically.

"So it's true? She's alive?"

I don't know how I'm going to manage this.

"She's very sick," he says. "Two winters ago she had a viral infection, and after that she was totally transformed. Like a new person. I suspect the virus settled in her brain. But the doctors she went to were skeptical and seemed to think it was psychosomatic somehow. She just got worse and worse, and I couldn't stand to see her in such pain, so I got her some pills."

He looks up. His eyes are wet.

It's all over.

"You told me she was dead."

I try to recall his exact words, and where we were. You'd have to be extraordinarily damaged to say such a thing about your wife.

"It was thoroughly horrid of me," Steven says. "If I'd known things would get serious between us . . . I never thought you'd want to keep seeing me. Or that I would fall in love."

His voice trembles.

I should spit in his face and kick him in the balls.

"Soon enough, Regina had increased the dosages on her own and became addicted," he says, sounding pitiful. "Now I don't know how much is illness and how much is the pills, but she's not the person I married anymore."

I look him straight in the eyes. So his wife is lying there tripping on tranquilizers in their fancy-ass house not fifty meters away from us.

My gut feeling was right. I knew something was fucking wrong.

"But she's alive, Steven. She's still alive!"

He runs his hand across his nose. He seems to be ashamed; his regret seems genuine, but it doesn't matter. I can never trust him again.

Cheating men. It's a curse that haunts me.

"I've wanted to leave Regina for a long time, but I can't. She's totally dependent on me. She has no one else. Plus, I'm the one who gave her the medications in the first place. I've tried to help her quit. On some level I still love her, but I can't do this anymore. I've told her all about you and me. I've explained that I want a divorce."

I turn to gaze out at the quiet park. The morning sun scatters silver on the treetops and to the west is a fluffy blanket of clouds, like cotton candy above the Oresund.

"What the hell have I done?" Steven cranes his neck to look up at the sky. "I've ruined everything."

When I revealed Ricky's infidelity at that party, he went on the defensive straightaway. He was drunk; he'd been seduced; you couldn't call that cheating. Dad, on the other hand, has never denied his "missteps," but he did try to get away with them by saying they were bagatelles, inconsequential flings that meant nothing.

An older couple is on their way into the park, a woman pushing a man in a wheelchair. Instead of stepping aside, I start to trudge up the path through the garden.

It smells like thyme and basil.

"Then I received that letter," Steven says, following close behind. "Regina seems to have convinced our cleaner that she's not sick at all and that I'm drugging her and keeping her closed up in the bedroom."

I stop in front of a low stone wall. On the other side is a billowing sea of red and pink flowers.

"Why would you do something like that?" I ask.

"I don't know what she told her. Maybe that I'm out after her father's money. I have to talk to the cleaner."

"Do whatever you like," I say, continuing past the sea of flowers.

All the times I've been betrayed. This must be the worst time of all. Even so, my fury just isn't there. I mostly feel empty.

"She tried to attack our last cleaner too," Steven says, out of breath. "Accused her of sleeping with me. It was right before she caught that virus. I think that's when it all started. She got paranoid."

"But then why do you have a new cleaner? And why another young girl?"

It just seems absurd. Like they were asking for more trouble.

I keep walking up the gravel path with Steven just behind me. Two students pass us on electric scooters, leaving behind the sweet vapor of an e-cigarette. I cough my way past the greenhouses with Steven on my heels.

"That's what Regina demands. She wants the house cleaned at least twice a week. At first I suppose it was like a test, to make sure I didn't touch the new cleaner. I know Regina spies on me."

Well, that's no wonder. He's cheating on her while she's deathly ill. I think of the pictures I've seen of Regina. Her Facebook profile. If she's keeping tabs on Steven, she must already know all about us.

"After you told me about your father's affairs, I tried to find a way to tell you about this." Steven walks faster and comes up alongside me. "I understand that my lies are unforgivable. I never thought I would meet someone like you."

I can't look at him any longer. I rub the shards of a shattered dream out of my eyes.

"You knew. You knew exactly how I feel about cheating."

A couple mallards quack off at full speed toward the pond. I take a left, heading out of the park.

"I just want you to know that everything that happened between you and me was real," Steven says. "This summer has been amazing. I've never felt this way about anyone else."

I close my eyes. Enveloped in darkness, a flaming dot whirls far in the distance. Smaller and smaller. Soon I can hardly see it. Am I watching my future as it disappears?

When I get to the gate, I stop to look at him one last time.

"I wish we had never met."

He drops his gaze and takes a few, dragging steps in the gravel. I move to the sidewalk, cross the street, and Steven vanishes in the other direction.

Something sharp and hard lingers inside me.

It's been years since I've broken down. I've been living like a god-damn brick house. A wall, a facade. Humans aren't built to survive earthquakes and hurricanes.

I'm about to come crumbling down.

Excerpt from Interrogation with Petronella Schimanski

Would you please state your full name for the record?
My name is Petronella Schimanski, but most people call me Petra.

How did you know Steven and Regina Rytter?
We were classmates at the university. Me and Regina. Or Gina, as we all called her. I was new to Lund and she became my first and best friend. For a while we were even roommates.

How would you describe Regina?
Before she met Steven? She was smart, charming, full of life. Men loved her. But of course some of them got scared off. Gina wasn't the kind of person you could order around. She knew what she wanted. I think that's why she had such a tough time with relationships. She was too bossy. She liked to say she needed an equal opponent. And then she met Steven.

How did it happen? How did they meet?
It was at some charity event, some kind of gala. Gina's dad is a multi-millionaire, you know. I seem to recall that he had gotten involved

in some project and it was a swanky dinner. That's where she met Steven.

And that's when she changed?

Not right away. She was definitely head over heels for Steven, but after a while it came out that he was already in a relationship. At first Gina was crushed, but Steven left the other woman, and after a few months they moved in together in that big house in Professorsstaden.

Then what happened?

I think they were too similar somehow. Both of them were control freaks and used to getting their way. Gina and I almost never saw each other without Steven there. She was totally absorbed in him. She had never liked art or theater before, she was a typical party girl who listened to techno. But suddenly she was going to concerts of classical music with Steven instead. They would go to gallery openings and exhibits. When I asked if she wanted to hang out, it was always the same thing. "I'll have to check with Steven first. Don't know if that'll work for Steven."

Did you bring this up with her?

Of course. I tried to be as tactful as possible, but Gina lashed out anyway. There was no talking about it. Not until the thing with the cleaner.

The cleaner? Karla Larsson?

No, no, this was long ago. Before Gina got sick. Steven hired some firm who sent a cute young blonde who was supposed to clean their house every week. At least, that's what Gina told me. One day she came home early and found Steven with the cleaner. He denied everything, of course, but after that, Gina was sure he was cheating on her. You know, he did the same thing to his ex, with Gina. Once a cheater, and all.

But he had hooked up with this cleaner?

Yes, and Gina sure went on a tear. The cleaner got fired, and Gina started snooping and spying on Steven. She lost control.

And then she got sick?

Exactly. She thought she had caught some sort of virus, but it all sounded pretty suspicious to me. Every time we talked, it was worse. She would rant and ramble. I know Steven took her for a psych eval. Eventually you couldn't have a normal conversation with her anymore. She was mixing up dreams and reality. It was scary to watch. She was psychotic. Paranoid.

In what way?

She claimed that Steven was drugging her.

Karla

The notification comes in an email. As soon as I see the sender on my phone, I know it's the results of my final exam.

I close down the app immediately without opening the email. My dream is so close and yet so far away. I've talked to Mom on the phone. She sounded frail and sad, but she was happy to hear that I was finally coming home.

"I need you more than ever, sweetheart."

Sally and Bill are up early. Boxes and crates are stacked on top of each other in the front hall. Sally has hung Miranda's old dresses on a clothes rack and marked them with little red price tags.

"You two are up already?" I say.

Bill has half a piece of plain toast in hand.

"The flea market starts soon."

"Are you coming?" Sally asks. "You can help us sell. It'll be super fun."

"I wish I could," I say. "But I have to catch my train this afternoon."

Sally turns away and pouts.

I'm not happy to have to leave her. If I'd only had some reliable adult to turn to when I was eight, maybe everything would have turned out different.

I feel like a traitor.

"Tomorrow I get to meet the client I'm going to work with," Bill says. "Then Sally and I are going to pay a visit to the Red Cabin."

"What's that?" I ask.

Sally shoots me a sidelong glance. She opens her mouth to tell me, but then she remembers she's supposed to be pouting.

"It's a kids' rec center that's open nights and weekends," Bill explains.

Sally can't hold back any longer. "You get supper there and you even get to watch TV."

She's incapable of pouting for more than five minutes. It's like she just doesn't have it in her.

"That sounds fun."

If I were staying, I could take care of her when Bill has to work nights and weekends. It would have been so cozy. We could have snuck some popcorn to pop and read *Harry Potter*.

"Come on, Sally." Bill nudges her canvas shoes with his foot. "We have to get going."

"Just a sec," I say.

They stop in the hall and look at me.

I so badly want to share this moment with Bill and Sally. No matter what the email says, I want them to be there when I open it.

"I got my results," I say, phone in hand.

"What? Haven't you looked yet?" Bill asks.

"Tell us what it says," Sally says.

They hang on me as I bring up the email. My eyes scan the lines of text. My name and personal ID number, my address, a lot of unnecessary stuff. At the very bottom is my grade.

I can hardly breathe.

All those nights in the worn easy chair in our kitchen. Me with my textbooks, Mom with her Marlboros. Roxette and Bon Jovi on the stereo. All that hard work—it paid off. I made it past every obstacle.

It's not just a result here in this email. It's a promise. History doesn't have to repeat itself. I can become a different person. As long as I don't move back to be with Mom.

I blink away a tear and rub my eyes with my finger.

"Did you make it?" Sally wonders.

I hand my phone to Bill, who studies the text up close.

"Grade: AB," he reads.

"Oh no!" Sally says. "Not an A?"

She throws her arms around me and my eyes spill over once more. "It . . . it's . . ."

"Don't be sad," Sally says. "You're still the best."

She holds me tight. The warmth of her body makes me go all soft. Eventually I manage to collect myself.

"I'm not sad. AB is the highest grade. I did it! I got in."

In the hour that follows, I ignore thirty calls from Waheeda and my chat on Snap fills with unread messages. But I don't know how to handle it, what to say. What if she didn't get in? I'm no good at this kind of thing.

I sit on the bed in Sally's old room, my suitcase packed. Mom's words echo in the back of my head. She sounded so happy when I told her I'd booked a train ticket. I don't want to disappoint her yet again.

I bring up Waheeda's number on my phone. Still hesitant. What happens if she wasn't accepted? Obviously I'll seem like the worst snob in the world, getting in but thinking about declining the offer.

At last I can't put it off any longer.

Waheeda screeches in my ear.

"Where have you been? Don't scare me like that! I thought you had moped yourself to death or something."

"I just needed to digest it."

"Oh no. No way. Tell me one of us got in!"

I answer on an inhale: "Yep."

"Bismillah, you're kidding! That's fantastic! You got in! You fuck-ing got in!"

I have to hold my phone away from my ear to keep my eardrum from bursting. My hand is trembling, but I can feel the corners of my mouth turn up.

"You're going to be the most badass judge in the world," Wa-heeda says. "You're so wise and sensible. You listen to people without prejudging them. This is wonderful!"

"What about you, though?" I say.

Now there's no way I can tell her that I booked a ticket for Boden. Only a dummy would close the door on a lifelong dream like this. Be-sides, Waheeda doesn't know about how things are with me and Mom.

"I didn't even get a passing grade," she says, with bubbling laughter. "I'm no bookworm like you. I'll just become a cop instead. Shooting nine-mils and whacking with batons, that stuff I can handle. So you can judge the hooligans I haul in."

I can't help laughing too, but soon my chuckle catches in my throat. I've fought so hard for this.

"We have to hang up now," I say. "I have to call my mom."

"What? You haven't told your mom yet? Yalla, get to it!"

She's right. I have to talk to Mom right away. But I still don't know what I'm going to say.

I lean back against the angled wall behind me and bite away the last bit of thumbnail I have.

The train goes in three hours.

Am I just supposed to leave all of this behind? Everything I've dreamed of and fought so hard for?

I thunk my head against the wall.

At last, I make the call.

"Hi."

I can tell right away that she's high. She practically *just* died of an overdose, and here she's taken something again.

"Oh, Mom."

Despite all the talk about methadone and change, she's high as a kite. It makes me feel so resigned. But you can't give up on your mother. If you get past all the drugs, there's a warm-hearted person who used to carry me through life in a sling on her belly, who fed me raisins and apple slices and put wet washcloths on my forehead when I had a fever. I miss that person every day.

"When are you coming?" she asks. "I need you here. Don't you get it?"

"The train leaves in a few hours," I say.

"Good. It will be so nice when everything is back to normal."

I'm not so sure. I don't think I want that.

"Mom, I got accepted into the legal studies program."

She doesn't say anything. I look at my hand. My cuticles sting.

"What? In Lund?"

"Right."

"But you're coming home. You're going to stay here, aren't you?"

I think of all our fights over the years, the shouting and tears, objects hurled to the floor and against the wall. The cigarette smoke and the odor of alcohol. Mom snoring from the couch. I don't want to go back to all that. Mom will never change. If, against all expectations, she manages to get out of all this crap at some point in the future, it won't be on account of me. I have to accept that.

"Will it really make any difference?" I say.

"What do you mean?"

"How will my moving home again make anything better, Mom?"

She mutters. I can't tell what she's saying, but it doesn't matter. We know the answer, both of us.

I've been mothering my own mother for so many years. She needs me there to help her breathe, to use me as a dumping ground, someone to unload all her crap on when she can't take it anymore, someone to wash dishes and take out the trash, call social services and find a way to get money. I can't do it anymore.

"This is my dream," I say.

Mom snuffles loudly in my ear.

"I wish you could be happy and proud," I whisper.

My voice nearly gives out.

I close my eyes.

Amid all the blackness, I see a ray of light.

When I open my eyes again, I'm crying.

"I am proud," Mom says. "But I miss having you here."

By the time Bill and Sally get home from the flea market, I've unpacked my suitcase and hung everything back up in the wardrobe. In addition, I've cooked us a meal.

"I thought your train left at three," Bill says.

"It did."

Sally comes dashing down the hall and throws herself into my arms.

"Please, say you're staying."

When she burrows her nose into my neck, I know I made the right decision. Mom is still there, but right now I am doing much better in the company of Sally and Bill.

"I'm staying," I whisper into her hair.

Bill smiles from the front hall as I spin around with Sally in my arms.

"You make me happy!" she sings.

It's some song from the Melody Festival.

Tomorrow I'll call Lena at the cleaning firm and give my notice. My program starts in two weeks, and I won't have time to clean as much as I've been doing. Waheeda has told me she can probably get me some hours at McDonald's.

Bill claims there's no evidence that can tie me to the theft or the extortion. He says he'll take all the blame. But he doesn't know how hopeless I am at lying if someone gets my back up against the wall.

I hope, at least, that Regina finds the strength to break free from Steven. I can't save her. Like Mom, she has to make that decision on her own.

After we eat, Sally asks if I want to read to her. Bill's about to protest, but I cut him off.

"Of course I'll read to you."

Sally has never been in such a hurry to get into her jammies.

As I read the first chapter, she shifts her pillow little by little, cuddling up so close that her every breath warms my cheek.

Once she's asleep, I gently tuck the blanket beneath her chin, turn out the bedside lamp, and leave a crack of gentle light coming through the door.

"Sweet dreams," I whisper.

Bill is on the couch. Slow piano music is coming from the TV. I stand by the open balcony door and fill my nose with the cool air.

"How you doing?" Bill asks.

"Good," I say, trying to aim all my attention inward. "I'm good."

To be sure, my shoulders are heavy and wish I could lie down and dream myself away, but my body is calm and my mind is quiet. It honestly does feel good. If only it weren't for that damn letter he sent.

"Have you talked to the cleaning firm?" he asks. "You're not going to keep cleaning for the Rytters, are you?"

"I'll call them tomorrow. I'm going to quit."

I brush my teeth and wash up, then say good night to Bill. In the bedroom I put on my headphones and settle my head on the pillow as I search my phone for something to listen to.

The phone barely starts to vibrate before I pick up.

"Is this Karla?"

I bolt up in bed.

Although we haven't talked all that many times, I don't have to wonder for a second who it is. I know right away.

"We have to talk about the letter you sent."

"What letter?"

The phone trembles in my hand.

"You know exactly what I'm talking about," Steven Rytter says. "Would you rather I go to the police?"

I close my eyes and picture the email from the law school. The top grade on my final exam. My dream of becoming a judge. Everything swirls past me. Mom, Sally, and Waheeda. Regina's pained eyes.

"Just throw it out," I pant.

Steven clears his throat.

"It's not that simple. We'll have to discuss it with Regina when you get here. Does anyone else know about this?"

I look at the closed door. Hopefully Bill hasn't heard anything. He doesn't need to get involved in this. We can figure this out.

"No, no. No one else knows."

"Good," says Steven Rytter. "Don't say a word to anyone, and we'll figure this all out tomorrow."

Jennica

bike home to see Mom. It's like I'm twelve again, and life is just too much. I bawl like a baby, and Mom strokes my back with comforting hands.

Just like when I was little, I refuse to appear vulnerable in front of Dad. As soon as he enters the room, I sit up and rub the mascara from my cheeks.

"That bastard," Dad says.

He and his belly stand in the doorway. Rage vibrates in his clenched fists.

"It was lucky you figured it out before this went too far."

Naturally, Mom has told him everything. She's always been ridiculously loyal.

In reality, I don't want to let go of the idea of Steven. Maybe the two of us still have a chance.

"My little girl," Dad says. "I could snap the the that bastard's neck. But right now it's important for you to concentrate on your studies. You know I have a number of international contacts. I'll see what I can arrange."

At first, I don't protest.

From the cradle on, I've been taught that all that matters is order, discipline, and hard work. My parents never played with me. My older siblings sighed when I was choosing my college track and considered becoming a social worker.

Ever since, I've always said I don't know what I want to be.

Being something has always been synonymous with getting an education and then a career. You are what you do, and so on.

Fuck that.

"Thanks, but I don't want to work in international relations. I don't even know what that is. I want to work with people. Regular people. Help folks who're having a tough time."

"A psychologist?" Mom says, her eyes darting in Dad's direction.

He won't even look at her. His eyes are small and skeptical. Dad has never cared about anyone but himself. Not really.

"You can do that stuff in your free time. There are tons of organizations you can get involved with."

It's like he's shut off his ears. He only hears what he wants to hear.

"I've already made up my mind, Dad. I don't even like traveling. And I can certainly imagine working with some nonprofit, like the anti-bullying coalition or the suicide hotline or something, but not on the side. I want to devote my whole life to that sort of thing."

Dad is seething. He fixes his gaze on Mom, although he's directing his words at me.

"Why do you always have to be so precious about your little fixations? Can't you just be normal for once?"

"There's no need to fight," Mom says.

That's one of her standard phrases.

"Fixations? Normal? And by the way, who are you to judge Steven?" I say, looking right at Dad without losing control.

"Please," Mom says.

For all these years she's hidden behind tears and despair whenever I try to take Dad to task.

I'm not giving in this time.

"You are at least as much of a pig yourself. Time and again you betrayed Mom. Treated her and the rest of your family like dirt."

"Jennica!" Mom says. "There's no need to poke at old wounds."

Dad is still in the doorway. Scorn surges over me. All those duped women I've talked to on the phone. Men like my father have ruined the lives of so many people. And merely for the sake of their own pleasure, without sparing a thought for their loved ones.

Only after what happened with Ricky, when I myself was the victim, did I truly understand. That betrayal hurts so much. That brutal violation when someone you love, someone you want to share everything with, offers himself and his heart to a stranger. Everything Ricky and I had turned into one big fat lie. It took me years to even consider trusting a man again.

"Steven actually wanted to get a divorce, but his wife is very sick," I say. "It's no excuse, but it's still understandable, he was acting out of some sort of strange concern. Did you ever think of Mom or me or my siblings when you were fucking around?"

Mom yanks my arm hard.

"That's enough."

"Children shouldn't interfere in adults' love lives," Dad says. "You're imagining things."

"Please stop!" Mom whimpers.

"Shut up!" I snap.

Mom backs away, her eyes full of horror. She lands in Dad's arms.

"You let him do it. Every time you took him back, it was like you were giving your tacit approval. As if you weren't worth more."

"You know nothing about it," Mom says, wiping tears from her cheek. "You have no idea what it was like for me."

Dad puts his arms around her waist like a padlock. His eyelids twitch as he looks at me.

"Have you forgotten to take your happy pills again?"

He thinks everything is about strength. About being strong enough to keep your emotions at bay, strong enough to keep yourself from being affected. Only wusses need therapy or pills.

"Some things have to be forgiven," Mom says. "That's how a family works. That's what it means to love."

That was what I believed during my upbringing. My view of love was warped from the start.

"What do you know about love?" I shove them out of the way and crowd past them into the hall. My Converse await me at the front door. I don't bother to tie them. "I've spent my whole life walking on eggshells for you. Nothing I have ever done has been enough. You've never accepted me. Know what? That is over. From now on, you can take me as I am or just forget about it."

"Please, Jennica, sweetie," Mom says.

She starts to come after me, but Dad catches her.

"I'm not all that sweet. I never have been. It's time for you accept that."

I hurry out and slam the door behind me. My bike is in the driveway, unlocked.

The wind tugs at my hair as I chug my way up the hill. I rise over the frame and push the pedals toward the ground, harder and harder. My thighs and calves ache, the wind bites at my cheeks, but I keep pedaling manically.

Images from my childhood flash and burn in my mind. Mom's shaking shoulders and tearstained cheeks. The shouting and arguing at night. Slamming doors. The sleep that never came.

I made up my mind back then.

I would never be like Mom. Never let a man treat me like that.

For all my life I've hated and battled infidelity. In my role as an adviser, I've told so many women that cheating can never be forgiven, that it's the same as giving in to the patriarchy and rejecting your own worth as a person. The shield I thought I had built up slowly dissolved when I met Steven. Everything was so different with him. So genuine. I thought I had found something new. I thought it was love, and I didn't notice that I was slowly being swept along into the same old lies and betrayal.

At some point, it has to end.

At some point, someone has to put a stop to men like my father and Steven. And women like my mother and Regina.

Bill

wake up early after yet another night of too little sleep, and sneak out, leaving Sally in the bed. In the hall are the items we didn't manage to sell at the flea market. It smells like Miranda. My chest immediately tightens with guilt.

Sally comes tiptoeing over in her pajamas.

"I had a nightmare, Dad."

It's been a long time. When Miranda was sick, and for several months after the funeral, Sally suffered from nightmares every single night.

"I had a dream about Karla. Something awful happened."

I hug her, pressing her little head to my chest to comfort her.

"It was only a dream. Nothing's going to happen to Karla."

"I know, but it felt so real."

I pour some Cocoa Puffs for her. Miranda always said those were like having candy for breakfast. Over the past year, there's been a lot of that.

"Did you remember you're going to Naemi's house today?" I say.

Sally lights up.

She's going to spend the day with her friend while I meet the client I'll be working with.

"Naemi and I are going to play Skitgubbe," Sally says, fetching the deck of cards from the drawer.

I find myself standing before the couch, with Miranda gazing down at me from her photo. I will always love her. It's never more than a few minutes before the next time she'll pop into my head. But there's something limiting about having her there on the wall.

"Hey," I say to Sally as I touch the frame. "What do you say I take this down now?"

Sally stops in the arch. "Um . . ."

"Mom will always be with us no matter what," I say.

"I know."

I hug her again, then take down the photo.

As we're putting on our shoes, the alarm on Karla's phone sounds from her bedroom. Sally looks at the closed door and then at me.

"Isn't Karla going to work today?"

"I think she has the day off."

At least, she won't be cleaning at the Rytters', which is what she usually does on Mondays.

Sally sits on the back of the bike, and the sun creeps up over the rooftops to the east.

"I really appreciate this," I say when Naemi's mom opens the door in a long nightgown, with a cup of coffee in hand.

"Oh, hush, Naemi is just thrilled to see Sally."

Sally hugs me and vanishes into the warmth of the row house.

"We were going to take a little trip to Bjärred after lunch," Naemi's mom says. "Is that okay?"

I should have planned for this.

"Unfortunately I didn't bring her swimsuit."

Naemi's mom smiles apologetically.

"We were actually just going to stop for ice cream."

Then she stops and looks away. As if she has realized the awkwardness of the situation.

I still haven't Swished her the money for Sally's lunch last time.

"Let me see if I have—" I say, digging in my wallet.

Naemi's mom stops me. "Don't worry about it. It'll all even out eventually."

We both know it's not true. Maybe I'll pay them back some other way. If there is anything like justice in the world.

I avoid looking her in the eyes as I hop on my bike and pedal off. Although the morning sun is shining, I've got a strong headwind the whole way.

The client lives in Planetstaden, as far east as you can get without hitting the highway to Malmö. Right across from his apartment is a hotel. Who would check in there?

Hanna-Linnea from the home-care agency meets me in the parking lot. She's not nearly as stressed as last time. She says she's been thinking of me and is sure I'll fit in perfectly "in the gang."

"You seem so calm and even keeled."

I don't know why, and it seems pretty dorky, but her words give me warm fuzzies.

Hanna-Linnea rings the doorbell, and we are let into the apartment by another PCA, a young woman with pink hair and a pierced eyebrow.

"Astor is in there. We just put on coffee."

In a cramped and dimly lit kitchen, he sits in his wheelchair.

Astor must be around fifty-five. His eyes are nut brown and sad. He has to support his right arm with his left hand when he greets me.

"Sometimes Astor has some trouble speaking," Hanna-Linnea says.

Astor nods. Saliva trickles down his chin.

"Pleasure," he says with great effort after I've introduced myself.

He needs help doing most things, and has the right to around-the-clock care, every day of every year. He can't make a cup of coffee on his own. In the evenings I'm to help him out of the wheelchair and into the custom bed. I will brush his teeth. If he gets thirsty, I'll give him water. If nature calls, I'll have to pull down his pants and help him into place.

Astor doesn't look at me while Hanna-Linnea rattles off all the instructions.

It must be completely devastating to be so dependent on other people. It was the same for Miranda, in her last few weeks. Palliative care is death's waiting room. Even so, I maintained a vague sense of hope up until the very end, although it was irrational and in direct opposition to what everyone was telling me. I suppose there are certain truths you simply can't accept until they are fact.

"You . . . have . . . kids?" Astor asks me.

When I tell him about Sally, he lights up. He pats my arm tenderly.

"See you soon," I say before we leave.

My first shift will be this very Wednesday. In the afternoon, Sally and I will head up to check out the nighttime rec center called the Red Cabin on Sölvegatan, a stone's throw from the humanities building where I studied film. Six months ago, it would have been unthinkable for Sally to spend a whole night away from me, but now I think it will work, even if it will be tough on both of us at first. Karla has said that she can step in sometimes too.

She's going to quit the cleaning firm. I wonder how Steven and Regina will react to that. They still haven't gotten the ring back, and it's not exactly hard to work out that Karla is involved in the extortion. But there is no proof.

I hope I can depend on Karla. But I can't be naive about this. She's managed to get so thoroughly dragged into Regina Rytter's misery. Karla is the sort of person who wants to help everyone and everything, at any price.

When I get down to the parking lot, I take out my phone.

"Bill!" Hanna-Linnea is hurrying out of the building. "There's something we forgot."

She's out of breath. I know exactly what she forgot. I've been trying not to think about it.

"Your background check," she says. "It's just a formality, but I still have to have a look at it."

"Of course." Suddenly I can feel my pulse. "Unfortunately I forgot it at home. Is it okay to email it to you?"

"That would be perfect. Just make sure I have it before Wednesday."

I promise I will. I haven't quite figured out what the deal is, whether my record has to be spotless. I need to find out. Tell me it won't all fall apart based on this one thing.

Hanna-Linnea waves and vanishes across the parking lot. I lean over, my arms on the handlebars, and text Karla. Just to be safe.

What are you doing? Where are you?

With my phone in my pocket and the sun on the back of my neck, I pedal westward. A strong wind hits me from the side, causing my bike to wobble. As I straighten out the handlebars, a white van zooms by at high speed. I cross Tornavägen and take a shortcut through the little park there, where two royally high junkie types are shouting at each other.

I speed up and follow Dalbyvägen downtown. From here, it's not far at all to the Rytters' house on Linnégatan.

I stop at the roundabout and walk my bike across the street. I fish out my phone. No response from Karla yet. She didn't lie to me and go to the Rytters' house after all, did she?

In front of the old deaf school, the weeping birches dangle their heavy branches in the water-lily-dotted pond. The magpies jabber in the grass.

My phone vibrates. Finally. I keep walking, one hand on the handlebars as I try to shield the screen so I can see anything. No text from Karla. Just junk mail from some fake customer service account.

What is going on? Karla typically responds within a minute, max. Her phone is like an extra body part.

I have to call and make sure everything's okay. I balance with both hands on the handlebars and the phone pressed to my shoulder. A baby carriage forces me to swerve, and my front tire brushes the garden fence. The ringing on the other end seems slow, an eternity passes.

At last she answers with a quiet *hi*.

"Karla? Where are you?"

"I can't talk right now."

She's whispering. There's no way she's at home. Is she at the Rytters'? She knows how risky that is.

"Is everything okay?" I say.

My bike rocks, the wheel turns hard, and I lose control. Slowly the phone slips from my shoulder and hits the ground.

"Hello? Karla? Are you there?"

All that's left is silence.

Excerpt from Interrogation with Jennica Jungstedt

How did you first come in contact with Steven Rytter?

We matched on Tinder. He was quite a bit older than me, but I agreed to go on a date anyway. Steven was really charming. Friendly, intelligent. Unlike other men I've dated, he could offer an intellectual exchange.

So you embarked on a relationship?

I suppose you could say so. We saw each other pretty frequently for most of the summer.

Did you know he was married?

No, I certainly didn't. I would have broken it off immediately.

How did you find out he was?

He'd tried to hide it online, naturally. There wasn't much information at all about Regina Rytter when you googled her. But he failed to consider that you could still find her if you searched her maiden name. And apparently she went by Gina back then.

What did you do when you found out Steven was married?

I confronted him. He confessed everything on the spot. As far as I could tell, this was far from the first time he'd had an affair.

And how did you take that news?

I was mostly just angry. And sad, of course. But angry, most of all. I told him I never wanted to see him again. It wasn't a hard decision to make.

So you never saw Steven again after this?

No.

Let's talk about the day we suspect Steven and Regina lost their lives. Can you tell me what you were doing that day?

I slept until probably eight thirty, nine. I don't have any particular commitments this summer, except studying for an exam I have to retake. After breakfast, I biked down to the botanical gardens to meet up with Bill Olsson.

Why were you meeting Bill?

He was upset about something we'd argued over earlier in the summer. Bill and I were both cheated on by our partners a few years ago, but we'd never talked it out.

So you had arranged to meet in the botanical gardens?

Yeah. That was basically the halfway point between us. And it's so lovely there in the summer. We took a long walk and had lunch at the café.

What time was this?

We met up around ten, I think. Bill had been at some meeting that morning, to see a client. He was just about to start working as a PCA.

And how long did the two of you stay in the botanical gardens?

Until twelve thirty or one, maybe. I can't quite recall. I'm sure it's possible to check what time I made a transaction at the café. I always use a credit card.

Where did you go after you and Bill parted ways?

No, no. We didn't part ways.

No?

No, I went with him to his apartment on Karhögstorg.

How long were you there?

Until late that evening. Ten or ten thirty, I would guess.

And Bill was there with you the whole time?

Of course.

Is there anyone who could corroborate this information?

There would have been tons of people who saw us in the botanical gardens. And on our way to Bill's we picked up his daughter, Sally. She had been with a classmate.

So you mean to say that Bill Olsson was with you from ten o'clock in the morning to ten at night on the day the Rytters were murdered in their home?

Yes.

You understand what this means, don't you, Jennica? You are aware of our suspicions against Bill. Are you absolutely certain of these times?

Sure. How could I be mistaken about something like that?

Karla

The morning is brisk. Even though it's the middle of August, the trees smell like autumn. I pull my zipper up to my throat. By the time I arrive at Linnégatan, I really have to pee. Steven's car is in the driveway.

On the phone he said we would sort out what had happened. Him, me, and Regina. What has he told her about the extortion? There's not a chance he's confessed to drugging her. If it weren't for the ring and that letter, I would be going straight to the police.

It's time to accept responsibility and make this right. I'm no victim; there's no reason to feel an ounce of pity for me. But surely we can work this out. I'll be starting my legal studies program soon, and I have no intention of keeping this still hanging over me.

I ring the bell. Although I know the code, it feels wrong to simply walk in. After all, I'm not here to clean today.

When no one comes to the door, I bend over and peer through the window. On the shoe rack are Steven's Gucci sneakers; his blazer is hanging from the coatrack. I think of how he stood there in the foyer glaring at me, coming so close that I felt trapped. Once again forbidding me to talk to Regina. This was just before I realized he was drugging her.

Now I squeeze my thighs against my full bladder while a *ding-dong* echoes through the house.

No one is coming. There's no movement anywhere.

To be safe, I check the time on my phone. I was supposed to be here two minutes ago. I look around, but there's no sign of Steven.

I think of Waheeda and start up the voice recording app on my phone. You never know.

Then I ring the doorbell again, but still no one comes. I press my legs together, shaking. My bladder is about to burst. I really shouldn't go in on my own, but I can't squat in the yard. It's burning between my legs. At last I enter the code and storm into the hall.

"Hello?"

I call out several times, but there's no response. I dash to the bathroom, and my relief is overwhelming. At the same time, I'm terrified that Steven will show up and find me here. I wash my hands quickly and am on my way out again when a loud thud from upstairs stops me in my tracks.

"Hello? Steven? Regina?"

I approach the stairs and strain to hear.

"Help!"

A soft cry from the bedroom up there.

"Regina?"

I take two steps up, then think of Mom. Her disappointment that I'm not coming home, but also her pride in what I've accomplished. Mom has, to a large extent, chosen her own path. Unlike Regina, who is being force-fed benzos by a psychopath.

"Help me!" she whimpers, and I pelt up the rest of the staircase.

With all the doors closed, the second floor is swathed in darkness. I rap my knuckles on Regina's bedroom door.

"Is that you?"

I depress the handle and enter. The blinds are down, as usual; it's pitch-black, only shadows on the walls.

"Regina?"

Two, three long strides into the room. It takes a while for my eyes to adjust to the lack of light.

On the nightstand is the pill organizer. A sheet hangs down from the end of the bed, but the bed itself is empty.

"Regina? Where are you?"

I've spent so many hours in this house. My whole summer. I've dusted and vacuumed every last corner. Yet now everything seems strange and cold. When I leave the bedroom, I don't know where to go. It's like I've never set foot here before. The closed doors and walls tumble toward me.

"Here."

Regina's voice again. It seems to be coming from Steven's bedroom.

"Are you in there?"

I knock quickly, then open the door.

The blinds are drawn here as well, but a small lamp shines from the windowsill. A tie dangles on a hanger next to Steven's light blue shirt. He has folded the bedspread over the ottoman in the corner with careful precision.

Regina is on the butterfly chair with her face buried in her hands. On the bed in front of her is Steven, lying stretched out and motionless. There's a peaceful stillness to his mouth; his eyes are closed. It looks like he's sleeping.

"What happened?"

Regina presses her fingers to her temples.

"I found him like this. He must have taken pills."

Slowly it dawns on me.

I grab his slack wrist. He's cold. His face is drained of color.

"Why? It makes no sense."

I fumble for something to grab on to.

"He must have realized it was all going to come to light," Regina says.

Her eyes are hollow and red.

Slowly she straightens up and points at the floor beside the bed. I bend down.

Just below Steven's right hand is a folded sheet of paper. It's landed so gently that it's standing like a pitched roof.

"I guess he didn't see any other way out," Regina says as I pick up the paper.

I already know what it is.

"It was you, wasn't it?" she says.

I gently unfold the paper and read the letter Bill sent.

"How could you?" Regina continues. "You promised to help me and I trusted you. Instead, you tried to extort money from Steven. You wanted him to pay for your silence."

"No, that's not what happened. It was Bill . . ."

I trail off. I can't blame Bill. I had a hand in this too, but he sent the letter without talking to me first.

"I was trying to help him," I say. "He was desperate."

I shoot another reluctant glance at Steven. His head is turned slightly to the side. His lips are icy blue. There's something inhuman about all of this.

This is the very thing I've always feared finding at home in Boden. I've never seen a dead person before in real life, but in my nightmares and in the terror of my imagination, those images have been sharply detailed. I have stood outside Mom's bedroom door, bracing myself. I have read up on first aid and CPR, I know how to take a pulse and check if someone is breathing. In my imagination, it's always been Mom. But now it's Steven instead.

I was just supposed to come here one last time to figure everything out.

"You sacrificed me," Regina says. She moans with effort as she leans forward in her chair. "Do you know how it feels, not to have a single person in your life? I have no one, Karla."

She clasps the collar of her pajamas tight at her throat.

"That's not true," I say.

But it is. I betrayed Regina, just like I betrayed Mom. I am one huge lie. And now Steven's dead. He killed himself. Because of us? I will never be able to become a judge after this.

"I was honestly trying to help you."

Regina won't meet my eyes.

I crumple the damned letter in my palm, walk to the window, and hide my face in my hands.

"What are we going to do?" Regina says.

I look at the door. No one knows I'm here. I could leave the house. No matter what, this is a turning point. I will be haunted by it for the rest of my life. But the alternative is even worse.

Regina eyes me closely. Her gaze is cool and watchful. She hauls herself out of the chair.

"We don't need to say anything." She reaches out to me. "Not about the letter or the ring."

My arm tightens as her cold fingers grasp my wrist. She strokes my hand slowly like Mom used to do when I was little. She looks at me with tenderness. Despite my betrayal, she's prepared to bury the truth for my sake.

"It's not easy, when a member of your family is so sick," she says. "People will understand why Steven couldn't go on. No need to mention the drugs or the extortion. Might as well let it be. At least I'll finally be free of him."

Bill

All the blinds are down in the house on Linnégatan. The yard is quiet. Not even the birds are singing.

I ring the doorbell and press my nose to the window in the door. Karla's shoes are upside down just to the left. So she did come here after all.

I tried several times to call as I rode the last little bit on my bike, but she didn't answer. Did Steven confront her? He might be capable of anything. I look at my phone, wondering if I should call the emergency number.

When I look up again, Karla is approaching the door. A sudden wave of relief is immediately replaced by fresh worry. Her eyes look wild and she fumbles with the lock before she manages to open up.

"What's wrong?" I ask.

"What are you doing here?" She looks past me, out at the street. "You have to leave."

Her feet are stepping in place.

"I got worried, obviously."

She shakes her head and moves the door handle up and down.

"What's wrong, Karla? Did something happen? Are they home?"

She doesn't respond, just stares vacantly.

"You're scaring me," I say. "What's going on?"

Karla's lips tremble and part. "Please, Bill, just go."

Her eyes crumple, and teardrops slip down her cheeks.

I try to look past her into the house. A wide foyer with dark wallpaper and a large brown bureau. Crystal chandeliers hanging from the ceiling. An almost ghostly mood.

Karla has sacrificed so much for me and Sally. Now it's my turn to take responsibility. I'm going to have a talk with this Steven and explain everything. We were desperate, I've had a horrid year.

"May I come in?" I ask.

Karla seems to be struggling not to break down.

"Something terrible has happened."

"What?"

I should have known she would come here. Why didn't I stop her?

"Steven is dead."

I try to absorb what she's saying. My mouth goes dry, and I can't control my tongue.

"Dead?"

Karla sniffles and fresh tears break out. A sound startles her and she turns around. My eyes follow her movement down the hall and over to the stairs. A woman in pajamas with a rat's nest of hair stands there with her hand on the railing. She looks like a living corpse.

Jennica

On summer days like this, the botanical gardens are busy and vibrant. I climb off my bike at the magnolia grove and lead it down the center path. A couple of students are sitting on the lawn under a tree and playing with each other's hair, textbooks open on their laps. On a bench in the shadows, a group has settled in with near beer and cigarettes.

Nothing but chill, cozy times here.

But my steps fumble in the gravel. I'm hardly holding it together.

I leave my bike by the southern entrance. A car honks as I cross the street toward Linnégatan.

I think about Regina Rytter. She must be so pathetically weak. What is wrong with women who allow men to treat them like shit? My own mother is one of them.

My wrath grows in my chest like a tumor when I see Steven's car in the driveway. I throw open the gate and storm up the path. I hit the doorbell so hard it hurts my thumb.

A shadow flutters by in the window. A face.

I cup my hands to the pane to see into the hall.

A couple of people are running back and forth. Agitated, urgent movements. At last one of them comes to the door.

She hardly opens it, a skinny little crack, and although she's radically transformed, I immediately recognize Regina Rytter from her pictures online.

"Yes?" She eyes me curiously.

"Is Steven here?" I say, trying to see past her into the house.

"He's at work," Regina says.

She tries to close the door, but I grab it.

"Who are you?" she says. There's something off about her eyes. She blinks and squints. "What do you want with Steven?"

I scrutinize her. She doesn't look well. She's wearing some sort of silk pajamas and her cheeks are pale and sunken.

"I think you know who I am," I say. "Let me in so we can talk."

"But Steven's not here."

She yanks at the door a little, but I maintain my grip.

"That doesn't matter. You and I can talk."

She tosses a quick glance over her shoulder.

"I can't. Not now."

I take the opportunity to crane my neck. In the foyer behind her I catch a glimpse of a young woman. Our gazes meet for a split second, and that's all it takes for me to see the fear positively radiating from her eyes.

What on earth is going on here?

Next to the wall behind her stands a man. His cheeks are puffy, his forehead red. He's gained weight. But there can be no doubt it's him.

"Bill?"

Bill

look at Karla. Her face is a mush of tears and makeup. Regina has just closed the front door. That really is Jennica Jungstedt standing in front of me.

"What are you doing here?" I had hoped never to see this person again.

"Steven and I have been in a relationship for the past few months," she says. "I need to talk to him." She looks at Regina. "And you."

This is nuts. I try to recall the evening I biked over to Linnégatan and saw Steven Rytter. His purposeful strides across the street and the young woman who was waiting for him at the intersection. I never saw her face, but she was pretty tall and thin. Sure, it could have been Jennica. She seems to have some kind of pathological attraction to cheating men.

"Shouldn't the question be what are *you* doing here?" Jennica says. She looks grim. Harsh and cold.

"Karla is renting a room from me. She works here," I say. "She's a cleaner."

Regina tries to stand in Jennica's way.

"You have to go. Anyway, Steven isn't here."

Jennica won't give an inch.

"I'm not going anywhere. Not until we've talked this through." She slaps Regina's hand aside and steps past her into the hall. "You might as well hear this too, Bill. You're part of the problem."

"What problem?"

She glances up the stairs and looks around, then heads right for me. Her nostrils are flared and her eyes are steaming.

"You are blind! Just like her." A long index finger in Regina's direction. "It's because of people like you that this stuff just keeps happening over and over."

"Stop," Karla says, rushing toward the kitchen. I follow her and throw my arms around her shaking shoulders.

"It'll be okay," I whisper into her hair, which smells faintly of shampoo.

It's a white lie, cold comfort. Nothing but words. We both know this isn't going to be okay at all. Steven Rytter is dead.

"What is going on?" Jennica says.

Both she and Regina are in the door to the kitchen.

Karla's breathing calms. An impenetrable silence ensues. Shifting eyes.

"It was *them*," Regina says.

She points at Karla and me.

I don't understand what she means.

"Steven is gone," she continues, sobbing. "He couldn't take it anymore."

She casts her eyes down and cries.

"What do you mean?" Jennica asks.

"It's their fault!" Regina shouts. "They tried to extort him for money."

Jennica

He took a bunch of pills," the young woman stammers between sobs. She sounds like she's from Norrland. "He's up there on the bed."

Slowly the fury in my body crumbles. A black void opens. A maw of nothingness. Steven can't be dead. He was just here. At restaurants and the theater, at Louisiana and Mölle, with me. In the king-size bed in his apartment. Missionary. His eyes on me when we'd just woken up. He can't be gone.

"You two drove him to it," Regina says.

Bill Olsson opens his mouth to protest, but he doesn't seem to know what to say. He's at a loss. He's always been so socially awkward. Could he really be behind the extortion? He did used to be into online poker and that kind of crap. I know he had to borrow money from Miranda's parents to pay off some gambling debts.

But Steven wouldn't have killed himself because of some blackmail letter. He hardly seemed to be taking it seriously. Maybe it was because of me? He said he'd never had such strong feelings for another person before. Was that why? The thought makes me dizzy.

I look around the kitchen. It's so clean you could see your reflection in the wall tile. Pots and pans and cooking implements hang from sturdy designer hooks.

Regina is leaning against the wall. Her gaze wavers. How much does she know about me? Steven said she was paranoid and accused him of a bunch of awful stuff. But he had told her about me. He had made it clear he wanted a divorce.

"It's not our fault," the young Norrlander sobs from Bill's embrace. "Steven was a total psychopath. He was drugging Regina. He's been keeping her closed up in here for over a year."

"You didn't know he was married, did you?" Bill says.

I shake my head. "He told me Regina was dead."

"Shit," says Bill.

But he knows nothing about Steven. I still can't absorb what they're saying. It must be a joke, a cruel attempt to get revenge on me. I turn to Regina.

"He told me about you the other day," I say. "He said he wanted a divorce."

She gives a scornful sniff.

"You believed him? You seriously believed Steven wanted you, out of everyone he's fucked over the years?"

My vision goes black. I blink and blink. The kitchen is shrouded in a fog, and I can hear her voice far off in some other universe.

Bill

t was Karla; she did it."

I put my arm around Karla as Regina takes a big step toward us. Her voice is loud; the sick, weak woman is suddenly gone.

"What are you talking about?" Karla says.

"You killed Steven."

She shoves her face just centimeters from Karla's.

"What are you talking about? Why would I kill Steven?"

I look at Jennica, who's leaning against the island. She seems woozy; she blinks several times and runs her hand over her face.

"Karla was in his bedroom when I woke up," Regina says. "She must have force-fed him the pills. First she stole a diamond ring from me, and then she tried to blackmail Steven. He caught her, and then she killed him."

Karla frees herself from my arm as Regina keeps hurling accusations at her. Is she telling the truth? Certainly Karla has been involved in a whole lot of crap. I probably only know about a fraction of her past. Now her education and dream of becoming a judge are in peril. And here I was terrified of losing Sally. All this ring and letter stuff. Could Karla have become that desperate?

"She's lying," Karla says. "She said we weren't going to tell anyone about what Steven had done. I bet she knew exactly what medications she was taking."

"Of course she knew," Jennica says, eyeing Regina. "Steven may have been a cheating asshole, but he didn't keep her locked up. He was doing everything he could to help you. That's why he got those medications for you. You ended up addicted to them, didn't you?"

"Bullshit. Steven was a tyrant, and Karla killed him."

"That's not true!" Karla fishes her phone from her pocket. "And I've got proof. I recorded everything you said."

Regina stares at the phone. Her eyes narrow and darken.

"Give me that," she says.

An instant later she's grabbed Karla's wrist.

"Leave her be," I say.

But Regina is surprisingly strong. She's got both hands on Karla and is trying to get the phone by force. Karla throws herself side to side and manages, at last, to yank loose.

"You lied about everything, from beginning to end. And I felt sorry for you. I wanted to help you."

Jennica is still by the island. I begin to think we've completely misjudged this whole situation.

Karla pulls away, her back to the counter, and Regina follows.

This is about to go off the rails.

"We have to call the police," I say.

Karla tilts her phone up and runs her thumb over the screen.

Just then, Regina darts into action.

Two quick steps, one blow, and the phone flies across the floor. Regina flings herself at Karla and twists her arm up behind her back. Karla bends and writhes, but Regina clamps her arm tight and presses her to the floor with all her weight.

"Let her go!" I shout.

My adrenaline is surging. Everything is topsy-turvy.

If what we've done comes to light, I can forget this PCA job. I can forget everything. The apartment? I'm screwed. And what will happen to Sally?

Karla whimpers, her cheek pressed to the floor. Regina's hands are around her neck and she's trying desperately to take a breath.

A quick glance at Jennica, and I rush over to grab Regina. I yank and pull at her arms, but she's tenacious.

Rasping sounds escape from Karla's throat. Frightening, guttural sounds. Time and again she tries to gasp for breath.

I can't do this on my own. I can't manage.

"Help!" I scream at Jennica. "Do something!"

From the corner of my eye, I see her take a cast-iron pan from the wall; it's so heavy she has to use both hands.

I'm tugging and yanking at Regina for all I'm worth, but she keeps pressing Karla's head to the floor. Her hands around her throat. Sweat and shouting. An elbow hits me in the face, and there's a burning flash of pain.

I only just have time to turn around and look up.

Behind me stands Jennica.

With full force, she swings the frying pan at Regina's head.

I close my eyes. It's over now.

Jennica hits her again.

Again and again.

NO OUTSIDE PERPETRATOR IN LUND—
"A FAMILY TRAGEDY"

The Evening Post, Lund

The preliminary investigation into the alleged double homicide has been closed, and the 33-year-old suspect who was in custody has been cleared of all suspicion. This information was made public during a press conference in Lund earlier today.

In August, a physician, 47, and his wife, 43, were found deceased in their home in central Lund.

The police now confirm that the woman died of blunt force trauma to the head, a fact *The Evening Post* revealed last week.

Just as *The Evening Post* has previously reported, the woman's husband, a well-liked pediatrician, died as the result of a narcotics overdose. According to the prosecutor, the death was by all indications a suicide.

The suspect who had been detained under suspicion of the homicides, a 33-year-old Lund father, has now been released. According to today's press conference, the man has been fully cleared of all suspicion.

According to a source close to the investigation, the police became interested in the 33-year-old because his live-in partner worked as a cleaner for the deceased couple. According to information provided to *The Evening Post*, the 33-year-old's fingerprints were discovered in the home and, because the man had a previous conviction for theft, the police suspected that the crime might be a case of robbery with homicide. The man's partner, who is in her twenties, has never been a suspect.

The police have now closed the investigation.

"We have conducted a thorough preliminary investigation in this matter," says the spokesperson for the police. "Along with the prosecutor we have reached the conclusion that the perpetrator is deceased and no outside person is suspected of involvement in these deaths."

Since no charges will be filed, the police investigation will not be made public, a fact that has caused a certain amount of controversy among the citizens of Lund.

"It almost seems like they're hiding something," says one of the private citizens who has gathered outside the police press conference. He prefers to remain anonymous.

The police also released information today that the murder weapon found in the house has been thoroughly examined and results confirm that the woman died under the circumstances put forward by police and prosecutor.

"There was no outside perpetrator present in the house when the couple perished."

Although the event has given rise to speculation, not least on various online forums, the police have declined to discuss in greater detail what happened between the pediatrician and his wife.

"Out of respect for the surviving family, we will not be releasing further details," says the police spokesperson. "There are many names for this sort of tragic incident. Unfortunately, violence of this sort is not unknown in close relationships. In some contexts we use terms like 'murder-suicide,' but I would prefer to say that what happened here was a family tragedy."

Karla

My throat is tight. I cough and clear my throat, stumble and grab the counter for support. Regina is lying on the floor behind an overturned chair, her right arm bent and her legs slightly parted. The frying pan is still next to her.

It was all over so fast. I still can't comprehend what happened.

Bill kneels beside Regina.

"What the hell have you done?" he says, looking at Jennica in horror.

"You were begging for help. I had to do something."

"We have to call an ambulance," I say.

Bill looks away, aghast, as he cautiously presses his fingers to Regina's throat. Disgusted, he leans toward her face.

I look at Jennica. We both hold our breath.

"It's too late," Bill says. "She's dead."

A bitter taste floods my mouth.

"No, it can't be. What have we done?"

I never should have come here. I could have gone home to Mom.

Bill staggers to the wall beyond the island. He leans back and slowly sinks to the floor, his face buried in his hands.

I put my arm around him.

"It was an accident. She attacked me."

My vision goes red and cloudy, and I cough up bile. From under my bangs I sneak a look at Jennica, who's pacing back and forth across the kitchen.

"The blackmail," whispers Bill. "The stolen ring. It'll all come out now."

Jennica stops at the island and stares at nothing.

"It was self-defense. Right?"

She sounds far from convinced. I don't know if she wants an answer, but Bill nods encouragingly at me.

"What do you think?"

"I don't know," I say. "I don't actually think it counts as self-defense."

"Of course it does!" Jennica slaps the top of the island. "She had just killed Steven. If I hadn't interfered, she would have hurt you too. Don't you get that?"

I don't think she understands how the right of self-defense works, but that's not my problem.

"Karla's studying the law," Bill says.

Jennica stares at me in surprise. She's taken me for someone totally different.

"Well, then, you know all this stuff, right? It's obviously self-defense."

I look at the frying pan and Regina's lifeless body. I refuse to look at her face. How many blows was it? At least three, maybe four or five. Way too many. She lost control.

"I'm sure you're right," Bill says.

I wish it were that simple.

Three young, healthy people versus one sickly woman. It will be immediately obvious that she was hit in the head multiple times. That's more like excessive force than self-defense.

I think of the discussion Waheeda and I had about this.

Never would I have imagined myself in this situation. Even back when I stole the ring, it was against everything I believe in and stand for. I can't blame Mom or my upbringing. Each person carries their own set of morals. I thought I had limits, but one by one they fell by the wayside.

"I saved your life," Jennica says.

She looks as terrified as I feel. She's pleading. Besides, she's right. Bill couldn't get Regina off me. I can still feel her thumbs digging into my throat. If Jennica hadn't acted, I don't know what might have happened.

"It was self-defense," she says again.

I don't want to lie to her.

"The law doesn't allow someone to use violence to defend themselves just any old way. It has to be proportional, and all other options must have been exhausted. I'm pretty sure this won't meet the standards for self-defense."

I look at Bill, who's sitting beside me with his elbows on his knees and his hands hiding his face.

Meanwhile, Jennica is stomping around the kitchen again. Her eyes rove here and there. She stops and stares soullessly, then starts pacing again.

I pat Bill's arm as Jennica stops mid-stride. This time she simply stands in the middle of the kitchen. She's noticed something; she resolutely steps right over Regina's body and goes to the sink. She lowers the blinds and grabs a microfiber cloth. Bill and I gape at each other in astonishment as she crouches down and wipes off the frying pan.

"What are you doing?" Bill says.

She meticulously rubs the pan with the cloth.

"Does anyone know we were here today?"

Jennica eyes us intensely, first me, then Bill.

"What do you mean?" He sounds frightened.

"Maybe there's another way," she says.

Bill

You could hear a pin drop in this kitchen. Is Jennica serious? She seems to think we're going to get away with this.

"It won't take long for the police to realize that you two were trying to blackmail Steven," she says. "Is it true you stole a ring too?"

I shoot a glance at her and turn to Karla. All three of us stare at one another. It's like a very strange trust exercise. As if we're trying measure how trustworthy the people before us are.

"Listen." Jennica comes closer. "No one needs to know we were here today."

I close my eyes. Everything goes black. An almost infinite, dark void. But at the end of the tunnel is the hint of a break, a place where the shadows give way to a crack that longs for light. On the other side of all that darkness waits Sally.

"It *was* an accident," Jennica says. "Self-defense."

She's right, no matter what the law says. There is such a thing as moral justice. None of us wanted things to turn out like this.

"Well, there's nothing weird about my being here today," Karla says. "I clean every Monday."

"What about you?" Jennica turns to me. "What are you doing here?"

I hesitate. Part of me wants to tell her to go to hell. She ruined so many years for Miranda. Now she has to face the music. But then I see Karla's face and soften. All of her dreams will go up in smoke if the truth comes out. And mine too. I might never get to see Sally again.

"I was at a meeting in Planetstaden this morning," I say. "I'm going to start working as a PCA. I was actually meant to bike straight home, but I couldn't get hold of Karla and got worried."

Karla touches my arm in gratitude. But soon her face contorts.

"The ring," she says. "The police might be able to trace it."

Jennica glances at her phone.

"Where's the ring now?"

"I sold it," I say. "The ad was taken down weeks ago. The police will never find it."

That ring has brought us nothing but misery.

"The ring probably won't be much of an issue," Jennica says. "But the extortion letter. If the police find that . . ."

"They won't," Karla says, standing up.

She digs in her pants pocket and fishes up a crumpled sheet of paper.

"Tear it into tiny pieces as soon as you leave here," Jennica says.

I have to protest. This is bad news. We're about to make everything a thousand times worse.

"I think we'd better just tell the truth."

I try to appeal to Karla.

"Our lives will never be the same," she says.

I know she's right. We're risking everything.

"So what are we supposed to do?" I say.

Jennica spins in place, looking around the kitchen. "Do you think the police can tell exactly when they died?"

Karla shrugs. "Maybe not down to the minute. Or even the hour. Really, they can probably only come up with an estimate."

"Right?" Jennica says. "They'll know it happened today, and maybe that it happened sometime in the morning, but they won't know exactly. I've seen an awful lot of true crime. It's only bad police procedurals where the pathologist can tell down to the minute when someone died."

I don't understand what she's getting at. This is starting to seem like something I want no part in.

"We can't do this. Call the police."

Jennica puts her hands on her hips.

"If the police find Steven's fingerprints on the frying pan, and he's the only one who was in the house today, they won't need to investigate any further."

"You're saying we should . . ."

I try to catch Karla's eye. I want her to put a stop to this.

"The police won't be able to tell which of them died first," she says.

"But . . ."

This is beyond the pale.

"Think of your little girl," Jennica says. "Think of Sally."

I press my hands to my forehead and picture Sally in my mind. She's laughing and asking about my dreams.

"What about our phones? The police can check up on where we've been."

"We can handle that," Jennica says. "You and I could have spent the whole day strolling around the botanical gardens. That's right around the corner. Maybe we met to have a heart-to-heart about Miranda and Ricky."

"But . . . I don't know . . ."

I'm still holding out hope for Karla. Is she really prepared to take such a risk?

"I'll delete the recordings from my phone," she says, touching the screen.

Jennica comes to stand in front of me and offers her hand.

"They'll find our fingerprints," I say.

"We'll have to do a thorough clean. Wipe down everything. Even that." She points at the body on the floor.

"It's no big deal if they find my DNA in the house," Karla says.

Jennica seems to be pondering something.

"I'm sure we can explain mine away too, if we need to. And when the police question you, you can say Bill came to pick you up sometime last week. Just to be on the safe side. In case they find evidence from him."

I put my hand in Jennica's and, my back to the wall, I heave myself up from the floor. The blood rushes out of my head. Fuzzy clouds block my vision and I sway in place.

"Take the frying pan," Jennica says, handing me the microfiber cloth.

The heavy cast-iron pan is on the island in front of me.

"Me?"

Jennica shoves me lightly in the back.

"We'll do it together, all three of us. We have to get Steven's fingerprints on it."

My mind is reeling. The clouds have settled like a thick fog around my thoughts. Somewhere in the background, I hear the echo of Sally's laughter as it becomes a wild shriek.

"Come on," Jennica says.

I turn to Karla, who grits her teeth and nods.

Then I simply do it.

It's like turning on the autopilot. I wrap the handle of the frying pan in the cloth. It weighs several pounds. My feet drag up the stairs. I close my eyes and Karla holds my arm as we enter the darkened bedroom. The stuffy smell invades my nostrils.

Karla cautiously holds the edge of the frying pan with a towel as I pick up Steven's hand and bring his fingers to the handle.

When we get back down to the kitchen, Jennica helps me arrange the pan on the floor beside Regina Rytter's body. Together we wipe down every millimeter of the counter, island, table, and chairs.

"Bill and I will take off first," Jennica says to Karla. "You clean the rest of the house. When the police ask, you can say Regina was sleeping while you were here. She usually stays closed up in her room, right?"

"Yep."

Jennica opens the front door, and I stagger after her out onto the path, where my bike is. It takes no more than two minutes to cross the street and slip into the greenery of the botanical gardens.

"It's best that as many people as possible see us," Jennica says.

The sun is high in the sky and its sharp light falls across the lawn. The sky is ethereally light, almost transparent, its blue color thinned out until it seems it might burst. The rays of the sun slice through the atmosphere and in those cracks the darkness breaks forth. Everything that was hidden seeps out and froths over.

Jennica looks at me.

We are both permanently transformed.

There are boundaries you feel so certain you will never cross that you don't even consider the consequences.

In the park, people in sunglasses are spreading out blankets and unpacking picnic baskets. Some children climb on a big log; one of them is laughing, another crying.

Life goes on as though nothing has happened.

I walk mechanically, each movement robotic.

"Are we really going to . . . ?" I say, glancing over my shoulder.

Jennica's hand lands on my back.

"Just keep walking," she says. "Think of Sally."

She nudges me gently ahead of her.

From now on, we are forever beholden to one another. Jennica, Karla, and me. We carry one another's fates in our hands.

THE MURDER OF A WOMAN IS NEVER A "FAMILY TRAGEDY"

Crime Column, *The Evening Post*

By Jonna Jensen

Each year, approximately fifteen Swedish women are murdered by a current or former partner. Most men who kill their female partners have a stable life and no previous criminal record. One in five of these murderers take their own life in connection with their crime.

This past summer, a 43-year-old woman in Lund was killed by her husband, a prominent pediatrician who then committed suicide. The police conducted a thorough investigation, and during a press conference held after the preliminary investigation was closed, the incident was described as "a family tragedy."

In law enforcement circles, this phrase seems to be used to denote situations in which there is no external perpetrator to bring to justice. It is used when a murderer has taken their own life after killing one or more family members. It's one thing, I suppose, that the police need an internal code word for this type of case, but it's highly problematic to use the same phrase in communications with the public.

A murder is never a private matter. Intimate partner violence concerns all of us. There are no mitigating factors whatsoever in the case of the Lund pediatrician. It's not a "family tragedy." A murder is a murder and a killer is a killer.

Subforum "Current crimes and cases"

TWO PEOPLE FOUND DEAD IN LUND HOME

Most recent entries in thread

Lundcitizen1977

Us Swedes need to fucking wake up. Yet again the police and justice system are colluding to hide the truth. No further info?! Everything marked confidential? Seriously, what happened in that house? I guess we'll never know.

Smolkie

Take off your fucking tinfoil hat!!! There is physical evidence to support that it happened just like the police and prosecutor said. What is it you don't understand about that?

Mockingbird2

Family tragedy? This is no family tragedy. The man committed a bestial murder and then he was cowardly enough to kill himself. A family tragedy is when something terrible happens to a whole family and all of them are innocent.

Xtracola

On Wikipedia it says "A family tragedy is a euphemistic expression for a serious violent crime committed within a family. It can refer to a parent or

parents who kill one another or their children; in the classic example a sui-
cide follows." I have no issues with the phrase being used this way.

Mountainking
Maybe it's a problematic term, but if the concept is going to keep its loaded
connotations it sure can't start to mean that you just get sick of your wife and
move out. So family tragedy is a perfect way to describe the terrible thing
that happened to this family.

Katti9090
I know firsthand Steven R*tter was a fucking psychopath.

JoVaLi
You know nothing of the sort. Steven was a lovely person and an amazing
doctor. He helped so many families. The tragic thing is that no one could find
treatment that worked for Regina. Apparently she caught some sort of virus
that settled in her brain.

BrutusEtTu
Someone should damn well track down Bill Ol**on and see to it that justice
is done.

Lundcitizen1977
There is no justice in this country!

Katti9090
There is such a thing as moral justice.

BrutusEtTu
I think there's a killer on the loose in Lund.

Bill

get to the school with time to spare and settle in to wait for Sally. After two weeks in jail, I don't want to miss a second.

She comes rushing over with her hair dancing in the wind. She has to hold her skirt up in one hand. Her face is determined, and as she throws herself into my arms we both lose it and burst into tears.

It's happening more and more often, that my emotions overwhelm me and tears start to fall. It's as though all the shit I've been carrying around is starting to leak out. I think it's helping me feel better.

"Dad," Sally says softly against my cheek. "Daddy, Daddy."

She weighs nothing, and my smile isn't one of joy but of relief.

Two weeks without her was torture.

I don't know how much she understands about everything that's happened, but right now it doesn't matter. All that matters is that we're together and nothing can change that.

The investigation was closed. The police came to the conclusion that Steven Rytter killed Regina and then took his own life.

Just as we planned.

A family tragedy, said the press secretary for the police.

He has no idea what a true family tragedy is. I can hardly sleep these days. At night I am tortured by the memory of loud blows, the heavy frying pan hitting the back of Regina's head. Again and again.

I toss and turn in sweaty sheets, trying to distract myself and to remain strong for Sally. I go to the balcony and fill my lungs with fresh autumn air. Then I go sit in front of the computer or the TV while the clock slowly ticks away the minutes.

Steven and Regina are gone forever, but maybe the truth can spare me this all-consuming guilt.

During the interrogations, I was sometimes seconds away from breaking down and confessing. I can't explain how I managed to resist.

But now every minute hurts.

I must have underestimated my internal desire to do the right thing. I cannot get away from it. There's only one way to cure moral pain. The alternative is a life of torture.

Naturally, I can't leave Sally at the nighttime rec center now. Hanna-Linnea has been kind enough to arrange some daytime hours here and there, both with Astor and with other clients. I was prepared for the worst when I handed in my background check. I was upfront about everything: my gambling debts and my theft from the movie theater. Hanna-Linnea understood; she says she will trust me until I give her reason not to. Now the electric bill is paid, and the rent too, and next week a math student from Piteå will be moving into Karla's old room.

We talk, now and then, Karla and me. In doing so we break our vow of silence, but it mostly ends up feeling forced and regretful. Not once have we come close to mentioning the house on Linnégatan.

I don't mention my sleepless nights. We talk past all the tough stuff.

But as soon as I put Sally to bed each night, I plunge right back down into all that darkness.

Time and again I see it in my mind, like a movie. Regina Rytter's hands around Karla's throat. Jennica raising the frying pan and bringing it down.

Again and again and again.

The sound of it has settled permanently in my eardrums.

I can hear those blows everywhere.

I will never be free.

After we left Karla alone in the house, Jennica and I sat down at an outdoor café in the botanical gardens. I went to the bathroom to throw up. I had the urge more than once to give up and call the police, but Jennica convinced me to be strong. For Sally.

She came home with me, to the apartment. As soon as Sally was asleep, I sat down on the couch and cried as the night washed over me with its merciless darkness. The pain took hold and spread through me.

Two days later, the police called me in for questioning. My first thought was that Karla had capitulated and told them everything, but it turned out the investigators found my fingerprints in Steven's bedroom. They searched the apartment and seized my computer. My bank account led them straight to the guy in Malmö who bought Regina's ring. I was on the verge of confessing everything when I remembered Miranda's last words.

Whatever you do, do it for Sally.

It was for her sake that I lied. And it's for Sally's sake that the truth must come out.

"Jennica?" I say on the phone. "It's Bill."

Our agreement was that we would have no contact whatsoever. Now that pact of silence is broken.

"Are you crazy?" she says. "You can't call me. Rumors are already flying."

I know that, of course. I too have read what people are saying online.

"But I can't take it anymore," I say. "We have to tell the truth."

"Shut up," Jennica hisses into the phone. "The worst is over now.

You made it through jail and all those interrogations. I didn't think you were this weak."

She sounds convincing. But Jennica knows nothing about weakness.

True strength means letting go.

"You don't get it. I'm falling apart here," I say. "We have to tell the truth."

"After everything I've done for you?" Her rage gives way to sheer desperation. "I gave you an alibi. Without me, you and that Norrlander would have been screwed."

She's probably right. But it doesn't matter.

"You'll go to prison, Bill. You're as entangled in this as I am. You and Karla put Steven's fingerprints on that pan. Then you cleaned up the scene of the crime and lied to the police when they questioned you. None of us will get off scot-free."

She's right, of course. The truth would have enormous consequences for all three of us. We all bear equal responsibility.

"I can't take it," I say.

Tears spring to my eyes.

"There is such a thing as therapy, Bill. I'm sure you have the right to have it subsidized."

"What is wrong with you?" I say.

Jennica raises her voice. "For Christ's sake, think of Sally! They'll take her away from you."

She hangs up and silence envelops me.

She's right. I have to keep it together and get through this.

I think of Sally. I always think of Sally.

Everything I do, I do for her.

Karla

Every night I wake up with something squeezing my chest and think I'm about to take my last breath. A whisper, and Waheeda dangles her hand down from the top bunk. It's enough to hold it for a moment, and my heart rate slows.

Sometimes Waheeda hums a lullaby from her homeland.

She believes that these nightmares are a relic of my childhood. I told her they're about Mom. The uncertainty of what might happen with Mom still scares me, but I have to learn to live with it. Only Mom can save herself. Once she makes up her mind to do it, I'll be there for her.

Five weeks ago, I started the legal studies program. Waheeda is studying adult ed. Each morning we take the bus together and I walk up the stairs at Juridicum. It's like walking straight into a dream.

"It's so nuts that the cops suspected Bill," Waheeda says one morning. "He could hardly even find a job. As if he could kill someone?"

"No," I say. "He couldn't."

I gaze out the window, where autumn leaves fly in the breeze.

"Anyway, I told them everything when they questioned me," Waheeda continues. "How that psychopath doctor locked up his wife and tortured her for over a year. If he hadn't already been dead he would have gotten the fucking death penalty."

I don't respond, and we say nothing more about it.

Day after day, I try to understand how things could have turned out the way they did. I try to explain it to myself, but deep down I know it's impossible.

There is no defending it.

But there are tiny, brief moments when other stuff takes over. Stuff that almost seems like everyday life.

Like evenings at Mickey D's.

The stench wafting off the grill and Waheeda cramming her hair under the tiny cap. Our manager, Momme, who shouts "Ajde, fries ASAP!" and me burning my fingers on the fryer for the fiftieth time.

Or Fridays, when we go out together. When we play soccer at Smörlyckan or dance in front of the mirror in our new apartment at the Sparta student housing complex.

All the hours spent poring over books and course readers, all the stress in front of the computer, my aching fingertips.

The student orientation days with pea soup and fun banquets and scavenger hunts.

There are lots of opportunities to forget.

But when the night comes and the darkness crowds in, it's no longer possible to escape that Monday morning in the kitchen on Linnégatan.

When the police detained Bill, I was beside myself.

The thought that he would have to sit alone in a jail cell while social services took Sally burned a hole in my brain.

It was my responsibility to wipe down all the surfaces in the house. I was the one who failed to remove Bill's fingerprints from Steven's bedroom. The first time I was interrogated, I said that Bill had been inside the house, and up to the bedroom, but according to the interrogator Bill himself denied this. He must have forgotten what he was supposed to say.

I made up my mind. Next time they questioned me, I would confess everything. Presumably I would never be able to realize my dream of becoming a judge, and in the worst case I would go to prison, but at least that was preferable to letting Bill shoulder all the blame.

I spent two feverish late-summer nights roaming the streets like a zombie. I quit my job at the cleaning firm and told Waheeda I'd come down with the flu.

Jennica was the one who made me change my mind.

In the wee hours, I found her standing outside my door. Her hair was stuffed into a knitted cap; her eyes were ice-cold.

We had made a pact never to contact each other again.

"Can I come in for a minute?"

She said it was for my own good. She was worried.

She knew, of course, that I had been called in for questioning again.

"Don't forget that what you elect to tell the police will affect more people than just you. This isn't just about your career. Think of Bill. And Sally."

By the time she left, I had made a different decision.

The interrogator was a middle-aged man with aviator glasses. He had hairy forearms and a gold ring on his left hand, and a way of holding your gaze for an extra long time. Eyes like an eagle, as if nothing got past him.

Mom always said I was like an open book.

I've never had a poker face. My emotions are written right on my face.

But I showed Mom.

She was wrong.

Jennica

send a message to Tinder Central.

8 PM, Klostergatan Vin & Delikatess.

Senior Project Manager at Tetra Pak, 43.

Then I leave my phone in my purse as I round the corner by the real estate firm. He's waiting under the restaurant's red awning. A wide stance, black jeans. His cap rolled up above his ears.

"Jennica?"

He's actually been pretty honest with his photos. A couple gray hairs at the very top of his head, but otherwise he looks surprisingly young and trendy for being over forty.

"Hi, I'm Magnus."

His handshake is firm, not the least bit of hesitation, just as I like it. My dainty fingers vanish in his big paw.

We follow a waiter through the dining room, and Magnus pulls out my chair. I check it carefully before I sit down. I have to return this Filippa K dress to the store on Monday.

"I'm so glad you wanted to meet," Magnus says. "It's such a pain to keep sending messages back and forth. If it feels right from the start, seems to me it's just as well to meet up as soon as possible."

He sounds like a seasoned dater. That's the nice thing about this older generation. They're like, boom, let's get to it, not interested in playing games.

"This might sound nuts," I say, brushing a lock of hair from my face as I lean across the table. "But want to make a deal? If you don't like me, you can just get up and go. Say you need to visit the bathroom or something. I don't want you to have to suffer your way through several hours."

Magnus laughs. His pale gray eyes light up.

We've only been exchanging messages for a week, max. Our tone has been pretty flirty from the start, and I've sent him pictures I wouldn't show my mother.

"But you're welcome to pick up the check," I add.

He laughs even more.

"Is that so? I though you said you were a feminist."

I smile and roll my eyes. According to a site I searched online, Magnus drives a BMW, last year's model, has a taxable income of more than one million kronor annually, and owns a home valued at eight and a half million kronor. Obviously he's going to pay for our meal. Steven never mentioned money. He simply paid. Because he loved me. He had never felt so strongly about anyone else.

"What strikes your fancy?" I ask.

Magnus runs his index finger down the glossy menu.

"I'm thinking maybe the fish. Braised char."

He fiddles with his chin and keeps thinking. I hate people who can't make up their minds. Besides, I have no idea what *braised* means, and I don't want to ask or google it.

"I'll have a meat dish," I say, tossing the menu onto my plate. "Beef tenderloin."

Magnus shoots me a quick glance, then looks back at the menu. I drum my fingers on the table.

"Okay, I'll have beef tenderloin as well."

Not much character at all, this one. I struggle to smile.

"What do you say about a Tempranillo?" I say. "Maybe a Portia Roble?"

I've done my homework.

"Okay, that . . . is that a red, or . . . ?"

I stifle a sigh. This is useless. I can't date anyone without comparing them to Steven, and no one will ever measure up to him.

A blond waitress, high-school aged, approaches our table and smiles with lips that have seen too many fillers.

"Are you ready to order?"

Magnus waffles a little.

"Yes," I say.

Magnus wonders if he can have his beef without the béarnaise, because apparently he can't eat egg. He also wants his meat well done. Steven would have a seizure if he heard this.

As the waitress sails off, Magnus's eyes linger a little too long on her ass. I take a few sips of water and clear my throat.

"Have you been single for a long time?" he asks, looking at my hands.

"Not really."

It's strange. We've barely even sat down and he already wants to discuss exes. Of course, I've already checked up on his ex-wife as thoroughly as possible. They have two kids together, and his wife seems to work at a day care. Despite the filters on her pictures, she looks tired.

"My boyfriend passed away," I say.

Magnus coughs and presses his napkin to his lips.

"My condolences."

I recall the first time Steven told me about Regina. He mentioned she was dead, but I was the one who asked for details. Of course he was caught off guard. He had only a few seconds to make a crucial decision, and that was where the lie sprouted. I wonder if he'd planned it. He must have gone through various scenarios in his mind.

What would have happened if Steven had told the truth from the start? No doubt about it: I would have walked out and never come back. Obviously, Steven was aware of this.

"It's okay. You couldn't have known," I say to Magnus. "I've moved on now."

It's true. Life goes on. There's no point in getting stuck in the past. You can learn to live with just about anything.

Maybe it's just as well it turned out the way it did. Steven determined our future. Or did Regina do it? I still don't know, and I never will. But it doesn't matter. Either way, Regina got what she deserved. I delighted in every single blow of that frying pan. After all, in my world, she was already dead.

Acknowledgments

I've had a lot of help writing this novel. First and foremost from my agent, Astri von Arbin Ahlander, who is my first reader, sharpest critic, and greatest support. I've also gotten help in every conceivable way from Matilda, Kaisa, Christine, Kajsa, and Mariya at Ahlander Agency. Many thanks. You're all fantastic!

John Häggblom has been invaluable during the work on this book. You constantly make me a better author. Same goes for Teresa Knochenhauer, who plowed through endless versions of this text with great patience and a sense of optimism that never waned. My fantastic editor, Lisa Jonasdotter Nilsson, cut all the cheeky words and helped me understand my own characters even better. I'm so glad I get to work alongside your sharp eyes and brains. Big thanks to everyone at Bokförlaget Forum.

A huge thanks to translator Rachel Willson-Broyles and my British publisher, Vicki Mellor, at PanMacMillan. I am also forever grateful to my American publisher, Deb Futter, and the rest of the fantastic team at Celadon Books: Randi Kramer, Frances Sayers, Vincent Stanley, Michelle McMillian, Erica Ferguson, Jeannette Cohen, Rachel Chou, Jennifer Jackson, Jaime Noven, Rebecca Ritchey, Anna Belle

Hindenlang, Sandra Moore, Anne Twomey, and Erin Cahill. And thanks to Kelly Blair for the amazing cover.

Extra big thanks to Birgitta Ekstrand, Monika Wieser, and Lotten Glans, who read the manuscript at an early stage and gave me extremely valuable feedback.

Thanks too to my author colleagues Johanna Schreiber, who gave Steven big hands, and Malin Stehn, who gave Bill a better backstory. Thanks to Petra Holst, Anette Eggert, and Mårten Melin for reading, chatting, and support.

I'd also like to thank my family and all my friends, in Skåne and Tenerife, who have been there for me as I worked on this book. Thanks, Mom and Dad, for all your love.

Finally I want to thank Dr. Emma Lindström for all the tips on how to drug your wife, even though I happen to be married to your sister.

Note: The crime column on page 363 is based on the articles "En mördad kvinna är ingen 'familjetragedi'" by Pernilla Ericson (["A Murdered Woman is Not a 'Family Tragedy'"] *Aftonbladet*, August 26, 2020) and "Ordet 'mord' behöver inga förskönande omskrivningar" by Britta Svensson (["We Don't Need a Euphemism for the Word 'Murder'"] *Expressen*, October 1, 2018).

About the Author

M. T. Edvardsson is an author and teacher from Trelleborg, Sweden. He is the author of multiple novels, including *A Nearly Normal Family*, his first published in the United States. He lives with his family in Löddeköpinge, Sweden.

CELADON
BOOKS

Founded in 2017, Celadon Books, a division of
Macmillan Publishers, publishes a highly curated list
of twenty to twenty-five new titles a year. The list of
both fiction and nonfiction is eclectic and focuses
on publishing commercial and literary books and
discovering and nurturing talent.

35674060269694